UNDEAD KELLY

SOMEBODY HAS TO STOP THE ROT

TIMOTHY BOWDEN

TAR
& FEATHER

Timothy Bowden/Tar & Feather Publishing.

www.tarandfeather.com.au

tarandfeathergroup@gmail.com

Cover design by Nick Hamilton

www.thehammo.com

Book Layout ©2019 Vellum

Undead Kelly. Timothy Bowden. -- 2nd edition.

ISBN 978-1-68411-980-6

for Sandra

PROLOGUE

Later
   afterwards
      in the quiet that exists when the burials and burnings are done and the weeping left for those private hells that exist in the dead of wakeful night

in the drawing of breath before recriminations, before shock and puzzlement gave way to anger

in that pause

no one was left to say how it really began...

There were theories. Always, there were theories.

Some said the source had always been here, hidden away in the malevolent dead heart of the interior. There in the hot red dust, the towering silent stones. Waiting for us.

Or maybe up there in the stinking foetid forests of the north, where the timber-getters said your very shirt would rot off your back in a day, and all the while, as you cut, this sense of something watching...

But those who knew the ways and stories of the natives – and trusted them – said that nowhere in their tales of the Dreamtime was there an evil such as this. And you would think it would rate a mention... No, this was something more recent. More modern.

So maybe it came ashore later, washed here among the mats of curled seaweed from the islands of the Javanese. Or borne on driftwood infected by the cannibals of the Guinean interior.

Others believed it was the punishment of God, brought against the sinful. But in that case, said others, shouldn't it be happening to say, the French?

Or was it a warning of Man's progress, a protest from Nature itself about the pace of change sweeping the world, when some new-fangled machine or another was seemingly being unveiled every day?

Partly, the problem lay in no one knowing too much about it. There seemed to be some cloying layer of silence smothering gossip, something more than just fear or the jibes of the unbelievers.

But still there were stories.

Stories told in hushed voices in the dark corner of the pub, where all would fall silent and lean back, sipping their beers at the approach of a stranger. Stories told at risk of a flogging behind the outhouse in the dusty schoolyard. Or on pain of dismissal at the washtubs in the city where the maids stretched their aching backs.

Swagmen, with rolling white eyes and hands shaking as if in the liquor deliriums, staggering into some town and raving about barely escaping one of *them*...

Them what?

Them Blighted ones. Them walking dead.

But it could have been different, oh so different, if not for one man...

ONE

I n This Author's opinion, the recent Example of the perverse story-telling of the Chinamen from Lambing Flat, wherein they claimed to have been Set Upon by The Dearly Departed, Now Returned, otherwise referred to as the Blighted, does nothing but reveal the Extent of Opium usage among our Yellow Brothers...

Harrumphing, as an educated man must when confronted by such rubbish, I turned the page.

The supposed corroborating account from the excitable band of Italians, Americans and Fenians at Eureka, who Swear they were forced to barricade themselves and Fire Upon members of Her Majesty's Armed Forces, recently Blighted, who they Maintain had come upon them with the Express Desire of Consuming their Flesh, is best explained by Moonshine and Madness.

Oh for God's sake.

Honestly. All I wanted was something juicy, something salacious. Something about a naughty little maid, or lonely sea captain's wife. Not this unholy drivel. You could normally trust the penny dreadfuls to feature stories designed to excite and shock, but lately they had been focussing more and more on these stories of madmen. Or rather, on *debunking* the stories of madmen, which was odd, since one would have thought such drivel was fodder to them... and meanwhile sane, decent men such as I who just wanted to steam themselves gently with some ammunition for the lonelier parts of the night went... unfulfilled.

I closed the volume and tossed it beside me onto the seat of the cab, where of course, it sent a cloud of dust rising. Dandruff and mould spores. At the same time, a fly blew in through the open window and went for the corners of my mouth and eyes. I crushed it. Filthy things. I glared out the window at the streets of Melbourne, which did nothing to improve my mood. Filthy place. What was I doing here?

Sydney had been better. Not much, but better. At least I had a friend there, of sorts. I frowned as I thought of Norris. Even he had been caught up in this craze for stories about the walking dead. I recalled our last whiskey-sodden dinner, when he had been brandishing a dog-eared journal containing some work of fiction by a colonial writer who I'd never heard of. No doubt the chap would have received short shrift in Charing Cross Road, but out here, if you could write at all, I suppose you were considered something of a genius.

"Look at this!" cried Norris, eyes fever bright. He threw the volume at me, rather than bother leaning forward and passing it. "Oh, sorry, old chap!"

"You complete ass, Norris." I bent and swatted at the magazine, aware of the rich food and whiskey making some attempt to run back up my throat as I hung upside down. Straightening, I glanced at the pages he had indicated, squinting to bring them into focus. "Yes? What am I looking for? Seems to be about some peasant woman..."

"Skip a bit, skip a bit!" he cried, fairly bouncing up and down in his seat. He frowned. "And pay attention, damn you!"

That was Norris. Could go from *hail-fellow-well-met* to *come-here-and-say-that* within moments when he was in his cups. That was part of the reason he was practising here in the colonies and not back in England.

"Yes, well," I said, buying time as I skimmed. "So she is alone with her whelps and does battle with a snake..."

Norris stabbed his finger at me. "It isn't a snake!"

I frowned and studied the words again. "No. No, it definitely says snake. Look, right here."

Norris wasn't having it, and shook his head violently. "They changed it, don't you see? They wouldn't let the cove publish a story about the Blighted, and so they changed it to a snake instead! It's *really* about a brave drover's wife and her dog defending her children from one of *them*! It turns up while her husband is away working, and she barricades her family inside. She reflects on her hard life as a colonial wife and then bashes the Blighter's brains to pulp with a log when it tries to get inside! But listen, there are copies of the original still out there, if you can find them..."

"Oh, for crying out loud, Norris. Do you know how that sounds? Anyway, who would go to the trouble of making some semi-literate nobody change his ridiculous story like that? It's fiction!"

Norris stared at me, leaned in close, breathing whiskey fumes into my face. "It isn't fiction."

What an ass...

"Here we are, sir!" called the cabby, and we swayed to a halt, horses stamping and twitching their tails, instantly beset by their own collection of insect persecutors. "Russell Street entrance."

I ducked my head out and looked up at the blue-grey slab of a building before me. Did I really need this? Were things quite this desperate? Melbourne gaol. Father would be pleased – he'd mumble something through his whiskers about me ending up where I clearly belonged. Ha! *That* to him – I snapped my fingers, causing my cabby to raise an eyebrow as he took my coin. I was here in a legal sense, alright – but a *working* legal sense. No, I didn't like the sound of 'working', make that in a *professional* legal sense. Yes. Better.

"No need to wait," I said, but the bugger was already tapping his horses with his crop, rather than wait for his better to instruct him. No matter. While I had no intention of this taking very long, I had little idea of what exactly may be involved. Perhaps, if I had actually attended a few lectures at college before being sent down my current role would be clearer – but then, if I had seen my studies through I wouldn't be here, would I? I'd be stuck toadying and grovelling to some grizzled friend of Father with extensions on his waistcoat just so he could close it over the port and gravy stains. No, horrid as this place was, at least I was free. Ironic, really, as I was about to enter a gaol.

I knocked on the thick smaller door set into the gate of the prison. After a frustrating wait, a bow-legged lackey opened the entrance amid much jangling of keys, and peered myopically at the letter I held out for him, but would not let him take. It took three attempts of him reaching out to pinch it between his nicotine stained finger and thumb, and me whisking it above his reach before he realised I didn't want him to touch it. Instead, he stood there, ridiculous with his hands on his knees, head tilted on the size, reading it. I stared – the man was actually mouthing the words as he read. Sounding them out.

"All good and correct, sir," he said, and stepped back for me to enter.

I ducked through, and found we were in the inner courtyard. All the buildings inside were built of the same depressing blue stone. I heard that Jebb, the prim prison engineer who built the place, had some theory on the merit of the colour blue for the soul, or some such rubbish. Damned reformists. Just can't leave you alone to get on with it.

"This way, please, sir."

He was gesturing towards the administration offices. I had automatically turned toward the massive main cell block.

"But the prisoner is in there... Isn't he?"

"Oh that he is, sir. Locked up good and proper. Murdering cur. But the Guv'nor would like a word before you go talk to him."

"Oh. So he knew I was coming?"

"Well, he knew *someone* was coming. Can't rightly say if he knew *who*. Specific, like."

I followed my guide, who seemed to lurch from side to side as much as forward as he walked, into one of the buildings on the right and up a flight of stairs. We reached a heavy panelled door upon which he knocked lightly.

"Come."

The lackey turned the handle, and gestured me through with a slight bow, and if I wasn't mistaken, a wink. Impudent twat.

The office inside was dominated by a large desk – too large, in fact. I was momentarily distracted, pondering on the appalling taste of whoever deemed this was the place for it – why, they must have had to winch it up through the windows...

"Good morning," said the man sitting behind the desk. "Be with you in a moment. Please, take a seat."

I sat, and watched the grey and balding top of the fellow's head as he made a show of flicking through pages of closely-written text piled on the desk before him. The minutes drew slowly out as he sorted and re-sorted, and I was wondering if I should clear my throat pointedly, when I caught him peeking at me from under his bushy brows. Hello, I thought. Making some kind of point, are we? So instead, I affixed my most aggravating expression of polite, bored disdain – the one best reserved for vicars, university dons and railway inspectors – and resolved to wait him out. It didn't take long.

"Now then," he said, finally gracing me with a smile and direct eye contact. "Here you are."

"Quite."

I flicked at some fluff on my good trousers and waited. Glancing around, I took in shelves filled with uniformly bound volumes, most likely bylaws and rules for the housing of Her Majesty's guests – memorised and thus unopened, I supposed – and not much else. No model ships, or framed medals, or even portraits of Grandpa during the Opium Wars, or the like. Nothing to suggest anything about the personality of the man sitting behind the desk.

"I hope you don't mind me pulling you away – briefly – from your legal duties, uh, young man," said the governor.

I shrugged. He reddened, just a little, at my casualness. As intended.

"Introductions? I am Governor Castieau, lord of this... humble little domain. My casa, your casa, that sort of thing."

I raised one eyebrow and his forced jolliness deflated. "You have a letter?" he asked.

"Yes, sir. Here." I handed my letter to him, and he brightened at once. As he read it, he licked his lips. I noticed with revulsion that his tongue was flat and bluish grey, not dissimilar in colour to the stone walls of his prison. It reminded me of the flat blue tongues of the wedge-headed lizards you found scuttling about in Sydney. I wondered whether working here meant slowly succumbing to the power of the walls and taking on their colour. And character. Solid. Dependable. Dull.

"Ah, so Gaunson is acting for him, then? It is decided?"

"Indeed."

"A great parliamentarian is Gaunson. And you are...?"

"Acting as Mr Gaunson's legal secretary. I'm to meet with the prisoner and obtain his statement."

Castieau fixed me with a suddenly piercing eye. "Does it matter?"

"It will matter very much at his trial. They do tend to like having the defendant's point of view presented too."

"Yes. Well." He pretended to look back at my letter. Again that vile tongue poked out and circled his lips.

"I do hope," he said, finally laying it aside, "that a gentleman, such as Mr Gaunson - and your good self, of course – realise the position I am in here. Having such an infamous prisoner in my gaol. On the one hand, I have elements of the press baying for his blood, and the Melbourne Club members pressing for no special privileges, and on the other, I have the reformists and Fenian sympathisers scrutinizing every move I make, ready to howl with outrage about prisoner's rights. Do you know there is even a petition circulating calling for his outright release? With thousands of signatures. Who knows what some of these sympathisers are capable of! An armed rescue attempt is not outside the realms of possibility. No one seems to note the additional pressure this puts on me."

"I do indeed sympathise with the difficulties of your position, Mr Castieau. You are undoubtedly one of the forgotten victims in this."

"The difficulties of my position?" he repeated. "I like that. The Difficulties of My Position. Where's my pen?" He went rooting through the papers on his desk until he found it, and then proceeded on a new hunt for his inkwell and then a fresh sheet of paper. Of course, the tongue came into action again as he concentrated on writing the words down. "I think you have just provided me with my title. I'm dabbling in a little writing, you see."

"Oh?" I responded, with as little enthusiasm as possible. I should have guessed it – all the papers strewn about. The man was an amateur writer, a very dangerous beast. Liable to drop everything and read to you from their turgid prose at the faintest hint of interest.

"These are important times. Very important. As well as diffi-cult. Difficult and important. I feel that a clear account of proceedings, the trial and execution and so on..."

"Execution?" I interrupted coolly. "Aren't we jumping ahead a little? He hasn't even been found guilty of anything."

"But... But you don't think he is innocent, do you? I mean, I know the man is your client – or your employer's client – but... come. His conviction is assured. And that will mean execution. You must realise that."

Actually, until that moment, I really hadn't. So far, this project had lurched between chore and game. That a man's very life was entangled in it gave me some pause. I tasted for just a heartbeat what it meant to face such responsibility. I didn't want this – wasn't this exactly what I had come out here to escape? I pressed a fingertip to my temple. I believed I was coming down with one of my migraines.

"Anyway, I am in the box seat, as it were, to provide a definitive account in my book-"

"My book!" I cried, suddenly remembering the penny dreadful I had left in disgust on the seat of the cab. It may have been dreadful indeed, but it was mine nevertheless, and repre-sented an expenditure – or would, were I ever to return to the same bookseller I had picked it up from and pay my account. I must say, it had actually been quite odd to find the silly story Norris had been banging on about. Not that it meant anything – so they publish one dull version and one ridiculous version of the same story. No law against bad taste, as Melbourne proved all the time.

"Your book? You are also a writer, sir?" Castieau asked, pumping himself up with hail-fellow-well-met, let's-form-a-writer's-group fantasies.

On an impulse, rather than correct him, I said, "Well, I cannot *fully* make that claim, as yet..." then tapered off, somewhat enigmatically. Keep them guessing, I say.

"Ah," replied Castieau, tapping a finger to the side of his nose. What the devil did he think I meant? "As fellow travellers in the wake of Homer, I wonder if I may beg an indulgence..." He leaned forward conspiratorially. "Should you learn of anything particularly... uh, shall we say, *interesting*...That may be considered outside the realm of what is appropriate for the trial, but that later, afterwards, may add a certain something to the story... Well, I do hope you may consider sharing it with me..."

"Good God, sir!" I cried, making him jump and glance towards the door. "You mean share details of the defence with you?" I can do righteous indignation as good as any Presbyterian clergyman.

"Not at all, not at all! Not details related to the trial... I am speaking of, well, other things." He all but winked at me – but then frowned. "Unless you are planning to write your own volume on proceedings..." The colour – grey as it was – drained from his face.

I maintained a blank face. Clearly, the fellow was a little unhinged; a little star-struck and puffed up on the fame of one of his current guests. Me, write a book about this nasty little murderer?

"Fear not, Mr Castieau. I am here for the prisoner's statement and nothing more. Now, I feel I must have kept you from your... from your papers long enough. Perhaps, you will be so kind as to have me taken to my client now."

The fellow flushed with relief and shook my hand warmly.

He squeezed around from behind his desk and called out the door. After an awkward minute in which we both stood in his doorway, smiling pointlessly at one another, a young lackey arrived with cake crumbs on his jacket. He was directed by the governor to deliver the gentleman to Mr Quinn. The boy nodded, swallowed – causing his Adam's apple to slide in and out of view beneath his tight collar – and then took off at a gallop down the hallway. I was obliged to put my long legs to use to keep his back in view. As I left, Castieau shut the door smartly, no doubt to record our meeting while it was still fresh in his mind.

The young man glanced back at me once or twice, then slowed and turned so he was walking backwards. His eyes bulged as he looked me up and down.

"Is it true?" he finally said, stopping, a spray of cake crumbs filling the gap between us. "Are you going to speak to him?"

"Speak to whom?" I asked sternly.

"Whom," he replied, dropping his eyes.

"Yes. If by him – or rather, whom – you mean your prisoner, who is my client."

His jaw dropped. "He ain't my prisoner. I ain't to go anywhere near him, says Mr Quinn."

He stared at me a moment longer, until I raised an eyebrow at him, and then we resumed our journey through the guts of the gaol. Mr Quinn turned out to be the senior warder, who in turn handed me over to Mr Nixon, an under senior warder or some such, who in turn handed me over to the original old soak who had let me in the gate. It was he who I finally followed down the echoing central hall of the cellblock, the rows of thick doors extending on both sides, for several floors.

"Now, if you want my advice, don't go mentioning his old mum. She's being held in the women's section, and if you get him started on that, you won't get any sense for half an hour."

I nodded. I had been poised to tell him his advice could go hang, but my mouth had strangely gone a little dry.

"Here we are."

He produced his prodigious set of keys and carefully counted along, then took one and inserted it into the door. There was a loud clank as he turned it, and with an effort, he heaved the portal open. Stale air wafted out. I glanced in, and fought a strange sense of panic before ducking and stepping inside. The feeling was not just due to my hatred of feeling fenced in. There was more to it: a sense that once I entered the beast's den, something unstoppable would begin. My client was lying stretched out on his narrow bed. So this was he. The revolutionary.

The murderer.

Ned Kelly.

TWO

"And who the devil are you?" asked the man on the bed.

I am not proud, but man enough, I hope, to admit that in that first moment, I was a little overcome. After all, it is not every day one comes face to face with a man who is simultaneously held up as the worst criminal in the colony and the salvation of the common man against repression.

"I..." I said, then again, "I..."

"Where is Gaunson?"

"He... He is unable to attend," I said. I mentally shook myself: I had nothing to fear from this man. "Detained on parliamentary business, I'm afraid."

"Is that so?"

"Quite."

"And you're afraid?"

"What? No... I... That is... Figure of speech..."

He swivelled his legs slowly and stiffly off the narrow bed and sat up, staring at me. I had the wherewithal to return his gaze – I fancied myself something of a master when it comes to staring contests.

"What do you want?" he asked at last.

"I've come to take your statement for Mr Gaunson, for your defence."

He chuckled, deep and low in his chest. We must have been around the same age, but I felt rather like a schoolboy standing before him.

"My defence, eh?" He laughed again. "Wait till Maggie finds out Gaunson didn't come himself. I wouldn't trade places with him then for all the tea in China."

"Maggie?" I asked.

He looked at me.

"And what manner of man are you? English, that much is certain. Old enough to be a lawyer yourself, yet here as someone else's clerk..."

"I am English, yes, and while I have not taken my final exams, I assure you I am highly trained in the legal arts. I am merely taking some time out from my studies."

"You've come a long way for a holiday, Mr..."

"I don't believe who I am or how I have come to be here has any real bearing on your case, Mr Kelly."

"How do you know? Do you even know what you are defending?"

"Of course. You are charged with the murder of several police officers."

He laughed. "Murder?"

"I gather the evidence against you is quite telling. I fail to see the humour in your situation."

"Ah, well," he said, and lay back down again upon his cot and closed his eyes. "You're a remittance man, aren't you?"

I was glad he was not looking at me, and so missed my aston-ishment. "How... How did you know?"

"I can smell it on you."

I fought the urge to sniff my own arm.

"It's all a piece of it. All the strings draw together and form a rope. You know what is at the end of that rope, don't you, Mr Remittance Man? A noose for my neck. But I am ready for it. So long as I get my say in court. With the gallery full and every reporter from across the east coast there hanging on my every word. So run along, now, there's a good fellow. Run along and tell your masters to play some other game. No matter what they try, the truth will out. And they are right to fear it."

The volcano that had been building within me finally broke through the remaining crust.

"Now look here, you damn colonial dog," I snarled. I kicked his cot – his eyes snapped open, fixing on me. "I belong to no man! I have no master, damn you! How dare you lie there and insult me like that? I've a good mind to... to..."

"What?" he asked softly, but there was no gentleness in his voice. What in God's name was I doing? The man was a murderer! Alleged murderer, I corrected myself.

I wiped a hand over my face. This damned heat.

"Look, I'm sorry about that. It's just that I came out here to get away from people trying to control me... You just touched on a sore point, is all."

"Well then," he said. "A bit of spunk. I like you the more for it. So, you really are here to help me then?"

"Well, yes."

"Then get them to give me a tankard of water, will you? My throat is parched."

I looked at him to see if this was some kind of test, asking me to do his bidding like I was some kind of servant. But behind his eyes I saw no mockery, only... pain?

"Are you alright, Mr Kelly?"

"Call me Ned. And no, I'm not. The least of it is the load of buckshot I took to the backs of my legs. Now get me that water, won't you? They don't always come when I call."

I nodded, and pounded my hand on the cell door. When the

turnkey – a pock-marked youth this time - finally deigned to appear – God help me if I had been in desperate need of assistance – I treated him to as haughty a demeanour as I possessed, and well programmed by the horrors of school life, he leapt to obey me as his better.

"So," said Ned, closing his eyes again and perhaps seeking to distract himself from whatever nagging pain lingered in his legs. "Tell me what stain you smeared on the family name, Remittance Man, to get you sent out here."

"Ah."

"You want me to trust you with my story."

So that was the price? I smirked, as I thought back. Not an endearing or very repentant reaction, I know. I really couldn't help it. "Well," I drawled, "let's just say I may have placed a cuckoo in the nest. In a very high nest."

He laughed a little. "Upsetting the supposed natural order of things, are we? You're a proper little revolutionary, eh?"

"Oh, I wouldn't say my motives were particularly political... Not so much left or right as straight up the middle, as it were, if you get my meaning." This time, he laughed aloud. "And you? Were your motives revolutionary?"

He quietened. "Revolutionary? I..."

The door rattled open and he fell silent. The pustulent one scurried in, tankard held in both hands, thumbs dipping into the water, slopping some on the floor. He looked at me and frowned, so I made a show of taking it from him and pretending to sip – while being careful not to let the water actually touch my lips, as no doubt he had spat in it. Or at least sipped it himself on the way. Once he had gone, I passed it to Ned, who took it and craned his head to take a long pull. I watched his beard undulate with the hidden motion of his Adam's apple. He sank back then with a sigh, resting the tankard on his belly.

I waited.

"It's a long story," he said. "To answer your question. For you to understand. I don't know how far to go back..."

"Why not start at the beginning?" I said.

I reached in my jacket pocket and produced some folded paper and a fountain pen – both from the same establishment that had provided my penny dreadful. I was pleased with myself that I had thought to add them to my account that morning.

"I'll take notes as you go, then write them up properly for Mr Gaunson to review and decide which aspects are worth highlighting in your defence. Don't worry, I have a fast hand."

"Alright. Alright, Mr Remittance Man."

There was a rickety chair and small table holding an empty washbowl. I put it on the floor and smoothed my first sheet of paper out, and scribbled in the corner to check the pen's ink.

"This is the truth," said Ned. "Some I know because I was there. Some I learned after. Some I saw." He touched a finger to his head. "Here."

I must remember I am dealing with a madman. Or a mystic. He was looking at me now. I nodded at him.

"You don't believe me."

"What I believe doesn't really matter, Mr Kelly. I am here to defend you – believing you has nothing to do with that."

"We'll see... We'll see..."

Should I knock and request a cushion, I wondered? The seat tended towards unforgiving.

"My upbringing was poor, but honest," he began, eyes drifting off me and up to the web-shrouded corner of the cell.

My pen scratched. 'His upbringing was one of poverty, and thus unenviable,' I wrote.

THREE

His upbringing was one of poverty, and thus unenviable.

The family – Ned, his mother, his six brothers and sisters – moved onto eighty odd acres of hardscrabble land beyond the pinprick of civilisation that was the town of Greta after the death of his ex-convict father. It was Ned himself, though still a boy, who took charge when old da passed away from exhaustion and bitterness, signing the letter that informed the local doctor of the fact. And if there was no single splash upon that heavy page from eye, or even nose- who is to say what that may mean?

What does anything mean when we are young? Is this where some great truth is to be found?

If a boy was to drown his sister's puppy, say, in a moment of blind jealous rage, what are we to make of that? What information do we glean, and what inferences and conclusions do we draw? That he is passionate? Or irredeemable? Best thrust into the cold care of sour Scotch governesses and harsh public schools, barely tolerated, until he begins to assume the mantle given, and take vicious delight in living down to what is ascribed him?

What if another boy, thanks to the great gods of Fate, chances on another lad drowning in a rain-swollen creek, and in that moment when there was no time for thought dove in and dragged the frightened, clawing lad to the bank, what then? This is a boy destined for greatness? For leadership? Let this boy be publicly feted and bestowed with a ridiculous sash by the tearful family that he kept for twenty years – twenty years! – and had tied about him at the end, when it all ended in blood and flesh and flame and horror-

No matter.

The young Ned grew, and tasted what it meant to be on the other side of the law. An assault charge here, an accusation of theft there. But these are meaningless, given the context – a police force made up of whatever the tide left behind and a hard-living, hard-drinking, hard-fighting community largely identifying as Irish.

However, there came a day that may have set the engine on the track...

Ned whistled as he walked along the road, kicking at stones, hands stuck in his pockets in that way his mother detested. It was getting late, the shadows were lengthening on the bush track, but Ned was unafraid. He was a strong lad, with knuckles to back up whatever foulness he let fly from his mouth, and fast feet too, if it should come to that. The sound of hooves, a single horse, came to him from up ahead, and he readied himself for what may come if it turned out to be one of them feckin' troopers. He'd give him a mouthful, and scarper into the bush - maybe throw a rock and try to panic the horse, watch the poor ass sitting on it – couldn't call it riding, generally speaking – try to stay mounted. His eyes were already scanning the ground for suitable ammunition when the rider came into sight – no trooper.

The man was riding a horse no policeman could ever hope to aspire to. To Ned's practised eye it looked like a thoroughbred, though it was dusty and in need of currying. The man riding it was equally powdered, and wore a kerchief tied around his nose and mouth, a hat pulled down low to just above his eyes. He had a small swag tied on the back of the horse, and – and this is what really drew the boy's attention – a small arsenal of guns. There were two different types of rifles in long cases attached to the saddle, a shotgun across the man's back and a brace of pistols in his belt.

As he jogged past, the man's head swivelled to return Ned's stare. The corners of his eyes crinkled, the skin furrowing into scores of deep wrinkles, and Ned felt the man was smiling at him. In return, he gave a cheeky smile and waved. The man nodded his head and rode on. Ned watched for a while, and then slowly lifted one hand, now armed with an imaginary pistol, aiming at the man's back. You had to keep steady when shooting at a man on horseback.

"Bang."

Ned turned – and jumped as a face and wild eyes and gnashing teeth filled his view, stumbling backwards till he tripped and fell upon his arse. He stared up at the figure before him.

"Dan, damn and blast you, one of these days I'll pound you to kingdom come."

Dan Kelly surveyed him coolly, hands on his hips. "You shit yourself."

"I'll shit you out. I'll swallow you whole and shit you in the dunny."

Dan laughed in outraged delight, and Ned grinned and held up a hand to be helped to his feet.

"Ma's lookin' for you."

"She's always looking for me. Alright, let's go."

"No, not through there. Let's go on the road."

Ned rolled his eyes in disgust. "Walk all that way extra when we can take a short cut? Are you wrong in the head?"

Dan looked down, around, mumbled. "Came that way. Saw somethin'."

"Saw something? Saw what?"

Dan shrugged uncomfortably. "Just some weird swaggie. Over a ways."

"Weird? What do you mean weird?"

"I dunno. Didn't get a good look at 'im. There was just something... creepy about him."

Ned cocked an eyebrow. "Well, come on then."

"Ned!"

"Now don't be turning yellow on me, Daniel. Let's take a look."

Ned dashed off the road into the scrub, and, as he suspected, after a moment, he heard Dan call out and come crashing after him. He let him catch up, and then put on a burst of speed, to make Dan work for it, easily dodging between trees and jumping roots and rocks. He laughed, hearing Dan curse, but then slowed to a walk. Then, something caught his eye.

There was a man standing in a clearing just ahead. Like a scarecrow wrapped in rags. A lone dark sentinel.

"That him?" Ned asked as Dan arrived behind him, and his voice came out in a whisper, though he didn't mean it to. Dan nodded, white faced despite the exertion. Rousing himself, Ned walked closer.

The man was standing, swaying slightly, his back to the two boys. His clothes were shredded, and so filthy it was impossible to tell what colour or style they may have originally been. He had no hat, and what hair he had was greasy and lank. Flies buzzed in a cloud about him, their whine filling the clearing, a sharp sound highlighting the eerie silence of the surrounding bush.

"He's just some drunk..."

At Ned's words, the man's head twitched, and he turned, and came stumbling towards them. Ned felt fingers digging into his arm, and glanced down to see Dan's hand squeezing him, white-knuckled. Dan cried out, and Ned's eyes snapped to his brother's terrified face, and then back to the man.

He was smiling-

-There was something wrong-

-no, not smiling - mouth too big, ragged blackened skin, no lips, teeth and bone exposed, no skin on one side of his face, and the flies all over, all over, in the mouth and in the eyes.

The man reeled towards them, his very movement like a crime, reaching out for them with withered arms, the fingertips like white lace gloves but not gloves, only tips of bone sharp bone and shredded flesh reaching-

Ned was frozen.

There came a booming shot, and the man's head snapped back and away, a spattering of material spraying onto the leaf litter behind him, and he collapsed like a stunned bullock.

The boys gripped each other and turned to look. The horseman sat on his mount across the other side of the clearing. He lowered the rifle in his hands, opening the breech and sliding another shell home as he urged his horse forward with his knees. The boys' eyes turned back to the man on the ground. The flies, disturbed by the shot and the collapse, were returning, settling upon him once more. Dan twisted and threw his guts up into the dirt. Ned patted his back absentmindedly, watching as the horseman stopped beside the body, studying it.

The man grunted, seemingly satisfied, and slipped his rifle back into its sling.

"No need to worry about that one, boys. Good head shot sees them right, every time." His voice, coming from behind the kerchief was gruff but gentle. "Are you right?"

Ned nodded. Dan made a croaking sound.

"Pays to be careful out here," said the man, looking into Ned's eyes. "You need to take care. Of yourself, and your brother there, and your family. Here."

He pulled the other rifle from its case, and leaned down, holding it out to Ned. "Go on, son, take it. If a boy is going to be walking around on his own, he needs to be able to protect himself."

Ned held out his hands, trembling slightly, and the man placed the rifle in them. His fingers closed about it, took the sweet smooth weight of it.

"It's only an old muzzle loader, but it's a .577 calibre – that'll put a hole in anything. Remember what I said – you see one of them things, you sure as sin make sure you put a ball through its head."

Ned nodded.

"You may not see one for months or years, but they're out there, walking around. And hungry – they're always hungry. Keep a watch. Don't let them get to your family. You mind me?"

Ned nodded again, unable to find his voice. The man seemed satisfied, touched his hat, and flicked his reins, turning the horse. Dan came over and stood beside Ned, looking from the rifle, to the body, and then to the departing rider. "Who was that?"

FOUR

"Who was it?" I asked.

"Harry. Harry Power."

"Is that supposed to mean something to me?"

Ned looked towards me. "I suppose not. He was a bushranger. Locked up now." He took a sip from his tankard. "I'm not used to talking so much. This is thirsty work."

I flexed my fingers, looking down at the lines of seemingly illegible scribble on the pages before me. Lucky I could read my own hand. "I'm not quite sure what to make of this. Though maybe we could claim that witnessing a murder at such a young age had a permanent effect on your..."

"Murder?" Ned frowned at me. "Harry Power saved our lives that day."

"By shooting some crazed inebriate?"

"Did you not hear what I said? It was one of the Blighted."

"Oh, not you too," I groaned, rubbing my eyes. Had the whole country developed this craze about walking corpses? I glanced at Ned, and saw that he was staring at me coldly.

"Oh, Remittance Man, if you had seen the things that I have seen..." Rather than angry, his voice sounded oddly sad.

"Couldn't it be," I asked, tapping my pen on the page. "Couldn't it be that to your childish eyes he seemed like some kind of monster? Maybe he had been badly burned in an accident... Rolled into a fire while he was drunk, for example – that kind of thing happens."

"I'm telling you, when I went over to have a closer look at the body – after Dan had run screaming home – it was like I was looking at a carcass that had been lying there for weeks. It was dried out and rotten."

"What did you do with it?"

"Left it. Figured I'd let the flies finish it off. Went home and got a licking from Ma for getting home so late. She never questioned my story, though. Let me keep the gun, too."

I grunted. "Seems a little unwise. Young boy with a gun."

"Ah, that's city talk. And the talk of one who's never come face to face with one of the Blighted. I still dream about that first one..."

"First one? So you are saying you saw others?"

"Oh, just you wait and see, Mr Remittance Man. By the time you've heard the end of this your hair is going to turn white and you are going to sleep with a pistol under your pillow."

"Back to your mother. If, as you say, she believed your tale, surely she would want to move you all out of the area? Or at least forbid you children to ever leave her sight?"

"Don't think I fail to pick up on the criticism, and I give you fair warning that if you go near there again, you will not leave this cell in one piece."

I glanced up, and met his eye. I looked down first, clearing my throat. Damned dusty cell.

"We couldn't move. Our whole future was tied to that scrap of land the government deigned to sentence us to. And she knew there was no keeping me home all the day. She just made sure we travelled together, and checked I had powder for the carbine. How I loved that carbine. Had to cut it down so I could use it – took the stock off and shortened the barrel. Too much, as it turned out. Damned thing kept threatening to fall apart; I had to tie it together with waxed string. Still. Still, it did the job when I needed it to at Stringybark."

"When you shot Constable Lonigan, you mean?"

He ignored me. "There weren't too many around those parts in those days, anyway. It was years before we encountered any others. See, wherever it was starting from, somewhere way out in the bush, well there just wasn't that much of a food supply for them. The odd bullock dray, swagman, so on. Not many made it all the way to more populated areas. Thank God. If one got loose in a good sized town... Or a city..."

"What about the blacks?"

"What do you mean? As food? No, the Aborigines weren't caught napping. Smallpox may have caught them, but not the Blighted. Even though that was why it was started out there, to get rid of them."

"Are you suggesting some kind of deliberate policy of extermination? A secret policy, using these so-called Blighted undead creatures? Do you have any idea how this sounds? And you want to stand up in court and repeat this? This is your idea of defending yourself?"

"I think," said Ned slowly, "I think you had better leave now. "

So. Dismissed, was I? I gathered my pages, rustling them crankily. What a waste of time. The man was a crackpot. Worse than Norris. I stood and pushed the chair under the table, making sure it scraped irritatingly. I banged on the door and waited, and happily heard the jangle of approaching keys.

"Come back tomorrow," said the man on the bed. A statement, not a question, curse him.

"Hmmmm."

As the door slammed closed behind me, and I followed the stooped back of the older warder, my mind was full of things I should have said... I would have to call on Gaunson and tell him that I wanted no further part in this. I did not want my name associated with it in any way, or worse, my image to appear in a newspaper. One shuddered to think what they would say... and if word somehow got home, things could get very tight indeed. Not that they weren't tight enough now – but not so tight that I needed to be part of this lunacy.

I was back out on Russell Street before I knew it, the heavy door clanging closed behind me. I took a moment to watch the bustle of the city, let it soothe me. But as I watched the men and women walking or riding past, I darkly wondered how many of them would leap at the chance to believe tales of the undead wandering the bush, seeking to eat good Christian folk. Probably all too many of them.

I raised an arm to hail a passing cab, but then thought to check my wallet first. The cabbie snarled something foul at me as I waved him off, charming fellow, but a quick count confirmed my fears. Best I catch the omnibus back to Fitzroy, especially now as this particular job was about to dry up. I set off down the street, towards the railway station on Flinders Street, where the omnibus started its journey.

Why did humans – even educated, seemingly rational humans like Norris – so quickly embrace ideas of conspiracy and the supernatural?

"Alright then," I had said to Norris. "Imagining for a moment your infected..."

"Blighted!"

"Blighted, then – imagining your Blighted exist, how does it spread?"

"Ah! A good question and one many have speculated on. It

may be an airborne infection, or perhaps spread by touch or the sharing of bodily fluids…"

"What? You mean someone comes across one out the back of beyond and *rides* them? I knew things were desperate out there, but I didn't know they were *that* desperate!"

"Don't be facetious."

"It could be evolutionary," said a new voice.

I turned, frowning. A small, nervous man with a quite despicable moustache was hovering nearby.

"Sir, this is a private conversation. I'll thank you to remove yourself."

"Oh, it's only old Spence," said Norris. "You know Spence. How are you, fellow?"

Indeed, I did not know Spence and did not care to. Apparently needing no further encouragement, he dragged a chair to our table, his knees butting mine, causing me to have to shift my own chair back. Norris signalled for a glass and poured him a generous measure of whiskey. I hoped he was going to feel just as generous about buying another bottle if he was going to splash it around like that.

"Now what were you saying? Evolution?"

"Yes! I've been reading that Darwin fellow, and it seems to me the Blighted may represent a natural progression in response to our increasingly modern lives."

I groaned. Darwin? Evolution? Blighted? I ask, was this what passed for club talk amongst men these days? Couldn't we discuss where to get the best tarts with the least chance of pox?

"Think about it! Man now rides more than walks, so has no need of swift movement…"

"They can't really run," said Norris, turning to me.

"As we are less and less in nature, it stands to reason we will slough off those animal traits that are surplus! We could be witnessing the genesis of a whole new species! *Homo Modernus!*"

"Ah!" cried Norris, thrusting a finger up in the air. "But the Blighted have not appeared in the city! It is in the bush that they have been encountered."

Spence deflated a little. "A puzzle, yes."

"But it is a good theory," said Norris, patting the man's hand. "Now drink up, there's a good fellow. Who's next shout?"

He looked at me. I pulled out my watch. "Time I made a move, I'm afraid."

But now, looking at the blank expressions on the faces of the people swirling past me, caught up in the urgent, rapacious life of the city, I wondered whether Spence may indeed have been close to the mark...

I slowed my pace, thinking. Probably the best thing to do was go see old Gaunson right away, and hand in my notice. He'd be sure to be at the Melbourne Club by now, sipping port with all his political cronies. It was laughable, really, this jumped up chorus thinking themselves a government. Everyone knew where real power still resided. Yes, best to do it now. Although not a member myself, I would send up a note. Perhaps he might invite me in and buy me dinner, try to convince me to stay on.

"Sir? Excuse me?"

A hand plucked at my sleeve. I turned to find a young woman behind me, staring at me intently. She was clothed decently enough in a dark skirt and white blouse, her brunette hair piled on her head, though a few wisps had escaped and hung down her face. I don't know why, but that appealed to me. That faint Irish burr to her voice, too – I'd always been partial to an Irish lass. A simple, clean country girl. Something earthy about them, something that suggested it wouldn't be too hard to get their clothes off them.

"Not today, thank you." I turned to walk on. She was attractive, but I did need to consider the state of my wallet.

"Sir?" She hadn't loosened her grip at all – she held me fast. Strong, too. I noticed her nails were broken. Pity.

"Go bother some other gentlemen, there's a good girl."

I smiled at her, and gave her a wink. Her eyes first widened, and then narrowed dangerously. She released her hold as if she had suddenly found me to be covered in ordure. "I am no street walker!" she snarled loudly. "How dare you?"

The poor thing was fairly shaking with rage. People were slowing and craning their heads to watch. I cared about that, even if she didn't seem to. I stepped in closer to her.

"My humble apologies. I just assumed you were some piece of cheap Irish trade. My mistake – it is of course a very common thing for respectable young ladies to approach gentlemen in the street unintroduced."

For an instant, I believed she was actually about to attack me, and my mind had already formed the appalling image of me having to fight her off while crowds gathered to watch. But then she slumped, and rubbed her face with her hands.

"I'd already called out to you, but you didn't hear. I got to the gaol too late to meet you at the gate."

"The gaol?"

"You were visiting my brother."

Ah, there it was. Her face resolved itself into its several pieces – the eyes, that forehead, the turns on the side of her mouth. Yes, this was his sister alright.

"My apologies, Ms Kelly…"

"It's Mrs Skillion, actually. But you can call me Maggie."

I didn't really want to call her anything. I glanced down the street.

"Why didn't Gaunson come himself?" she demanded.

"Well, he is a Member of Parliament. Very busy man…"

She harrumphed at that. "Look, Mr..."

"You can call me William."

"Look. I'd rather not stand talking in the street – respectable or not. I want to hear about my brother."

So they were restricting his visitors. Afraid of an escape attempt? Or assisted suicide to avoid the noose? Sometimes happened.

"Let me buy you a drink at the Royal."

I suppose a true gentleman would have refused the suggestion on several grounds. However...

I made a show of consulting my watch. "I can spare you a little time."

She gave me a tight smile and set off at a cracking pace. I caught her up, and she led me down Russel Street to the premises she had mentioned, a glorious building several stories high. I was looking for the entrance to the lounge when she pushed through the main doors before I could stop her - I was set to call her back when the smell from inside hit me: coffee.

God damn it.

FIVE

The coffee palace. I ask you, what greater hell can there be than this? A building that lures the unwary in by presenting itself on the outside as a normal hotel, even calls itself names like "The Royal," only to reveal a hidden nest of teetotallers inside. Worst of all: religious teetotallers, like the Independent Order of Rechabites or some other such nonsense, intent on saving the rest of us, one liver at a time whether we liked it or not. Well, they weren't getting mine.

This one had a generous sized lower level, and stairs leading up to function rooms and accommodation. They even had billiard rooms I could see further out the back – what a way to ruin a gentleman's fun; suggest a game of billiards and *coffee*?

Kelly's sister attracted the attention of a dago waiter fairly dripping with pomade, and we were shown to a table in the busy front room.

"Do you mind?" she asked as we sat. "I could murder for something hot."

I was eyeing off a cart laden with cream cakes coming our way. "I suppose a coffee would not be out of the question."

"I can't stand that muck," she grimaced. Her mouth turned down in that way again – a smaller, feminine version of her brother's frown. "Tea for me. And I'm paying, no argument."

She'd get none from me. I signalled to our oily friend and repeated our order twice to be sure he understood. I was wondering if her generosity would extend itself to a nice pastry but she waved the cart away in impatience.

"Now, tell me everything. How is he?"

"He is quite well. He seemed to be a little troubled by the wounds in his legs."

"That bastard sergeant."

"Uh, quite. Apart from that, he seems well enough. A little drawn, maybe."

"And his spirits?"

"As good as can be expected, given the circumstances."

She sat back, as at that moment our beverages arrived. There was an awkward pause while our waiter made a great show of pouring her tea, and presenting me my dark brew, then a bowl of sugar cubes, then a small jug of cream. He appeared to wish for applause, as if he had conjured them out of the air, rather than from the doubtlessly vermin infested kitchen out the back. I used the moment to look again at the young woman's face, only to find her cool eyes already studying me. At last, the unctuous fellow could find no more reason to dawdle, and withdrew.

"Given the circumstances," she repeated, stirring her tea. "You don't seem very positive about his chances of getting off."

I choked, spluttering some coffee across the tablecloth. "Getting off? He isn't going to be getting off. Surely you realise they are going to hang the poor sod?"

The eyes flashed again. I wondered what they would like in the moonlight.

"Fine talk coming from his defence!"

"I'm only being realistic..."

"Well, you are the one who calls himself a lawyer! It is your job to think of something!"

"Actually, I don't... Well, it is up to Gaunson and whoever acts as his barrister to prepare his defence. But really, Ms Kelly, Mrs Skill... Maggie. The evidence against him is very tight, I gather. And so far, well, I wouldn't exactly say that your brother is helping himself..."

She stared at me over her cup, lips puckering. I thought she was going to speak, or blow me a kiss, but she merely blew onto her tea. The silence stretched out. I couldn't help notice a fat banking type out of the corner of my eye biting into a particularly moist looking slice of cream cake.

"My God," she said at last. "You don't believe him. You don't believe it's true. You don't believe in Blighters."

The fellow chewed with his mouth open, which rather dissolved my interest. She leaned across the table, capturing my eye.

"William, I have seen them with my own two eyes. Seen them rend a man into pieces. They should be giving my brother a medal for what he has done, not stick him in that hole. When this colony hears what has been going on..." She leaned back, perhaps embarrassed by showing such passion, and made a show of pushing a stray piece of hair behind her ear. "I just need you to hear him out, William. Hear the whole story. Help him have his chance in court. Then we'll see who will hang."

I didn't know what to say. Tell her I was intending to walk away? Have no more part of this? She was watching me again, as if reading my thoughts. I shifted uncomfortably. Mystics and mind readers, walking undead and conspiracies...

"Will Mr Skillion be joining you?" I asked.

"Mr Skillion is in gaol. Has been for years. That's the price you pay for being associated with the Kelly's." She counted coins from her purse and placed them on the table. She rose, and waved me to stay in my seat as I made to stand. She stood beside me and gripped my arm. "We don't have many friends in the city, my brother and I. We need all the help we can get."

With that, she left me, picking her way between the tables. I watched her go, and then glanced up to find the waiter also admiring her retreating form. He looked at me and grinned, revealing a gold tooth. I frowned, and rooted through the coins on the table, carefully removing the gratuity that Maggie had left. I enjoyed watching his grin turn to a scowl as I sauntered from the place.

What to do? Legally, the situation was hopeless. Ned was guilty of murder, and the murder of police officers at that. There were many in the legal profession who would avoid such foregone defeat like a dead rat, men who prided themselves on winning stakes and percentages. Mind you, there were always others who claimed a higher moral calling and made a name for themselves defending the defenceless, and I could see a certain cachet in that. But to be involved in a case based on such lunacy, that was another thing altogether.

I set off towards the station and the omnibus stop. On the other hand, I was pretty skint and couldn't rely on receiving any more money from dear papa any time soon. And while I could cable him with the threat of returning home unless I received a bonus, that was a shot I preferred to hold back as an absolute last resort, particularly when I didn't have the wherewithal to go through with it if the crafty old bugger called my bluff.

More to the point, I couldn't get the sight of Maggie Skillion's quite delectable posterior as she left the hotel out of my mind. Needing all the help she could get, indeed.

I slouched along down Russell Street and found I was just in time for the next omnibus. It actually wasn't that far out to Fitzroy, where I was lodging, but it was hard to shake that ingrained attitude that a gentleman doesn't walk, except out along the heath with an over-and-under resting broken open over one arm, while one's tenants beat the scrub for pheasants. The bus was crowded, of course, and smelled – but to their credit, they made sure the horse teams were changed regularly, so you didn't too often have the annoying sight of every passing pedestrian actually overtaking you.

Probably the best thing about the bus – apart from its reasonable three penny fare – was that it terminated in Fitzroy at the Birmingham Hotel. It was quite natural for the majority of the passengers to pile off the bus and head straight inside. Normally, I would have joined them, but I did not yet have any acquaintances firm enough to stand me some drinks, and I was displaying an admittedly out of character concern for the state of my finances.

I cursed and slapped my head as I realised I had forgotten to go see Gaunson. There wasn't time now to go back and track him down – who knew where he may have moved on to after the Club. Besides, here I was. By going with Maggie and then catching the bus, I had more or less made my decision. I needed the money, and to be honest, I could probably do with the distraction. Melbourne was not London. Wilde might have opined that when a man was tired of London he must be tired of life, but let him spend a month trying to amuse himself here.

Decision made, I increased my pace, threading my way past tired working men trudging home from the nearby factories. There was the smell of sweat and oil about them, that kind of modern smell taking over from the older working smells of horse and leather that I recalled fondly as I larked about on my family estate, watching the staff go about their work and generally getting in the way. I turned off down a quiet side street and was shortly pushing open the gate that led into the front yard of the mansion where I was residing.

As usual, the door stuck as I tried to push it open, requiring some thrusting on my behalf. The carpet inside was too thick and carelessly laid over older shabbier floor coverings, no one troubling to do the job properly. The air inside smelled of mildew and decay, but the place was clean enough. There were raised voices coming from somewhere out the back, down the narrow passage by the staircase, but this was nothing new.

I had a foot on the first stair when the door to the parlour swung open.

"Mr Adams."

"Now, Mrs Mackie," I said, swinging around with a smile. "You know I have asked you to call me Robert."

"And I have asked you to be prompt with your rent. Where is it?"

"Why, you know, Mrs Mackie, in the excitement of my day, I clear forgot to go to my bank! A terrible oversight, forgive me. But let me tell you..."

"Excitement, is it? Most likely chasing some floozy around a booze hall."

"Nothing could be further from the truth, dear lady. Why, I was sampling the wares in a delightful temperance hotel. Nothing stronger than coffee has passed these lips." On an impulse, I stepped towards her. "Smell my breath!"

I breathed out in her direction, and she recoiled, butting up against the parlour door.

"And as for floozies as you term them, well, you should know that an educated gentleman such as I, prefers ladies with a certain, shall we say, substance to them." I treated her to my best smile.

She frowned. I was beginning to wonder if the cow had any blood flowing through her veins at all. I had been trying to bed her in the hope of a sharp reduction in rent, for some weeks. I had expected an easy victory, the besieged city opening its gates wide in surrender, as it were, but had been met so far with an impenetrable wall of rejection. An iron-clad bodice.

"You do understand how this arrangement works; do you not, Mr Adams? This is a boarding house. I provide lodgings in return for regular rent. No payment, and you are out in the street, gentleman or not."

"Of course, of course. Honestly, it is just that by the time I was finished speaking with my new client, Mr Kelly... You know, *the* Mr Kelly." Had this woman never opened a newspaper? "Ned Kelly..."

"I know who he is. Am I meant to be impressed that you are representing such a cur?"

"Well..."

"All that does is proves to me what a pack of jackals you legal types are, running after men such as him."

"Everyone's entitled to a fair trial, Mrs Mackie."

"Did he give a fair trial to those poor policemen he executed at Stringybark?"

So much for using my potential new found fame to bring her on; here was another firmly in the 'hang him high' camp. I smiled and continued up the stairs, careful to step lightly as she hated the upstairs tenants "clomping up and down like a battalion of Frenchies." She was a difficult woman to like, it had to be said, and not at all what you would call attractive. I had been hoping that she would, however, prove herself to be a tigress in the dark, which would make up for her other missing charms. I had thought her a widow and she had never corrected my use of Mrs, but I was beginning to suspect she was a spinster, and may have been totally oblivious to my wooing.

On the second level, I padded down the short hallway and opened the door to my room. In the building's glory days it was probably a child's room – and not a favoured child at that. Now, its cramped gloom was what I called home. It did have a small window, looking out onto the dank passage that ran beside this home and the next, and I stood there now, gazing through smeared glass at the red bricks across from me. There was a window in a similar position in that house, but I had never seen anyone through it, never seen any signs of life. I stood here sometimes in the dark, watching, faint fantasies of bohemian female artistes sitting and drinking gin in their underclothes playing across my mind. But the room remained empty. Or else whoever lived in it never looked out or lit a lamp. A recluse, perhaps? Was there a watcher in the darkness, staring out at me?

I shuddered and turned away, my growling stomach reminding me I had not eaten since luncheon. Pity to have missed out on that cake... And there, my thoughts were back again to Maggie Kelly. I really must avail myself of one of the area's working girls, and get rid of some of this pent up lust, if it meant that otherwise every young woman I spoke to was going to haunt my thoughts for hours afterwards.

But it was more than that. There was a hollow ache growing in my chest that I recognized as an old acquaintance, if not a welcome one.

I lit a candle, and found a hunk of stale bread I had saved from breakfast, and sat on my narrow bed gnawing on that. If only I had some alcohol. I rubbed at my chest. Shadows flickered on the walls. Swirling memories of dinner parties and dances crowded my head. Careless, greedy laughter and red shining faces. Drifting cigar smoke and my feet up on the couch. Their tearful faces and bile in my throat. And always my secret burden, my monster, carried through it all. Screaming into my pillow. The counterpoint weight of the gun wrapped in oilcloth beneath my mattress – not enough. Relentless.

It sat there now, this gaping, aching hole in my chest, unsatisfied, untouched by food, waiting to be filled by something...something...

A free man. Such a free man.

SIX

"I knew you'd be back," he said.

"I was rather under the impression you told me to."

"But you were tempted not to come, weren't you?" He smiled. "Don't play poker, Remittance Man, you're an easy read."

"How delightful to know. Pity no one told me earlier; could have saved a bundle."

"I don't mean to give offence. I'm pleased to see you. Talking to you yesterday brought some memories back to life... brought Dan back to life, for a short while. It is nice to think of him as that young boy."

"Yes, well. We'll have to speed things up a bit today if we are to be ready in time for your trial."

He nodded. "I was...tired yesterday. I'm feeling better today. We'll make good headway."

I pulled the chair out from the table and set out my paper and pen. Ned sat smoothing the coarse material of his trousers across his legs. He did look better. A touch more liveliness about his eyes, though they still appeared a little sunken. I noticed his lashes, and the gentle broad arc of his brow. They were brother and sister alright.

"What are you looking at?" he asked.

"I met your sister yesterday."

His hands stopped and lay still in his lap. He gazed down at them. "You saw her?"

"Yes. We had tea."

His head lifted, and the eyes weren't like hers at all. Hers were all fire and passion – these were like the dead eyes of a shark. I'd seen one once, on a Sydney beach, dragged ashore by fishermen. Though it thrashed and gnashed its triangular teeth, desperate to live or at least to kill, the whole while, its eyes remained empty, blank. That was the most terrifying thing about it.

"Did you indeed?"

"Yes. But that's all. Of course. She asked to see me." Why was I explaining myself to this man? "To talk about you."

"It would probably be for the best," he said carefully, "if you stayed away from her."

"Really?"

"Yes. You see, I have your measure."

"You did hear me say that *she* sought *me* out?"

He was silent, brooding. I wondered if I ought to go, come back tomorrow. I could go find Gaunson and try to get some money out of him.

"You see, it is difficult getting used to being here. Without any power. I can tell you to keep well away from her, Remittance Man, but how can I make sure that happens? I could break your neck, but then would anyone else come and take my story? Would I still get a chance to have my say in court? No, there is too much at stake... But I tell you this," And I did meet his eyes now, and found myself held by them. "If you do wrong by her in any way, it will come back to bite you. Do you understand?"

I nodded. Was every session doomed to be so uncomfortable? Perhaps the best thing to do was to get it over and done with as quickly as possible. I shuffled my papers and licked the tip of my pen, and with a jolly tone that did not reflect how I was feeling said, "Well then. Shall we begin? Where were we? You were a young boy..."

"We can skip a few years. I didn't have any more contact with the Blighted until I was about 20. In the intervening years, I had a few run-ins with the law – horse stealing and the like - but I'd resolved to become an honest working man, for the sake of my ma... And then something strange happened..."

My pen scratched. He was a tearaway, I wrote.

He was a tearaway. A horse and cattle thief, and Irish besides, and so attracted the attention of the local constabulary. Petty enough stuff, but you had to keep on top of them, these wild colonial boys, or before you knew it, you had a real problem on your hands. Such was the opinion of the local superintendent, Nicholson. The Greta Mob, they called themselves, and pretty much all of them, all the main players in the story - Aaron Sherritt, Joe Byrne, Steve Hart - took their turn breaking their backs doing hard labour for six or twelve months stints at Beechworth Gaol.

They broke the law for sport more than anything else; something to relieve the tedium of life on the land. But this summer Ned had just returned from Pentridge gaol, where he had done three years. As such, he was held in a little awe by the other Mob members. This was serious gaol time, not like the sentences they had been receiving. As such, when Ned told them all that he was going straight, they took him at his word, and did not seek to change his mind. Indeed, as the unofficial leader of the group, his decision had a steadying effect on them, and the young men settled down.

That just left two problems: how to supplement their meagre incomes, and how to find a spot of fun.

That summer, the answer to both questions appeared to come in the form of the Greta Show. An annual event, it was the highlight for the district. Farmers got to display their prize produce, graziers showed their best beef and the young men tore around on horseback, racing and jumping, seeking in equal parts to impress the young ladies of the district and win the approval of their mates.

This year, there was even something a little more exotic – a travelling boxing troop; although troop was a bit of an exaggeration. For curious locals who read the sides of the wagons noted that there seemed only to be one fighter featured. The Wild Man. A boxing troop surviving on the ability of a single pugilist? He would have to be something special indeed.

Five young men stood looking at the faded adverts painted on one of the wagons, their hands thrust deep in their pockets, hats sitting back on their heads.

"Come see Jimmy Charming's Wild Man," read Joe Byrne.

"Says here the fellow is unbeaten," said Dan Kelly.

"They always say that," said Joe. "They're hardly going to say Old Plonker Tomkins, Knocked Cold More Times Than You've Had Hot Dinners, are they now?"

"Reckon you could beat him, Ned?" asked Aaron Sherritt.

"Course he could!" said Dan. "Couldn't you, Ned?"

Ned shrugged, but his eyes glittered as he read the words "Huge Cash Prizes." It would be a fine thing to come riding home to Eleven Mile Creek with a purse full of coins. Wouldn't Ma be pleased with that?

"I've a mind to try," said Ned.

"Maybe I'll have a crack, too," said Aaron, and the others laughed derisively. Ned ruffled his hair and walked off. Aaron was the last to follow, and none noticed how his face went dark and red.

Instead of the usual tent, the fight was set to take place in a stockyard, which had been surrounded by a high canvas wall. People were already standing around or seated on the wooden benches when the boys arrived. Though it would be easy to cheat and slip under the canvas, people had their pride and were content to pay their coin for the prospect of a good beating. On the far side, there was a gap in the yard fence, and a closed wagon had been backed up to it. The boys found a sweating man in a faded red jacket, and Ned registered himself with a handshake and a fee.

"Jimmy Charming," said the man. "Think you can survive the Wildman, young fellow?"

Ned shrugged. "I hope to at least make a good show of it."

"Ned's pretty much a wild man himself," said Dan. The showman gave him a tight smile.

"Well, we'll see, won't we?" He turned back to Ned. "Now don't be too put off by his appearance. It's all in the name of theatricality, you understand? Makes it a bit more exciting, and to be fair, his style is more grappling than boxing. But you can feel free to hit him, fair enough?"

He clapped Ned on the shoulder and climbed over the rail, while Ned started stripping off his shirt and jacket. He passed them to Steve, who folded them carefully across his arm.

"Ladies and gentlemen!" cried Jimmy, turning slowly with arms outstretched in the centre of the yard. "Ladies and gentlemen, the time has come!"

Most of the loud conversations around the fence quietened, and there was a scattering of applause.

"Ladies and gentlemen, if I could have your attention! The time for combat has arrived! The time for one of your own to take on the Wildman in a display of courage and martial skill! From Eleven Mile Creek, I give you..." He consulted the paper in his hand. "Edward Kelly!"

Ned walked up the railings of the fence like it was nothing, swinging a leg over at the top and dropping lightly down onto the other side. There were a few cheers and whistles, and cries of "Get 'im, Ned!" and "Go the Kelly's!" Ned started jogging around the yard lightly on his toes, swinging his long muscled arms. He danced around behind Jimmy, shadowboxing him, and the crowd laughed.

The showman smiled, but his eyes were dark. "Ladies and gentlemen! I urge you – no matter what may happen in the ring – do not enter this space when the fight begins! The Wildman is a dangerous foe! No matter what befalls Mr Kelly, please allow my team to act. They are professionals. Please do not get in the way."

The crowd laughed. The showman glanced behind and realised Ned was mimicking him. He smiled again, lips pulling tightly back over his teeth. "This fight continues until Mr Kelly submits!"

"When he beats the brains out of your wild man, more likely!" shouted Dan, and the crowd cheered.

Jimmy bowed slightly, and then suddenly stepped nimbly sideways towards the wagon. "Without any further ado – I give you... the Wildman!"

He stepped up onto the side of the wagon and pulled a lever. With a groan, the back fell with a crash. Necks craned as people tried to peer into the darkness of the interior. Those closest suddenly exclaimed loudly, and a woman screamed. Those further away called out "What? What is it?" Ned ceased his movement, and stood, watching, fists raised.

"There's something in there!" someone yelled.

"Here he comes!" cried someone else.

The wagon shook and a dark figure burst out into the light. He lurched down the ramp, and there was a terrible metallic jangling behind him – three long chains ran from his back, into the hands of a trio of muscular men standing on the top of the wagon with Jimmy Charming. There were cries from the crowd – some of horror, some of derision. For the man who stood there now, swaying slightly, was a very strange looking fellow indeed. He appeared to be clad entirely in a suit of leather, tightly strapped about him. His hands were covered in leather gloves, his face covered in a mask except for two glass eye holes. There appeared to be a mouth hole, but that was tightly stitched shut. He did not appear overly large – he certainly wasn't as big as any of the men who held him by the chains locked onto a large ring in the back of his suit.

The Wildman craned his head around, and then seemed to suddenly notice Ned standing in the centre of the yard. There was a muffled growl, and he lurched into movement, arms held out before him. With a jerk, the three men snapped their chains, and the Wildman was held, reaching for Ned.

"Theatricality," said Ned to himself.

"Behold the Wildman!" cried Jimmy, and the crowd was silent, unsettled. "No mercy! No fear! No hope for any who face him!" He turned his gaze down onto Ned, who seemed somehow smaller as he stood with his bony fists next to his face. "Good luck to you, son."

With that, the carnies let the chain slide through their calloused fingers. The Wild Man staggered forward, recovered, and came at Ned on stiff legs. He stood his ground, and just before the Wild Man reached him, easily ducked below his arms and let go a savage rip to the solar plexus.

"Ho!" cried Dan, who had been the victim of a similar

punch from his brother many times. That was the thing with Ned – he always kept his head, and when you came in swinging wildly in a fury, he'd watch for the opening and drill you.

The Wild Man, however, appeared unfazed. He spun around, and one of his outstretched arms cracked across Ned's face. Ned stepped back, and dabbed at this nose where a thin trickle of blood began to flow. The Wild Man paused for a moment, seeming to lean towards him, then surged forward again. Ned gave way, and let go with a series of jabs – one, two, three – straight into the masked face. Each snapped the Man's head back, but did not slow him. Ned ducked and weaved the other way, coming around behind him, and caught him a prodigious straight right to the back of the head. The force sent the Wild Man overbalancing and falling face forward into the dust.

The crowd erupted. Ned held his hands above his head and turned, accepting the applause.

"Ned!" cried Joe.

The Wild Man barrelled into Ned from behind, wrapping his arms around him and mashing his masked face into the side of Ned's neck.

"Head butt! Head butt!" cried Dan and Joe.

"If he gets pinned he loses!" cried Jimmy from on top of the wagon.

"Stay up, Ned! Stay up!"

Ned, legs buckling under the relentless grappling of the Wild Man, managed to turn so they were pressed chest to chest. He then suddenly dropped, and rolled clear, springing to his feet before the Wild Man could react.

"He went down!" cried Jimmy. "He loses!"

The crowd booed in fury. An apple core bounced off Jimmy's shoulder. Ned, meanwhile, had danced back in and sunk a series of blows into the Wild Man's head and kidneys. Again, the leather-clad figure spun around with a muffled roar.

The three carnies gripped their chains, looking to Jimmy, who was in turn surveying the baying crowd with a shrewd eye. He made a tiny gesture, and the brawny men relaxed their grip, giving the Wildman more slack to move with.

"He can't last in that suit," said Joe. "He must be baking!"

Ned himself was streaming with sweat, making it harder for the leather mitts of the Wild Man to find purchase, which was as well, since he was breathing hard and moving slower. His opponent, on the other hand, continued at the same slow but inexorable pace, pursuing him back and forward across the yard. Strangely, the Wild Man made no moves to defend himself, and Ned was able to hit him with impunity. There was no smile on his face now. Rather, he battered the Wild Man with a grim determination, his knuckles bloody from contact with the leather.

Then Ned found himself backed into a corner of the yard, and the Wildman lunged at him, nearly pinning him against the thick wooden planks. Ned just managed to slide himself free and past, his chest scratched red from the leather suit. But as he went, his foot caught in a divot and he went sprawling, completely unbalanced. The Wildman twisted and roared. He moved to throw himself on Ned, who was crawling backwards desperately, but then – stopped. He turned his head in confusion, and tried to lunge at Ned again, but again seemed unable to move. He strained, and there was a tearing sound – his suit had become hooked on a nail, and now tore free, opening a gash in the leather torso. The sudden release brought the Wildman crashing down onto his hands and knees.

Ned meanwhile climbed to his feet, breathing laboured, raising his shaking bleeding fists beside his head. He stepped in, and delivered a vicious downwards punch to the side of the Wildman's head – then recoiled –

"Jesus Christ!" He turned away, bent over, and vomited prodigiously into the saleyard mud.

His cry was taken up by all the spectators sitting around that part of the stand. Handkerchiefs went to noses and people leapt to their feet and a few even moved away.

"What is it?" asked Aaron. They were on the other side of the yard and could smell nothing. Dan was staring intently at Ned, who in that moment turned and met his eye. Ned nodded. Dan nodded back, lips tight and grim.

"It's a bloody Blighter."

"What?" asked Aaron.

"It isn't alive," said Dan.

"What do you mean?"

"I'll explain later."

"Is Ned in trouble then?" asked Steve.

"Not now that he knows what he's up against," said Dan, and his confidence reassured the others, even if they did not yet understand fully what he meant.

The Wildman had regained his feet, and was following Ned, who, in a burst of new found energy was jogging backwards, back toward the wagon and Jimmy, just outside its reach. Again, the leather clad figure came on in that same unstoppable way. Ned suddenly spun around, and seized the closest chain. He whipped hard, and the burly carnie pitched forward into the yard. With a shriek, he scrambled to his feet and threw himself at the wagon, feet kicking and scraping as he attempted to climb up. His mates threw their chains down, and grabbed his flailing arms, straining to haul his weight to the roof of the wagon while Jimmy cursed at them.

Ned moved backwards, gathering the long length of chain into his hands. The Wildman paused, head swinging from Ned to the beefy legs of the carnie, swinging wildly before it. Ned whistled sharply, and the leather head turned back towards him.

The Wildman charged in its awkward staggering fashion, covering the ground surprisingly quickly. Ned darted forward, spinning past, and neatly dropped a loop of chain around the Wildman's neck. Then, as if it were nothing, with the chain held over his shoulder, Ned walked up the slats of the stockyard fence, balancing on the top. He swiftly gathered the chain tight to his chest – and jumped. The chain snapped tight, and the Wildman slammed head first into the fence, right into the sharp hard corner of a fence post, shaking it with the impact.

The crowd gasped. Jimmy and his workers stared, as the Wildman slid slowly down the post. There was a noticeable dent in its head, its skull fractured. Ned dusted off his hands and climbed slowly back over the railings. He walked into the middle of the yard, and waited.

Jimmy stared at him, and said, "Knocked cold. Looks like a tie?"

The crowd was outraged. Joe and Dan were on their feet, yelling. Steve shook his head.

"Perhaps the fellow needs some air, under all that leather," said Ned. "Shall I loosen his collar?"

If you weren't looking for it, you would miss the look that passed between the two.

"Well, then," said Jimmy through gritted teeth. "Looks like we have a winner."

The boys surged into the yard and lifted Ned onto their shoulders, and he threw his head back and laughed, and laughed again shortly after when Jimmy dropped a prize purse into his hands.

And later, back home, if Ma's hands were none too gentle, and the carbolic stung, well, all in all it was still a fine thing.

SEVEN

"So you had a boxing match. With one of the Blighted."

"Yes."

"An undead pugilist?"

"Well, to be fair he was more of a brawler. What he was before he was Blighted, I can't say. He may have been a fair man with his fists, but once Blighted... Well, they turn into biters, then. I'm the first to admit I was lucky he was wearing a mask. You have to remember, these were the early days of the Blight. Nobody knew exactly how it was passed on. Jimmy just wanted to stop his freak from biting bits off of people. And to disguise it, of course. Lucky for me."

"But why... why..."

"Low overheads? Who knows? Maybe the Wildman was one of his original troop, and got bit one night... Jimmy worked out a way to keep him, and make use of him, while hiding the truth of what had happened."

"To what end, though?"

"Apart from the money, you mean? I told you, there's a conspiracy. If he advertised he was using a Blighter in fights, he'd have been shut down faster than I could down a pint. And he probably would have disappeared into the bargain."

"It just doesn't make sense..."

"To you, maybe. But we aren't anywhere near the end of the story. Keep an open mind. Wait and see what you think."

I stroked my chin. "So what did happen to this Jimmy? You just let him go?"

"That's right. Warned him not to come back round Greta way if he valued his whiskered chin. Hopefully, the bastard was dumb enough to go out looking for another Blighter and got bit himself. Or eaten outright."

I mopped my face. My stomach growled loudly, causing Ned to chuckle.

"All this talk making you hungry, Remittance Man?"

"I confess I could use a break."

"Well, I'd invite you to stay and share my noontime slop, but there is barely enough for one, let alone two."

"Quite alright. I'll return in an hour or two, if you like."

He nodded, but his mercurial mood seemed to have soured again, as it seemed capable of doing at the drop of a hat. Must have been a moody brat to raise. I banged on the door, but was kept waiting some minutes until Father Time, my original warder arrived, grumbling.

"It's mealtime," he said, glowering at me.

"Yes, but is there any link between that statement and your current activity?" I asked, pointedly looking up and down at this tunic, which was covered in many splashes and drops of some foul muck. I was rewarded with a faint chuckle from the bed behind me as I brushed past. I strode down the central way of the gaol, Father Time scurrying to keep up, while the rest of his cohort banged around on the other levels with dented tureens.

Out in the courtyard, I was relieved to feel the sun hit my face. It was one of the best things about this country, the sunlight. It felt healing. Nothing like that runny uncooked egg sunshine of England, this light was a virile, vibrant thing. I recalled the voyage out here, when the other first class passengers largely kept to their cabins, groaning and sweltering in a fog of laudanum. I much preferred the open deck – as far up the bow as the crew would let me, and the combination of warmth and stinging spray had been like a blessing, like forgiveness.

There was a sudden jarring crash, causing both the warder and I to jump. A book smashed through one of the upper windows of the administration block, fluttering heavily to the ground like a shot pheasant, amongst a snowfall of shattered glass. The warder swore, and clutched at his chest. I looked upwards, shading my eyes, at the dark hole from whence the book had come, ringed with pointed shards. A wan face appeared, gazing miserably down at the book on the ground: Castieau.

I made a show of hastening over and recovering the volume, holding it gingerly and brushing at the dirt and glass. I held it aloft and waved limply at Castieau, who hesitated for a moment then waved back. He disappeared from view, and I heard angry voices and a slamming door. I turned the book to read the spine: it was indeed assorted articles as to the keeping of Her Majesty's guests, volume nine or some such. It figured. I opened my hand and let the tome fall back to the ground with a thud. My shadow tut-tutted and lunged past me, picking it up and holding it to him like it was a small child. Or a full bottle.

The door of the administration block crashed open, and a Fury burst out.

"I hope you rot in hell, you fuckin' English pig!" she screamed, and stormed towards the gate.

"Maggie!"

I started, for the voice that called to her was not mine, though I had just been about to speak. A lanky bushman with a thick beard had followed her out of the block, and was hurrying after her. The outer door was swung open for them with a scowl by a sallow warder I hadn't seen before.

"Maggie," I croaked. She didn't hear me. I ran after them. "Maggie!"

I came out onto the street, to find her standing white faced and trembling with rage. The fellow with her was standing in front of her, arms moving in strange patterns, unsure what to do, whether to take hold of her or not – his arms went out to the side, towards her, back down – the great oaf. Her fine dark eyes were darting from side to side – then she saw me. She pushed past the bushman without noticing and ran to me. My own arms started to rise towards her of their own accord, but of course she wasn't coming to me for that, and it took great effort to stop them and hold them steady. I saw him notice the move though, and hate me.

"William!" she cried, grabbing my sleeve. "Have you seen him? Were you with him?"

"Yes. Yes, I just left him. Whatever is the matter?"

Tears glittered in her eyes. "I'm still not allowed in to see him! My own fuckin' brother!"

"It's the governor, isn't it?" I asked gravely, patting her hand, pressing it. "Castieau?"

"The dirty fucker." She came back to herself, and released me, sliding her hand out from under mine. "Where are my manners? You'll think me some kind of... William, this is a dear friend of mine. Tom. Tom Lloyd."

I shook his calloused hand, and smiled as he tried to grind the bones in mine. He was a good size man, but ill at ease in the suit he wore. His oiled hair glinted in the light.

"Shall we take tea?" I asked Maggie, and she rewarded me with a small smile.

"We could go back to the Royal..." she said.

"Oh no." said Tom. "I'm not going there. I need proper food. I want steak and eggs."

Maggie frowned, and looked back at me. "Do you mind, William? Will you come with us? He gets in such a state if he doesn't eat half a cow a day."

"I don't mind at all," I told her. I smiled at Tom. Lunch is on you, cocky, I thought to myself, even if you don't know it yet.

At Tom's suggestion we walked together down towards the river, where we were more likely to find the kind of restaurant where a yokel like him would feel comfortable – but which he no doubt would think was the height of sophistication. Maggie walked between us, and as a gentleman, I took position closest to the street. I hoped to subtly drift closer to her, and thus force Tom uncomfortably close to the shopfronts, but when I bumped against her, she didn't seem to mind and didn't move away as I expected. Strange, the impact of these small contacts, small collisions, usually meaningless in a busy city. Almost like a language now, a conversation. Though I wasn't sure exactly what was being said, and by whom.

Close by the station on Flinders Street, we found a place with a carpet of dead flies in the window that seemed to suit Tom. He led us in and shouted unnecessarily loudly at the waiter for a table. I writhed internally with embarrassment for Maggie, but she hid it well and even smiled indulgently at her tame cocky. The food, however, turned out to be very good indeed. The steaks were large, and it had been so long since I'd enjoyed such a fine piece of meat that I was almost completely able to tune out the smacking lips and belches from the third wheel at our table. Maggie proved to have a good appetite, which I appreciate in a woman. Dining is not a spectator sport – if you are in company, you are best to show yourself a willing part of the fellowship. Besides, I believed a healthy appetite for food reflected a healthy appetite for other of life's pleasures.

"Tom has been such a support," Maggie told me.

Just not in bed, I hoped fervently. "Lovely," I said. "Are you married, Mr Lloyd?"

He shook his head, sucking on a bone. "Tom."

"I don't know what I'd do without him," Maggie continued. "He's my rock, with Bill – Mr Skillion – in gaol."

"Staying long?"

He shrugged. "Dunno. Long as Maggie needs me."

"And you have that other matter," Maggie said to him, somewhat pointedly. He shrugged, and would not meet her eye. "Tom, William can help us. He has been in to see Ned twice now..."

"And I'm going back this afternoon," I volunteered. Tom scowled.

"Let him take the message! Tom!"

She had his sleeve, twisting it, imploring him. Suddenly, a single tear rolled down her cheek and splashed onto the stained white cloth covering the table. I watched it form a flower of dark dampness, the edges softening, spreading, as the moisture was absorbed by the threads.

"How do we know we can trust him?"

I shook myself, and drew up in haughty disdain, but Maggie beat me to it.

"Tom! He's defending Ned! Besides which – I say we can trust him. That's how we know. And that had better be good enough for you. He's my brother, after all."

Funny, isn't it, how people flesh out details in their heads. It's like all you have to do is provide an outline, like a paper doll cut-out, and the foolish and naïve will rush in to colour it the way they want to see it. Here was Maggie, now adamantly certain that I was a champion of her brother, eyes flashing as she defended me to whoever this was to her - what was he to her? – when just yesterday she had been furious at my apparent lack of belief.

"Staying nearby?" I asked.

"At the Robert Burns Hotel," he said. A pause, then he looked at me. "Same as Maggie."

Oh, you bastard.

"Tell Ned," he said, suddenly leaning forward. "Tell Ned... the horses are on the track."

"The horses are on the track?"

"The horses," he repeated, slowly, like I was an ass, "are on the track."

"That's what I said," I snapped. "I heard you the first time."

"Thank you, William," said Maggie. "It will mean a lot to Ned, having someone like you to help him."

And what about you, I nearly asked out loud, but didn't. We finished up, and the waiter brought over the bill. I picked it up – not too bad, but more than I could comfortably deal with – and Tom offered to pay. I beamed my thanks and promptly handed it to him. He took it, frowning at it, seemingly unable to believe I had accepted so quickly. I thanked him warmly and swiftly stood, pulling my jacket back on.

"Well!" I said. "Must get back! There's a man's life to save!"

Maggie smiled at me and I tipped my hat to her. Then with a wink at Tom, who was still holding the bill in confusion, walked boldly from the café and back up towards the gaol.

"Good lunch?" asked Ned.

"Not bad."

"You had meat. I can smell the grease on you."

"Sorry..."

He waved a hand. "Eat alone?"

"Uh... yes."

Those damned eyes of his. Worse than my first form master.

"Nobody spoke to you? No one?"

"No..."

There was a pause that stretched out between us then, stretched out tighter and thinner until it fairly screamed in silent vibration. He was not the only master of silence within that dank cell. Where others would have rushed and tripped in to fill the void with awkward words, I held my tongue and held my ground. Waiting.

The horses are on the track...

"Let's keep going," he said roughly.

I sat, and took up my pen. My hand shook slightly, but I breathed slowly to still it.

"Meat!" he said, as he arranged his long legs on the bed. "What I wouldn't give for some roast beef..."

EIGHT

"What I wouldn't give for some roast beef," said Ned, as they took a break from the sawing and stretched their cramping muscles.

"Now, Ned, where are we going to get that?" asked Dan. "I thought we was going straight."

"I'm not suggesting we run anything off. I'm just saying."

Dan's face fell a little. Working in a sawmill was honest, upstanding work that made Ma proud, there was no doubt about that... but it did tend to be hot, dusty and not overly fun. Aaron and Joe, who were working with them, put down their axes and joined them for a tin cup of tea.

"How much tea is there in China, Joe?" Aaron asked, swirling his dregs.

"What? How the devil am I supposed to know that?"

"Well, I just thought, you being the resident expert on all things oriental, maybe you'd know."

Joe had grown up next to an old mined out area, recently inhabited by the Chinese. They would regularly set up camps in such areas and meticulously work through the discarded rock, slowly accumulating flecks of gold. White diggers hated them, because with their tireless work ethic they were able to make a tidy profit from fields conventional wisdom said were dug out and exhausted. Joe was one of the rare few who took an interest in their culture, and had even learned to speak a little of their lingo. And didn't that make the other blokes laugh, to hear those funny singsong nasal sounds coming out of the bushy beard of their mate.

"Why do you care how much bloody tea there is in bloody China anyway?" asked Joe, unsure if Aaron was taking the piss or not.

"It's just that people say it all the time, don't they? Not for all the tea in China? They must like it over there, do they?"

"Yes, Aaron. They like tea over there."

"I thought they just liked opium."

"No, Aaron. They don't all just sit around smoking bloody opium. For God's sake..."

"Maybe you should get one of them pigtails, Joe. You'd look sweet."

"Aaron... Just leave off."

"I'd kiss you. What do you reckon, Ned?"

Ned smiled slightly, but said nothing.

"That's it, Aaron!" Joe leapt to his feet. Aaron tried to run, but Joe had him down on the ground within a few yards. "Come and sit on his head for me, Ned!"

"Show us some of those Chinamen tricks, Joe," Ned said instead.

Joe grinned, and seized one of Aaron's hands. He selected a finger and twisted. Aaron shrieked.

"Now, this one is called Wild Chicken Spreads its Wings."

"I love the names," said Dan to Ned, "makes me hungry."

"Get off! Get off you rat bastard! I'll do you! Fight me like a man!"

"This is the manly art of *chin na*, Aaron. It's very old; older than the crumbs in your beard and the stains in your drawers."

"Maybe I should learn some of that," said Ned.

Before the fight could develop further or tail off, Steve came running up. The others watched him with interest – Steve was a natural horseman, who had a bowlegged gate, which, when combined with his penchant for high heel riding boots and strapped moleskins, meant he was fascinating to watch run. Like a duck on loose gravel, said Joe, but not nearly as graceful.

Steve ran past them all, straight to the bucket of water they kept hanging on one of the posts supporting the roof. He scooped a cup of water and poured it over his head, and shook himself, gasping, like some old dog. Joe climbed off Aaron and joined the Kelly brothers. Steve stood there, staring into space.

"What's up then, Steve?" asked Ned.

Steve turned at his voice, and blinked, his eyes coming back into focus. He smiled at Ned, and took a sip of water. The others waited. You couldn't rush Steve to talk – the more you pressed him, the quieter he got.

"Sure was something," he said now. He noticed the water droplets covering his shirt, and started to brush at them with a frown.

"What was, Steve?" Ned asked gently.

"Bull."

"Bull? What bull?"

"Big bull. Big white one."

"White... You don't mean old Harrison's bull? Harrison's *prize* bull?"

"Yup."

"What about it?"

"Something's been and eaten it."

"Something ate Harrison's bull?"

"That thing's a monster," said Joe. "It must weigh... hell, a lot!"

"Show us," said Ned.

Steve nodded, dropped the cup and started walking back the way he'd come, followed by the other three.

"Hold up!" called Ned. He ran to the side of the shed and pulled his carbine from his swag. "You going to sulk or come, Aaron?"

Aaron was sitting in the same spot, flexing his hand. "No. No, you go on without me. I've got some things to do."

"Suit yourself." Ned jogged over to the other three, and they headed down the track into the bush.

The track they were following led along the boundary of Harrison's scrubland, where the wealthy grazier ran a fair sized herd of cattle and some horses besides. He had been a tempting enough target over the years, but had been enjoying a period of calm, where few, if any, of his valuable animals had mysteriously wandered off, since the Greta Mob had settled down. Ned could often be heard railing in the past about the injustice of wealthy squatters like Harrison being able to acquire such large tracts of land, while the poor had to make do with small plots of back-and-heart breaking bush. For these rich nobs and toffs to then complain when one of their fences fell down and an animal or two took the opportunity to trample someone else's patch, well, that was a bit rich, wasn't it?

They continued along the track until Steve pointed to a broad section of the fence, broken outwards towards them. When they had been in the game of faking stock escapes, they had always made it look like small parts of a fence had collapsed from age and wear – but this looked as if someone had driven a herd of cattle right through it. Steve turned off into the scrub, and they followed, noting the broken saplings and churned earth that showed at least one large animal had charged through here, quite recently. As they continued, the scrub became denser, and the land started to rise and become rougher. Soon they were breathing hard and wet with sweat, though all were fit young men.

Then up ahead, there was a glimpse of white among the trees and the tell-tale droning of the flies. The smell hit them soon after – the rich tang of blood, and dung, and meat on the turn.

The bull, or what was left of it, lay tangled in a gulley where it must have become trapped. And there, something had caught up with it. And attacked it.

As Joe had said, this was a prize bull, and huge, but now it lay ruined, a gaping cavity where its intestines should have been, ringed with flies, gouges of flesh torn from its hide. The huge head lay splintered, empty-socketed, the skull cavity clean.

"What in the name of hell..." said Joe.

There was a metallic click. They looked to Ned, who was scanning the trees, the carbine cocked in his hands. "Come on," he said, and without question, they followed him up the slope.

Not far above the carcass, the ground plateaued, and the going was easier for a ways. They moved quietly among the cathedral columns of the trees. Up ahead the land rose again, before rising up almost sheer. And it was here that they caught up with them.

There were four.

Once, they were something else. Perhaps drovers, who had once been sitting on their swags, yarning away the dark night while out mustering on the extreme edge of some squatter's property. Or shearers travelling from station to station, keeping each other company on the lonely roads. Or swagmen, sharing bottles and looking out for each other, sundowners in search of an easy feed.

But they weren't that any more. Somewhere, something

dark and dead had found them. They bore the injuries still, their flesh torn. But the wounds were old and blackened and troubled them no more. They were together now, but not in true comradeship, merely driven by the same hunger. They clawed at the loose scree on the rock face, trying to haul themselves up, but then sliding back down to the bottom. Their ragged, skinless fingers scrabbled, and their clumsy booted feet kicked, but they could not climb. They grabbed at each other, seeking to use one another to climb higher, but showed no anger as they were each in turn hauled down by the efforts of the others. Moans emanated from their gaping lipless mouths, stale rotten air forced from their useless lungs.

"What on earth are they doing?" whispered Dan.

"Trying to climb up," said Joe. "But why?"

Ned pointed. "There. About six feet higher."

They squinted, and saw a young Aboriginal boy, naked, standing silently on a small rocky ledge. He was watching the dead calmly with his liquid brown eyes as they fought to reach him and tear him to pieces.

Ned aimed, and fired.

The ball took one of the Blighters in the neck, spinning it around and slamming it into the rock face.

"Damn," said Ned.

The other three stopped. And turned around.

"Damn!" said Ned.

"Load!" cried Dan.

"It was the noise!" said Joe. "They can hear!"

The dead eyes of the Blighted fixed on them, and they came on together, a ragged charge. Ned's fingers worked feverishly, pulling the ramrod from the barrel, digging in his pocket for another ball. With a guttural roar the Blighters juddered on, their relentless stiff legged gate, their grasping hands, and their gaping teeth-filled mouths.

"Run!" Joe yelled.

However, there came a whirring, and something flashed through the air, and the closest undead lurched, head askew, shattered, and sank onto its knees then down onto its face. The others didn't slow, but then one suddenly sprouted one, two, long dark poles from its back, overbalanced, and went down too. A third pole – a spear - pinned it, vibrating, right through the abdomen and into the dirt. Ned reversed his grip on the carbine, waiting for the final one, as the others instinctively moved back, behind him.

"Come on, you dead bastard," he muttered, bringing the gun back ready.

There came a wittering through the air again, and the Blighter's eyes bulged as a black spike suddenly burst through its ruined mouth, impossibly long, protruding four feet like some monstrous tongue, and it crumpled to the ground.

The four living men stood transfixed by the scene before them. Shadows slowly detached themselves from the surrounding trees, and the men drew together. Ned reversed the carbine, and kept reloading.

The shadows resolved themselves into half a dozen warriors, with dark skin and spears and clubs. They wore little, but carried themselves erect and proud, their skin puckered with neat lines of ceremonial scarring. They moved among the fallen Blighters, to the one pinned through its back by three spears, vainly trying to stand, and their short heavy clubs rose and fell in a series of sickening crunches that caused the white men to flinch and look away. They pulled their long spears from the bodies, using their feet to hold them steady while they pulled. Another picked a boomerang from alongside the shattered head of the third.

There was a groan from near the cliff face, and the fourth Blighter staggered to its feet, its head lolling at an angle where half its neck had been shot away. The Aboriginal warriors yelled and leapt aside, hurrying to fit spears to their woomeras, but Ned already had the carbine up to his cheek. He squeezed the trigger, and this time the ball entered the undead thing's forehead and the back of its head blew apart. It sagged to the ground like a bundle of old clothes.

"You got to get them fellas in the head," said one of the warriors, an older man with white hair and beard, but still well-muscled and fit-looking.

"I know," said Ned. "I missed the first time."

"You fellas alright? None of you been bit?"

The four white men looked at each other questioningly.

"No. No, we're all fine."

"You show us, eh?"

Ned looked at the warrior, then at the rest who had formed an arc around them, spears now fitted, or heavy boomerangs held over their shoulders. Their dark eyes watched, unreadable.

"You fellas show us now. Take off them clothes."

Ned glanced at this carbine, now empty. He looked to the others, shrugged, and started unbuttoning his shirt. The others followed suit, stripping to their undergarments in some bemusement. At the leader's insistence, they held their arms out and turned in slow circles, scrutinised from all sides, before the warrior leader nodded and waved for them to dress again. The band relaxed, stacking their weapons and dragging the bodies away into the bush. One reappeared with a wallaby, already dressed, while another started a fire. The leader called to the young boy, still standing on the ledge, and he came scrambling nimbly down the rock face.

"What was that about?" Dan asked Ned. "We would have told them if we were hurt."

Ned shook his head. "There's something more to it..."

"You fellas hungry?" asked the old warrior. "Give you a feed for any tobacco."

They pooled what they had, and were soon joined in a circle around the fire, watching the meat sizzle on the flames, while most of the natives smoked pipes pulled from small pouches.

"Helps get the smell out of your nose," said the leader, tamping down his tobacco.

"Who are you?" asked Ned.

The leader surveyed him through wisps of white smoke. "We are warriors of the Yaitmathang; these are our lands."

"We haven't seen any Aborigines in these parts for a long time..."

"No? Well, we still here, and we see you. Lucky thing for you, eh?"

Ned shrugged. The leader chuckled deep in his chest.

"What's your name?" asked Joe.

"You can call me Billy."

"That's your name? Billy?"

"No. That is not my name, but that's what you can call me. That the name white fellas on the mission give me. It'll do for you."

"That's where you learned English?"

"That's right. Learned lots of things on the mission. Want to know number one lesson I learned? Keep away from you white fellas." Billy laughed loudly at this, showing nicotine stained teeth. "Now what you fellas doing up here? Plenty dangerous."

"We were looking for them," said Dan. "The Blighters."

"With only one gun? No other weapons? You fellas not too bright, eh?"

"They're pretty slow moving," said Joe. "They can't really run."

"Depend how old they are. Fresh ones, they faster. One at a time, they not so bad," said the leader. "But you get a bunch all together, fresh ones, and you in trouble. They don't stop."

"We've only ever seen one at a time," said Ned. "Till now."

"Used to be, that's how we see 'em too. But now we seeing more and more. In groups like this, too. Reckon they're spreading."

"Where do they come from?" asked Dan.

"Where they come from?" The leader spat in the fire. "Where you think they come from? From white fellas. You fellas."

"*What*?"

"That right. Surprise you, huh?"

"You mean like a disease though, right?" asked Joe. "People catch it..."

"Disease like smallpox, you mean?" The leader's eyes narrowed. "That another story. People bound to catch that when they get blankets full of it, blankets been used to wrap fellas who died of it. Big piles of them blankets given out as gifts. "

Dan gasped. "Who would do that?"

Ned looked at him. "We would."

"But why?"

"Think about it. Settlers. Squatters. Miners..."

"That right. You fellas is always hungry. Just like them. Always want more, more, more. Never have enough anything. You fellas see the land, and want all of it. Black fellas in the way. Hard to shoot 'em all, so maybe kill 'em another way. Smallpox be one. Them never-fall-down-fellas another. Song lines are full of the story. Black fellas see wagon pull up – big, strong wagon - men untie horses, unlock back then ride off fast. Black fellas go have a look, and the wagon opens and them fellas come tumbling out, try to eat everybody. First black fellas to see them wagons got hurt bad. Now all the tribes know."

"And yet you saved us..." murmured Ned. "Why not let them kill us? Aren't you angry at all white men?"

There was a pause. The leader reached over and tousled the hair of the young boy, who was chewing on a piece of meat.

"Oh, we plenty angry. I lost family. Wife. Children. This one all that is left. You know how that feels? No, you fellas still pretty young, you don't know. But listen, them things, them never-fall-down-fellas, they got no place here." He scooped up a handful of earth, and let it trickle between his fingers. "This land is our mother. Them fellas is like shit on her. It's our job to kill 'em off. Clean her up. You fellas just lucky we was here."

"Are all the tribes doing this? Hunting them?"

"Reckon so. Reckon you all be dead by now if we didn't. All you white fellas. Eaten, or maybe turned into them fellas yourselves. But..." He paused, looking sadly at the boy. "This no life for young fellas. Too many gone. Maybe soon we stop... Go up in the mountains..."

He trailed off into silence, eyes suddenly welling up with tears. They all looked away in embarrassment.

"How do you catch it?" asked Joe finally. "How do people get Blighted?"

"If you get bit. If them fellas don't eat you right up, you fall down and pretty soon get up again. As one of them."

"That's why you wanted to check our skin? See if we were bitten?"

"That right. Have to check. Or else you burn up with fever, fall down and same thing happen."

"What if any of us had been bitten?"

The leader chuckled and leaned forward, tapping Joe between the eyes. "Then you catch a spear right here. Or a boomerang."

The white men glanced at each other, and shifted uncomfortably. It was like getting into a card game for fun, and then suddenly finding the stakes have risen dangerously high.

NINE

"You've stopped writing," said Ned.

"Yes, well, I'll be doing you a favour if I don't include it. Honestly. Tales of undead swagmen wandering the land attacking young boys is one thing, but this... this conspiracy theory is just too much. Especially when it's coming from some Abo, as told to an accused murderer..."

He regarded me coolly. "Don't call them that."

"Which?"

"They are a warrior people. A people truly of this land in a way I can never be, and you can only dream of. Show some respect."

"Oh, God. The romanticism of the Noble Savage strikes again. England's full of people like you. I confess I'm more of a White Man's Burden fellow, myself, considering how pathetic-"

I hardly saw him move. Suddenly, I was off my chair, and slammed against the rough stone wall of the cell. The breath left my lungs in a rush and I sagged in his gasp.

"Just because you see me in my cage, don't let that fool you into thinking I'm tame," he ground out into my ear from between clenched teeth. I could feel them pressed hard against the side of my head, his breath hissing between them.

"I'm sorry, I'm sorry," I said, or I might have been saying it nonstop since he grabbed me. Then suddenly, he stepped away, and pressed his fingers into his temples, his eyes fluttering closed. Should I hit him, I wondered? But the strength in those corded arms was obvious – I doubted I could best him, wounded though he was. I stayed hunched and still against the wall, waiting.

He stepped back, and sank down onto his bed.

"Right," I said, straightening myself up. Luckily he hadn't damaged my shirt, or I would have had to go looking for a tailor who extended credit. He didn't look up – was he ashamed? "That's probably enough for today, anyway... My hand could use a rest. Well... see you tomorrow, then." I banged on the door.

"Remittance Man?" he said quietly, and I turned. "Do you have anything to tell me?"

I met his eye.

The horses...

"No," I said, and left him there.

Outside, the weather had changed for the worse. Very typical of Melbourne, I thought, as I turned up my collar against a cool wind that threatened rain soon. At least, unlike England, poor weather here could be over and done with by the next day, rather than dragging on relentlessly until you felt the very colour of your skin washing away in the drizzle and the fog.

I looked for her. Pathetically, I even stood outside the bleak walls of the gaol for some time, waiting and hoping she would appear. Didn't she want to hear more about her brother? Didn't she want to see me? But she did not come. No doubt she was somewhere with that bushy-bearded streak of brilliantined excrescence, Lloyd. I forced myself to relax, to try to breathe deeper into my chest. I could still feel traces of my attack the night before, and didn't want to bring on another turn. I realised I had probably missed the last omnibus by now, but I found I didn't care and was in the mood for a walk. So I set off from the gaol, without a final look around, though I confess my ears were straining in case I should hear her call after me.

I headed down La Trobe Street, and then turned up Rathdowne. The Carlton Gardens were on my right, and within them, the giant edifice that was the Royal Exhibition Hall. When the International Exhibition opened in about a week, the city fathers were expecting thousands of visitors. Some optimists were tipping numbers to pass the million mark. All those people. Suffocating. If the trial was finished by then, maybe I would be better off returning to Sydney for a while. Catch up with Norris.

"'Scuse me, sir?"

I jumped, and my hand clapped to my pocket. Empty. I backpedalled, straight into the fence around the garden. But then I relaxed – the fellow before me was not that large, and what I had taken to be a knife was actually a pencil, and in his other hand, he held bundle of paper.

"Sorry, sir, didn't mean to alarm you. You right?"

"I'm fine."

"Thought I gave you a heart attack, I did! Lord, I was sure you seen me coming. Nervy, ain't you? Mind elsewhere, eh?"

"What do you want?"

He was rather rat-like, I thought, with eyes that were a little wild. Socialist, maybe?

"I'm collecting signatures, sir. For the petition."

"What petition?"

"To free Ned Kelly, sir."

Ah. So this was the petition Castieau had mentioned. They even had workers accosting people on the street! Who on earth was organising this? Not Gaunson – too populist by half. Maggie? Lloyd? Not the latter, that didn't seem all that likely.

"We 'ope to present it at his trial. To the judge, so he can see there has been a terrible miscarriage o' justice."

"Oh, really?" I asked. "And what is that? There's pretty solid evidence he murdered those policeman..."

The man shook his head vehemently. "That's all a cover up. Ned only done what he done to protect the people."

"You mean he killed people to protect people?"

"Somebody had to *stop the rot*, if you take my meaning, sir."

The fellow all but tapped his nose as he said this. Dear God, was this specimen the best they could get?

"And how was he going to do this?"

"Why, by setting up a land where a man could *live*. Free of them *brain dead* fellows...where you going...? Sir?"

Enough; I had heard enough. I stalked off, shouldering rudely past him and ignoring his calls then curses. I felt like an idiot – it was all so obvious, now. The whole thing was a sham – well, I had known that the talk of walking undead was spurious – but I hadn't put two and two together to come up with the whole picture. It was a code, all this talk of the Blighted. They meant us, the English, those cunning, arrogant, ignorant bog-stinking Irish. The whole thing was a coded plot to establish some farcical Irish republic in Victoria, where no doubt the potatoes would be free and heavy drinking compulsory, especially for the women and children. I'd got myself mixed up with a bunch of Fenian agitators. Oh, Father would be pleased.

Actually, that would probably be the best thing about the whole sorry mess, should the story get back home. It would be enough to make him choke on his beef tea.

I stamped along, leaving the massive Hall behind me, and entering the streets where I doubted the tourists would set foot. Unless they liked dust, soot and sewerage. That's probably what offended me about the exhibition – it was all so manufactured, so much part of the world I thought I had left behind. All that artifice.

I found myself nearly back at my lodgings, faster than I expected. I walk fast when angry. I paused to spend more than I should on a somewhat stale pie from a cart, and tried not to think too much about what may be in it as I chewed it down. Then I loitered outside my address, watching the lights in Mrs Mackie's windows, and when it appeared she had gone to bed – pretty early, Thank God, since she had nothing else to do – slipped in the front door and upstairs to my room.

I made it to my door unnoticed. My neighbour on this floor, a mostly unemployed actor by the name of Rawson, was mumbling behind his closed door. Either he had company, had finally secured a role and was rehearsing, or he was talking to himself. He was quite the bohemian, good for the occasional glass of raw red wine and chat about anything but our pasts and our current circumstances, but I did not feel like talking tonight and so let myself quietly into my room. My feelings once inside, as usual, were a mixture of depression looking at the grimy grey surrounds and my meagre belongings, and a sense of relief at being inside and alone. I actually physically shuddered as my spine and shoulders unlocked and I let myself slouch. I lit a lamp for comfort, kicked off my shoes and lay down on my narrow cot.

Here, alone, in this sprawling mass of humanity; my one little haven among the suffocating throng. Almost as invisible as if I was lying amid the red dirt in some distant desert. And yet somehow, here I was, being sucked into mad plots and mad tales.

The floorboards on the landing creaked. I glanced at the door. A shadow moved along the bottom edge.

"That you, Rawson?" I called softly. There was no reply.

"Mrs Mackie?" I added, somewhat hopefully. The silence thickened. The lamp on the landing went out – but Mrs Mackie never filled them very full, apparently happy to risk her guest's necks on the stairs at night to save a few pence, so whether this was by accident or design, I couldn't say. Then did my eyes deceive me or did my door handle turn slightly in the dim light? My hand trailed down to the edge of the mattress, and my fingers dug underneath for the stiff oilcloth package hidden there. I drew it out, and opened it to reveal my derringer pocket pistol. It wasn't much of a weapon, but it had two barrels, and was good enough in close quarters. I held it across my chest now, suddenly finding my limbs heavy with dread.

"Who's there?" I asked, my voice coming in a shamefully hoarse whisper... Or did I really mean 'what's there?'

There came a rustling at the bottom of the door, and I fancied I saw white bone fingers sliding under, seeking purchase, seeking entry, and now at last my limbs responded and my arm unfurled, pointing the twin barrels at the entrance, grateful to find them steady. I held my breath, fearful as a child that any noise on my part would unleash a nightmarish attack. And then came the creaking of the staircase as someone ran quickly down the stairs, and by the time I rose they were no doubt long gone, and then I saw that the whiteness I had seen was not bone, but a folded slip of paper thrust under my door.

I snatched it up in my free hand, and toyed with opening the door. Should I go as far as the front gate, see if I could spot anyone fleeing? But somehow, I could not bring myself to open the door – its thin wood provided security against an imagined malevolence still hovering on the landing, and so instead, I took the note back over to my lamp and opened it.

Oh ho.

You bastard.

"You bastard!" I shouted, as I stormed into the cell the next day.

"Pleased to see you, too," said Ned. "What the hell is that?"

He was pointing to the red velvet cushion under my arm. Damn it. When I had arrived at the gaol that morning, the Ancient Mariner had come tottering after me and told me with much heaving and coughing that Castieau – that is, "the guv'nor" - wanted to see me. So I had followed his stooped form into the administration wing and along to the governor's bland office. The man himself was standing fidgeting by the window, and fairly leapt towards me with hand extended when I was presented.

"Ah! Good day to you, sir!" he beamed. "Please, take a seat. I would like just a moment of your time, if I may. Tea? Yes?"

He shooed the old boy out the door and we sat across his gleaming desk. He had made some effort to stack his papers. I hoped he wasn't going to ask me to give his manuscript a quick peruse and offer feedback.

"How goes the preparation?"

"You know, sir, that I am not at liberty to discuss matters pertinent to..."

"Yes, yes, quite alright," he said, waving my words aside. He sat beaming at me. "I, uh, took the liberty of looking your family up in the Who's Who. I thought I recognized the name."

I should have been more careful.

"Might I just say that it is an honour to have you here, sir, both in the colony and even more so within this, my humble domain."

I inclined my head graciously. Tea arrived at that point, the tray carried in by the pimpled youth I had met on my first visit. Castieau dismissed him and poured himself. There was a saucer with five biscuits set out in a rough circle. I reached across and grabbed up three, sat back, and then rose again to take a fourth. I dunked studiously – it was necessary, the biscuits being dry and stale – and watched the governor stare with dismay at the lone biscuit left on the plate.

I shoved the rest of mine into my mouth. "May I?" I asked, around a mouthful of soggy dough.

He waved his assent with a tight smile, and I took the final biscuit. I took one small bite, and then left it on the edge of my saucer, where Castieau stared at it mournfully.

"Was there anything else you wanted, Governor?" I asked.

He was gazing toward the door, frowning, but his gaze snapped back to me and a smile slid back across his face – or at least across his mouth.

"I just wanted to make sure you have everything you need... Paper? Pens?"

"I have those... Although some more paper may come in handy – he is a bit of a talker, Ned."

"Really? I always thought him rather quiet. He has never said much to me. Except to swear at me, of course... He can be quite inventive. And hurtful."

Castieau gave me a bundle of paper from his own stock – it was good quality, too. Seemed a shame to waste it on the tales of a lying murderer, but I could at least rest assured I was saving it from being covered in the governor's ponderous, predictable prattling about his life to date. I wondered what else I could get...

"Also, Mr Kelly's cell is not the most salubrious of locations. Quite uncomfortable, really. Might you find an office you can put at my disposal?"

He shook his head sadly. "That, I am afraid, will not be possible."

"Oh," I said, and let the silence sit.

He stared at his desk, shaking his head solemnly back and forth.

"I have it!" he cried suddenly.

Shortly afterwards I was presented with the very cushion I had beneath my arm as I entered Ned's cell. Lord knows what its usual job was, but I really did find the wooden seat in the cell uncomfortable on my backside, so I accepted it with formal grace. Though it had rather undercut my entrance...

"You are not being plain with me, sir, and if you do not do that, then I will not be able to help you."

I had it better in my head on the way to the gaol – the meeting with Castieau had ruined some of my best lines.

"What are you wittering on about?"

"Oh, just the small matter of being heard to threaten the life of one of the constables you are accused of murdering – *in front of witnesses.*"

"What?"

"Constable Lonigan. Did you or did you not say to him something like, 'if I ever shoot a man Lonigan, it will be you'?"

"So what if I did?"

"So what if you did? Good God, man! You threaten to kill a man, and then later he turns up dead? You might as well have admitted to pre-meditated murder and saved us all the bother."

"Remittance Man, listen carefully. And put that bloody cushion down, will you? I never said I didn't shoot Lonigan and the others, but it wasn't murder."

"What was it? Self -defence? It isn't self-defence when you have threatened to... Oh no, you are not going to tell me they were Blighted, are you?"

Ned's eyes narrowed. "How did you hear about this anyway? I hadn't got to that part yet. Who have you been speaking to?"

I hesitated – who had stuffed that note under my door?

How on earth had they found me, and why was it so important to give me that information? Something kept me from wanting to reveal the truth of the matter to him, I don't know what. Some strange sense of embarrassment. Instead, I sniffed and said, "I have my own resources, you know."

"Your own resources... And did these resources explain what was going on when I said it? And that it took place months before he was infected and I had to put him down like a sick dog?"

"No... No I didn't quite get all the details... Or not in as much detail as I would like, say... Perhaps you could-"

"Tell you what happened? Certainly. Why don't you take a seat on your Auntie Madge's haemorrhoid cushion, or whatever it is you have there, and I'll continue."

TEN

Things hadn't gone well when the boys returned from the bush. Harrison was screaming blue murder about the theft of his prize bull and other of his stock, and suspicion naturally fell on the young men with known records for this kind of caper. Nicholson, the old superintendent in the area, facing replacement, heard Harrison out and promised to do what he could to lock the Greta Mob up and keep them locked up – but he would need some evidence. He began to wonder if it would be possible to turn someone, find someone with a grudge against Ned or one of the others and persuade them to turn informer. The trouble was the brute Irish were as thick as thieves with each other. But still, wouldn't hurt to keep an eye out, would it?

Orders were given – if not entirely formally – that there was to be no tolerance of any skylarking by the Greta Mob. Their families, especially the Kellys, were to be considered highly suspect. Take some of the flashness out them, said Nicholson. And if that meant operating with "loaded dice," as it were, well, so be it. It wouldn't have come to this if they had been decent law-abiding folk in the first place.

Within the Mob itself, there was some disagreement how to best proceed.

"We need to warn the people," said Ned. "Let them know about the Blighters. You all heard Billy – they're spreading. We can't rely on the natives to hold them back. People have to know."

"They've all heard the stories, Ned, surely," said Joe.

"They need to know the stories are true, or be told which parts of the stories are true. There is a lot of nonsense out there. They need to be able to defend themselves."

"We'll sound like crackpots."

Ned shrugged. "It's a risk I'll take for my family. What about you?"

"You'll have to do most of the talking. People will listen to you more than me, Dan or Steve."

"What about me?" asked Aaron, who was sitting with them.

"I was definitely including you in the list no one will listen to, Aaron. Alright?"

Aaron nodded, but his face was troubled.

"Where do we start?" asked Dan. "Riding round house to house?"

"No," said Ned. "We go where people gather to listen. The pubs and the churches."

It was decided that Ned and Joe would ride out to some of the further towns like Benalla and Mansfield the next day. Dan and Steve would stick around Greta, where they knew more people. Ned in particular gave them the job of talking to Ma Kelly first. She loved to grab hold of Steve whenever she could and attempt to fatten him up, and while he sat smiling quietly and tucking in with a will to plates of rabbit stew and fresh bread, that would give Dan a good chance to talk.

"You're her favourite," said Ned, and Dan looked down and went red. "She'll be a captive audience. Make the most of it."

When Ned rode up to Joe early the next morning, Aaron was sitting on a horse beside him. Joe caught his eye and shrugged slightly.

"Morning, Joe," said Ned.

"Morning, Ned," said Joe.

"Morning, Ned," said Aaron.

"Didn't know you were coming, Aaron."

"Yeah? Well... I'm here!"

Ned looked at a vein pulsing in Aaron's jaw rather than his eyes, and then nodded. "Let's go, then."

They headed south, at an easy canter, and rode into Mansfield not long after. It was a fair sized place, made all the larger by the width of the main street, built to accommodate bullock teams needing to turn around. There were three hotels and two churches, the larger belonging to the Church of England. That was also the closest to the side of town they rode in on.

"Wait a minute," said Aaron, "it isn't Sunday. Will anybody be in church?"

"We can't just go busting into a service talking about walking dead bodies, Aaron," said Joe.

"That's the man we need to see," said Ned, pointing.

The vicarage was built alongside the church, a large brick building with a bull-nosed veranda. A grey haired man was sitting there now in a wicker chair, polishing a long object in his lap.

They rode up and swung off their horses, Ned and Joe in unspoken unison, Aaron lagging a little behind. Ned led the way, opening the creaking gate that led into the vicarage grounds.

"Morning, Father," called Ned. "Is that for chastening the ungodly, then?"

The object in the priest's lap was a heavy double barrelled shotgun. He continued to clean it as he answered.

"That's Vicar to you, or Reverend Sandiford, not Father. This is not one of your Catholic temples."

"Still and all, Reverend, it's a mighty fine looking piece."

The vicar snapped the breach shut and squinted down the barrel.

"Aye, it is that."

"Could come in mighty handy with all that's going on."

"Oh?"

"I'm Ned, and this here is Joe. Can we have a word?"

"Talk is free, son. Though I only give advice to parishioners."

"Right. Now, Fa...Vicar, this is going to sound strange, but we were wondering if we could come back on a Sunday and have a word with your flock?"

"As what? Lay preachers? On what subject?"

Ned and Joe exchanged a glance. "The Blighted, Vicar. The walking dead."

"No need, son."

"But Vicar..."

"If you'd bothered to come and hear me preach, you'd know I regularly sermonise on the rising of the sinful and the ungodly..."

Joe raised an eyebrow at Ned.

"Well, that's good to hear..."

"...and the coming of strife, and the end of days. When all good Christian men will stand by His side and Satan will be cast down. The only question in my mind is – on what side will the Irish Catholics be standing?"

Joe bristled, but Ned put a hand on his arm. "Now, then, Vicar. No need for that, surely. But we're talking about now, not the end of days. The dead truly are walking."

"Sinners are dead. Their souls are black and rotten, those who drink, and gamble, and steal, and fornicate. Those who think only of living a flash life now, and give no thought to the hereafter." The Vicar looked up at them with shrewd eyes. "If you'll forgive me for saying so, I'm talking about young men like yourselves. Men who are dead to God."

"You aren't listening," said Ned quietly. "There is a real threat out there. Something that could tear your precious flock apart unless they are ready to face it..."

"No, you aren't listening, boy." The Vicar leaned forward. "Your only hope is redemption. You and your ilk must repent before it is too late. Turn back to the Lord."

"Too late..." muttered Ned. "Father, I pray it isn't so."

He turned and walked off, leaving Joe and Aaron to hurry after him.

"Stupid, ignorant puppet!" Ned hissed as they untied their horses and mounted up. "Dedicated to keeping everyone in their place for the pleasure of his masters. I hope he does get eaten!"

"Maybe this isn't such a good idea..." ventured Joe.

"Let's try at the pubs," said Ned.

So they went into all three, the Exchange, Kelson's and the Delatite, and in each they had a beer or two and spoke to the publican and the old soaks who frequented the places, and any passing stockmen or tinkers or ne'er-do-wells who happened to be there. Here they found a more receptive audience – because everyone had heard the stories of the Blighters, everyone knew someone who had a cousin who had had a narrow escape from a bony dried up ghoul on some distant track. But when Ned talked of the risks of the Blighted coming into town, their eyes would wander around the solid bar, or glance out the window at the telegraph office, the flour mill, the police station, all those solid pieces of civilisation. You could see the scepticism rising – sure, there were nightmarish things Out There, in the bush, but here? In broad daylight, with a cool beer before you, it was more than a little hard to swallow.

"Let's ride on to Benalla," said Ned, as they rode out of town. He turned – Joe and Aaron were riding alongside each other behind him, laughing and trying to shove each other out of their saddles. He shook his head. "How about you two larrikins head home – I'll do Benalla myself."

"No, no, Ned. I'm fine, fine," said Joe, frowning. He yelped as Aaron leaned over and punched him in the arm, and nearly slid off his horse. "Whoa..."

"Ah, come on, Joe," said Aaron. "He's right. Let's go."

"Well, if you're sure, Ned..."

Ned was sure. He rode on alone.

The Kelly family knew Benalla well. It was the closest size-able town to Greta, and where they came to do their shopping. It was also the headquarters for the area police operations. Ned rode down Bridge Street, the main street, which was split by the Broken River that ran through the centre of town. There were six hotels in all. He knew that there was one at least he would stay well away from – O'Leary's. It wasn't his speed anyway, with its crisp linen tablecloths and doormen – pretentious tommyrot. Worse still, it was where the officers of the police stayed. Ned doubted he would get much of a hearing there.

That still left five pubs. Ned licked his lips and chose the first – the Commercial.

———

Some time later, Ned sat bolt upright with a start. He found himself sitting at the bar in the Shamrock, his cheek sticky from the counter top. His throat felt raw, like he had been shouting. Behind him at the tables a crowd of red faced men sang "The Wild Colonial Boy." He rubbed his face. Had he been sleeping?

"What's happening?" he mumbled. He couldn't remember getting there.

"Oh, ye've been having a lovely time of it," said the barman. "Ye've been talkin' a fair treat and the boys have been standing ye drinks."

The song trailed off behind them as the singers reached the end, but someone started it again and the voices joined in lusty chorus.

"Mind you, ye've got the lads all overexcited, now, and... oh shite."

Ned looked up. The barman was staring at the door. In the reflection of the mirror behind the bar Ned could see that four troopers had entered. The song faltered and fell as the other men around the tables noticed the new arrivals.

"Not to worry, lads," said the first trooper, Lonigan, as he walked forward. "It's just a song. Mind you, if there was a law against murdering a tune, you'd all hang for sure."

There was a little nervous laughter.

"Why, look who's at the bar, Fitz. The madman himself."

"Aye, so it is," said the next trooper, Fitzpatrick. "What do you know, boys? Was he sprouting nonsense about ghosts and ghoulies again?"

The four had Ned ringed in against the bar.

"Nah, not ghosts," cried an old sot in the corner. "It were them Blighters he were talkin' about!"

"Blighters?" scoffed Lonigan. "You believe in fairies, too, do you Kelly? Leprechauns? Do you have a pot of gold?"

"They're real..." mumbled Ned. His head swam. Had he really drunk so much? "The Blighted are out there... Coming..."

"They're what? Coming?" Lonigan put on a falsetto. "Oh, look out boys and girls! Ned says the Blighters are coming to nibble your toes!"

"And yer testes!" added Fitzpatrick.

The troopers all laughed. A few others joined them. The rest sat silent, watching.

Lonigan stepped in closer. "What is this sick fascination you have with these stories, Kelly? The idea turn you on, or something?"

"Ned Kelly, lover of the undead," said Fitzpatrick. "Kelly of the Undead. Undead Kelly!"

They laughed some more, Lonigan right in Ned's ear. Ned shoved himself up. "Give me some air, can't you. I don't feel right..."

"You're drunk," said Lonigan in disgust. "Do it, Fitz."

Fitzpatrick stepped forward and clapped a hand on Ned's shoulder. "Edward Kelly, I am arresting you for public drunkenness..."

"No!" cried Ned, spinning around. Fitzpatrick went sprawling backwards and fell. "I'm not drunk, I tell you. Someone's drugged me... You bastards..."

"Resisting arrest now, is it, Kelly?" said Lonigan with malicious glee. "Oh, thank you, you Irish bastard. I'm going to enjoy this!"

He stepped in and punched Ned low, in the kidneys. Ned grunted from the unexpected pain of it, and in reflex, trapped Lonigan's hand against his side with his arm and spun in towards him, his elbow up and connecting with Lonigan's head with a loud crack. Ned stepped away, hands outstretched.

"Ach, I didn't mean for... Stop it, stop it."

But the other two troopers were on him, fists flying, and Fitzpatrick had bounded back onto his feet and waded in, too. The only thing that saved Ned in that moment was how they all got in each other's way, so no one could land a really telling blow. Ned set his feet and shoved in hard against them – best thing was to put your head down and go like a bull, get inside the other fellow's guard and shove him off balance. But there were four of them, and tables and chairs to collide with and splinter, but finally amidst the snarling swearing and bludgeoning fists, Ned made it to the front door and the whole knot of them spilled outside onto the road.

Ned came up, pulling clear. "Come on then, you bastards!"

Fitzpatrick came at him low, trying for a tackle, and met Ned's knee in his face. The others came on, right over the top of him, and Ned aimed careful jabs into whatever face was closest, and felt the gratifying crunch of knuckle on nose. But for all his skill, he was one man against four, and drugged besides. He could scarcely get his arms to move fast enough, and the only thing protecting him, he figured, was that he was numb to the pain of it all from whatever had been slipped into his drink. He grabbed hold of someone's fingers, and tried to bend them the way Joe had shown him, but was suddenly stopped by a God almighty blinding pain that shafted like white light across his eyes. Lonigan had come in from behind and grabbed his testicles in a vice-like grip. Ned tried to grab at his hand, but Lonigan twisted and he shrieked, and hot bitter vomit jetted from his mouth.

"Oh, you filthy bastard!"

The troopers stepped back in disgust, leaving Ned curled and sobbing on the ground, hands between his legs. The world was black with streaks of red, but he turned his head up and picked out one man's face among his attackers.

ELEVEN

"And that's when you said it?" I asked. I realised I had crossed my legs.

"So they say. I don't remember. I probably did, though. 'Black balling', they called it. And my balls were truly black for a week or more after. The bastard."

"Did you mention police brutality at your trial?"

"Trial? There was no trial. I paid a fine for public drunkenness at the courthouse and they let me go. Mind you, I could barely sit in my saddle, and every step that horse took was pure agony. Took me hours to get home."

"And are you saying this all means something? That this was an attempt by the authorities to silence you?"

He looked at me. "There's that tone of voice again. The one that says I'm nothing but a mad Irishman."

"Mad?" I pretended to study him shrewdly. "No. I'm beginning to suspect you are an extremely canny individual, Mr Kelly."

"I told you to call me Ned. Only my enemies call me Mr Kelly. And you aren't one of them, are you, Remittance Man?"

What to say? That I suspected he was a revolutionary, using

all this talk of the Blighted as code for plotting insurrection? Did it help if I knew? It certainly wouldn't do his case any favours. They wanted him charged and tried as a common murderer. The last thing the big boys of the Melbourne Club would want would be for this trial to be politicised. Jesus, if this case became a rallying point for the home rule types in Ireland... Although, that being said, it would be one in the eye for my old man that I doubted he would ever recover from... But then, if I was cut off, and written out of the will, penniless...

"Well?"

"No. I'm not your enemy, Ned."

But I don't think I'm your friend, either.

When I was leaving, the gormless young warder from Castieau's office bounded over to me.

"Note for you, sir!"

I took the folded slip from him, and absently patted my pockets in my usual dumb show of wishing to tip but finding myself embarrassingly without coin – but then I remembered I didn't need to tip the bugger anyway. I turned my back on him in dismissal and opened the paper, squinting at the looping writing within. It was from Gaunson.

With my bundle of papers under my arm I strode down Russel Street and turned right into Collins St. The Melbourne Club was located here, in the heart of the city. An imposing three storied block of a place with tall shuttered windows – designed for looking out, not in. No, the rich men here were not on show – on the contrary, the rest of the world was placed outside these windows for their pleasure.

It was late afternoon, and the two lamps beside the heavy narrow main entrance were already lit. There was a doorman there, in hat and tails. I gave him a name, and he nodded at me soberly and ushered me inside. Another overdressed servant with

a bearing like a Major bid me follow him, and took me up a
secondary staircase to one of the dining rooms towards the back
of the second floor. The smell of the rich food and cigar smoke
made my mouth water. Men sat about in pairs, or alone, dining,
with large wine glasses or whiskey tumblers set by their arms. My
native guide didn't stop, but led me clear through the restaurant
and into a short panelled corridor set with doors. Private dining
rooms. He stopped beside one and knocked, then opened it and
ushered me ponderously inside into the intimate, candlelit interior. One small table and two people sitting quite close together.

"Ah, dear chap," said Gaunson.

"Hello, William," said Maggie.

You dirty old bugger.

"William?" said Gaunson. "William? You mean Charles."

"Either is fine," I lied smoothly. "William is my middle
name. I reserve its usage for friends." Maggie looked at me
askance, no doubt remembering that I had given it to her as soon
as we met. "And for social use. Charles is my father's Christian
name as well, as you know, and I reserve its use for business and
professional activities."

"Separation of the public and the private self, eh? I like that.
I like that very much." Gaunson rubbed his whiskers. "Very
useful for a man in public office too, I should think."

"Are you joining us?" asked Maggie. Her face and eyes were
open – it appeared I had got through that potential hiccup
unscathed.

"Where are my manners?" cried Gaunson. "Sit! You must
have a drink. Are you hungry?"

He pulled on a silken bell rope, and within minutes, a
starched waiter appeared. I ordered the fish and a glass of
Riesling.

"Not a fan of white wine myself," said Gaunson. "Popular

back in London, is it? Perhaps I should educate myself in it. How about you, my dear?"

"Oh, I rarely touch wine," said Maggie. "It's wasted on me. Tastes all the same.""All the same? Oh my dear! Did you hear that, Charles? All the same! We shall have to see to the education of our young friend."

I certainly wanted to teach her a thing or two. The candlelight was catching in her eyes in a most pleasing way. I felt an odd flutter in my stomach, different but similar to the monster that squatted so often in my chest. This was quite pleasurable.

"Do you have your notes, Charles?"

I handed them over and smiled at Maggie as Gaunson fished spectacles out of his jacket pocket.

"And where is Tom, this fine evening?" I asked her.

She shrugged. "In the bar of the Burns, probably. Like most evenings." Ah. Bored, was she? Dear Tom preferring to spend time with more manly company and leaving her twiddling her thumbs upstairs in her room? "Mr Gaunson was kind enough to agree to meet so we could discuss strategy."

Over dinner in a private room? What a pet. He was scanning my spidery scrawl with a frown, chewing absently on his lower lip. Maggie reached over and put her hand on mine.

"We very much appreciate what you are doing for us, William."

Her fingers pressed lightly against my hand, and I opened my fingers, allowing hers to slip in and lock between them. She squeezed and I glanced at her face. She smiled, and I noticed how moist her lips were. My God, this was an incredibly erotic moment, and one I would be sure to revisit when I was alone later that night!

Then Gaunson seemed to choke and she pulled her hand away.

"So," said Gaunson, tapping the pages back into a neat pile. "So..." He wouldn't meet my eye.

"This is what Ned... Mr Kelly... has told me so far. As you can see, I am at this point just recording his version of events. I haven't seen it as being my place at this stage to... ah... query him on them."

"Quite right, quite right," Gaunson said, nodding.

"I thought it best to leave it to you... to come up with the best defence strategy." I glanced back at Maggie. She was watching me carefully. God, it made it hard to talk, her being there. "The thing is... The thing is..." I left off as the waiter reappeared and placed a dish before me, aromatic steam rising.

"Leave them with me, dear boy," said Gaunson, looking up and smiling at me. He whisked the papers off the table and stuffed them into a leather case sitting by his chair. "You just continue as you have been. How is the fish?"

"Delicious," I said. I had hardly tasted it.

We finished our meal with Gaunson holding forth about the various troubles currently confronting the Victorian parliament. I let his words wash over me, while watching how Maggie removed her food from her fork. Occasionally, I was treated to the sight of her small pink tongue, and wondered what it would be like to feel it swirling with my own.

Finally, Gaunson mopped his mouth with his linen cloth, dropped it on his plate and fixed me with an intense eye. "It has been wonderful to have this opportunity to catch up, Charles."

"Yes," I said.

"But we wouldn't want to keep you from your endeavours."

"I'm fine," I said.

"I'm sure a keen young man such as you has things of import to do... Or maybe you are giving yourself a well-deserved night of rest."

"Well, actually..."

"In either case, we don't want to keep you." And he stared at me from under his bushy eyebrows.

Right.

"Well, I will say goodnight, then..."

"Actually, I had better be going too," said Maggie, rising. She leant over and gave Gaunson a peck on the cheek. "Thank you so much. No, don't get up. William can escort me back to the hotel. Or help me find a cab."

Gaunson's jowls quivered and he watched her gather her things with such a look of despondency on his face that I almost laughed.

"Oh, one more thing, Mr Gaunson," I said. "I wonder if you wouldn't mind paying me for the work done so far. If it is no bother?"

Still watching Maggie, he slowly withdrew his billfold from his inside pocket and counted out some notes. He hesitated.

"Thank you so much for treating us to dinner, too," said Maggie, and the poor old boy brought out more notes to leave on the table.

"Shall we?" I said to Maggie, and offered her my arm. She laughed, and walked from the room, leaving me to follow. I didn't glance back at my employer, but fancied I could feel his eyes drilling in to the back of my head.

We didn't speak until we were outside on the street.

"Oh, thank God!" said Maggie, practically skipping down the walk. "Thank God you showed up! Old Blowhard... Jesus, farmers and old blowhards..." She looked up at the night sky, and turned in a circle. "Sometimes a girl just wants..." She fell silent, and I felt her eye was on me even as she gazed heavenward. I took a step toward her. She started walking. "Come on, William or Charles or whoever you are. Let's find a cab."

"It's a fine night for walking," I said, coming up beside her.

"Alright," she said. "Alright, let's walk a bit and see how the road finds us."

We strolled along Collins Street. There were others walking about, and the gas lamps had the area well lit.

"Where are you up to with Ned?" she asked.

"Must we talk about work?"

"You mean, must we talk about my brother? Yes, we must."

"Of course. I do apologise."

"Oh, Lord, don't apologise!" she said with sudden heat. "Don't..." She growled with exasperation and swiped at the air with her hands as if to conjure understanding from it. "It's just that when you talk like that, it doesn't sound like you. It sounds like you're – we're – in some play."

I was unsure what to say, not really understanding the waters I suddenly found myself in, and not wanting to turn her against me in any way. So I nodded and walked on, frowning at the sidewalk.

"Oh, William," she said, and her small hand grabbed my elbow. "I'm afraid I'm not a very nice person. If you knew me better, you'd see that, too."

"Nonsense," I replied. "You seem perfectly lovely to..."

"There you go again!" she twisted my sleeve in her fingers and shook my arm. "The character! Don't be a character with me. Be you. Can we..." and she stopped and made me face her. Her eyes were dark, wide. "Can you and I at least be honest with each other?"

Honesty? Honesty?

I opened my mouth to speak, but saw her face, and finally managed to mutter, "I'll try."

That seemed to satisfy her. She nodded, and released me. She smiled, and gestured with her head, and we continued up the road.

"Ned?" she prompted.

"He was telling me about Lonigan. When he was fined for drunkenness, and Lonigan... uh..."

"Grabbed him by the balls?"

"Yes. That."

"Does my language offend you?"

"No. It's honest."

She smiled – I could see it from the corner of my eye – and slipped her arm through mine as we crossed a lane.

"Lonigan was a pig," she said. "Most of them were. Mind you, they were encouraged by the superintendents.""Nicholson?"

"Yes. Him and then the other one."

"The other one?"

"Hare."

I glanced at her. Her face was troubled.

"Ned hasn't mentioned him."

"He will."

"So... It was hard? With the police?"

"Hard? Yes, it was hard. You know what they called us all? The Kelly Gang. Not a family, a gang, as if we were all criminals. And they treated us like rubbish."

"Well... Ned and Dan had stolen livestock... In the past..."

I felt a change through her arm – she didn't remove it, but it went slack, dead. God damn it. Why was it so difficult with her? Why so much easier with a whore, tittering at your every utterance, or some dull socialite out for her first season, staring at you and hanging on your every word?

"So?" she asked, her voice ragged. "Did that give them the right to harass all of us? To poison our dogs, so they couldn't warn us when the traps were coming? " And she choked on a sob. "Our dogs! Do you know what that is like? Did you have a dog as a child?"

And there is the puppy. Wriggling in my arms, milky

breath, warm round stomach, paw resting gently on my nose. And my sister's shrieking voice: give him back! He's mine! He's mine! Mama! Papa! And the stern rebuke: how old are you, boy? There are manly things and womanly things – if we're ever going to make a man out of you... Focusing on the downward turn of his mouth, the small patch of dried egg yolk in his whiskers... My empty hands, the vicious triumph in my sister's eyes... And then later, the puppy again, and the well like a gaping hungry mouth, ready to swallow someone, something... There are manly things... Mother's face, cold as rock as she held my shrieking sister. Monstrous boy, monster. Father with the strap. Manly things.

"And my ma..." she continued, crying. "To take my poor old ma and lock her up..."

I stopped. Generally, I hated women's tears. Normally, they meant they wanted something. Do this. Stop doing that. Feel bad. Make me feel the most wanted. Make me feel special, better than you, much more important than you. Each one a hot little drop of acid that fed the aching monster in my chest until one day there was no room for anything else, any feeling for anyone else...

But...

"Maggie," I said, in a voice not my own.

She looked at me, and the night slowed into wax. She could do it. She could fall into my arms. Here we would find something. Here was the time.

But the gossamer thread pulled tight, and snapped.

She dashed an arm across her eyes, pulled a handkerchief from her bodice and blew her nose heartily into it. She half turned away, breaking the pull, creating an awkwardness of space that felt impossible to surmount.

"I'm not..." she said. "I'm not..."

Please, I thought, say it. Whatever it is, find the words and say it, and I will find another combination of words that proves it not so, that unlocks it, that opens you up.

"I find myself out of sorts, William. Perhaps a cab is a better idea after all."

I didn't argue. I hailed one quite quickly, and it was understood between us that she would ride alone. I watched as she settled herself inside, waiting to see if she would look at me, but she did not. I gave the address to the driver and found myself paying from my little treasure trove of notes. She didn't see.

TWELVE

Constable Fitzpatrick rode along the track, not in the best of moods. He was more than a little hung over, and had been unable to take a hair of the dog this morning before he was summoned by the new superintendent, Hare, and given this job.

Fitzpatrick didn't much care for Hare. Not that Old Man Nicholson was in any way his favourite, oh no. Gruff old bastard. But there was just something about Hare. Sure, he was already popular with the rest of the lads, and it was true he didn't lord it above them, instead speaking to them as if they were equals, but still... there was something. Fitz couldn't quite put his finger on it.

This morning, when he had stumbled in to the super's office in Benalla, unshaven and still buttoning his tunic, Hare hadn't said a word about it. Instead, he had smiled genially, and announced he had a job for Fitz to do – a job to help stick it to the Kelly gang. Fitz was to ride out to the homestead at Greta and arrest Dan for horse theft.

"Warrant?" asked Fitz, concentrating on the pounding in his head and the sour taste at the back of his throat.

Don't need one, Hare informed him cheerfully. Don't worry, all above board – or it will be, by the time you bring him in. Pressure, Fitz, that's the key. Got to keep the pressure up on these rats. Keep them off balance. Keep them reacting rather than acting.

That morning Fitz couldn't give a fuck what the key was, and just stopped short of saying as much, but Hare had clapped him heartily on the arm and sent him on his way.

———

"Look," I said, turning in my chair to look at Ned. "I'm having a problem with this. At best this is hearsay..."

"It's the truth," he said mildly. He was in his customary position, sitting back on his bed, his stiff injured legs out before him.

"Yes, but you weren't there. You can't know."

"Have you ever been to Africa, Remittance Man?"

"What? No. Can't say I have. Wouldn't want to anyway."

"But you don't doubt it exists? Even though you haven't been there, and can't know?"

"Oh, very droll. Try that one on the judge, he'll love it. We are talking on a point of law here! Will this fellow – Fitzpatrick – will he attest to all this?"

For some reason this made Ned chuckle, harshly, without humour, till he started to cough. "Oh! That I would very much like to see! Fitzpatrick on the stand! Oh yes!"

"Well... We'll subpoena him..."

"Wait, Remittance Man. Wait and listen."

———

Fitz leant over and spat. His mouth tasted truly foul. To make matters worse, the baited calf's liver he had in his saddle bag to take care of any dogs at the Kelly place was already pretty high. He had a cloud of flies following him, and had to keep swatting them away from his face. He was in a foul enough mood just to shoot Dan dead when he found him and claim he was resisting arrest. The prospect of dragging a prisoner all the way back to Benalla again – especially one as mouthy as a Kelly - was not appealing.

So caught up in his own misery was Fitzpatrick as he rounded a bend on the bush road that he was almost upon the girl before he spotted her.

She was walking along the track ahead of him – though staggering would be a better description, as she lurched unsteadily in her little boots.

"Drunk," grunted Fitzpatrick.

Her clothes were stained and torn – clearly, she had been on quite a bender, and now here she was, miles from anywhere, trying to walk back home, or walk herself sober.

Miles from anywhere...

Fitzpatrick glanced back over his shoulder. There wasn't another soul to be seen on the track. He felt his manhood stiffen within his breeches.

Dirty as she was, he could tell from her long blonde tresses hanging down her back, and her slight figure, that she was fairly young – at a guess, he would say early twenties. Old enough. Old enough to know the ways of the world, and be a sensible girl.

On horseback, he was slowly gaining. He sat straighter in the saddle, lifted his helmet and dragged his fingers through his oily hair.

"Miss?" he called. "Excuse me, Miss?"

She didn't hear him, or was choosing to ignore him, instead continuing on her unsteady way down the track. Fancied herself as something special, did she? Fitz was in no mood for games.

"Stop right there," he called. "I must examine you for public drunkenness."

Always helped to throw around a few legal terms. Most girls were keen to do anything to avoid serving a spell inside.

But this one kept walking. Fitz swore, and kicked his horse until he was right alongside her, catching a glimpse of her pale cheek. She was thinner than he would have liked, but, oh, this was going to be good sport. He reached down and took hold of her arm.

"Miss!"

Finally she stopped and turned towards him, but there was a mistake, there was something wrong. One half of her face was young, pretty – time enough to notice that – but the other the other gaping eye socket lips and cheek torn away scalp hanging off blood like thick dark tar dripping so wrong...my God...my God-

Her one eye fixed on him, and she snarled, and her head darted forward like a snake, and those teeth, so long with no lips to cover them, latched onto his arm, and she bit so hard. Fitz felt the skin part, felt her work down into the meat of the muscle. He wrenched his arm away, and to his horror saw a strip of skin, his skin, ripping away. He cried out, and grabbed the searing wound, blood running around his fingers. And the girl - the girl's teeth worked and her throat convulsed and he realised he was watching her eat his flesh. He screamed then, high and loud, and she was coming at him again, bloodied mouth gaping. The horse shied though, skipping sideways, and he scrabbled at his holster but his arm was so painful and fingers slick with blood. Here she came, reaching for him, that abomination of a face, the mouth working hungrily. He lashed out with his boot, missed, but the horse spun, terrified, and kicked. Fitz didn't see it, but one great hoof stove in her skull, and she was flung backward in a crumpled quiet heap, but he was already lashing at the horse and urging it on.

It was many minutes before he eased off, and looking back, convinced himself that he wasn't being chased. Dear God above and all His saints preserve us...

He peeked at his arm. It was throbbing, but the grip he was keeping on it had slowed the bleeding. His legs were aching from gripping onto the horse, and it was hard to hold the reins. He needed help, but there was no way in Hell he was riding back down that track. He looked around, getting his bearings. There was another looping road near here he could take back to Benalla, but that would take a long time, and what would he say when he got back? That he had been attacked by one of Them? He had heard stories about Blighters like everyone else, but knew that as a constable of the law, if he reported having had a run in with one, he could kiss his job away.

Christ, he could murder a drink.

He realised he was actually not that far from the Kelly property. It occurred to him he could get some help there – maybe even lure Dan into helping him back to Benalla, and then arrest him when they got there. He could claim Dan injured him resisting arrest... Aye, a good plan. He kicked his horse, then stopped, and first reached with his good hand into his saddle bag and removed the calf liver. Wouldn't want the Kelly's to get the wrong idea about his visit. He cast it as far as he could into the bush, and then rode on.

The Kelly family homestead was a sprawling slab-built affair. Chickens scurried as Fitz rode into the yard, and a dog barked at him from behind a shed. A little boy and girl who had been playing in a puddle stopped and stared at him as he swung painfully from the saddle.

"Is y'er ma at home?" he asked, and gasped. He steadied himself against the warm side of the horse.

Both children stared at him mutely. He was about to try again, when an older girl, a pretty teenager, appeared in the doorway. "What do you want?" she asked.

"Is y'er ma in? I need some help." He held his arm up to show her, and tears came unbidden to his eyes.

"Ma!" the girl yelled over her shoulder. "What did you do?" she asked Fitz.

"I had an accident..."

"Devil take you!" bellowed a voice from inside the house. "Am I not busy in here? What is it now?"

Ellen Kelly appeared beside her daughter, a baby in her arms. Another teenage girl peeked around from behind her.

"Morning, Mrs Kelly..." said Fitz.

"Mrs Kelly, is it? Well, aren't ye the perfect gent? And here's me been calling all you traps a no good pack of lying bastard curs. What with all the harassment and the killin' of our dogs and chasin' of me sons. What do you want?"

"I..." said Fitz, but then a wave of dizziness hit him and he staggered. He reached for his horse but it stepped away, and he went down sprawling in the mud. The young ones all laughed. He swore, and sat up, holding his bloody arm clear of the muck.

"Oh, Jesus, look at you. Ye'd better come in then, I suppose," huffed Ellen. "Kate, Grace, give him a hand."

Once helped inside to the kitchen table by the teenage girls, and with a mug of tea before him, Fitz started to feel a little better. He was grateful for the tea, as his mouth was drying out, and he felt a fever coming on. The two youngest children – not counting the baby, now minded by Kate, the eldest girl – stood staring at him, snot running from their noses. Fitzpatrick was finding the sight quite nauseating. Ellen fussed with a pot of water on the fire.

"So," she said without looking up. "What happened?"

"I had an accident..."

"What kind of accident?"

"I... I fell."

"Here's a cloth, Ma," said Grace, coming into the kitchen. Fitz let his eyes rest on her instead of her disgusting siblings. She was a peach, that was for sure. As was her older sister. Both ready for the plucking, soon. Wouldn't that stick it to the Kelly brothers, then?

"Here, show me." Ellen took hold of his arm in her strong grip, and frowned as she examined the oozing wound. "Ye've lost a fair amount of hide off of you. Caught it on something?"

Fitz nodded. He felt like he was floating a few inches above the ground. He was aware of pain as Ellen dabbed at his arm, but felt strangely disconnected from it.

"What brings you out this way, Constable Fitzpatrick?"

"You know my name?"

"We make it our business to know all the troopers. I don't much like the look of this arm. I'll bind it for you, but ye'd best see the doctor... The edges are going black. Ye said it just happened?"

"Yes..."

" What did ye say the reason was for your being out here?"

"Looking for Dan..."

"Were ye now?"

Fitzgerald gasped - her voice was soft but the grip on his arm was very strong.

"And what did ye want Dan for? He's done nothing wrong."

Fitz tried to focus. "Just wanted to talk... That's all... No trouble."

"Are ye sure of that? Ye wasn't going to try to arrest the poor boy?"

"Arrest? No... No..." He stared at Kate and Grace. Must

change the subject, he thought. "You have such pretty girls, Mrs Kelly." He frowned. An image of teeth and bone superimposed itself over both girls. "No..." He shook his head. "Not like... Not like her..."

"Her?"

"The girl on the track... She was horrible."

Fitz didn't notice Ellen release his arm and sit slowly back. "What girl on the track?"

Fitz squinted. His head was hot. There was something he had to be careful of - what was it? Ellen had gone back over to the fireplace. He wondered if he could ask for some whiskey. He tried to lick his lips, but his tongue was like a piece of leather. How his arm throbbed.

"Constable? What girl on the track?"

"Don't want to think about her... Teeth..."

"Did she bite you?"

A warning penetrated the hot fog in Fitz's mind -why did she ask that?

"Ma," said Kate. "Like the boys said?"

"Take the baby inside, girl. Quickly now."

He should go. He fumbled with his helmet, pulled it onto his head, vaguely surprised to find it still fit, since his head felt so swollen. Then everything spun and a light flared through his eyes, and he was aware of a dull thudding noise, and his head was on the table and warm sticky blood was pouring from his nose.

"Hit him again, Ma!" cried Grace.

Fitz thrust himself up and away from the table. Ellen stood across from him holding a coal shovel. His helmet lay rolling on the floor, a sizable dent in it.

"Quickly, Grace! Fetch the axe!"

The girl darted past Fitz and out the door.

"What are you doing?" he asked.

"Believe it or not, but it's nothing personal, Constable. Ye've got the Blight and we need to put ye down. Now just hold still..."

She came at him, swinging that damned shovel. He fumbled for his pistol, but she caught him a blow on the arm and it went dead.

"I've brought the saw!" cried Grace, running back into the room.

"I said the axe!"

"It was stuck too tight!"

"What good will the saw do?" asked Kate, reappearing from the inside doorway. "Are you going to ask him to please hold still while we saw his head off?"

"We could hold him down!"

Fitz finally managed to pull his gun clear with his left hand. He brandished it wildly. "No one is going to be cutting my head off!" he yelled, his voice sounding shrill in his own ears. "There's nothin' wrong with me!"

"Oh, be a man, can't ye?" scoffed Ellen. "Ye're done for anyway. It'll be quicker like this! Now, Kate!"

He spun - the girl had a large carving knife and was coming at him. He pointed the pistol at her and fired. The shot went high, smashing into the top of the wall, sending splinters flying. The girls screamed. Ellen dropped the shovel and scooped up the two children, who had been watching calmly the whole time.

"Are ye mad? There's children here!"

"Me mad?" spluttered Fitz. "Me?"

Seeing his chance, he raised his pistol and fired again for good measure, up into the roof. They all screamed again as debris rained down, and he dashed for the door. He was vaguely aware of the knife clattering off the wall beside him as he as tumbled from the house. He grabbed the reins of his horse and pulled himself up across the saddle, calling to it to get a blessed move on. Hanging upside down, he looked back as it trotted towards the track, his last view of the Kelly homestead was one of the entire family standing outside, armed with a variety of kitchen implements.

The ride back to Benalla was a nightmare. It took an eternity to get upright in the saddle. He had to ride down that section of the track at a mad gallop, for fear of encountering *her* - though the question of who was worse, that dead thing, or the Kelly women, was a vexed one. He thought he caught sight of what looked like a bundle of clothes lying by the side of the road, but he didn't slow to look, keeping his focus fixed grimly ahead. By the time he rode into Benalla, he couldn't tell if he was upright or upside down. At the police station, he slid from his horse, not bothering to tie it up, and stumbled inside. There was no one about in the front office, so he lurched through into the back. He heard a cough from one of the offices and stumbled in. It was Superintendent Hare.

"Constable Fitzpatrick," said Hare in surprise as the dishevelled trooper fell into a chair. "Whatever is the matter?"

"I've been shot," said Fitzpatrick, with sudden inspiration.

"Shot? Shot, did you say? Who shot you?"

Who shot him?

"Dan," he said. "Mrs Kelly," he added.

"Dan Kelly and Mrs Kelly shot you? They both shot you?"

"That's right. Here." And he dragged his chair forward and dropped his arm onto the superintendent's desk. It looked terrible. It was a mixture of angry red flesh and blackened edges. A viscous dark blood was seeping from it, and the veins on the rest of his arm were raised and sore.

"That doesn't look like a bullet wound to me," said Hare. "Unless it happened a week ago and you have been keeping it hidden?"

"I think I need a doctor," said Fitz, staring in horror at his arm. His head suddenly felt much clearer – no, colder.

"All in good time, my dear fellow," said Hare, "but first, I need your report."

"There's something really wrong with me..."

"I dare say there is," said Hare, "but I'm not sure a doctor is the answer. Now, report. Where's Dan Kelly?"

"He wasn't there..."

"No. But someone - or something, to be more precise - was at the house, hmm? Or on the way there? Something a little difficult to talk about, perhaps? It is alright, constable. You can be honest with me."

Fitz stared at the superintendent. "How do you know that?" he asked hoarsely.

"Come, come man," said Hare. "I think I would know the difference between a gunshot and a bite. You don't take me for an idiot, I hope?"

"A bite..."

"That's right. You've been bitten by one of them, haven't you? By one of the Blighted? There, I've said it."

"Blighters aren't real... Not supposed to say..."

"Oh, they're real alright. As you can well attest to. I know, official policy is to deny and repress - blame the odd incident on lunatics, bushrangers, wild natives, and so on... But they definitely do exist. Now, what happened to the one that bit you?"

"Not sure... Christ, what is going to happen to me? Am I going to die?"

"I shouldn't think so," said Hare with a smile.

"Hurts like a bitch... Sorry, sir, 'scuse the language."

"Quite alright, Constable, given the circumstances. Well, best we take care of you, eh?"

"Thank you, sir." Fitzpatrick sagged in relief. It was good to hand yourself over into a superior's care.

"Let me help you up," said Hare, coming around his desk and taking hold of Fitz. "Easy does it. That's good. Let's go this way..."

"Out the back, sir? Aren't we going to the doctor?"

"Better to have someone come to you, I think. This way."

Out the back of the police station were a series of sheds, rarely used except to store old equipment. One, right up the back, was sometimes used as a drunk tank or an overflow cell if there had been a big brawl at one of the pubs. It was towards this door that Hare propelled Fitzpatrick now.

"I don't want to go in there," said Fitzpatrick plaintively as Hare fished about on a large ring for the right key.

"You'll be snug as a bug in here! Here we go." He unclasped a large padlock and swung the door open. Fitz peered into the murky interior.

"Can't I wait inside the station?"

A heavy blow - the second of the day - sent him sprawling into the shed. He landed on his face on the bare dirt floor and groaned. His head was killing him. He was dimly aware of the rattle of chains, and of Hare gripping his leg and pulling something tight about it. When at last he felt able to roll over and try to sit up, he found he had been chained to the back wall, the chain being padlocked to his ankle and bolted to the wall.

"Chain is from when we had Mad Jack in here after his last blinder," said Hare, dusting off a stool and sitting down. "You remember Mad Jack? Big, big fellow. And a very mean drunk."

"What did you do that for? Why hit me?"

Hare blinked at him. "Bit slow on the uptake, aren't you, Constable? I had to get you in here, and chain you up. You're a danger to others, and I had my doubts you would just sit still and cooperate while I bound you. Couldn't take any chances. Apologies for the head, but I rather think that is small potatoes anyway, in the face of what's going to happen."

"What's going to happen..." repeated Fitz, a heavy feeling settling in his stomach.

"I don't really know," said Hare cheerfully, "but I doubt you'll enjoy it. I don't know much about Blighters - I don't know who does, and I can hardly ask, can I? That wouldn't sit very well with my superiors in Melbourne, and I have my career to think of. No offence to you, as a local, but I have no desire to see out my working life in this backwater. So, we must consider ourselves amateur scientists in this regard, Constable. Together, we are going to come to a greater understanding of the Blight." He leaned forward, staring at Fitz in a way the constable didn't care for at all. "And see whether it could be useful to me..."

THIRTEEN

"And yes... 'useful to me'... Got it." I looked up at Ned. "Right, ready."

He remained silent, staring at the wall. Christ, the man was as moody as a debutante.

"You can go on," I said, but then fell silent myself. Were his eyes glistening? Were those tears? Oh, if the mob could see their revolutionary hard man now!

He dashed his arm across his eyes, and then kept it there, shielding himself from my gaze, or hiding from the cell itself, perhaps. Or the painful images of memory – on that score at least I could sympathise.

"They charged my Ma with attempted murder after that and locked her up in this filthy place. She's so close by, Remittance Man, but the dirty stinking bastards won't let me see her!" His voice built to a roar. I watched his bottom lip tremble with emotion. But then he continued in a voice so soft I could hardly hear it. "Maybe the bastards have it coming..."

"Have what coming?" I asked.

He rubbed his face with his hands, and leant over to clear his nose, noisily, onto the floor. Bloody peasant.

"Nothing," he muttered.

I could see that there was no shifting him from his present mood, and I was keen to head to the Robbie Burns to see if a certain young lady might be more in the mood for some company tonight. I wasn't sure if this was the best way to approach her, but it worked back home - just keep showing enough interest in a girl and she would come around eventually. After all, they were terrified of finding themselves old maids - at least, this was the case with the ones I targeted. The one advantage of my frequent monster in my chest was for some reason, it gave me the ability to recognize its kin in others. So while there was no point in pursuing the brash, gorgeous girls dripping with confidence, jewellery, and sexual appeal, there was a lot to be gained in looking to their quieter friends standing in the corners. Not the ugly wallflowers, I didn't mean them. I meant the ones who were quite attractive on the outside, but full of doubt and self-loathing within. The ones with the air of brittle despair about them. The ones grateful when approached by a young man. The same ones who would not make a fuss - who would indeed accept it as what they deserved - when turned out of a hotel room the next morning, their dress as crumpled as their self-worth.

But with Maggie? All I could do was pursue her like an amorous ox and hope that at least by comparison - what had she said? Old blowhards and farmers? - I may shine. Like gold. Or Fool's Gold perhaps, to be more precise.

So I was happy to leave Ned chewing on his beard and tell him I would see him on the morrow. Once out of his cell, I headed swiftly for the gate, hoping to avoid spending any time with Castiaeu. Outside of the main gate I turned left, but then remembered I was flush by my standards, and could easily take a cab. I was looking up and down the street for just such a conveyance, when a carriage that drew up before me, its window shades drawn down, blocked my view. I was craning to look around it when the door swung open and two men slipped out. They were not large, but looked handy, and had hard-set faces. The thing that really caught my attention was their eyes - dead and expressionless. I hated eyes like that. It was a look I wished I could develop myself - I felt my eyes were absolutely a window to my soul and gave too much away.

"Someone wants a word with you," said one of the toughs to me now.

"Who, me? Gentlemen, you have the wrong man, I'm afraid."

The two glanced at each other, and then looked me up and down like scullery maids choosing beef.

"No, we got the right man. Get in the carriage, please, sir."

"But who do you work for? Are you the police?"

They didn't answer, just gestured towards the open door and the dark interior of the carriage. I glanced back at the closed prison gate behind me. If I threw myself on it and hammered, would someone come before these cherubs slit my throat with the razors they no doubt had slipped inside their coat pockets?

As if sensing my thoughts, one moved to stand between the gaol and me. "Don't be silly, sir. Now come on, he doesn't like to be kept waiting."

"He who?" I croaked, still trying to play the part of the unruffled hero. Why did I suddenly need to urinate so badly? There were people about on the street, but I couldn't see myself calling for help. Somehow, making a scene seemed worse.

"You'll see soon enough. He just wants to have a little chat with you, is all."

A little chat? Well, that didn't sound too bad, unless that was razor gang code for slicing off parts of your body, and then feeding them to you. Hoping the toughs wouldn't see how my hands were shaking, I shrugged and climbed aboard. They followed me swiftly inside, one sitting beside me, one across. They both folded their arms and sat in silence. I wasn't going to give them the pleasure of not answering my questions, so I sat quietly. With the blinds pulled down, it was impossible to be sure where we were heading. I didn't know Melbourne's streets well enough to track our journey mentally. There was also the issue that I had a particularly bad sense of direction - I was forever getting totally turned around. Indeed, I recalled an old governess who was in the family employ when I was a boy - she had later come back when I was in my adolescence, more grey and gaunt, and seeking re-employment as a housemaid. While my father was off talking to my mother, in an attempt to ingratiate herself, she told me with a laugh how she used to like to let me walk out of buildings in town when I was little, as I would invariably turn the wrong way. She used to find it quite diverting, apparently, and told me how when she told the rest of the staff, they joked about how I would probably get lost on the way to my wedding, one day.

Quite.

I wondered whatever happened to her. Father was very gracious and didn't press charges when items of the family silverware went missing, and turned up stashed in her suitcase. I remembered her wailing entreaties and assurances of innocence and even now, in my current state, they brought a smile to my lips.

We made several turns, of that I was sure. It was tempting to lift one of the shades to peek out, but I gathered the twins would not sit idly by and let me do that. Clearly, they didn't want me to know where they were taking me. Were they going to kill me? What for? What had I done? I wracked my brain. Were they some of Kelly's misguided revolutionaries? They didn't seem the type - too organized for starters - lying in wait outside the gaol to affect a public kidnapping... Didn't seem the style based on the sad pale specimens I had encountered in low bars on the continent. All wild hair, wild eyes, sour breath, and shattered expectations, those fellows.

So perhaps government flunkies? Except they seemed generally too handy to be public servants. My mental wrestling had at least filled the time and helped me keep quiet. I realized the sound of the horses' hooves dragging us, was echoing strangely, but then the carriage stopped and the man sitting beside me pushed the door open and got out. His friend gestured at me to follow, and came out hard behind me. I saw that we were in a very narrow lane squeezed between the backs of a series of large buildings. I looked about, but couldn't recognize any of them - but the backs of buildings always looked different to their fronts. Like the difference between the face you saw on some women at the ball, and then what you wake up beside in the morning.

One of the fellows rapped on a door before us, and it swung open to reveal a nondescript man in a fairly expensive suit. He stared at me, and then said, without taking his eyes off me, "So this is him, is it?"

"It's him alright," answered one of my new friends.

"Hmm," said the man in the doorway, as if somewhat disappointed. "Follow me."

As he disappeared back inside, I realized he was talking to me. I glanced back at Bib and Bub, who were standing behind me with folded arms and expressions that suggested they might be yearning for a little excitement. I stepped through the doorway.

Inside, I found myself following the man's back down a narrow passageway. We passed an open doorway leading into a large laundry room on the left, and somewhere behind other closed doors was a kitchen, going by the rich smells and clatter of dishes. I wondered if we could be in the back of a hotel, perhaps.

My guide proceeded to lead me up a narrow staircase, up two floors. I felt as if I was penetrating the labyrinth, and wondered if I should have been taking more careful note of which way we came in – leaving Ariadne's thread - in case I had to beat a hasty retreat. But then I remembered the fellows waiting downstairs outside the door - no, whatever minotaur awaited, it looked like I was going to have to see this through.

I set my shoulders and drew up taller. I'd survived some pretty horrible meetings before. The last discussion with Father jolted into my mind - that cold, miserable day, him standing behind his desk pretending to look out the window at the view, but really finding it almost impossible to look at me... The letter lying open on his desk... The ticket beside it...

We exited the staircase through a narrow door, and found ourselves in a wide hall with a thick carpet. My guide led me to a heavy door and raised his hand to knock - he paused. "Do try to keep a civil tongue in your head," he said, and added, "I'll be right outside the door." But whether this last was meant to be threat, or reassurance, I didn't have time to ponder, as he rapped briskly on the door and stuck his head inside.

"Ready, HP?" he asked quietly, and, receiving a grunt in reply, took my arm and propelled me inside. The door clicked closed behind me.

A small sitting room with a pair of high leather wingback chairs facing a fireplace lay within. There was a small blaze in the grate - and quite welcome it was, too, not just for the warmth - this was Melbourne after all, where the weather never seemed to quite commit itself to anything - but because of the cheer it leant the sober book- lined walls. Nothing very bad could happen somewhere so civilised, could it?

I realized there was someone sitting in the right hand chair -

HP, I presumed, whoever that was. I could just make out a cloud of white hair above the chair back, and then whoever it was blew a plume of cigar smoke into the air. He raised a hand above his head and waved me forward.

I walked slowly around and sank onto the other seat with a creak of leather. My buttocks were perched on the edge of the chair - I had no wish to find myself having to clamber out of its deep embrace in a hurry. I studied the man seated across from me - he was a large fellow, with a craggy face, his belly now softening and rounding with age. He wore a beard of the same quality as his hair - indeed his face was surrounded by this mane of white hair, giving him the appearance of a kindly old lion. He twiddled his cigar between his fingers, and had his legs stretched out fully towards the fire in an air of relaxation. He seemed harmless enough, and I allowed myself to sink slightly further back into the chair.

"Manifest destiny," he growled, staring at the fire.

I wasn't sure what to make of this, whether it was a statement or a question, so, chose to remain silent.

"Manifest destiny," he said again and harrumphed. "A Yankee idea... But apt. The belief that it is your nation's destiny to expand and grow. You ever heard of it... Charles?" and he looked across at me for the first time and I could see the intelligence in his eyes. Whoever or whatever he was, this was not one of Maggie's old blowhards that was for sure.

"You know my name, apparently," I said instead of answering. "Might I have the honour of enquiring as to yours? Your man called you HP, but I assume that is not for common usage."

He grinned around his cigar, an act which gave his smile a certain carnivorous quality. "You may enquire all you like. But no, Charles, this isn't a social engagement. You don't need to know my name. HP will suffice."

I nodded. "So this is business, then?"

"I'm not sure I'd classify it as that, either. It rather depends on where you stand."

"In relation to what?" I was battling to keep my tone light, bored almost, but was struggling. I was becoming a little tired of secrets.

"Tell me, Charles, were you born here? In Australia?"

"No, I wasn't. A fact that should be readily apparent from my accent."

"Not necessarily. There are many natives of this land who identify very strongly with the mother country, even down to affecting the accent."

"Well, I can assure you I am not one of them. I am a fairly recent arrival to this land."

"And so you see yourself as English? Not Australian?"

"Why must I see myself as anything? Why can't a person just be allowed to be himself? What is this great urgency to have to belong to this group or that group? This tribalism?" I stopped, a little embarrassed to find myself up on one of my soapboxes.

"I suppose I could say it is human nature," he answered. "But it is more complicated than that - at least in relation to the other part of your question, as to why you can't be left alone to *not* choose sides."

He fell silent, brooding, sucking on his cigar.

"So what am I doing here?" I asked, "Apart from receiving the lesson in civics?"

"Listening carefully, I hope." He blew a great cloud of smoke into the air. "One day," he said, "this will be a great nation. One day, it will truly mean something to say 'I am an Australian.' These squabbling, disparate colonies shall come together, and together forge a nation the equal of any in the world. A new nation, young and vigorous, unshackled by the chains of history. A beacon to the world." He studied the ash on the end of his cigar, and dislodged it into an ashtray beside him. "And nothing must be allowed to get in the way."

I stared at him. "Wait a minute...you think *I* am in the way?"

He held a hand out, and waggled it. "Could go either way, Charles, is our thinking. That's why we are having this little chat."

"This is absurd! I don't understand what you are talking about. The only thing it could possibly be about is Kelly's trial, but he is just a broken down bushranger, sure to hang..."

HP stared at me from under heavy brows. "Is that all he is, Charles?"

"Well, I think he may well be a madman, too, with delusions... Look, I shouldn't really be talking about this. You might be working with the prosecution."

"You just said yourself that he is going to hang. Harsh words from his defence."

"Realistic words. And that's beside the point. The man still deserves a fair hearing; he has to have his day in court..." I stopped as I got the awful picture of how the trial would go, me sitting trying to fade into the background at the defenders table, while Kelly railed to all and sundry about Blighters and conspiracies...

"No one is suggesting otherwise, my boy." I flinched at that - I was no one's boy. Not noticing my reaction, HP continued, "but there is more to this trial than this one man's guilt or innocence. This trial - which must not be interfered with as to justice - must be managed very carefully. Very carefully indeed. And you are in a position to help do just that."

"Managed? What are you suggesting?"

"This trial is about the murder of three police officers at Stringybark Creek. That is all that this trial should concern itself with. There should be no other matters brought up that may cause obfuscation. Especially matters that may have political ramifications beyond this trial. Ramifications that may delay or even stop federation of this nation ever occurring."

My God, I thought. He means the plan to establish a republic within Victoria - Kelly's plan for an Irish state. Yes, I could see how that would not go down well with Her Majesty's government back home.

Or...

He couldn't possibly be talking about Blighters, could he? Would anyone - apart from me and my fear of the ensuing public ridicule - really be afraid of Kelly getting in the stand and subjecting us to his views on a huge conspiracy involving the walking dead?

Unless... Oh, surely not. I was getting as bad as he was.

I looked up at HP, to find him watching me intently.

"So, Charles," he said, "what kind of assurance can you give me that when the time comes, you will do the right thing?"

The right thing? In relation to what? And at what time? My confusion must have spilled over onto my face, and HP didn't seem to like what he saw, for his great brow furrowed and his eyes went hard. Then, as if the sun had passed briefly behind a cloud, his face relaxed and he smiled at me benignly.

"Well, then," he said, "that's enough of all that, eh? We'll consider the matter duly discussed and decided for now. You're a smart young fellow. You'll do the sensible thing. Now how about a drink?"

I did not feel the matter - whatever it actually was - to have been discussed much at all, let alone there being any kind of agreement reached, but a drink certainly sounded very welcome indeed. HP rose from his chair - I saw by his movement that he was a younger man than I had at first thought - and pulled on a rope by the fireplace, and when the same suited lackey appeared, ordered him to fetch us a drink.

"Hope you like port, dear fellow," he said, sinking back into his chair. "I always enjoy a glass before dinner. Aids the digestion."

Frankly, I didn't care, so long as it had alcohol in it, but murmured my agreement with him. When the glasses appeared, borne on a silver tray, no less, I accepted mine with gratitude and sipped away. It was red and rich as blood. A pleasing warmth spread through my body, as HP droned on about the differences as he saw them between Sydney and Melbourne. I nodded and smiled at the right times, but felt no urge to speak at all.

"My goodness, look at the time. You must forgive me, Charles, but I have another engagement. My man here will see you back to your abode." He stood, and seemed to loom hugely over me. I felt him grip my shoulder briefly. "I'm sorry, my boy."

I assured him that was quite alright, or meant to, but by the time the words were coming out of my mouth, we seemed to be already gliding down the back stairs. I felt the cold outside air like an immersion in water, and overhead, the stars wheeled in a narrow panel of sky. And the next I knew, I was in the carriage and it was starting with a jolt, throwing me against someone, one of them. I slid sideways, unable to hold myself upright, and found my face pressed into a less-than-clean jacket. I giggled, the sound muffled and echoing in my ears, which made me giggle all the more. Rough hands grabbed me and dragged me upright, slamming me back against my seat. I bounced, falling forward, and laughed with delight, though my face seemed suddenly to stop against a bony knee. I was held there, in the cosy dark, until the next I knew, my feet were banging against steps and my arms were feeling strained, wrapped as they were around two men's necks. I heard the angry sound of Mrs Mackie's voice, and a lower soothing tone talking to her, and then I was lying on my bed and it was quiet at last, though the room was spinning and I was the axis, and I slipped away into sleep...

...and fevered dreams took me to the ends of the earth. My cot was at the bottom of the ocean, and I struggled against the weight of the depths, the cloying, clasping lengths of weed that wrapped about me... But then I was walled within the depths of the earth, and volcanic heat roasted me as I strained to dig my way out...

...and then I lay, imprisoned, chained, in the dark, alone - no, not alone, for the Watcher sat nearby, smoke curling from his pipe, the ember in the bowl an angry red eye in the gloom...

"God, help me," said a voice, and it was not my voice, but that of another man, a man wracked by a terrible fever, a man who could feel his life boiling away. "God help me."

...and it was as well that he appealed to the Almighty and not the man sitting watching, for there was to be no help, no hope, from that quarter.

"Shush now. Shush," said the Watcher, but his tone belied the care of his words, and his eyes, if the dying man could have seen them, glittered with greed.

And when the last desperate, ragged breath wracked its way into the man's ruined lungs, and burbled out as black liquid seeped from his mouth and he was still, then the Watcher leaned forwards and said, "Constable? Are you dead? Can you wake up? *Can you wake up?*"

FOURTEEN

"Can you wake up? Or do I need to help you? Jesus, man, how drunk did you get?"

Cold water drenched me, and I came awake bawling and gasping. I looked about wildly - I was in my room, and Tom Lloyd stood over me, a pitcher in his hand.

"Get up, curse you, and stop that noise, it's only water. I could have used your chamber pot."

I groaned, holding my pounding head. Sour bile threatened at the back of my throat.

"What the devil are you doing here?"

"Maggie sent me."

"Maggie? Why? Where is she? What's wrong?"

"They're moving Ned."

"What the hell do you mean, they're moving him?"

"They're on the way to the railway station. They're taking him to Beechworth. Maggie's gone to find Gaunson and sent me after you."

Beechworth? What the hell? How could they move him somewhere else when his trial was due to commence in a few days? I realized I was still fully dressed, down to my boots.

"Is there any water? Or did you throw it all on me?"

He looked into the pitcher. "Threw it all on you. Come on, get up."

I dragged myself upright - then a thought struck me. "How did you find me?"

He smiled at me smugly. "Now that's interesting. I followed you the other day, see-"

"Followed me?"

"-so I told Maggie I knew where to find you while she went looking for Gaunson. Funny thing, though. Your landlady didn't seem to think she had a William here. When I described you, she knew you well enough, though. 'Cept she thinks your name is Robert.'"

"It's my middle name," I said, grabbing a valise and stuffing what clothes I could into it, and my shaving kit. "Turn around, would you? I need to use the pot."

While his back was briefly turned, I dug under my mattress for my derringer, and stuffed it in the bottom of the bag.

"Shy, are you?"

"Shut up," I said, and then proceeded to urinate noisily into the chamber pot. "Why exactly did you follow me?"

"Just curious about you..."

"Well, spare me your interest."

"I've seen the way you look at her."

I'd finished my brief packing, and looked up at him. His colour was a little high, and his hands were clenched. Oh no. I was in no state for a fight. I groped for something to say but could think of nothing, except denying it, which he wouldn't believe anyway. He stalked to the door instead.

"There's no time for this now. Ned needs you."

I followed him out, pointedly locking my door behind me - though he didn't really look like the lock-picking type. More likely my friends last night had left it open... Hmm, last night.

Either that port was damn near a hundred proof, or there had been a little something extra added to it. I was distracted from following this train of thought further by Lloyd, who suddenly loomed over me, very close in the narrow landing.

"By Christ, you just watch yourself, though. Or when this is over... "

He left the threat hanging, and stamped down the stairs.

"Well, when this is over, maybe I'll just shoot you dead," I said softly, aiming a finger at his retreating back, then followed him down. "Ah, Mrs Mackie..."

My esteemed landlady was waiting at the bottom of the stairs with a face like thunder. She was glowering at Lloyd with great dislike - well, he was like a herd of elephants on her stairs - but then her eyes swept to me and I shuddered. She drew a breath - a pinched hiss of air, mixed it with the poison swirling within her, and opened her mouth to unleash hell.

I beat her to it.

"Dear Mrs Mackie! Rent! My rent!" I fumbled in my jacket pocket - God, let them not have robbed me last night! But no, my fingers closed on my money clip and I swiftly drew forth my bundle of pounds. At the sight of the money, the good woman pinched her lips closed tight, and held out one of her taloned claws. "I do apologise for making you wait," I said as I counted what I owed into her hand. I toyed with paying ahead, just to see if I could make her smile, but decided to be sensible.

Lloyd was already out the door and waving to the cab he had waiting. I hoped he didn't think I was going to be paying for that.

We rattled through the streets towards the rail station at Newmarket - it was some distance from Fitzroy, certainly not a walk. The motion of the cab wasn't helping my stomach settle. I took some pleasure in belching up some foul gas and trying to breathe it in Lloyd's direction, but couldn't tell if it was having any impact, since he always seemed to have the same sour look on his face. I tried to get my thoughts in order. Hopefully, Gaunson would be at the station with Maggie and we could clear this all up. They couldn't go moving Ned at this point. Then my thoughts turned to the mysterious government man – for what else could he be? – HP. What had he said as he left? Apologized, hadn't he? For drugging me? The port must have been drugged, to cause me to miss them moving Ned. I didn't understand why I was that important to events - though I supposed I should be grateful they hadn't seen me as important enough to kill. Maybe the drugging was also to serve as a warning, to bring me to heel. My lips curled into a snarl.

As we arrived at the station, I could see a small train consisting of an engine, a carriage, and a guard van. There was a knot of men standing near it, some in the uniform of troopers. As soon as the cabbie came to a halt, I grabbed my bag and leapt onto the road.

"Quick, Tom!" I cried. "They're leaving!"

As I ran for the platform, I heard the cabbie yell and Lloyd curse. I glanced back to see him digging furiously in his pockets for coins. Of course, when I arrived on the platform, there was no sign the train was going anywhere soon. Ned was standing defiantly, arms crossed and jaw jutting belligerently. He nodded when he saw me, I think with some relief in his eyes, and the action caused the five or six troopers to turn and look at me.

"Who the hell are you?" demanded a sergeant, his hand on the butt of his holstered revolver.

"He's with me," said Ned, "legal representation."

The sergeant screwed up his face. "Legal representation? I don't know nothing about transporting no legal representation."

"And why are you transporting my client anywhere, Sergeant?" I gasped. My head was pounding and my stomach was churning. Perhaps a bullet in the head would have been preferable. But I was at my most imperial, and it worked as always. The lower classes always instinctively know their place - you just have to remind them of it from time to time.

"All legal and proper, sir. Prisoner is to be taken to Beechworth for arraignment." He turned to Ned. "Now don't be difficult, Kelly. Get on the train. We don't want to have to drag you on, but we will if we have to."

"You have a mind to try as long as I'm wearing these?" Ned lifted and shook his hands, displaying the heavy manacles wrapped around his wrists. "You big brave men."

"Listen, Kelly, you don't have any gang here. There's just you and us. So just mind your lip."

"I'll get aboard as long as he comes with me." He pointed his chained hands at me.

"Not a chance. Orders said nothing about taking anyone else on board. Stop larking about and get on."

"Just you and me, eh?" said Ned, looking past the sergeant's shoulder. "Hi! Boys!"

We all turned to look. Three boys were riding past the front of the station, on some magnificent looking horses. Probably racehorses getting some exercise. The boys stopped and looked in.

"Some fine looking horses you have there!" Ned yelled. "I'd love to give you a hand training them, but I'm a bit tied up at the moment!" He shook his bound hands above his head.

"Shut up, Kelly," hissed the sergeant, "we don't need a scene."

"Who's that?" yelled one of the boys. "Who you traps got there?"

"Don't you do it," growled the sergeant, "you keep your mouth shut."

"Either my legal chum comes with me now, or I send those

boys to raise the neighbourhood and cause a bloody riot. Your choice, Sergeant Steele."

Steele glowered. Ned smiled at me and winked. Why not do it, I wondered. Why not call up the people and get away in the fracas?

"Alright, alright. You win. Your lawyer can come with you. Just get on the bloody train!"

Ned nodded, and consented to being led across the tracks to the special train awaiting him. I spotted Lloyd lurking about at the back.

"No sign of Maggie and Gaunson?"

He shook his head.

"Find them. Tell them I've gone with Ned, but they need to get to Beechworth as quickly as possible."

He nodded morosely and went to find himself another cab. With that, I soon found myself seated beside Ned in a carriage, empty except for six troopers as the engine hissed and slowly hauled us away from the station.

I glanced around. The officers had spread themselves out and none were nearby. I moved to sit across from Ned, to give him more room, as I had noticed him rubbing his leg and wincing.

"Thanks," he said, and shuffled along so he could swing his legs up onto the seat. He exhaled and leaned back.

"Has the prison doctor looked at your legs lately?"

"Don't need him."

"They look like they are pretty painful."

"That's what comes of being shotgunned in the backs of them."

"It's their duty to provide you treatment."

"Remittance Man, my legs are the least of my problems right now."

He had a point, I suppose. What good would medical care be when he was soon to be dancing on the end of a rope?

We rattled along, passing through the suburbs and into the countryside, and I suppose I slept, for I was next aware of the train lurching and my head bouncing against the window. I sat up with a start, and saw that we were travelling through wooded hills. Ned was twisted in his seat so that he could stare out at the view.

"I was born around here," he said quietly; when he saw I was awake.

"Oh?" I managed.

"Over behind those hills you can see there. I don't suppose I'll ever walk those ranges again."

"You don't know that..."

He smiled at me mirthlessly. "Spare me any pep talk, Remittance Man. I don't think it is your style."

I nodded, and he went back to looking out the window.

"What happened back at the gaol?" I asked.

"Well, last night they fetched me from my cell and took me down into the prison kitchen. They had a magistrate there, and he said they were taking me to Beechworth to be arraigned - because that was the bailiwick in which my supposed crimes had occurred."

"I suppose that makes some sense... It just sounds odd, holding a hearing at night, in the kitchen. I'm surprised they found a judge who would go along with it."

"He was a member of the government as well as a judge, that's why. You can see it, can't you, Remittance Man? All this effort to cover up, to cover me up, have me done away with as quietly as possible?"

"It is peculiar, I'll grant you that... But it is still a lot of trouble to go to. They could have just let you rot in your cell. Or just killed you - surely that would be simpler?"

He smiled. "What do you think was going to happen on this train?"

"Oh, come now. Surely..."

"You can bet on it. You can bet that news would break tomorrow that bad Ned Kelly attempted to escape from the train taking him to trial, and he was gunned down by the tracks like the dog he is."

I shifted uneasily in my seat, glancing at the bored looking troopers sitting about the carriage.

"You don't think they..."

"With you here? Maybe. Maybe not. You're my lottery ticket, Remittance Man. Are you feeling lucky?"

Jesus. It would surely be easy to shoot me too, if it came to it, and claim I was hit in the crossfire. Or that I was aiding and abetting Ned's escape. I remembered I had my derringer, but it only held two shots, and I doubted its effectiveness against six officers with revolvers.

"I'm not afraid of dying," said Ned. "I just want my chance to speak. To sift all this to the bottom."

"I am afraid of dying."

He laughed. "Don't worry, Remittance Man. Dying is easy. Joe and Steve did it. Dan did it. We all do it... Though, there is what comes after..." he trailed off, looking uneasy.

"Heaven and hell?" I asked.

"Something like that."

"I didn't have you pegged as a religious man."

He grunted, and fell silent.

"Why don't you tell me more of your story?" I asked. "Why don't you tell me about what happened at Stringybark?"

"Ah," he said.

It was announced in the papers that Ellen Kelly, aided by her two sons, Edward and Daniel, had tried to murder a police officer who was simply going about his duties, making enquiries after a missing horse. A massive force of troopers had duly struck back, raiding the farm, and although the two boys had ridden off, abandoning their mother like the shabby cowards they were, the brave officers were able to apprehend the matriarch of the crime family after a brief struggle and fair degree of property destruction. She was charged, tried, and packed off to Melbourne gaol in short order.

In the hills, Ned was incandescent with rage. It took all of Joe's reasoning, and Dan's pleading, to stop him from riding into Beechworth to free her by force before they could load her on a train. That was just what they were waiting for, said Joe. They'll gun you down like a dog. Please, Ned, said Dan, let's help her legal-like.

And so Ned was convinced to stay away. It was the right decision. Aaron acted as their go-between, and reported that Beechworth was crawling with armed troopers.

"How was Ma?" asked Ned.

"She was looking tired, Ned," said Aaron. "But she kept her chin up, and wouldn't let them help her up into the train. Shook their hands right off her."

"That's Ma," said Dan, and sniffed.

"Aye," nodded Ned, "she's a tough old bird. A Kelly through and through. Doesn't change the fact that someone is going to pay for this."

"I can go visit her in Melbourne if you like, Ned," said Aaron. "I don't mind. It would be no bother."

"Ned," said Dan, "you promised."

"It truly would be no bother, Ned. Truly."

"Don't worry, Dan. We'll fight it in court."

"Ned?" asked Aaron, but Joe signalled him to let it go.

Lawyers were expensive, and it wasn't like anyone had that kind of money just lying around. There were few ways open to the boys to make money - at least, few legal ones that would net them the return they needed, especially as they were wanted men themselves. So they turned their hands to what they could - prospecting for gold dust in the streams of the Wombat Ranges, and setting up stills to make illegal alcohol. Lord knew, a decent drop was worth its weight in gold in those parts.

Ned was still restless. They were all well used to camping and living rough, but the lack of activity was telling. It felt like losing. And while he didn't say anything to Dan and the others, he was less than hopeful about Ma's chances of beating the charge. No, they really had it in for the Kelly's... And who 'they' were, was a question exercising Ned's mind a great deal recently. He had thought at first it was just the local constabulary's bias against his family - their Irish heritage, and, if he was honest, their past activities. Ned could understand them being angry at having noses thumbed at them. However, this was beginning to seem bigger than that, and it seemed to him things had started to change when he began to campaign against the Blighters. He hadn't forgotten Billy's claims that the government was involved, and that was appearing more and more likely.

The Blighted themselves were another issue. While the boys felt fairly safe from the police in the Wombats, since it was a long way from their usual haunts, it did seem to place them in an exposed position as far as the walking undead were concerned. Worryingly, they had seen no signs of any natives, suggesting the tribes had moved further inland and were no longer patrolling these parts, as Billy had threatened may happen. So, as well as working hard during the day, either on the stills or panning, they also had to take it in turns to watch through the long nights, to make sure they weren't taken unaware in their sleep.

It was a hard duty, to sit for a couple of hours at a time, outside the tent, no fire - they were worried a blaze would draw any nearby dead to them like moths to a flame - with Ned's old carbine across your knees. Staring out into the darkness, hearing the rustle of movement, the screams of the possums, well, it could do things to a man's mind. You'd stare at the ghostly whiteness of the gums, and fancy them to be moving bones and pale skin, an army of Blighters taking single steps forward every time you looked away, like the old children's game. It was always with great relief when you could rouse the next man swearing from his slumber, and pull your blankets up over your head, feeling somehow safer that way - not that you'd admit as much to the others. And finally dawn would come, the light slowly driving back the horrors, and a fire could be lit, and hot tea brewed, and someone would say "Well..." and the others would nod and blow on their tea, and the day's work would begin the cycle anew.

"We need more guns," said Ned, "repeaters, if we can get them."

"Bit hard to ride into town and buy them. And those kinds of guns are hard to get."

"We could raid some farms," said Dan.

"We'd mostly get old shotguns. I'd like something that could take down a Blighter at a distance. And revolvers, too. Six shooters."

"We'd have to go into Melbourne for all that - which we can't do, obviously," said Joe. "Send Aaron?"

Ned shook his head. "I reckon we can get what we need closer to home."

"Horse," said Steve.

The other three looked at him. His head was cocked to one side. He nodded, certain now. Ned picked up the carbine and cocked open the hammer, checking the powder in the pan.

They had axes and staves of wood at hand, too, if it came to that. Soon they could all make out the sound of a horse picking its way up the rough track to their campsite.

"Looks like Aaron," said Joe. "Must have some news."

"No," said Ned, putting down the gun, "that's Maggie."

She was laughing with delight when she rode up to them, her cheeks flushed. She was wearing trousers, and a man's shirt. She slid from her horse's back and ran to embrace Ned and Dan, then Joe and Steve as well.

"It's great to see you, girl," said Ned. "Did you see any troopers? Were you followed?"

She rolled her eyes. "Of course I was followed! They follow all of us. They'd follow us into the shitter if they thought it would lead to you!"

"You got away from them?" Dan was frowning.

"No, they're right behind me and I invited them for tea. Is the billy on?" She laughed as Dan glanced over her shoulder. "Oh, come on, Dan! You know I'm a better rider than any of them. I'm a better rider than any of you, too. Except maybe Steve, there."

Steve hung his head and smiled.

"They kept up for a while, and then I pulled so far ahead I had to stop and let them catch up..."

Ned burst out laughing. "What? You saucy devil!"

She grinned at him. "That's right. I sat myself down on a log and was looking ever so calm and grand when they came puffing up. They were nearly done in! 'Hello, boys,' I said. 'Don't you know better than to keep ladies waiting?' Then I jumped back on Socks and took off again. You should have heard the language! Enough to make a young girl blush, it was. Then when I was sure I had lost them good and proper, I made my way here."

"And it is grand to see you, it really is. But Maggie - what news?"

And her face fell at a stroke. "They took William. They arrested him and some other friends of the family. Said they were in on the plot to kill some traps. And without Ma, too... I'm all alone, Ned."

"The bastards. The bloody bastards."

"What should we do, Ned?" asked Dan.

"If they want a war, they'll get one!" With a shout, Ned kicked at the fire, and sent embers flying in an explosion of sparks and ash. An embarrassed silence fell. Steve walked around, stomping on any small fires threatening to break out.

Joe cleared his throat. "Pretty piss poor army with one old gun, eh, Ned?"

Ned barked in a manner that could have been laughter. "Don't worry. I'm not about to suggest we ride into town to our deaths. I'm just frustrated and angry."

"It's alright, Ned. We all feel it, though of course it's worse for you and Dan and Maggie, with your old Ma and all."

"Why are you wearing pants?" Steve asked Maggie, and it was such a long question coming from him, the others paused for a moment to look at him, but he was concentrating on grinding an ember beneath the heel of his riding boots.

Maggie laughed. "Oh, I was pretending to be Aaron. Since the traps have been following me everywhere, I asked him to wait and let me see if I could give them the slip dressed as him."

"Aaron was over?" asked Ned.

"He's always stopping in to see how me and the girls are. He's been making himself sick with worry looking out for us. I told him not to worry, that we were Kellys, and perfectly able to look after ourselves, but... he keeps coming."

"Does he now?"

"Didn't work anyway. Traps realised it was me and came on,

like I told you. I'll have to give him his shirt back sometime." Maggie plucked at the shirt, pulling it out from where it was tucked into her breeches.

"Gave you the shirt off his back, did he?"

"Yes," said Maggie. "Mighty generous of him, too. He'll be having to ride home shirtless."

"Ah, he'll be fine," said Joe. "He'd be glad to have a chance to do something to help. He'd better be careful, though, if they're arresting people who are friendly to us. Jesus, Ned, does that mean we're going to have to earn enough to hire lawyers for all them too? We'll be stuck out here for years!"

"No," said Ned, "no that's not the way this is going to end. It isn't going to be long speeches in court that reveal the black heart behind all this. No, things are going to have to be brought to a head. One way or another."

Maggie stayed for a bite of tea with the gang, and then swung up in the saddle to begin the long circular ride back home.

"I'll have to make sure I pick up the troopers somewhere," she said. "Wouldn't want to leave them floundering about in the dark."

"Serve them right," said Dan. "Goodbye, Maggie."

She leaned down to kiss him, and blew kisses at Ned, Joe, and Steve. They watched her move easily in the saddle as Socks picked her way back down the track.

It was less than a week later when they were awoken by the sound of gunshots.

Joe was on sentry duty, and stood outside the tent draped in a blanket. He was doing some breathing exercises that he had learned from his old neighbours, the Chinese miners, moving his hands and arms slowly up and down before him - "Like you in a river," as old Ah Feng used to tell him. It was a good time to practise, being on watch. It helped Joe stay awake, and to be honest, even though the others no longer teased him when they saw him "making like a Chinaman," as they called it, he was self-conscious about doing it in front of them. Since the whole point was to get out of his head, feeling embarrassed and wondering what the others were thinking was the last thing he needed.

The first shots came as a rolling double booming, echoing up from the valley below. They were followed by a fierce fusillade of sharper cracks, and as Joe stood frozen, the tent flap thrust open and the other three piled out. They stood in a silent line before the tent, listening as the shots gave way to silence again. Ned picked up the carbine, and his motion broke the spell and the others armed themselves with tools or heavy branches. But the silence dragged on unbroken, and they eventually sat - no one felt like going back into the tent. And finally, the sky began to lighten, and they began to feel like they could breathe.

"What the devil do you suppose that was?" asked Dan, his voice barely above a whisper.

"Well, we won't find out sitting here," said Ned. "It's light enough. Come on."

They made their way in single file down the narrow trail that hooked its way down through the scrubby slopes and into the valley below. The bush opened up here, and they made their way carefully forward. A creek ran beside them, and there was a clear path along its bank. They knew it led to an old abandoned miners' cottage. They had debated using it as their base, but when they inspected it, they found it in ruins, and besides, they felt if they knew about it, so must others, and as such, it would be an obvious place to search.

"Wait," said Steve, stopping, "listen."

They stood still, but there was no sound but the slow gurgle of the creek - but then-

"...Help..."

The cry was hoarse, and the sound dampened by the

towering trees. It was coming from up ahead. They moved forward slowly, forming an arrow with Ned at the front with the carbine.

"In God's name, help me," sobbed the voice.

They could smell a campfire now and there was the faint acrid tang of gunpowder in the air, growing stronger as they went. This was where the shots had come from. Moving up slowly, they came upon a clearing, and a campsite. There was one tent standing, and another lying in a collapsed heap. The campfire, obviously unfed for some time, was trailing a thin blue line of smoke into the air. A billy tin lay overturned nearby.

A man, his white shirt drenched in blood, stood swaying at the base of a tree, staring upwards. But it was not him who had cried out, for just at that moment, the voice came again, quieter now, from up within the tree.

"Oh, God, help me," came the voice, and they realised that there was another man maybe twelve feet up the narrow gum, his arms and legs wrapped around the trunk. As they watched, they could see him drop a foot or two lower, then clamp on harder to arrest his descent. As he moved, the figure at the bottom of the tree stirred, reaching up, his fingertips leaving red bloody lines on the white bark of the tree. "Oh, fuck off, Lonigan, can't you?"

"Lonigan!" said Ned.

"He's Blighted, Ned," said Dan.

At that moment, the man in the tree could take no more, and lost his grip. With a wretched cry, he slid down the rest of the trunk, colliding with Lonigan and sending the dead man staggering back. The living man landed in a sprawl, and scrambled to get up, but his weary limbs would hardly respond. The Blighter recovered its balance, and lurched toward him with a guttural growl.

"Stay down!" cried Ned, and he ran swiftly forward, cocking

and bringing the carbine up to his shoulder. The man shrieked, and covered his head in his hands as the undead figure clawed at him. From barely ten feet away, Ned stopped and fired. The carbine kicked, there was a splatter of dark blood and flesh upon the tree, and Lonigan staggered sideways.

"Find a gun!" yelled Ned, pulling a paper cartridge from his pocket. Steve and Dan ran to the tents, while Joe ran forward with an axe. "Careful, Joe!"

The Blighter spun around, and they saw that Ned's round had torn a great portion of its scalp and ear away, and they saw too how the front of the creature's shirt was torn open, and the terrible gaping wounds in its chest. Dark bloody air bubbles popped from within as they watched. It stared at them and at the man on the ground that was desperately clawing his way behind the tree, and then it went for Joe on swift jerking legs. Joe stood balanced on the balls of his feet, and swung the axe in a great overhead motion, chopping at it, but the blade skittered down the side of the Blighter's head and buried itself in its shoulder. It staggered under the weight of the blow, but kept its feet, and grabbed Joe's wrists in its terrible grasp.

"Ned!" Joe cried, pulling away with all his might, but unable to break free from the monster's grip.

"Hang on!" cried Ned, cursing as he tried to pour powder down the carbine's barrel with shaking fingers.

"Joe! Hang on!" And up ran Dan, and he put the barrel of a revolver to the side of the Blighter's head and pulled the trigger. There was a bang, and a spray of dark matter, and the creature that had been Lonigan, collapsed onto the ground.

Joe wiped at his gore-spattered face with trembling hands. "Th-that w-was close..." he stuttered, then clamped his mouth tightly shut against the shaking of his jaw. He raised his hands, and examined the welts where the Blighter had gripped him.

He nodded his thanks at Dan, who was staring at the ruined dead man lying at their feet.

"Good man, good man," said Ned, and he gently wrested the pistol from his brother's grip.

"Jesus Christ, Ned," said Dan.

"I know."

Steve joined them, a shotgun in his hands. "Took a while to find shells," he said sheepishly.

Ned frowned, looking at the gun he held. "Mighty fancy shotgun you got there, Steve. Looks familiar. Let me see that."

He lay his own old carbine down, and took the gun. He cracked it open. "Slugs, eh? Not exactly going duck hunting with this, were they?" He turned towards the tree. "You can come out now, Constable."

"C-constable?" said Joe. "He's a trap, too?"

"Why don't you ask him?"

The man half stepped from behind the tree, surveying them and the body at their feet with equal horror. "You... You're not going to shoot me, are you?"

"Only if you plan on trying to eat us," answered Ned. "Who are you?"

"Constable MacIntyre... And that..."

"I know who that is. Or was, rather. What were you doing out here? Looking for Blighters? Or looking for us?"

"You..." MacIntyre whispered. "We were sent here looking for you."

"And where are the others?"

"The others? My God, the others! They could be back any moment! We have to get out of here!" He went to move, but Ned casually trained the shotgun at his midsection, and he stopped. A wet patch slowly spread across the front of his trousers, and he sank to his knees, oblivious. "Oh, please, you have to let me get out of here."

"Not till you tell us what is going on. Why were you sent here? What were you told?"

"We... we were just told there were reports you were hiding in this area. They told us to find you..."

"And then? What? Arrest us? Bring us in?"

"Please, I beg you... The others..."

"Ned," said Joe, looking around nervously. "Others?"

"Speak up, McIntyre, or we'll tie you to that tree and leave you here for your friends. Were you going to bring us in?"

MacIntyre paused, then shook his head miserably, snot running from his nose down into his beard.

"Bastards!" cried Joe. "So you were just going to kill us?"

"And take a look at this shotgun, Joe. Look familiar to you? It's that vicar's."

Joe laughed hollowly. "What? He loaned it to the traps? So much for the man of God."

"What happened, McIntyre? What happened to Lonigan?"

McIntyre squinted up at them out of the corner of his eye. "I don't know."

"Yes, you do know, McIntyre. Don't try to be clever. We know all about the Blighted. No point pretending you don't know about them, too."

McIntyre shuddered visibly. "It just wouldn't stop... It turned up while we were asleep. Christ, it was foul. It just kept coming... Ripping into the tent to get us. We shot it and shot it - you could see parts of it being blown off, but it just kept coming, and it grabbed Lonigan and ripped him open... God, I'll never sleep again... The screams..."

"You have to shoot them in the head," said Dan. "Like...Like I did."

"We did. Eventually. We just about blew it to hell by the end. But it was too late for Lonigan. We lay his body outside the tent, and threw the remains of that... that thing into the creek.

We tried to sleep - then Sergeant Kennedy said he heard some-thing moving, and he went out to look, and he called to us that we'd made a mistake, Lonigan was alive, come and help, and then he started screaming. Scanlon tried to save him, but Lonigan got him, too. I only just got away myself. I climbed a tree - I didn't have time to pick a good one, Lonigan was right behind me. And then he had me treed like a possum. I hoped he'd get hungry, and go back and eat the other two and give me a chance to get away, but he seemed to lose interest in their bodies once they were dead. Or while I was still alive, anyway. Then after a while, Kennedy and Scanlon got up, too. It was horrible. Disgusting. They noticed the horses and went after them, but the horses broke their traces and ran off. You should have heard the noises they were making - they were terrified. That's where the other two went - they followed the horses down the track. And then you came along, thank God, or I'd be eaten alive by now..."

McIntyre put his face in his hands and wept.

"I guess it's a kind of justice," said Ned, "that you traps are killed by your own evil."

"How can you say that?" sobbed McIntyre. "It isn't my fault!"

"Keep searching," Ned said to the others. "We need all their guns and ammunition."

They split up, Dan and Steve pulling the collapsed tent open, Joe crawling into the other and tossing out bits of useful gear. Ned stood studying McIntyre, and keeping an eye on the bush.

"You're a sorry specimen, McIntyre. Why would you want to go and join the troopers? And you an Irishman and all."

McIntyre looked up at him through bleary eyes, and opened his mouth to speak, but Ned held a hand out in warning and dropped to his knees. "Hurry up with those guns, lads," he called softly over his shoulder. He cocked the hammers on the shotgun. McIntyre's eyes bulged, and then he glanced at Ned's face and turned to look in the same direction.

"It's them!" he shrieked, and struggled to rise.

"Keep still and shut up, man!" hissed Ned - but too late.

Down the track, two figures walked slowly into view. They paused, swaying slightly back and forth, appearing undecided. But at McIntyre's noise and movement, they stilled, and then they lurched forward, coming down the track at a fast, stiff legged walk that was almost a run.

"Damn you, McIntyre," muttered Ned, and he aimed carefully down the barrel. Loaded with solid shot, the weapon was devastating, but inaccurate when fired at any target more than a dozen yards away. He fought to control the impulse to pull the trigger. "Grab my carbine - but don't be an idiot if you want to live."

McIntyre crawled off - but then jumped to his feet and ran wailing down the track. Ned cursed - the nearest Blighter was close now, close enough that he could see the terrible wounds that had ended the man's life. Ned aimed low, guessing the gun would buck, and slowly squeezed the trigger. With a deep boom, it went off, and the Blighter was knocked clean off its feet and onto its back. There wasn't time to see if he had got it in the head, as the other one was coming on fast. Ned pulled the trigger all the way through, and the second barrel fired, but he saw through smoke the savage snarling face, devoid of any human remnant, coming on - he'd missed. He jumped to his feet and ran. Dan was standing not far behind him, the revolver in his hand and another stuck in his belt. He had a box of cartridges open and was spilling them all over the ground as he struggled to feed them into the chambers.

"Run!" shouted Ned, but Dan snapped the revolver shut and aimed just past Ned's shoulder. Ned swerved as the pistol fired, and he heard a meaty slap right behind him. He spun around -

the Blighter was rocked by the shot, and Ned saw the bullet had torn its jaw off, but not done enough damage to stop it. A guttural rasp of air escaped from its lungs through its ruined mouth. It was close enough that Ned could see the sergeant's stripes on its blue jacket - this must have been Kennedy. It turned its focus on Dan, and suddenly leapt forward in a surge of speed - a part of Ned's mind had time to note that the fresher Blighters were much faster than the dried out husks they had seen previously. Dan had the pistol up, but the Blighters hands grabbed at it. Dan fired, and the shot tore off parts of Kennedy's hands, but where a normal man would have dropped from the pain of it, the Blighter kept coming.

With a yell, Ned ran at it, reversing the shotgun in his hands. He struck the monster across the back of the head, and drove it forwards onto its knees, giving Dan time to backpedal furiously away.

"Ned!" It was Joe, kneeling in the open tent mouth, a carbine in his hands - it was a warning. Ned just had time to turn and there was the other Blighter, a massive hole punched in its chest, right on him. It grabbed him by the arms, and he just had time to bring the shotgun up across his body before it bore him to the ground. Its teeth bit into the steel of the barrel, inches from his face, and he was sickened by the grinding sound as it bit down hard. He stared into the thing's dead eyes, and it was a void deeper than any waterhole, colder than the blackest night sky. There was a crack, and its front teeth sheared off. Ned pushed desperately, forcing the barrel harder into its mouth, pushing its head up and away.

"Hold still!" cried Joe, and Ned thrust with all his might, raising the creature higher away from him. The barrel of Joe's carbine appeared in his view, inches from the Blighter's head. There was a bang, a red explosion, and it jerked away. Ned rolled clear, and lay gasping as Joe worked the lever. A hot shining casing landed right in front of his face. Joe cocked the gun and fired again into the Blighter's head.

"Help!"

"Dan! Here!"

They saw Steve holding the flap of the tent open and Dan dive inside. The other Blighter charged into it in pursuit, thrashing and getting tangled up, pulling half the tent down on top of them all. Joe worked the lever again, but there was no clear shot in the billowing canvas – it was not possible to say which squirming figure was which. There was the sound of tearing, and a knife blade cut through the wall of the tent. Steve squirmed out, Dan almost on top of him.

"Shoot it! Shoot it," yelled Dan.

Joe fired into the tent, working the lever again, and again, and again. The carbine clicked empty. The thing inside continued to thrash about. Ned ran to the fire, and picked up a stick with a glowing point. He blew on it, and the end glowed hot and red. He ran to a corner of the tent, thrust the stick into it, and blew again. At first, there was nothing, then a trickle of smoke, black and oily, and then the bright burst of flame. He jumped back, and the fire took hold. It seemed the more the Blighter thrashed, the faster the flames burned. The billowing canvas went up with a roar, and from the midst of it, a walking torch emerged. It blundered about, but whatever senses the creatures still had the use of, were to no avail. It was blind and deaf. There was a terrible stink that made them gag, as the things clothes burned from its body, along with its hair and beard. And finally the scorched thing staggered, and fell, as the tendons that drove it cooked and tightened, and whatever lay within its brain boiled away. It lay on its belly in the dirt, oddly looking like it was trying to swim, and then was still.

The flaming tent had collapsed in on itself, and smouldered, the fuel nearly spent. They came together, and wordlessly formed a circle, linking their arms around one another's shoulders. They bowed their heads, if not in prayer, then in thanks for comradeship and courage in the face of unspeakable horror. With a final squeeze and clap on the shoulder, they broke apart.

"Anyone hurt?" asked Ned.

Apart from scrapes and bruises, powder burns and singes, surprisingly, thankfully, no one was.

"So nobody bitten?" Ned asked quietly, and they fell silent as they considered that question, and what it could have meant.

"We were lucky," said Joe.

"It helped having more guns," said Dan. "Why couldn't they have kept them all loaded, and had the spare ammo close by?"

"Best gather all we can find. Where's McIntyre?"

But he was long gone. They busied themselves ensuring the fire was completely out, and combed the wreckage of the camp for ammunition and food. They now each had a revolver, as well as the vicar's double barrel shotgun and the carbine, which turned out to be a seven shot repeater, a Spencer - far better than any rifle the police would normally have had. Along with Ned's old muzzle-loader, they finally felt they had the firepower to defend themselves - though seeing what just one Blighter could do, stumbling upon a camp in the dark, gave them pause. There would be no grumbling about guard duty in the future.

FIFTEEN

The train lurched, and I almost fell forward onto Ned. I lost my grip on my pages, and they spilled across the floor. As we ground to a final halt, the locomotive hissed and spat out an enormous gout of steam that rolled past the window like a London fog. I dropped to my knees, gathering up the pages as quickly as possible.

"Alright, Kelly," Sergeant Steele called from the end of the car, "get ready. We're here."

I glanced out the window, and saw that we had indeed pulled in to a rural station. A solitary man stood on the platform - a dismal looking fellow in a dismal looking suit. Like some kind of Fate in a Greek tragedy. Welcome to Beechworth. Abandon all hope...

At least they hadn't shot us.

I had to help Ned up. The troopers were impatient, and went to lay rough hands on him, but I could see how stiff and painful his leg was after the long journey. I waved them off and put my arm around him, helping to lift him, and tried not to react when I caught a whiff of his sour breath in my face. He was lighter than I expected. If those who feared him as some kind of monster could see him now... But no, there would be little mercy. They would probably gloat at his fall from the flash young hooligan he had been to this... And yet, he still had his pride, and I respected him for the outward show he gave the troopers as we limped from the train, his face impassive, and only I could feel the way his fingers dug into me and trembled. And I, for my part, tried not to show the pain his grip caused me.

Out on the platform, the official waiting for us formally took possession of "the prisoner", though he still needed the Melbourne troopers to escort him to the lock-up behind the courthouse where Ned would spend the night. It was late afternoon, and as we left the station, there was quite a throng waiting, and more people came running every minute.

"Hang him!" screamed some.

"God save Undead Kelly!" screamed others. The two sides snarled and goaded each other, and gave the swearing troopers one more thing to worry about as they forced a path through. Punches were thrown, as people pushed in to get close. Some leaned in to spit, one woman tried to kiss him, another threw flowers. Ned slipped his hand from my shoulder and walked unaided, looking neither left nor right, all the long way to the courthouse. Here the police were finally able to stop the crowd, and led him down a narrow lane to the stone lockup.

Sergeant Steele stopped me with a hand in my chest. "Your company has been just grand," he said, "but that's far enough, now."

"I'm his legal representative. Just let me see him settled."

"Oh, don't you worry, sir. I'll be sure to tuck him up good and snug." He turned and walked off down the lane laughing.

"Ned!" I called, and saw him stop and his pale face turn back towards me. "I'll bring Gaunson as soon as I can! Don't worry!"

He lifted an arm in acknowledgement, and then the

troopers hustled him from my view. There was a sudden burst of noise as the crowd started talking amongst themselves, some even rudely pointing right at me and making comments. I was not comfortable being in the middle of such a throng, and boldly stepped out, swinging my valise to help clear the way. I had no idea when Gaunson was likely to arrive, and felt tired and hungry. I resolved to find a room for the night.

The closest - and nicest - hotel was the Hibernian. I pushed open the door to find a little weasel of a fellow behind the counter being harangued by a rather red-faced individual.

"You can't do this!" shouted the man. "It isn't right!"

The little fellow bobbed his head. "Indeed, sir. Oh, indeed." And he looked up at the man with great sorrowful eyes.

"Well..." continued the guest, a little taken aback by his agreement, "I want my room!"

"Ah, if only, sir..." murmured the Weasel.

"I booked it! It's mine! You can't just give it to somebody else!"

The Weasel nodded sympathetically. "Perhaps, I can recommend another hotel?"

"Another hotel? Are you mad? Half the bloody shire is already in town for the trial, and the other half are on the way! All the rooms are bloody gone!"

Weasel pursed his lips at the pity of it all.

"Look, are you going to give me my room? No? Then get me the manager. I want to speak to the manager!"

"Ah, alas, sir, he is not here."

At this news, I feared the man may have a coronary attack and collapse, but he instead spun on his heel and stormed for the door. He stopped beside me, and gripped my arm.

"Don't bother with this place!" he snapped. "Swindlers! Thieves!"

He slammed the door behind him. I turned back, in time to

see the Weasel mouthing the word "peasant" at his retreating back. I smiled warmly at him as he looked at me, his face slipping back into an ingratiating mask. I strode to the counter, dropped my valise and pressed the palms of my hands onto the counter top.

"Good afternoon," I said, allowing my accent to roll richly from my tongue.

"Good afternoon, sir." he replied, one eyebrow lifting slightly.

That's right, boyo, you have quality here.

"My office will have wired through a reservation. Name is Spencer. Henry Spencer."

A tiny furrow appeared between his eyes. "I do apologise, Mr Spencer, but I don't think we have received anything. Let me check."

He rifled through some cards on the counter, countenance growing increasingly morose as he did so.

"I'm afraid the only wire we have received is from Mr David Gaunson, MP."

"Ah. David, of course. He will have booked several rooms."

"No, only one I'm afraid, sir. And I must say, that one was a little... difficult to arrange at short notice."

Ah. So they kicked out one of the plebs to make way for the parliamentarian. How democratic.

"Oh dear," I said, mimicking his tone of voice. "How awfully, frightfully embarrassing."

I reached into my jacket pocket and pulled out my pound notes. I peeled one off and placed it on the counter, smoothing it out flat, and then taking my hands away. We both stared down at it silently. He sighed. Oh, just take it, you bastard, I thought to myself. Then, as smooth as silk, his hands glided forth like snakes, and the note disappeared below the counter.

"I do believe," he said, somewhat more brightly, "that I can help you out, sir."

Later, after depositing my valise in my room - which was quite nice, really, especially as I intended to skip out without paying, the bribe being enough, I felt - I finally went in search of some food. It was still early when I went into the dining room, but I hadn't really eaten anything all day, and the ill effects of the night before had well and truly warn off, leaving me starving. There was only one other diner at that hour - a fairly dishevelled, whiskered fellow with nothing but a half-eaten plate of bread and butter before him, and an empty glass in his hand.

"Service!" he slurred as I chose a table and sat down. A neatly dressed waiter appeared and flicked out my serviette, and handed me a menu.

"There you are, you bastard," grumbled my dining companion. "Why don't you come when I call? I want service, damn it!"

The waiter bowed slightly to me and glided over towards the lout. "Sir?"

"More whiskey."

"If sir would like to order something to eat, I would be happy to-"

" I told you I can't stomach your fancy grub! I'm eating your lousy bread and butter, ain't I?"

"Sir is free to go through to the bar, if he just wishes to drink-"

"Listen to me, would you? I told you, my nerves can't stand the crowd in there! And stop calling me 'sir'. It's Constable to you!"

I cleared my throat. "Constable...McIntyre?"

He swung around and stared at me. "Who wants to know?"

"A friend of the force, I assure you. Allow me to introduce myself. My name is Spencer. I'm with the court."

"Huh. Another lawyer, eh? If you bastards helped us instead of getting in the way all the time... Ah, forget it."

"May I join you, Constable?"

"Actually, it's Sergeant now. Sergeant McIntyre." He belched. "At least, it will be."

I sat down across from him. "A promotion? Then congratulations are in order. And you must certainly have your drink."

I snapped my fingers at the waiter and pointed at McIntyre's glass. He bobbed his head and disappeared. Ah, the power of command. Maybe I should have gone into the military.

"You achieved some fine result? Captured a miscreant?"

"What?"

"Your promotion. I'm asking how you earned it."

"Oh. That." His eyes took on a shifty look. "Never you mind about that."

"Oh, I see. Top secret, eh? Cloak and dagger?"

The waiter reappeared with a whiskey, and set it down before my companion. I ordered the roast beef and a nice red. It was much easier to choose when you had no inclination to pay: just pick the most expensive and enjoy.

I watched him slurp his whiskey. His hand was shaking.

"In town for the trial, are you?" I asked.

"That's right."

"I guessed as much. A police officer - a sergeant - in civvies, I would guess you are appearing as a witness for the prosecution?"

He squinted at me suspiciously. "Not supposed to talk about it..."

"No, of course not. Never know who may be listening." I made a show of turning around and surveying the empty room. "Dangerous blighters, aren't they?"

He choked, spraying whiskey across the table, and me, and falling into a paroxysm of coughing. I leapt from my chair and thumped him soundly on the back, hard as I could. The waiter appeared, eyebrows disappearing into his hairline. I waved him away cheerfully with one hand while continuing to punch McIntyre in the back with the other. Finally, I could no longer pretend I wasn't hearing his spluttering demands that I leave off, damn me, and returned to my seat, leaving him red faced and coughing. He stared at me malevolently.

"Alright now, old chap? There's a good fellow. Ah! Food!" I paused as the waiter glided to our table and gracefully slid a deliciously full plate of beef and vegetables before me, the aroma causing my stomach to growl like a living beast. Then he was back again, presenting me with a bottle and pouring a taste. I made a great show of smelling it, tasting it, rolling it around my mouth, while McIntyre stared at me. I nodded and the waiter filled my glass with deep red pleasure. "And another whiskey for my friend." That at least caused him to relax a little.

I gave my plate my full attention for a few minutes. The beef was tasty, if a little on the tough side, but not bad overall for a country town where, let's face it, everyone was no doubt partially related to everyone else, either through wedlock, adultery, or other sinful practices. Then again, the same could be said for a large portion of London society, so who was I to throw stones?

"So," I said to McIntyre, now deep into his cup, "where were we? Ah, yes, bushrangers. I was saying how bushrangers are such dangerous blighters. Don't you agree?"

He flinched at the word, and his eyes flicked up to look at me, but I kept my face open and impassive and chewed my way through a mouthful of beef.

"Yes," he finally said, "they're evil... bastards all right."

"Hanging too good for 'em, eh?" I asked cheerfully.

He stared down into his drink. That's right, man, I thought. You think about it... What happened out there? Did Ned really murder your colleagues in cold blood? Or did he save your worthless hide from the undead?

The door swung open, and McIntyre looked up and blanched. A tall man stood there, uniformed, full-bearded, and heavy lidded. He did not look happy.

"McIntyre!" he snapped.

"Sir!" McIntyre sprang to his feet, knocking his chair over backwards in the process.

The man stared at him, and then his cool eyes drifted over me. I met him with my own expressionless gaze. Our eyes slid over each over, ice on ice. He looked back at the trooper.

"Go to bed, for God's sake, McIntyre. We need you bloody sensible in the morning."

"Sir!"

The bearded officer glanced once more at me, turned, and walked out. McIntyre leaned forward onto the table, resting on his hands.

"Bastard!" he hissed.

"Who?"

"Him. Hare."

"That was Hare? Superintendent Hare?"

"I got to go..."

"Wait!" He looked at me, frowning. "Let me get you another drink. I hate to dine alone. Please, stay."

I'd placed a hand on his arm. He shook me off. "Leave off, curse you. I got to go."

Damn it. There was no way to detain him and question him more without arousing his suspicions. Or those of the Superintendent, Hare. I held my tongue and watched him walk unsteadily to the door. I supposed he had a room upstairs - being kept near to the proceedings, as the key witness.

I sat back and swirled the last of the wine around in my glass, dark as blood. Why make him a sergeant? The obvious answer, if Kelly's version was to be believed, was to reward him for sticking to whatever story they had concocted to explain the deaths and frame Kelly into the bargain. And there was the way he jumped when I used the word 'blighter'... But... It was just too hard to believe. Like being told that fairies and the monster under your bed were real after all. Surely, it could all still be explained by the political machinations I sensed moving beneath the surface. The tectonic plates of power, grinding on, seeking advantage. *That* I could understand: humans were capable of all kinds of things in the name of their beliefs.

I drained off the last of the wine. So that was Hare. I had the sense that he had more of a part to play in the story, whichever version was true.

I determined to take an evening stroll before turning in. Beechworth was a large town, even boasting macadamised roads and gas lamps, at least along the main street. As for buildings, it seemed to consist primarily of banks and hotels - the latter being no surprise, but the former suggesting the wealth in the region from mining and farming. Certainly supported the idea of why Melbourne would be unhappy if this corner seceded from the colony. The courthouse dominated the middle of the town. I stood across the street from it, thinking. So this was where so much of the story began. This was where the boys had their first brushes with the law, which did much to set them at logger-heads. It was here that Ellen Kelly was tried and convicted - of a crime she was truly innocent of, in Ned's tale. And of course, it was here that one William Skillion was also sentenced, leaving a certain young lady alone in the world.

I walked on. I was not alone; there were quite a few people about, entering and leaving the various drinking establishments, arguing on the corners, taking in the sights as I was. But strangely, even though I was at the centre of the current events, I felt somehow on the periphery, like some eternal spectator. A watcher of the watchers. Never actually part of things. But that was nothing new, was it? I stopped walking. I had come right through the main part of the town, and looming up ahead was a building I had overheard described as the local lunatic asylum. Its grey gloom caused me to shudder. That was where I felt I would end up if Gaunson and I presented Kelly's defence as he wished.

I don't want to be locked away.

I noticed I was rubbing my sternum - I could feel the ache building within. I turned, and walked briskly back towards the well-lit centre of town, and the Hibernian. I suddenly longed to get into the privacy of my own room. I began to feel as if everyone I passed was looking at me, and that caused me to lengthen my stride. But the faster I walked, the more they looked. Their eyes seemed both blank and searching, while I felt mine shone like windows in the night, exposing everything I had or lacked. I kept my gaze down, not wanting to make eye contact with anyone. My breathing was coming faster and shallower. It felt like a black balloon filled the lower part of my chest, forcing me to fight for breath with the narrow space at the top of my aching ribs – like being in a submerged box, with a bare inch of air at the top. Straining.

My old friend. My old monster.

Don't start running. Hang on, hang on.

Finally, finally, at the hotel. Through the door - a terrible buffeting of noise and laughter from the bar, women's voices from the restaurant. I pounded up the carpeted stairs to the accommodation, turned down a corridor, too fast, knocked a vase off a stand, couldn't catch it, shattering pieces across the floor like fragments of bone. A door opened and a man looked out. McIntyre. Our eyes met and he sees me and I see him and we see the sameness, God damn him to bloody hell. He nods once, slowly, and the door closes and I lurched past, looking for my bloody room, and dragging the awkward key from my pocket, caught on something, tearing the lining, and get it in the blasted lock and turn it. Then the door closed behind me and a gasping, tearing breath and I sink to the floor in my little room and am safe. Head covered in my arms.

After a little while, when the vice around my ribs had lessened and I could think, I considered the solution that lay nestled in the bottom of my valise beneath a clean undershirt. How simple a thing to get up now, go and get it, press it to my temple, it's cool touch like a parting kiss, a little pressure, and then to be free of all of it. Just to let go. And yet I continued to sit, congealed on the floor against the door.

Coward.

At some point, I dragged myself over to my bed and collapsed upon it. Impossibly, I slept, for I jerked awake some time later. Someone was knocking on the door.

I got up, and opened it a crack.

"Hello, William," said Maggie. "Can I please come in?"

I stepped back, and she came inside, a small case in her hand.

"You're here," I said stupidly.

"Yes," she said. "We followed as soon as we could... William, I hope you don't find this too forward, but can I stay here with you?"

"What?"

"David said he had rooms booked, but when we got here, it turned out there was only one room. With a double bed. He seemed to think... Well, I told him I would see him in the morning and came looking for you." She gave me a funny smile. "Lucky I know your little games. Of course there was no one staying here by your name, but I batted my eyelashes at the clerk and described you, and he told me which room Mr Spencer was occupying." She suddenly sank onto my bed, her humour draining away. "I'm sorry... What am I doing? Of course you don't want me here. I should just stay with David... If it helps Ned..."

"Nonsense," I said, "stay here. On no account spend the night with that randy old walrus."

Her use of Gaunson's first name was bothering me greatly. She laughed.

"I can pay my way," she said. She fished in her bag and held aloft a bottle of wine. "Or you can consider it a gift. Only I don't know if it is the kind you like."

I walked over and pretended to squint at the label. It was piss. "It will do admirably." And she smiled.

There were no glasses, so we passed the bottle between us. God, there had been few moments as fine as sharing that bottle. Pressing the glass to my lips, my tongue touching the rim, watching her take it and do the same, neither of us wiping it clean, sharing this distant kiss. And somewhere, somehow, it just became right to lean across and kiss her, and though she did not move, and her lips were still and cool as glass beneath mine, but then I dared to tickle them with my tongue, and her mouth opened to me, warm, wet, and inviting.

Oh those moments when we can totally, thankfully, blessedly, be free of our heads. When we can have the freedom enjoyed as a matter of course by every living being on the planet, except our own advanced damned species... Union. Wholeness.

For a short while...

Later, she lay sprawled wantonly across the bed, arms thrown behind her head, hair disarrayed around her.

"My God," she said, sighing.

"I think He already heard you earlier."

She poked her tongue out at me, and curled like a cat. "No one has ever done things like that to me before."

"Benefit of a university education," I said. "Bound to pick up some Latin along the way."

She frowned, and crossed her arms across her chest. "I don't understand you."

"It was just a little joke."

"That I can't understand. It makes me feel stupid. I hate that."

I wondered if she was now joking, but in the candlelight, could see how dark and dangerous her eyes were. I felt like I had some wild animal in the room with me, and one wrong move would cause it to flee. Or eat me alive.

"I was talking to Ned on the train trip out here," I said cautiously. "He was telling me about your visits to the gang in the Wombat Ranges. About out-riding the troopers."

I saw her shoulders relax, and her arms lowered enough that her nipples were exposed again. She giggled.

"That was fun. Did he tell you I'd even let the traps catch up to me, then leave them for dead again?"

"You must be quite the rider."

"You tell me," she said, and held her hand out to me.

The night was enchanted, and endless. Later still, she sat in the chair before the basic washstand, looking at herself in the mirror. The candle was down to a mere nub, and soon we would be in darkness until the morning. She had found a hair brush, and was brushing her hair in long strokes as I lay on the bed, bone tired, and more content and at peace than I could ever remember being.

"Am I beautiful?" she asked, looking into the mirror.

"Yes," I said, and meant it with all I had.

"I don't see it."

"Most women never do. And the ones who can, are insufferable. It's true, though. You are. More beautiful than anything I've ever seen."

"Those are just words, William."

"Then come back here and let me show you, my love."

"Don't call me that."

She began to cry then, first a few tears, which then turned to sobs. And just like that, the glass ball we inhabited shattered. The candle guttered and went out, and I lay for a moment listening to her wet snuffling. I went to her then, and held her, but she did not respond to my touch, and I was unsure whether to let go or hold on. Somehow, we ended up back on the bed, and then she did react to me, curling around me tightly in the narrow bed, and I lay still as I could so as not to disturb her, though part of me wanted to shove her away onto the floor.

When I awoke, she was gone.

SIXTEEN

I shaved and dressed, and headed downstairs to the dining room, unsure how I felt. Both flat and excited at the same time. I pushed through the swinging doors, the smell of bacon and coffee rolling warmly around me. There were a good few people at the various tables, and over in the corner sat Gaunson himself, taking up a table meant for four, with a pile of papers spread before him. I walked over, signalling the waiter to bring me coffee.

"There you are!" He exclaimed as I pulled out a seat and sat down across from him. "What a to do! What a mess!"

"How are you going?" I asked.

"I'm not ready! I need more time!"

My stomach flipped. "What do you mean, not ready? The committal is starting today, isn't it?"

His bottom lip quivered. "I've been busy..." His eyes darted about - looking for Maggie? Look all you like, you pig, I thought. She was with me.

"Well... I'll be with you. It's just the committal at this stage."

"It isn't fair though. I need more time. Can't expect me to

travel all the way to billy-oh at the drop of a hat. I'm an important man! I'm a member of parliament!"

His voice had risen, causing the other diners to stop and stare. I patted him on the wrist.

"We'll be alright. You can always ask for an adjournment, can't you?"

He suddenly seized hold of my wrist. "Have you seen Maggie?"

Oh, I've seen Maggie, I wanted to say. I've seen every square inch of Maggie, golden in candlelight, quivering beneath my touch.

"No. Here, have some more coffee and let's sort through these..."

───

The courthouse was full to bursting when we arrived. We had to thrust through a large crowd outside, and the noise inside was incredible as we took our seats at the small table reserved for the defence. All the public benches were crammed; ladies had been given seats in the small gallery by the more noble men. If an orange seller had appeared spruiking her wares up the aisle, I would not have been surprised. Gaunson nudged me and pointed out the Crown prosecutor, Smyth, as he arrived. I watched him deftly withdraw a sheaf of papers from an attaché case and pat them into a neat pile before him. He then set up pen, ink, blotter, and pocket watch in a neat row before him. He had two other men, Gurner and Chomley, assisting him - didn't they look like the undertakers their names suggested - and a couple of gormless errand boys at his back. When he had everything just where he wanted it, he sat perfectly still, not deigning to give us the most cursory of glances.

I looked at Gaunson, who was patting sweat off his forehead with a handkerchief. We were in trouble, no doubt about it.

There was a sudden upsurge from the crowd, and I looked up to see Ned being escorted into the court. Troopers led him to the dock and shut him in. He looked pale, but his face was impassive. He looked about the court, nodding briefly at me, before finding the face he wanted in the crowd. He smiled, and I could see his shoulders sag with a deep sigh. I twisted in my chair, craning about, and there she was, Maggie, a few rows back. She was staring back at Ned with great concern.

At that moment, the court officer bade us rise for the entrance of the magistrate, Foster, who blinked at the sight of the packed courthouse, and looked for a moment like he had thought better of the whole thing and wanted to go back into his chambers. But he took his seat, adjusting his powdered wig, and fixing Ned with a serious gaze.

We sat, and the officer read out the charge. That Edward Kelly was charged with the wilful murder of Thomas Lonigan in the Northern Bailiwick of the Colony of Victoria, on the twenty sixth day of October, 1878. We were reminded that these proceedings were to establish whether there was enough evidence to support a guilty verdict, and thus allow the case to go to a full trial.

"Edward Kelly," said Foster, in sonorous tones, "how do you plead?"

Ned pulled himself painfully upright from the stool they had provided him with, and answered clearly, "Not guilty, your honour."

There was a buzz throughout the courthouse. Idiots, what did they think he was going to say? I supposed they would chatter just as much if he pleaded guilty. Some people just like to talk - saves them thinking, I supposed.

Ned sat back down, and the magistrate nodded at Smyth,

who slid to his feet and cocked a thumb in his jacket lapel - his version of an ancient Roman rhetorical stance, no doubt. But before he could speak, Gaunson had clambered to his feet and addressed the judge.

"Your honour, I wish to move for an immediate adjournment of this case."

Smyth harrumphed loudly. Foster sighed and rested his chin on one hand. "Grounds?"

"Why, there are too many facts, your honour..."

"Too many facts," Foster repeated.

"Yes. It is utterly impossible to digest them all in the short time I have had. I have only been able to see my client briefly this morning..."

"Mr Smyth?"

Smyth smiled. "Your Honour, there is no reason why my learned colleague should find himself so unprepared. The facts of this case are well established. I trust my learned colleague can, in fact, open a newspaper."

At that moment, someone handed a folded slip of paper to Gurner, who read it and tapped Smyth. Smyth read it, and his smile broadened further. He looked back into the gallery and nodded in thanks. I followed his gaze, and saw Hare sitting several rows back. He turned and looked at me, and he smiled coldly. I swivelled quickly in my seat.

"Besides which, your Honour," Smyth continued, "a professional gentleman has in fact visited Mr Kelly in his cell in Melbourne gaol on a number of occasions. And this man is in the direct employ of Mr Gaunson. He is in fact sitting at the defence table at this very moment. It follows that Mr Gaunson has had ample time to consider his defence. If there is one to be had, of course..."

There was laughter at this, and I was aware of people craning to get a look at me.

"Mr Gaunson?"

"Your Honour... I beg you for more time. While I am indeed in full possession of the facts of the case, it is the details I am unacquainted with."

"If you can read a newspaper, then you have all the details and facts at your disposal, sir," observed Smyth drily.

"We shall resume, I think."

"They haven't let the poor wretch see his family!"

"Request denied. Mr Smyth? Pray continue."

Gaunson deflated next to me and sagged into his seat. I hissed quickly into his ear, and he bounded up again.

Foster stared at him wearily. "Yes, Mr Gaunson?"

"Your Honour, your pardon, forgive me, but the prisoner is well secured. What can be the point of having armed officers stationed about the court except to influence proceedings and intimidate witnesses?"

I had spotted several troopers when we came in with pistols at their belts. Foster drummed his fingertips on the polished wooded bench, thinking. Hare stood up in the gallery.

"Your Honour, the men are mine. They are present as we have received credible threats of a rescue attempt planned to secure the prisoner's release through force of arms."

I looked at Ned, but he was giving nothing away.

"Well," said Foster, "it is unusual, I will grant you that. But prejudicial? No, I rule not. Let us resume, gentlemen."

Hare and Gaunson exchanged a look, and both sat. Smyth finally got the chance to launch into his great opening speech, accompanied by deft hand movements and the occasional ironic arching of the eyebrow towards the gallery. I wished my neighbour Rawson was here to see it - as an actor, I believe he would have appreciated the subtle nuances Smyth added to his performance: a little cough here to signal disbelief, a pulling down of the shirt cuffs there, suggesting finality. In his brief opening, he painted Ned as a career criminal from the moment he was born, raising Cain and raining terror across Victoria. He said the Crown would show that Ned was known to have threatened officers going about their lawful duties, and was already charged with attempted murder - and now came this heinous, callous display...

At this, someone far back in the crowd could stand no more, and shouted, "He ain't none of them things! He's Undead Kelly!"

"Silence!" roared Foster, banging his gavel hard enough to break it. "One more outburst like that and I shall clear this court!"

He need not have worried. Troopers stationed in the court had spotted the individual - a scruffy looking little fellow - and lifted him from his seat. He was marched through the doors of the court, which were shut firmly behind them. I wondered what they would do to him. There was some applause, while others hissed. Foster banged his gavel again, and the noise subsided. Nobody else, it seemed, wanted to risk missing the fun.

"Your Honour, we call our first witness to the stand. Constable Thomas McIntyre."

McIntyre duly appeared, with pale skin and bloodshot eyes. He sank into the wooden witness chair, and made his oath in a barely audible whisper. His eyes darted furtively about the room, passed over me, then darted back. He sat up, open-mouthed, and turned to the magistrate as if about to say something, then sank back, instead, fixing me with a baleful glare. I gave no hint that I recognized him.

"Please identify yourself," said Smyth.

"Thomas McIntyre," he choked out, then coughed and said it again more clearly. "Sergeant... Constable Thomas McIntyre."

"You were based in this region in 1878?"

"I was."

"You were sent on patrol in the Wombat Ranges, in October of that year?"

"I was."

"And who else accompanied you?"

"Sergeant Kennedy, he was in charge. Then there was Tom Lonigan, Scanlon, and me."

"And what were your orders?"

"We were told to search for the Kelly brothers, Ned and Dan, as there was a warrant out for their arrest."

"I know this is difficult for you, Constable McIntyre, but please tell the court the events of October twenty six."

"Well, we had made camp by the Stringybark. I was sitting by the fire making tea. Tom Lonigan was there with me, and the other two had gone off patrolling. Anyway, I heard someone call out 'Bail up', and looked up to see four armed men at the edge of the bush."

"And are any of those men in court today?"

"That's one. Ned," said McIntyre, pointing in Ned's direction without looking at him.

"What did you do?"

"Well, my revolver was in the tent, and they had the drop on us good and proper, so I put my hands up. Tom tried to make a run for it, and they shot him."

"As he ran?"

"Yes."

"So they shot him in the back?"

"Uh, yes."

"Did Constable Lonigan die straight away?"

McIntyre stared at Smyth, the blood draining from his face. Smyth frowned. There was a cough from the crowd - it sounded like Hare.

"Did Lonigan die straight away?"

"No. I heard him say, 'Oh Christ, I'm shot', then he

collapsed. He thrashed around for a while after that, and then he was still."

"What happened next?"

"Ned asked me about the others. I said they would be back soon, and asked what he intended to do. I was worried he was going to shoot them down in cold blood, and said so. He told me to tell which direction they went. I said I would rather be shot a thousand times than tell him that, if he was going to kill them. I said one was the father of a large family."

"What did the defendant say?"

"He told me he wouldn't kill them if they gave themselves up. I said he should let me talk to them when they came back, so there wouldn't be any more killing. He and the other three hid themselves, and told me to sit by the fire or they'd shoot me. When Kennedy and Scanlon came back, I jumped up, but Kelly and the others leapt out too, and shouted for them to bail up, and started shooting."

"They started shooting? They didn't give Kennedy and Scanlon time to surrender?"

"I don't think so, no. I think they just started shooting."

"So it was cold blooded murder?"

"It was."

I elbowed Gaunson in the ribs.

"Objection!" he bellowed, and then hissed at me, "I was going to object!" He climbed to his feet and drawled, "I doubt that the constable, learned as he may be, happens to be an expert in matters of criminal law. He is in no position to make such definitive statements."

"Sustained," grunted Foster.

Smyth nodded. "Then, Constable McIntyre, can you tell the court whether you saw Edward Kelly and his associate's gun down three defenceless men?"

"Aye..."

I elbowed Gaunson again. He stared at me in disbelief. I leaned over and whispered in his ear.

"Objection!" he shouted.

"Yes, Mr Gaunson?"

"It hasn't been proved that the dead men did not, in fact, present a significant threat to the Kelly brothers. At least in their eyes."

"You'll get your chance to cross examine this afternoon, Mr Gaunson. I'm going to allow it."

The day wore on. McIntyre provided further details of the day in question, and then was allowed to slink from the stand, twisting his hat with his hands. As he drew alongside the defence table, he slowed for a moment, and I feared he was going to make some scene, but then he kept going, thrusting through the crowd gathered outside the doors of the courthouse.

It was after midday, and everyone appeared to be wilting, when the magistrate called for an adjournment of two hours. Kelly was hoisted, wincing to his feet, and led out the back of the court. Smyth gathered his papers into a neat pile, and thrust them back inside his case. Beside me, Gaunson stretched and yawned.

"Spot of lunch, I think," he said.

"Shouldn't we go and talk to Ned?"

He lifted an eyebrow at me. "I cannot be expected to cross-examine on an empty stomach. Besides, if we don't go now, the best tables will be taken."

I caught sight of Maggie in the swirling press of people. She was looking after Ned.

"You go ahead. I just want a quick word with Ned."

"Suit yourself."

I made a show of packing slowly, waiting for Gaunson to leave and the courtroom to clear - though there were some who obviously did not wish to risk losing their prime seats, and some of them had even had the foresight to bring along some supplies for a picnic. I looked around, but to my disappointment, Maggie had left. I had thought she would hang back to talk to me.

I opened a door near the magistrate's bench, and found a corridor running to the back of the building. Doors led off into various offices and vestibules. There were clerks flitting about, but no one questioned my right to be there. Foster was long gone, no doubt to a reserved table at whichever was the best restaurant in town. I wouldn't have been at all surprised if Smyth was dining with him. Out the back, stood the sturdy brick lockup, divided in two, for male and female prisoners. At the moment, there was only one resident, guarded by no less than three armed troopers.

"RM!" Ned called with a wave. He was sitting on the floor of the lockup behind a heavy iron grille. I joined him, squatting on my heels. I glanced up at the troopers, and they had the good grace to take a step or two away.

"How are you doing, Ned?"

"I'm alright. How's Maggie? Have you spoken to her?"

"She's fine. Fine." I paused. "Listen, Ned, I don't think it is going so well for you in there..."

"Doesn't matter."

"But..."

"It doesn't matter what happens here, Remittance Man. I want my time in court - a proper court in Melbourne, with reporters from the world over. That's all I want - a full and fair trial, with a chance for my side to be heard. Up to now, the police have had it all their own way. If I get a full trial - and I don't care how it turns out - then the public will see that I am not the monster. I'm the one who saves them from the monsters. And it is the more monstrous ones still who started this, and allow it to keep going, who should be called to account and made to pay."

We sat in silence for a few moments, Ned swirling patterns in the dust with his fingerprints, me not knowing where to look, feeling oddly embarrassed.

"That Smyth," I said at last. "I'd like to give him his comeuppance, though. Smug little git."

Ned laughed tiredly. "That's a good fellow. I thought there was a fighter in there somewhere."

"Still, Gaunson should be able to pull McIntyre apart on the stand. He looked shaky enough this morning. Even Gaunson should be able to handle him."

"Remember, I'm not aiming at getting off, Remittance Man. Save some of that spunk for the full trial."

We sat together a while longer, then a constable brought Ned a tray of food for his lunch, and my stomach suddenly reminded me that I'd had nothing since breakfast. I bid him goodbye, and walked back to the Hibernian. The dining room was full when I got there, and I stood awkwardly in the doorway, scanning the room for Gaunson. Instead, at a small table off to the side, I spied Maggie. She smiled and waved excitedly, and my heart lifted in my chest as I weaved between diners to her.

"William!" she said, fairly grabbing my arm and dragging me into the chair beside her. "I've got such great news!"

"Oh, yes?" I leaned over and brushed my lips against her cheek. She waved me off.

"Look down here!"

She pushed her chair back, and fussed between her legs. I looked swiftly around the room, not sure if she was playing some dangerous game.

"Here!"

She had pulled something up from a bag I now saw on the floor beneath her chair. It was some long leather strap. I felt a sudden rush of lust, picturing her strapped and writhing on the bed upstairs. I swallowed.

"I spoke to someone. A friend of Tom's, actually. He knows a man who owns a property near Stringybark. He found one of the trap's mounts wandering on his land - and this! There were four of them."

Now I was confused - what?

She looked at my blank face. "Why, don't you see? Don't you see what this means? They're body straps."

I shook my head. She leaned in, staring into my eyes. "For tying bodies down onto horses..."

Ah.

I tried to find Gaunson before the hearing resumed, but was unable to locate him in time. I had just taken my seat when the magistrate reappeared and settled himself behind the bench. Looked a little sleepy, to me. McIntyre was led back to his seat and reminded he was still under oath. He looked better, now. Either someone had given him a stirring speech to bolster his courage, or he'd sunk a few drinks over lunch. Either way, he eyed Gaunson with some smug disdain as he rose to his feet to take his turn at questioning.

"Do you know Constable Fitzpatrick?" asked Gaunson.

"Aye."

"What kind of man would you say he is?"

Smyth was up."Objection, your Honour. What possible bearing can Constable McIntyre's opinion of a fellow officer of the law have?"

"Mr Gaunson?"

"If you will allow me, your Honour, it goes very much to the heart of the matter. The whole reason Constable McIntyre and company were in the Wombat Ranges looking for my client, was due to the testimony of Constable Fitzpatrick that he had been attacked by him and his brother – oh, and of course, his poor old mother."

He earned a laugh for that line, and turned to beam at the crowd.

"I'll allow it - but get to the point quickly."

Gaunson nodded. "So then, Constable. What kind of man is Fitzpatrick? Is he an upright and honest man?"

"Well, let me see," said McIntyre, scratching his neck and pretending to think, but I could see he was desperately trying to get a glimpse of someone in the court, probably Hare. But Gaunson had positioned his bulk - whether by accident or design, I couldn't say - fair in the trooper's line of sight. "He was... He is maybe not the best of men, as he has been dismissed..."

"Dismissed? He is no longer an officer of the law?"

"No, he...he's gone. Dismissed. Drank too much, that was it, drank too much."

"I see. And yet it is upon his testimony that the charges against my client of attempted murder are based. Not to mention the conviction of Ellen Kelly. Makes it a little difficult to verify his statement if he isn't around, don't you think?"

McIntyre nodded thoughtfully. "Aye, you may have the right of it there. But Kelly did still shoot everyone. He didn't ought to have done that, if he was innocent of trying to kill Fitz."

"Is it not fair to say, though, Constable, that the local constabulary were rather biased against my client, and indeed were most keen to see him hang?"

"I wouldn't say that."

"No? There is no bias? What are we to make of the decision, then, not to allow him any contact with his family members? Including his beloved sister, who even now sits there in the court, looking as though her very heart would break..."

Gaunson stared at Maggie, and chewed his lip. I jumped to my feet.

"When Kelly shot Lonigan, what did you say he was doing?"

Gaunson frowned at me, but I motioned him to wait, imploring him to let me speak. He shrugged and allowed me the floor, taking his seat behind our desk. McIntyre frowned at me.

"He was at the tree... I mean, he was trying to get to a tree."

"And he was armed, yes? He had a pistol?"

"I don't remember."

"But if he was armed - or if our client thought he was armed - then running to seek cover behind a tree rather than surrendering suggests he was preparing to fight, doesn't it? Did he want a bite, I mean fight?"

McIntyre stared at me. "I don't know."

"And tell me about the other guns you had."

"Other guns?"

"You had a shotgun, didn't you?"

"For hunting, yes."

"With slugs? I didn't know the wildlife around these parts got so big."

"Well..."

"And you had a rifle with you, too, didn't you? A Spencer? Is that standard police issue?"

"No... We had to borrow that. From the bullion escort."

"Pretty well-armed for an arrest party, weren't you? And what about these?" With a flourish, I pulled one of the long leather straps from a bag under the table and brandished it above my head. McIntyre went white.

"What is this, Constable?"

"Just some strap..."

"No, not just some strap. Four of these were found on one of your horses. They're body straps, aren't they Constable? For tying bodies across a horse?"

McIntyre was silent. He was looking into the crowd, but I copied Gaunson and positioned myself in his way. "Your Honour?"

"Answer the question, Constable."

"They... They could be used for that, I suppose."

"Constable, I put it to you that you were not an arrest party, but an assassination party."

"Objection!"

"You were sent to find and murder Ned Kelly and his brother."

"No... We..."

"Objection!"

"Ned Kelly fired on your party in self-defence, isn't that right, Constable!"

"Your Honour! Objection"

"Or did something else happen? Did something else happen out there, Constable?"

"Mr... Who are you? Mr Gaunson, restrain your colleague!"

"McIntyre, what happened out there? Was it *them*? Tell me! *Tell me!*"

"Sit down, young man, right now!"

"Charles! Please! Enough!"

I stopped.

God.

McIntyre was leaning back in his chair – I was standing right over him, I practically had him by the throat. I looked around. Gaunson and Smyth were both on their feet, staring at me. The crowd was staring too. I suddenly caught sight of Hare, his eyes boring into me. I looked across at Ned. Our eyes met, and he nodded, ever so slightly. My hands were shaking; I wiped sweat stains down the legs of my trousers.

"Your pardon, Your Honour... I..."

"Just sit down at once, or I will have you thrown out of this hearing. Mr Gaunson, I advise you to instruct your assistants on how to conduct themselves in a court of law. I will not have witnesses harangued so."

"Of course, your Honour."

I walked stiffly back over to the desk and sat, wishing I could shrink away to nothing.

It didn't look good to me. The next witnesses gave evidence of Ned's criminal ways, stretching right back to his youth and his days of stealing horses and running off livestock. Others recalled his threat to murder Lonigan in the brawl in the streets of Benalla. Smyth made a big point of this. Gaunson tried to show that Ned was under duress at the time - the dreaded black balling - but Smyth was able to counter that it was a legitimate police technique for controlling the unruly. Hearing it all positioned like that, it seemed a fairly open and shut case - a desperate man on the run from the law, cruelly killing three men acting in its service. I kept stealing glances at Ned as he sat in the dock - his self-control was admirable, for he didn't interject or make a sound. Unless, of course, what he was hearing was the actual truth of the matter, and either on some level within his madness, or because he was not mad at all, he knew it to be so.

The proceedings drew to a close for the day. Foster ordered that the prisoner be taken back to the holding cells for the night. Troopers came forward and lifted Ned under his armpits, and I saw his stoic mask crumble as he winced with pain. Maggie jumped to her feet and pressed forward, and Ned looked over at her and smiled ruefully.

"It looks as though they won't let me see you, my dear."

"Never mind, Ned," she said, chin jutting belligerently, "they are a great lot of curs!"

"Aye," he said, "but there is one native of this land that is no cur, and he'll show them that yet!"

And with that, they dragged him away, to hoots, catcalls and cheers from the public gallery. For a strange moment, I felt that he had been referring to me in his last statement, as if he had some prescient notion of some future role I had yet to play. And I felt strangely saddened when I realised he was of course talking about himself, for I was no native of this strange land.

"A good first day," said Gaunson, interrupting my thoughts. "Always puts me in the mood for a hearty dinner."

"A good first day? That was disastrous!"

"Nonsense! Oh, they scored a few runs, and that was an own goal from you if I may mix my metaphors. But we'll come back tomorrow."

"You mean when we put Ned up on the stand?"

"Hmmm...well, we'll see."

I nearly grabbed at his sleeve, but I held myself back and let him go. It sounded like he was contemplating not putting Ned up to speak in his own defence. At first, the idea seemed monstrous, for it was what Ned wanted most. But then, I wondered if it was wiser to leave his stories of the Blighters out of proceedings for now. What would happen if he told his version of events at this hearing? Wasn't there a chance they would declare him criminally insane and lock him up in the very madhouse that stood on the edge of town? So maybe it was safer at this stage to stick to the story the police were unfolding and claim self-defence.

And if I was honest with myself, I was still not keen on being publicly associated with such wild claims. But I hoped self-interest was only a small part of it.

"Oi! You RM?"

I looked up. A trooper was standing at the door leading to the hallway.

"'e won't cooperate and go easy back in his cell till he tells you something. Sarge wants you to come quick so he shuts up and don't cause no scene."

"That's a double negative. I think you mean you don't want him to cause a scene."

"That's what I said."

I quickly crossed the court and walked into the hall.

"Fuckin' toff," the trooper murmered as I passed him.

Out the back, I found Ned on his knees at the entry to the cell block, head bowed, his arms were locked together through the bars of the grate.

"Get in there, Kelly, you thick Irish bastard!"

There were about six troopers and the sergeant gathered about him, and there was real tension in the air. I could tell they would love nothing more than to beat the snot out of him, and damn the consequences. I pushed rudely through and knelt by him.

"Ned?"

"Remittance Man," he rasped. There was blood on his lip. "Are you alright?"

"Am I alright? Am *I* alright?"

"You seemed to be getting a little excitable in there."

"Well, because... because..."

"I told you, this isn't important. But I can see you don't like losing, so I'll give you a gift."

I want your sister.

"What gift?"

"Try calling up as witnesses the troopers who arrested me."

"Why? What good will that do?"

"Trust me. It'll be a laugh."

"There now, Kelly," shouted Sergeant Steele, "you've had your kiss from your gentleman friend. Now get in your cage, like the dirty dog you are."

Ned looked at the man with dead eyes, but allowed me to

help him to his feet, and he stepped into the cell. They slammed the grate shut behind him, the massive key turning the bolt of the lock with a note of finality. God, how I would hate to be locked up like that. I had felt constrained in some way my whole life - but this, to lose one's freedom like that. I would lose my mind.

I walked down the narrow alleyway beside the courthouse and back onto the bustling main street. With the show over for the day, normal life resumed: shopping, drinking, barbering, wasting time, boasting, cheating, and big noting. Humans at their work.

Maggie stood waiting for me.

"Hello, William."

"Maggie. I didn't know where you went..."

She shook her head, rejecting my question, it seemed. Her face was dark for a moment, then, as if the sun came out from behind a cloud, she smiled.

"Shall we dine?"

I answered her carefully, "Yes, I'd like that very much."

Her smile turned to a grin, and for a moment, I could see a younger girl in her eyes. One with dreams for the future, maybe, before thankless toil and motherhood ground all spirit out of her but bitterness.

"And maybe we could have dessert back in your room?"

She spoke lightly, but as I looked at her, I could see colour in her cheeks. There was a stirring in my trousers in response. I choked out an affirmation. She took my arm and we strolled down the sidewalk, much like any other couple on the outside, I imagined.

"That McIntyre," she said, "what a fuckin' gobshite."

That was one difference, I guessed. No lady, yet no street trollop either. A new kind of woman. A new kind of woman for a new land? And would there be a place for me, maybe a new version of me, in such a place, with such a woman?

"He is a slimey one. How I'd like to-" A sudden thought hit me. "Maggie, do you have any makeup?"

She touched her fingertips to her cheek. "Why?" she asked, her voice like a young girl.

"No, I don't mean you need some. I need some. I have an idea."

"Oh?" she asked, raising an eyebrow at me. "Should I be alarmed?"

"No! No, I have an idea for an experiment. One that might help Ned."

That galvanised her into action, but we could not find an open store that had the kind of things I was thinking of. I told her to never mind, I would think about it, and we went off to eat instead. She was annoyed with me for not telling, and punched my arm, but I placated her by saying she could help me later with another jaunt, if she liked, which may give a comeuppance to Smyth and his fellow vultures.

We ate well - why steal for one when you can steal for two? - and then retired early to my room. As soon as we were through the door, she grabbed for me, and we fairly tore the clothes from each other like wild beasts. We devoured each other, pulling at flesh and muscle. She was animal-like that night, and at one point, bit my cheek, right at my moment of climax, and the sharp pain mixed with the rising heat and the hiss of her breath in my ear, to bring me to a most exquisite outcome.

When we were quite spent, she lay asleep against me, but I lay listening to the sounds of the town gradually falling silent outside my window. I gently began to pull myself clear, but, as I expected, she came awake.

"What are you doing?" she mumbled. "Do you need the pot?"

"I'm going out for a little. I shan't be long, I hope."

She sat up. "You said I could help you!"

"And so you can, if you want. But Maggie, it is a little risky. If we get caught..."

"If it's to help Ned, I'm fierce as a tiger!"

"Very well. Here, best you put these on."

I handed her my spare trousers, and her own little jacket, which was quite dark. I had my own jacket on, but no white shirt beneath to catch the moonlight.

She giggled as she dressed. "I feel like a housebreaker."

"Well, courthouse breaker in this case, to be more precise."

That stopped her. "Are we going to free Ned?"

"Good heavens, no. He'll be guarded. And he can hardly walk - haven't you noticed? No, we are breaking in to the court-house to find some information."

"What information?"

"Your brother suggested it. I want to find the names of the troopers who arrested him, the ones who were at Glenrowan."

At the name of that place, her eyes went far away for a moment. She shook herself, and asked, "Why break into the courthouse? Can't we ask someone?"

"I don't think so. Firstly, we need to find out tonight, and I can't see us marching up to the police station to demand they tell us. Say - you have lived around these parts all your life - do you recognise any of the troopers that have been on duty at the court?"

"I don't know. I never paid much attention to any of their ugly mugs. Why?"

"Something is going on here. Something that links with Fitz-patrick."

We pocketed some candles and matches, and I took some thin pieces of wire from my valise. I hesitated as my fingers brushed the rolled up bundle that was my pistol, but left it there. I couldn't picture us shooting our way clear if we were caught.

We left the Hibernian by one of the side doors, having not encountered anyone as we slipped down the stairs, our shoes in our hands. Out on the street, I was at first dismayed to see there were still a number of figures staggering about, but what can one expect in a gold mining town with upward of two score hotels? At least no one paid us any mind as we walked rapidly down the street, keeping to the shadows as much as possible.

What concerned me, were the glowing gas lamps outside the court itself. With those at the front, and armed guards at the lockup out the back, this was going to be a chancy thing. I was counting on a door I had spied that opened into the narrow little alley beside the building. It would be dark there, and far enough from the lockup that I hoped any sharp-eared troopers would not hear me at work. For Father was quite wrong, there were some things I was good at - though I don't suppose lock picking would be high on his list of preferred skills. It was on my voyage over that I picked it up. Boredom is a powerful motivator for me - I like my mind to be as occupied as possible. No, maybe it is more honest to say, I need my mind to be as occupied as possible. I knew the price I could pay if I allowed my thoughts to pool around me, congealing into thick black mucous. As luck would have it, there was a grizzled career housebreaker on the same ship, fleeing a warrant, a bad marriage and mounting debt. We got to talking and playing cards to pass the time, and finally took turns trying to educate the other. I taught him foul insults in Latin, and he taught me how to pick simple locks with a couple of bent pieces of wire. I was deeply indebted to him. The only other amusement on the ship would have been trying to seduce the women on board, but there were few enough of them; a pastor's wife, all powder and buttons - I'd have wagered any man would choke to death trying to find warm flesh - and a fairly pretty young woman who unfortunately was not a good sailor, and had the perpetual reek of vomit about her.

So now, as we slipped quickly down the side of the court-house, and I knelt by the door, I was fairly confident of success. By touch, I guided my picks into the keyhole, feeling for the tumblers. And I was right - a side door in a country town like this was lucky to be locked in the first place, let alone have a decent modern lock. No, the only problem with this one was the stiffness of the workings. As I jiggled my picks, I worried they may bend out of shape, or jam and force me to leave them there. But then, loud as a gunshot as it seemed to me, the bolt slid back and the door opened easily with a turn of the handle. We slipped inside, and I made sure to close the door quietly behind us. It was very dark, and we advanced carefully, Maggie holding my hand and following behind me. I knew there were desks in here, and that the room was open to the central hall.

"Where shall we start?" Maggie breathed into my ear.

"Court records," I whispered. "Somewhere down the back, I would guess."

In the main hallway, I risked lighting the nub of candle I had in my pocket. The match flared, sending crazed shadows chasing each other down the walls, and then we had the warm light of the candle to guide us. I shielded it as best I could, and resolved to stay well away from any windows looking out onto the lockup out the back.

We found a clerk's office, and once inside, Maggie was able to light her candle as well. Now, we set about leafing through piles of papers heaped on desks and held in cupboards.

"What are we looking for exactly?" asked Maggie. "You are hoping to find a list of traps employed at the time?"

"I don't think we'd be that lucky. No, I'm hoping to find something like... Aha. Like this. Look, it's the record of a case brought against an apprentice blacksmith in Benalla last year. See the arresting officer? Constable Stanton, based at Benalla."

"What about him?"

"You'll see. Write his name down, we need a list... Here's another one... And another... This is a goldmine, Maggie, a goldmine!"

While I read her the names, Maggie carefully wrote them onto a sheet of paper she took from a desk. Before the candles had burned down, we had at least a dozen names of men who would have been on duty in the region at the time Kelly was taken at Glenrowan.

I blew out both our candles and breathed, "Let's go," in Maggie's ear. I followed her dim shape out the door and down the hall. Suddenly she stopped, and I ran into her back. I looked about worriedly in the gloom but couldn't see anything. I was about to ask her what was wrong when she turned and pressed herself against me, her mouth searching for mine. I felt her hot breath as she laughed through her kiss and for a moment, we squeezed each other tightly. Then I took her by the hand and led her by touch to the door where we came in. I opened it a crack and peered through; it seemed so much brighter after the dark of inside. We squeezed out, and I closed it quietly behind us. But here lay a problem - I was unable to use my picks to relock the door. We were going to have to leave it unlocked and hope no one noticed. Back at the top of the alley, we paused and looked out again, Maggie fairly quivering beside me with the excitement of it all. The streets were quieter now, and it was no great difficulty to step out onto the sidewalk and start walking back towards the Hibernian. Maggie kept walking faster, threatening to break into a run, but there is nothing more suspicious looking than someone sprinting down the street at night, and so I hauled her back beside me every time.

"That was fantastic!" she said. "What fun! And the list is going to help Ned?"

"I believe so."

"Excellent! I'm not even going to ask you how - see? I trust you, William."

I squeezed her hand by way of reply.

"You were so brilliant picking that lock! Who'd have thought you had it in you? You seem such the gentleman. At least, out in public. I've seen another side of you." She was gabbling, bless her. Not used to the adrenaline. "Maybe you could pick a lock in the hotel and find us some wine."

"I didn't think you cared that much for wine."

"It's growing on me. I like the way it makes me feel. Or maybe we could steal some food - I'm suddenly famished..."

"Brilliant!" I said. "Of course - the kitchen!"

"That's the usual place to find food, yes..."

"Oh, we can find a snack alright. But I've got another idea, too."

I told her as we walked along, and she clapped her hands with delight.

The Hibernian was mostly in darkness when we let ourselves in the side door. The odd lamp shone on the stairs and in the hallways, but the guests had retired and most staff departed for the night. We made our way stealthily to the dining room, wending our way carefully between the tables, through the doors at the back, down a short staircase and into the kitchen. I relit our candles, confident no one would see the light. Maggie peered at canisters on the bench top, selected one and turned to me.

"Open your jacket."

I unbuttoned it as she bid and spread it wide. She dipped her hands in the canister and came up with a handful of flour.

She rubbed it into my face, neck, and chest, until my skin was deathly pale.

"What else?" I asked.

"Your hair," she murmured. "Has to be dirty... Lank."

She found a tub of lard, and massaged the fat into my scalp, till my hair stuck out in wild disarray. A tin of jam was next: she scooped our red fingerfulls and daubed it around my mouth.

"Yum," I said, dabbing at it with my tongue. She slapped me lightly.

Ash from the stove smudged beneath my eyes, and on my cheeks, making them appear sunken. She found a balled-up apron on the floor in the corner, stained and grimy, and had me slip it on. Next she nicked it with a knife, and quietly tore great rents in it, then rubbed on more jam. She stepped back.

"Well," I asked, "how do I look?"

She shivered, and looked away, arms folded across her midsection.

"That good, eh?"

She shook her head, not speaking.

"Help me get to his room, and then you can go and wait for me."

We blew out the candles, and stood for a while until our eyes grew more accustomed to the dark. I had Maggie scout ahead, while I followed behind, nervous now of discovery or of damaging my costume. We made it up the stairs, to the guest rooms, undetected. I touched Maggie on the arm.

"This is it. You go on."

She squeezed my hand, and tiptoed down the hall. I waited, and then took hold of the doorhandle. My hands were greasy, and it was hard to grip, but I could tell it was locked. I slowly knelt, reaching beneath my apron into my jacket pocket for my lockpicks. This lock was much harder than the courthouse, and I knelt there cursing silently until my legs went numb. But just when I was close to giving up, I felt the bolt shoot back. I rose on creaking legs, and quietly entered the room.

He lay snoring in his bed, on his back, one arm thrown across his face. I hesitated, strangely feeling almost bolted to the floor. There was a strong urge to flee, to slip out of the door before he saw me and run to my room. But I stood firm, and gained mastery over myself. After a couple of deep breaths, I walked softly over, and stood by the side of the bed, looking at his face in repose. It was a full moon, and plenty of light spilled through the open drapes to light the room.

Strange to look at another human while they sleep. It is one of the few times we see an unguarded face, and can look without need for guard ourselves. It is an intimacy normally only shared by lovers. This was an unlovely face - careworn, and troubled. Dreams pulled at the corners of his eyes and lips.

I bent over. I reached for him, and touched his arm. He mumbled something. I touched him again.

"McIntyre..." I growled. What else would one say? I wasn't even sure if they could talk. Ned never said... "McIntyre... brains..."

"Lonigan?" said McIntyre, and his eyes flickered open.

"Yargh!" I yelled, gaping my mouth wide and lunging forward.

He shrieked, high and loud, flailing at me, flailing amongst the bedclothes. There was the sudden hot stink of faeces - my God, he had literally shit himself! I growled, and battered at him, tearing at his vest. He screamed, and scrambled away, pulling himself onto the floor on the far side of the mattress with a bang. I dived onto the bed, in time to see his legs disappearing underneath it, and for a moment, we were a bizarre reversal of old childhood terrors - the monster on the bed, the boy under-neath. I fought to control a giggle.

Suddenly there was a muffled bang, and the room exploded

into a snowstorm of feathers. I fell back, confused, and saw blue smoke rising from a hole in the mattress. Shit! He had a gun down there! I leaped backwards and away, stumbling and sending furniture flying. I was at the door in moments, dimly aware of shrill shrieks still coming from beneath the bed. I slammed his door shut behind me and tore down the corridor to my room. As I grabbed the handle, the door whipped open and a pale-faced Maggie pulled me inside.

"Fuck!" I said, standing quivering in the middle of the room. "Fuck!"

Maggie was peering into the hall, and then quietly closed the door and locked it. She held a finger to her lips. I clamped my jaw tight, my teeth threatening to gnaw my tongue to pieces. We could hear a distant keening, then someone banging from the floor above and a distant shout of, "Shut up!" Gradually, the wailing subsided, as did the banging, and we stood listening. No one came to investigate the gunshot. Comforting to know. What did that mean - that no one knew what it was? Or that it was such a regular occurrence that it excited no interest?

"Bastard had a gun," I whispered to Maggie.

"I know! I heard! I thought you might be..."

"Bastard!"

"Yes. Did it work?"

I chuckled evilly. "Oh yes. Oh, very much yes. I think he nearly had a heart attack."

"Good. Now wipe all that muck off yourself."

"I'd rather you wiped it off for me..."

And she did. I stood naked, shivering slightly, as she washed me clean with the basin and a towel.

"Goodness," she said, running her hands across my skin, "look at these goosebumps. You're coming up everywhere." Her hands dipped lower. "Goodness," she said again, taking hold of me. "Goodness."

I dreamed.

I was walking down a cobbled city street - back in London, I suppose. As I walked, I became aware that everyone was looking at me. At first, it was a quick glance, then a furrowed brow, and then open looks of hatred and revile. People began to step aside, some even crossing the road to avoid me. Women covered their faces, and pulled their children close. Men braced themselves and cursed. And finally they turned, and ran from me – a whole crowd fleeing before me, looking back with terror. I turned and looked behind, where a thick fog came rolling after me, and in that fog lurched hideous dead things. I tried to run, to join the others as they fled, but my legs were stiff and unwieldy. I could make no sound. Tendrils of fog curled around my feet, and though I strived with all my might to go faster, the terrible fog overtook me, and with it came the stinking creatures who stumbled all about me, a mass of decay. Though I was jostled and bumped by them, they did not harm me. And I found myself at the window of a house, and within I could see Maggie, a candle in her hand, staring out in horror. I raised my hands to beat upon the glass, but she pulled the curtains closed and was lost to my view. And then I could see my reflection in the glass, my hideous reflection, and I realised I had not cleaned off my makeup – she thought I was one of them. I grabbed at the dry sticky jam on my face and pulled, and screamed in horror as a strip of my own dead skin came away in my fingers, revealing teeth and jaw beneath...

I woke.

Just a dream... For God's sake.

Sweat beaded my heaving chest. My head felt hot. I pulled myself away from Maggie and climbed from the bed, going to the window and wrenching the curtains open. The moon stood high and full in the night sky. I turned. The pale light fell into the room, and upon Maggie as she lay sleeping. I couldn't breathe. The soft light gave her skin a bluish tinge. Like marble. Like alabaster. She was carved and perfect. Her full breasts. Her thighs. Her throat. The darkened room like a tomb, a temple. The bed an altar. I ached in my core, my heart broken, for she would never be this impossibly lovely again. I could not even tell if she was breathing. Perfection.

So much. So much of life a disappointment. So much time waiting for something. What was it for? What was the point if the moment you let yourself care for something, it was snatched away? For she would be taken from me too, wouldn't she? Everything I wanted, everything I loved, always taken in the end. How could I let her slip from my fingers and tumble down into the darkness?

Tears burned my eyes, hot acid. A great sob welled within me, and burst like a bark though I tried to muffle it with my hands. She stirred, frowned, and this moment too was lost to me. Stolen from me.

"William?" she asked sleepily, and I tried to answer, but sobbed instead, standing by the window, my face in my hands. "What is it?"

What is it? It is everything nothing something. I am weak. I glance at her, expecting to see my own loathing mirrored, but her face is concerned, confused. Could I tell her? Everything?

Could I?

The chance hung between us. I fancied she felt it too. A moment when I might make my full confession. To tell who I really was, what I was, why I was here. To share that burden, and perhaps, impossibly, put it down? To have at least one moment of freedom.

But-

"You know, I don't think I've ever seen a man cry," she said suddenly, into the space, filling it with wet cement. "I've never seen Bill or Tom cry. Or Dan. Certainly not Ned."

You pathetic fool, I told myself. She is just some girl. That is all.

"Bully for them," I managed.

"Oh, don't be like that, William. I just meant you're different. You know, not as manly."

"Manly enough to make you fucking come."

She frowned, coming awake. "Don't be so sensitive. Come on, even you have to admit you can't touch Ned..."

"You stupid ignorant bog Irish slut."

Her face went dead. "If Ned was here and heard you talk to me like that..."

"Well, Ned isn't here, is he? And he isn't going to be hearing anything anymore pretty soon. You know, your adoration of him is a little sick. But that's the way with the Irish, isn't it?"

"What?" she said, flat and hard.

"You know what they say. An Irish virgin is a girl who can outrun her brothers. Unless of course, she wants to get caught..."

She came at me, all teeth and claws, like a harpy. I grabbed her, but she squirmed and fought with no sense of her own safety. I had to throw my head backwards to avoid her grasping fingernails raking my face. She spat at me, and her knee suddenly darted into my groin. I dropped her shoulders then and leapt forward, hands closing around her throat. Her eyes went wide then, as she stared into mine, saw all the way down, down into the black pit where the monster shook and howled. She caught at my hands, pulling at them with desperation, and the look of fear I saw made me sick to my stomach. I let go, and she scrambled backwards, falling onto the bed, then spun about, grabbing for her clothes.

"*Nobody touches me!*"

"Wait," I croaked.

She launched for the door, half-dressed, wild, and scrabbling with the key. "*Nobody!*"

"Wait. Maggie, stop. I'll tell you. My name..."

She threw the door open, glanced over her shoulder at me with pure venom, and then the dark maw of the hallway swallowed her.

There was a mewling in the moonlit room. Christ, it was me. I turned in a stiff circle, looking at the emptiness. What had happened? I shuffled over to the bed, and sat upon the edge. No point trying to sleep.

The sun would rise tomorrow.

I am a patient man.

SEVENTEEN

Gaunson was irritatingly chipper when he joined me at our desk in the courtroom. I'd been there since they opened the front doors. Before that, I had been walking. Before that, I had searched for her, in vain. Not that I had any idea what I could say to her. Dawn had slowly lit the room and revealed it for what it was, exposed the stained sheets. Exposed me again for what I am. Everyone saw it in the end.

"Good morning, Charles," said Gaunson. "Our turn today, eh?"

"Call McIntyre," I said.

He frowned. "He is a witness for the prosecution. We already cross examined him."

"Call him anyway. Tell the judge there was something you forgot to ask him."

"Something I forgot to ask him?"

"Stop repeating me. And stop looking at me with those cow eyes of yours. Just do as I say and call McIntyre back up. Say you forgot. The judge already thinks you're an idiot, so it won't matter."

"May I remind you, Charles, that *you* work for *me*?"

"And you work for the Kelly's. And that's who I am trying to help. This farce needs shaking up."

I was ready for a fight. Instead, he sat back and smiled patiently.

"You're a little overwrought. Happens to all at their first trial - especially such a one as this. It is a hard thing having another man's life in your hands..."

With an effort, I bit my lip.

"Unless something else is bothering you, Charles?" There was something sly about the casual way this question was posed. "Not disappointed in love, perhaps?"

"No, Gaunson. I am not some love-sick puppy. Or ridiculous bloated oaf sweating after a girl young enough to be my daughter. Unless, of course, that is the attraction."

He clamped his jaw shut in fury, making a big show of slamming his documents down onto the desk. We spoke no more as the court slowly filled, and Smyth and his cronies descended like so many crows on the other side of the room. There was still a decent crowd, but there were definitely fewer people than yesterday. It seemed that some, eager to get a view of the great Ned Kelly, had been satisfied and were now content to go and do whatever pointless activities they normally did to fill in their vapid, vacant lives.

Foster arrived, and we went through the motions, pretending there was something special about him, rising and waiting for him to settle his arse. Law and Order, here made flesh and blood in the form of this constipated turkey relegated to the backwaters of the colony.

Ned was brought in, limping heavily, looking like he had not slept. We made eye contact and nodded briefly. As I sat, I had the feeling of eyes boring into the back of my skull. I turned to look, imagining it might be Hare, but he was gazing up at the ceiling. I scanned the room, wondering if I might spot Maggie.

Instead, my eyes lit upon the face of Tom Lloyd, staring at me with absolute murder in his eyes. I blew him a kiss. His eyes widened and he went to stand, attracting attention from a couple of troopers. Lips moving as he silently cursed me; he sank back into his seat. I nodded at him, and then gave my attention back to the front of the court.

"Mr Gaunson?" said Foster, tone one of complete boredom.

"Your Honour," said Gaunson, rising, "we will today prove that my client, Edward Kelly, was acting in self-defence. As such, the most he can be charged with is manslaughter."

"Proceed," said Foster.

"Your Honour... My associate here wishes to recall Constable McIntyre. There is something further he wishes to ask the witness."

"He wants to attack him some more?" asked the magistrate dryly.

"No, no. It is simply that in his overexcitement, there is something he forgot to ask."

Predictable, really. No matter.

"Mr Smyth?"

Smyth shrugged. "The prosecution has no objection, Your Honour. As long as we can redirect afterwards."

"Of course. Call Constable McIntyre, then."

"Constable Thomas McIntyre!" shouted the clerk.

And of course we waited. Everyone looked about, expecting him to rise and come forward. Everyone but me. A buzz of conversation filled the air.

"Mr Smyth?" said Foster. "Where is your witness?"

"Ah... I don't really know..." Smyth was looking back over his shoulder at Hare.

"This is ridiculous. Send some troopers to wherever he is staying. If he is drunk, he is going straight in the cells."

Several troopers rushed off. Hare stood for a moment, then

sank back down as the magistrate cast a baleful eye on him. The he turned his attention to me.

"Young man, this had better be worth the wait."

I nodded, a study of serious professionalism.

Just then, there was a bustle at the back of the court, and a babble of voices. There were grunts and curses, and interlaced through it all, a high keening. Two troopers stomped up the aisle, dragging a sorry bundle between them, which they deposited in the witness chair. It was indeed McIntyre, and he looked horrible. He had not washed or shaved, and curled into a foetal position upon the chair, fingers in his mouth, drool running down onto his chest. I fancied I could detect the smell of excrement.

"Constable McIntyre," said Foster, "I remind you that you are still under oath... Constable McIntyre?"

But he may as well have been talking to the chair itself, for all the response he got out of the trooper. Ned looked towards me, and I risked a wink. He shook his head a little in response.

"What is wrong with this man?" asked Foster. His nose was twitching.

I took this as my cue and stood. "Constable, I would like to ask you some more questions about the events at Stringybark Creek. Could you repeat what you were doing when you say the defendant came upon you in the camp?"

I stood waiting, all patience. McIntyre twisted in the chair, raw red eyes clenched shut one moment, then looking wildly about the courtroom the next.

"Constable?" I asked. "Your Honour, so please you, could you direct the witness to answer the question?"

"I don't think we are going to be able to get him to do anything," muttered the magistrate. "Constable? Constable! Mr Smyth, come over here and do something about your witness."

"Um, I'd rather not," said Smyth.

"Your Honour!" I stode forward. "If this is the best the prosecution can do, to hang their case upon this... this lunatic... then I demand my client be set free at once! This is a joke! Look at him!"

I turned to the crowd, relishing their attention. Hare was, I think, trying to kill me with his eyes.

"Steady on," said Foster. "I agree the witness is not in possession of all his faculties. But he appeared to be so yesterday."

"A parrot or a madman may learn a speech by rote, Your Honour."

"The hearing will proceed. Someone take this unfortunate straight to the asylum."

The same troopers sighed, and took hold of McIntyre again, whisking him from the courtroom in the blink of an eye.

"With your permission, then, Your Honour, I will call our first witness."

I was aware of Gaunson trying to attract my attention. I ignored him.

"The defence calls Constable Stanton!"

I folded my arms and waited. Again came the hubbub of discussion. Ned raised an eyebrow at me. Gaunson frowned in confusion.

"Your Honour," said Smyth, standing, "what is this? Why are they calling officers to the stand?"

"It will all become clear, Your Honour. If the Constable could come forward?"

But he did not. Hare cleared his throat and stood.

"Your Honour, I regret to inform the court that the Constable is engaged in duties in the field. If the defence had given us warning that he was wanted, of course we would have ensured he was present."

"Not to worry," I said. "is he the only officer so engaged?"

"He... Yes, I believe so," said Hare slowly.

"Goodo. Then let's call Constable Emmett to the stand."

Again there was a pause. Hare slowly stood again.

"Constable Emmett has been transferred to another district..."

"These things happen," I said. "Then let's have Constable Baker."

"He has sadly left the force..."

"Oh. Live around here, does he?"

"I don't believe so."

"Not to worry. I'll be satisfied with any of the following: Constable Thompson, Constable Thackeray, Constable Biggins, Constable Taggart, Constable York... Any of them here? How about Taylor? Perkins? Collins? Any of them? Any of them at all?"

Hare stared at me. The court was in silence.

"Young man, I don't understand," said Foster.

"Your Honour, these are the names of officers serving at the time of my client's arrest at Glenrowan. That arrest was a large scale police operation. Some, if not all, of the constables I named must have taken part. And yet not a single one is here today. Why not, Your Honour? Where are they? What happened to them?"

I looked around. Hare was walking out of the courtroom.

"I call Inspector Hare," I yelled. "Inspector Hare!"

But without a backward glance he strode from the building. I spun around.

"Your Honour!"

"I am adjourning this hearing for the day!" said Foster.

"Your Honour!"

"*We are adjourned!*"

And he banged his gavel on the bench before sweeping from the room, clerks in hot pursuit. The room was a chaos of noise. Smyth and his cronies made a tight phalanx and thrust out of the court, while the spectators argued and shouted and whistled. Troopers began thrusting people from the room. Others descended on Ned. I strode over to him before they could take him away.

"Full of surprises, aren't you, Remittance Man?"

"And so, Ned? What about Glenrowan? What happened out there?"

"That's a tale for another time. Alas, I have a pressing engagement at the moment." He grinned at me as they dragged him away.

I walked from the courthouse, feeling lightheaded and a little nauseous. When the light hit my eyes, I felt a sharp pain above my temple - no doubt a migraine was coming on. I used to be absolutely crippled by them back in London, but since coming to Australia, had been somewhat free of them. This one felt like it was going to be a blinder. I resolved to get back to my room as quickly as possible and lie down, before I encountered Lloyd. I wondered if I could get hold of some opium - that was how I would treat myself back home. There were many Chinese on the periphery of Beechworth, this being a mining town, but I didn't fancy putting up with any dumb show of ignorance due to my lack of connections in the community. No, I was just going to have to deal with this one with peace and quiet.

When I got back to my room, I found my bed had been made, but the sheets had not been changed, and so after I closed the curtains and threw back the covers, the musky smell of her body rose to torment me. As I slipped into the sheets, I wondered what the cleaner had made of the dusting of flour all over the floor.

I lay back, but sleep eluded me. The throb of blood in my temple was like the beat of some infernal drum, or the clashing together of huge destructive engines. I crossed my arms over my face, blocking out the last of the needling light, the pressure at least affording a different sensation. My legs were restless, kicking at the sheet, and that brought to mind her legs, but that was a thought best thrust away at this point. What had I done? It was like a dream – a nightmare followed by another nightmare. Surely, I hadn't tried... I rubbed at my face and tried to focus instead on the trial, and McIntyre in particular.

My pretence of being a Blighter had certainly thrown him, if not sent him permanently insane. I almost felt some pity for him, being cast into the institution - for how did a man prove his sanity in a place like that? I could imagine nothing worse than being under such scrutiny, where every action, every utterance, would be recorded and nodded over, given symbolic importance, until you would fear doing anything - but then doing nothing would be seen as grounds to keep you there, too.

So what did this mean? That the stories were all true, the dead really did walk the lonely country roads? But on the other hand, surely a man who has had three comrades shot dead all around him, even if it was indeed in self-defence, was allowed to be traumatised by the event - left in one of the nervous conditions that were becoming all the rage in Europe. My antics may have proved nothing beyond the fact that he was a man on the edge. Besides, had I really been out to prove anything? It was more for the chance to strike back in some way, wasn't it, against the smug smooth machine of the powerful. So he was simply a pawn, so what – why not take him, if the bishops, king and queen were out of reach.

On top of that, there was Ned's hint to look at the officers present at his arrest. All those men conveniently out of the way for the trial. And Hare was particularly discomfited by my calling of them as witnesses. I would renew my call for the inspector to appear when the trial resumed the next day. We had not closed our argument, so I could see nothing stopping me from trying again.

At some point, I slept - dreamlessly, wonderfully - until a tight rapping woke me with a start. I lay for a moment, trying to recall where I was. My head had receded to a dull ache. I needed water. The floorboards creaked outside my door, and the rapid knocking came again. Maggie? I stumbled to my feet and over to the door, unlocked it, and pulled it half open. A man stood there, in a cheap suit and bowler hat, an envelope in his hand.

"What is it?" I asked.

"Mr Spencer?"

"Yes-"

There were three of them, of course - the other two out of sight on either side of the doorway. I caught a slight smile on the face of the one in the hat, then his hand lashed out and my head exploded. I staggered, and was carried backwards into my room on a wave of muscle and cheap cotton. They were good, they knew their work. The door was closed swiftly and quietly behind us, and they fell upon me with professional thoroughness. I crashed about the room, struggling to stay on my feet as their fists thumped into my stomach, my ribs, my kidneys. I kept getting rapid snapshots of different parts of the room at different angles, and realised it was because my head was snapping back and forward as they struck me. I fell towards the closed window, and with perverse gentleness, they caught me and pulled me away. I vomited, and still could not find breath to call for help or curse them. There was pain there, but it was like flashes of red lightning behind mountainous walls of cloud. My vision was shutting down, my nose full of snot and blood. Jesus Christ, were they planning to kill me? A shaft of fear ran through me, and I began to lash out, flinging my fists about, but it was like a nightmare, my blows weak and meaningless. And then finally, I did fall, and their feet began to kick me. I tried to crawl away, tucking my buttocks to try to protect my scrotum. Someone stamped on my back, and I was flattened - or almost flattened, I was lying across something that seemed hard, yet gave way beneath me as they struck. I was glad of that, wondering if it might save my ribs from breaking, whatever it was...

... my valise.

I thrust my clumsy hands beneath my body, clawing at the top of the bag. I could hear them grunt with effort as they struck me, but my hand was snaking into the bag now, digging, digging. And there it was, little heavy package waiting down the bottom. And now coming clear, and my sausage fingers pulling the socks away, thank God it had no trigger guard to contend with. And rolling to my side, right arm under me, pointing the derringer back and up from under my left arm.

I fired, and there was a yell of pain and curses and alarm.

"Fuck!" yelled one. "He shot me!"

"Out!" cried another. "He's got a gun! Out!"

And their feet were thumping as they headed for the door. I rolled, and pointed my arm, and squeezed again, the second trigger pull firing the second barrel, but there was nothing but a click. Misfire. But thank God they did not notice, and I heard them crashing down the stairs.

In their haste, they left my door swinging open, and it was that which saved me, as consciousness fled.

I became dimly aware of voices, and hands upon me, and gentle admonishments to be still, and I was tucked in my bed. I felt a cool cloth on my forehead, and something sharp and stinging dabbed upon me. At some point, I was sat up, and my shirt removed, and something tight was wrapped around my ribs. A spoon was forced between my teeth, a sickening liquid poured down my throat, but moments later a feeling, as familiar and welcome as an old friend, lifted me clear of the muddy pain besieging me, and I rolled joyfully around in sweet clouds high above the bed.

Later, clarity came to me, and I was conscious of darkness, a candle burning, and a man sitting by the bed, reading. I moved my hand, to show him I was awake. I would have spoken, but my jaw was tight and painful and my tongue swollen in my mouth.

"Hello, son," he said, putting down his book. He was a thick set man with greying hair and a shrewd gaze. "You don't have to try to speak. You feel terrible, I know. But don't worry, you'll pull through. My name is Dobbin. I'm a doctor. Lucky for you, I was nearby when they found you - treating an acquaintance of yours, actually, by the name of Edward Kelly."

I grunted.

"I'm guessing you want to know what for. Well, the judge wanted me to take a look at his wounds before they moved him. Don't know what they expected, moving a man about like that when he's been shot in the legs. I'm not a miracle worker - of course he has a fever. Told them they shouldn't be moving him again already, but they wouldn't listen."

I moaned.

"Oh yes, they're shipping him back to Melbourne. Probably on the train as we speak. I gave him a restorative to perk him up enough to get there... Now just hold still. You aren't going anywhere in a hurry. You've got some cracked ribs and some pretty extensive bruising, but you will live. You'll be sore as hell for a good couple of weeks, I'd say. Any idea who did this to you?"

I shook my head - slightly.

"Well, I imagine the police will want to question you. I won't tell them you're awake yet - plenty of time for all that tomorrow. I've got something here for the pain, and it will help you sleep, too. If I leave it, can I trust you not to just go and drink it all? It's laudanum. Take too much, and we'll be burying you here in the morning."

I nodded in understanding.

"Alright then. Just about a spoonful at a time is enough for your hurts." He rubbed his eyes. "And so I shall take my leave, Mr Spencer. I'll drop in tomorrow afternoon to see how you are, then we'll see if you are ready to be interviewed. Goodnight."

He fussed with the bottle he had placed on the bedside table, nodded, and bent to blow out the candle. I moaned. He nodded in understanding, and left it burning, quietly closing my door behind him as he left. I lay there for a moment, testing each limb and muscle. My body felt numb and swollen, but it was actually not as bad as I feared. I had felt, when they were beating me, that they were doing real permanent damage, but I was either lucky, or they knew their craft and were seeking only to hurt me and cause me pain. I was aware that I was lucky I had been found quickly, for if I had lain longer on the floor unconscious, untreated, there was a chance I would have been more ill and impaired.

For I had to go. I had to get back to Melbourne, to Ned. I did not want to be stuck here facing questions I had no answers to about my attackers.

No answers?

There were several possibilities. They could have been friends of Tom Lloyd, sent to teach a lesson. But I had the feeling that he was one of those irritating "salt of the earth" types who would want to do everything themselves. No, he was more likely to appear demanding satisfaction than set some goons onto me. Alternatively, they could have been troopers, intent on getting vengeance for my courtroom antics. But they had something of the city about them - they just didn't seem like small town hoodlums.

Or they could have been sent by someone else, to disconnect me from Ned...

I dragged myself into a sitting position, head thumping, ribs aching, and I laughed.

You stupid bastards. I wasn't going to believe him. I wasn't going to care. But you couldn't just leave me alone. If you had kept out of it, let me collect my little amount of cash for writing down the words of a madman, you'd have got what you wanted. But you had to push me, try to steer me, control me.

HP, if this was your doing, you had made a mistake.

EIGHTEEN

Getting out of Beechworth was not easy.

I had to dose myself liberally with laudanum so that I could move, but not so heavily that I staggered or stood staring at the lights. I carefully packed my valise, slipped the bottle in one coat pocket and my useless derringer in the other. I looked out the window, and dropped my bag into the evening shadows below. It was too high for me to jump, unfortunately, and I doubted I could climb in my increasingly stiff state. So, affecting my best careless attitude, I limped slowly down the steps to the foyer.

The Weasel was on duty behind the desk. I gave him a slight smile and nod, and sauntered for the door.

"Going out, Mr Spencer?" he enquired after me.

"Mmm," I said.

"Lovely night for it," he said. "Though a little late."

I shrugged. Suspicious little rat bastard.

"I see Mr Gaunson already checked out earlier."

"Hmmm," I agreed.

"We - the staff, that is - weren't expecting to see you up and about so soon?"

I raised an eyebrow at him, indicating bemusement at his doubts about my fitness.

"A terrible business, sir. A sad reflection of the times we find ourselves living in, when ruffians assault respectable men of the bar in such a prestigious establishment as ours, sir."

"Indeed," I said, slowly and carefully, all the while moving backwards to the door.

"Well," he said, "I won't say goodnight. No doubt I'll still be here on duty when you return from your stroll."

I smiled again, and yanked the door open. I made sure to pause for a moment, as if taking in the evening air, and then casually sauntered off. Once out of sight, I broke into a lurching, limping run and got to the alley as quickly as I could. My bag lay where it had fallen, and I retrieved it quickly and headed for the railway station. It was a cold evening, and that, plus the obvious ending of the committal hearing meant fewer out on the streets. I had no idea when the next train was likely to depart.

Of course, it wasn't until early the next morning. I spent the remainder of the miserable night sitting on a narrow bench in the small draughty waiting room on the platform, terrified that at any minute, a trooper would appear and I would be ordered back to the hotel. There was also a little fear that my three chums from the previous day would reappear - though of course, they now knew I was armed. So I sat, staring out into the darkness, taking the odd sip from my bottle of laudanum, again wishing for dawn to come.

And so, eventually, a rather surprised station master found me the next morning. He appeared to believe my story that I had been involved in an accident, and that I had to return to Melbourne immediately. He sold me a ticket and shared his breakfast with me as we waited for the earliest train. He was also able to tell me that the committal had indeed been concluded rather swiftly, because news had come of a growing swell of agitated Kelly supporters in town, and the authorities feared a break-out attempt or riot.

I scoffed at this. It was my observation that the numbers in town had been steadily dropping since the first day of the hearing. And while Lloyd had been showing his ugly mug, he did not in himself constitute a dangerous mob. No, this looked like a useful cover story to whisk Ned back to Melbourne gaol. I guessed that their plans for a quick, uneventful committal and trial had come rather unstuck, thanks mostly to me. It was rather an odd feeling. I suppose it was...pride.

The train to Melbourne was mostly empty, and I was able to lie down and sleep until we pulled in to Spencer Street station in the early afternoon. I took another swig from my bottle, and hailed a cab to take me straight to the gaol. I was frittering money away in a fashion I hadn't enjoyed since I quit England, but I was feeling strangely unconcerned about that. I felt as if huge gears and plates were moving, an intersection of components set to occur, with me as a small spinning cogwheel of teeth within a vast engine, dragging things forward. I would chew my way through this to the end.

At the gaol, I was admitted by my old friend Father Time, who stared at my swollen face in consternation. He stepped back to let me through, and I found a number of agitated warders standing about in the yard, with Castieau amongst them. He was in conversation with his two senior warders, Quinn and Nixon, but when he saw me, he blanched.

"My dear sir!" he cried, bustling over to me. "What has happened?"

"Never mind that, Governor. I need to see my client, at once."

He hesitated, licking his lips with his reptilian tongue. "That may not be possible at the moment. There have been some problems..."

"Are you denying me access?" I asked. All this talk was making my jaw ache. It was hard to enunciate properly.

"Well... It's just that Kelly is rather agitated at the moment..."

I shook my head. "Don't worry. I take full responsibility for my safety."

"And... This is rather difficult..."

"What is it?"

Castieau glanced about, and then leaned in close. "I am being pressured not to let anyone in to see him."

"Including his legal representation? Surely not."

"Including a certain young man who bears a rather strong likeness to you, though a different name, apparently. I must confess, I am a little confused by the whole thing..."

My little games were catching up with me, it seemed.

"Governor Castieau," I said. "One thing that is widely known is that you are a fair man. A fair man in a very difficult position. Indeed, the particular stresses of these times probably won't be known until you have had a chance to have your memoir published - how is the writing going, by the way?"

"Oh! Well, well, to be honest, I was a little disappointed when Kelly was removed from my care. I thought that made for a fairly disappointing end, not to be there at the finish. You may rest assured, sir, that I have taken up my pen again with a flourish."

"And you may rest assured, sir, that I have had correspondence with some of my family connections in London who are involved in publishing. I shouldn't be surprised if you received a positive response to any submissions you were to make to them."

He inflated like a puffer fish. "Which publishers?"

I smiled at him and remained silent. His eyes narrowed, and he called over one of his warders to take me at once to see my client. When the cell door was swung open, I was taken aback to see the room full of debris. There was not a stick of furniture left intact. Ned sat on floor where the bed had been, staring at the wall.

"Been redecorating?" I asked. "Must be some strange Irish style."

He started, then looked at me and smiled. "What happened to your face? Been making friends, RM?"

I ignored him, and stood looking about at the mess. "You've smashed my desk. Oh, and shredded my cushion, too. Did it put up much of a fight?"

"Maybe more than you did. Or should I see the other fellow?"

"I may have hurt their knuckles with my head. And what was this temper tantrum in aid of?"

He shrugged. "They wouldn't let me see ma. I told them, fine, you have me now, I'm committed, I'm not going anywhere, so you might as well let me talk to her. But the bastards still said no. And so I... I seem to be having some trouble controlling my temper lately."

"Are you alright?" I asked him seriously.

"Yes," he said. "You?"

I nodded. "It only hurts to walk, speak, and breathe. But I'll live."

"Well, isn't this a tough new version of the Remittance Man I knew? If I'd only known that being beaten would be so good for you... I could have helped you out days ago."

"I'm sorry I missed the end of the hearing, but as you can see, I was a little busy."

"You didn't miss much. That Smyth bloke got up and said it would be impossible for me to be properly tried in Beechworth, because the whole jury would be in fear for their lives from my supporters. So Foster ordered me to be remanded back to Melbourne for trial. Don't look so glum - it was always going to play out this way. This is how I want it... no, that's not right - this is how I need it to be."

"What did Gaunson say?"

"Not a lot. Just complained again about not getting his adjournment."

"Do you trust him? You don't think he's working with them?"

"Them?" Ned chuckled. "Jesus, RM, what's this? Conspiracies, now?"

"Something is going on..."

"I know something is going on. That's what I have been telling you. Not beginning to believe me, are you?"

"I don't know. I don't know."

"Nice job on McIntyre, by the way. What did you do?"

"Just a little research. And thanks for the tip about the police. That certainly set the cat amongst the pigeons. So... tell me."

"About?"

"Glenrowan."

He shook his head. "No. Not yet. We aren't there yet. There's more you have to understand first."

"Then tell me."

"Don't you want to write it down?"

"I just want to hear it. I can make notes later."

"Well, please find a seat. Sorry about your cushion. Your arse will have to suffer along with mine."

The chickens were in uproar, flapping about the hen house in a frenzy of feathers. The cause squatted in the corner, a hapless bird gripped tightly in each of its claw-like hands. Only one chicken was alive - the other had already had its head bitten off, and the Blighter sat chewing on it now, a faintly disappointed look on its face, as if there was some sense within that this wasn't exactly the kind of sustenance it craved. Once it was a man, as evidenced by the tattered remains of the clothes it wore, but where it had come from, who it had loved, what it had feared, all was lost now, all gone but the gnawing hunger in its shrivelled belly, and enough reptilian spark to respond to sight and sound.

The door to the coop was kicked in violently, and the Blighter looked up, jaws still working on a crunching, feathery mouthful. A pistol blazed twice, and the creature's head erupted against the wall behind it. The hens went into even greater paroxysms at the violence, spattering the floor with shit, and flapping away from the figures in the doorway,

"Thank you, son, I really appreciate it," said one, a middle aged man.

"No worries," said Ned, "all part of the service."

"I thought the bugger was going to clean me out. Already ate about two dozen of my best layers. And who's going to compensate me, eh? Answer me that."

"I'll give you what I can spare..."

"No, son," said the farmer, patting Ned on the arm. "I don't want your money. You've done enough for me already. God knows, I didn't want to try to take it on. That's how poor Marty bought it last month. Reckon this might be the same one who did for him."

"What became of Marty?" asked Ned casually.

"No need to worry about that one. We burned his house down around him. That sorted him. Poor bugger. He would never have wanted to become a Blighter."

A horrible thought occurred to Ned. "You did wait until he turned, didn't you?"

The farmer shifted about. "Well," he said at last. "He was as good as..."

"Jesus. Just send for us next time, will you?"

There was a clatter of hooves out in the yard, and they turned to see Dan and Steve ride up.

"How did you go?" asked Ned.

"It was no Blighter," Dan spat in disgust. "It was just some drunk swaggie, staggering around with the tremors."

"What did you do?"

"Well, here's the tricky part, Ned. We didn't know what to do, so we came back to talk to you. I told the old duck that called us that we weren't going to kill him because he wasn't dead... Well, you know what I mean. And she said if we didn't kill him, then he was only going to be got by some Blighter one of these days, wandering around like that, then turn into one himself, so why not save time and shoot him now?"

"Sounds a fair argument," said the farmer.

They looked at the farmer until he shrugged and shuffled away.

"Cheeky bugger," said Ned. "Ate two dozen of his chickens? More like half a dozen."

"So?" asked Dan. "What now? What about the drunk?"

"Well, let's go and take a look."

Ned swung up onto his horse, and they cantered down the road to another small farm nearby. Steve led the trio into a field bordered by scrubland, then reined in and sat back scratching his head.

"This is where we left him."

Steve was gazing toward the small slab cabin and pointed out some scuff marks in the dirt.

"Shit," said Ned.

They flicked their reins and galloped into the small yard.

"Oh, Jesus!" cried Dan. "You stupid mean old cow!"

An old lady stood outside the cabin door, an axe in her gnarled fists. She blinked up at them belligerently. A body lay in the dirt at her feet, blood flowing from several deep gashes in its head.

"Why'd you go and do that? He wasn't a Blighter!"

The old lady shrugged. "Had to protect meself if you lot weren't going to do it."

"But he wasn't bloody dead!"

"Is now," she said, and cackled, revealing the gaping holes where most of her teeth should be.

"Ned!" cried Dan. "These people!"

Ned stared. "Maybe she had a point," he said after a while. "Maybe we have to get more proactive..."

"What, by killing every vagrant in the colony?"

"No, Dan. I don't mean like this. But we can't blame the people too much when they're poor, or frightened, maybe. Come on, let's go find Joe."

"Hey!" cried the old woman. "What about this body?"

"You're pretty good with an axe," said Ned, turning his horse and kicking it on. "Let's hope you can handle a shovel as well."

At a crossroads, they dismounted in a small stand of trees, and after an hour heard a horse approaching. Hands on their revolvers just in case, they waited, and were soon relieved to see Joe riding towards them.

"Get any Blighters?" called Dan.

"No. But I've got word of one - and wait till you hear this! It's being kept like some kind of pet!"

"*What?*"

"It's true, bloke I was speaking to swore to it. Out on Faithfulls Creek Station. The manager has one in the shed."

"But that's crazy! Why?"

"To repress the workers," said Ned.

Joe nodded. "Got it in one, Ned. They have the staff on that station working flat out for fear of being thrown to that thing."

"They couldn't do that!" cried Dan. "It's murder! Is it? It

must be. I mean, if it don't eat you outright, then what's left of you would come back, but you're still dead, really... so..."

"What it is," said Ned, "is the ruling classes treating the worker as if he is nothing but a possession. This is perfect. This is just what we needed, a chance to hit back against those who brought this plague down on us. Mount up."

The four of them were soon riding down the road, bound for Faithfulls Creek Station. Steve was in the lead, as usual, his natural prowess in the saddle always placing him there. Ned rode slightly behind, with Dan and Joe behind and to either side. They were unafraid of encountering any troopers, being well mounted, well-armed, and well-hard young men.

The station was located to the north of the small town of Euroa, just off the main road running from Albury, high up on the border of the colony, down to Melbourne. It was a large place, with a brick homestead and a number of slab outbuildings, sheds and quarters for the men.

"You hang back here," said Ned to the others, and road into the empty yard alone. He swung from the saddle and tied the horse to a railing, then, seeing no one about, casually walked up the stairs to the veranda and in the open front door. A cool, dark hallway led into the interior, with rooms coming off on both sides. He headed towards the back of the house, and found the kitchen. A middle-aged woman was kneading dough, and cried out at the sight of him.

"Don't be alarmed," he said. "We aren't here to hurt you. I'm looking for the manager."

"Mr Macauley? He isn't here."

Something was bubbling on the stove. Ned sniffed appreciatively.

"Ah, you're a fine cook, missus, or so my nose is telling me."

She smiled a little, and dusted her white hands on her apron.

"I'd better call my husband."

"What's his name?"

"Mr Fitzgerald. I'm Mrs Fitzgerald, the housekeeper."

"You call him, then. Tell him Ned Kelly is here."

She looked at him, and then disappeared through a door behind her. He could hear her thin voice calling, and the deeper rumbling of a man in reply. Shortly afterwards, a stocky bearded man walked into the kitchen, still chewing on his dinner. He stopped abruptly at the sight of the pistol Ned held loosely by his leg.

"Aye," said Ned. "I just wanted to show you that, so you know we are in earnest. We have no quarrel with you, or any of the workers, but it will go hard for anyone who gets in our way. Understood?"

Fitzgerald nodded. "What do you want?"

"Are you expecting Macauley back for his dinner?"

"We are."

Ned nodded towards the range. "Then I think we'll start with a bite to eat ourselves. And for our horses, too."

While the Fitzgerald's set the table, Ned went out onto the veranda and whistled the others in. Once seated, they set to with a will. It had been a while since they had the luxury of a sit-down meal such as this. Mrs Fitzgerald went back to work, making more dinner for the station hands, who would be arriving soon. When they had finished eating, the gang kept out of sight, watching for them to arrive.

"I think you should know," said Fitzgerald, standing behind Ned, "that if you mean to shoot Mr Macauley down, then I shall have to try to fight you first."

Ned glanced back at the solemn man behind him. "You'd risk dying for him?"

"He's a good man, and doesn't deserve murder."

"Not even if he uses a Blighter to keep everyone working?"

"Ah," said Fitzgerald, nodding, "I thought you might be here because of that."

Just then, a small group of men rode into the yard, sweaty, and covered in dust. They sent their horses off with a stable hand and walked up to the main house, conversing loudly, till the click of a revolver being cocked brought them up short.

"Bail up," said Ned, and their arms went up like a forest.

Each of the stockmen was given a plate of food and then locked into one of the storerooms, the young stable hand too once he had seen to the horses. They took it in good spirit, nudging each other and pointing out the members of the gang. Their fame was spreading.

"Not you," said Ned to Macauley, as he went to get his plate. He gestured outside, and the manager nodded and led the way out into the yard. "Stop," said Ned, and Macauley turned to face the gang. There was a sob behind them, where the housekeeper had appeared, a handkerchief held to her face. "Go back inside, Mrs Fitzgerald." He turned back to the manager. "You know why we're here?"

Macauley nodded. "You're Undead Kelly. I know why you're here. I'm not going to beg. Just do it quick, damn you."

"I haven't decided if I'm going to kill you yet," said Ned. "Show us the Blighter."

Macauley stared at him for a moment, and then led the way over to a huge slab shed. The door was secured with a thick chain and massive padlock. Macauley pulled a key from his pocket.

"They're over in the far corner, in a kind of pen we built..."

"They?" asked Joe.

"Yes. We have two," said the manager. "If you keep your voices down, and don't let them see you, they stay fairly quiet. If they do notice you, well, they get a little upset."

Macauley opened the lock, and pulled the chain free slowly. The door swung open on greased hinges, and he led them through. Light spilled in through the gaps in the slab walls, revealing a mostly empty shed but for an array of leather harnesses and tools. In one corner, some kind of extra walls had been added, and these were covered over by hessian bags tacked all across them.

"They're in there," whispered Macauley, and he stepped lightly and softly across to the pen. He plucked at a corner of bagging, not nailed down, and peeked through, then waved them over. The gang found it impossible not to copy his care, and tiptoed over the wooden floor, and bent to peek through the small gap.

Inside, in the gloom, sat two figures. One was very big, and was sprawled across from them, leaning back against the outer wall. The other was sitting with knees drawn up against the palings to the right. Ned stood longest at the gap, waiting for his eyes to adjust to the poorer light. The smell of dust and sacking filled his nose, but it did not completely cover the stench of corruption coming from inside the pen. He stared at the nearer figure sitting slumped on the floor, a frown suddenly creasing his face as he discerned long raven hair and thin shoulders. He reached up and took hold of the hessian.

"Don't!" cried Macauley.

Ned wrenched the sacking, and a huge sheet of it tore away with a popping noise. The others took his lead, and seized the rest, pulling it away. Light spilled into the pen, built of closely nailed timbers.

"There's a girl in there!" cried Dan. He pointed at the nearer figure, sitting forlornly.

"Get her out!" roared Ned, and he seized hold of one of the boards and heaved at it, the wood splitting as the nails started tearing free. Joe was beside him in an instant, adding his weight, and the first board came free. They grabbed the next. Steve turned and sprinted from the shed.

"What are you doing?" Macauley flung himself on Ned's back, grabbing at his arms.

"You evil fucking bastard," shouted Dan, and he hauled the manager off and levelled him with a punch to his face.

There was a gurgling roar from inside the pen, and the big Blighter sitting across from them came to its feet. It launched across the small space and slammed against the wall of the pen, the force shaking the walls and cracking boards. It thrust its arms through the gap they had made, encircling Joe's waist and pulling at him. Joe cried out as he was slammed against the rough wood, while inches from his face, the thing's teeth gnashed against a gap, unable to reach him. Long dead air escaped from its dried lungs and washed over Joe. He gagged, and vomit sprayed the wood beside him, adding its own sharper acid stench.

Ned grabbed at the Blighter's arms, trying to pull them free, but the dead thing had been a big man in his time, and had that weight still now. Ned felt a clawing at his feet, and glanced down in horror, but it was Macauley grabbing at him, while Dan tried switching between kicking at him and trying to drag him away.

Steve raced in, an iron crow bar in his hands. He ran to the side of the pen, away from where the fight was taking place, and began swiftly levering boards free.

"Ned!" screamed Joe. "Shoot it! Fucking shoot it!"

Ned let go of the Blighter's arm, and drew his revolver. He jammed it up against the wood, but the gap was too small - the bullet would have to tear through too much wood, showering Joe with splinters. He swiftly dropped to his knees and instead, reached through the gap they had made, pressing the barrel into the softness of the thing's stomach.

"Hold on, Joe!" he roared, and fired. He squeezed the trigger rapidly, cycling though six shots in half as many seconds. The first of them shook the Blighter's grip, and Joe tore himself free, falling backwards across Macauley and Dan. Ned's last shots thrust the monster back across the pen. But it kept its feet, and it shook its head, as if trying to understand what had happened. A huge hole had been opened in its side, shattered ribs showing amongst blackened intestine. In the middle sat its stomach, obscenely red and distended.

"Miss!" cried Steve, and he had his whole torso through the gap he had made, his hand reaching towards the girl who had sat as if terrified into stillness the whole time. And now her head came up, the hair falling away from her face, and she reached her arms out toward him, and he cried out and recoiled in horror, for she had no hands, but raw blackened stumps, and her eyes were dead. Steve shoved himself backwards, but his belt became hooked on a nail and push as he might, he was stuck fast in the hole he had made.

"Ned!" he cried.

Ned was up, and running around the corner of the pen towards him, as the female Blighter sprang upon him. Steve desperately got hold of her head as she leaned in to bite, and held her off, arms shaking with the effort. Ned grabbed hold of his feet and threw himself backwards, tearing Steve clear of the Blighter, the hole, and half his clothes in the process.

Joe had his revolver out, but before he could aim, the male blighter charged forward again, this time crashing all the way through the weakened wood. It barrelled into Joe, driving him back, bits of planking crushed between them. Joe tripped and went down, with the Blighter on top of him, his pistol hand trapped between their two bodies, the thing's stained teeth coming for his face. With his left hand, he caught hold of a splintered piece of wood and thrust the point into the Blighter's mouth. His muscles bunched and shook as he held the splinter between them, and the monster, with mindless hunger, bore down upon him, forcing the wood deeper and deeper into its own head. Then Dan was beside, swinging wild kicks.

"Wait!" grunted Joe, but too late, as Dan knocked the Blighter off, the wood stuck in its mouth but not terminally deep. Joe rolled clear, coming up beside Dan as the Blighter rose slowly to its feet, mouth working. "I nearly had it!"

"Sorry! I couldn't see!"

Off to the side, Ned bodily threw Steve aside, and snapped his revolver open, shaking out the tinkling empty cartridges. The female Blighter was crawling through the gap, awful stumps tapping on the wooden flooring, looking like some grotesque giant spider. Ned backpedalled, fishing more bullets from his pocket. He had time to slide two home before she was through and on her feet. He raised the pistol and pulled the trigger - there was a dull click – an empty chamber. She was running at him, and from the side a pistol blazed - Steve on his knees, his own gun held in two hands, firing as she ran. One bullet found its mark, and spun her light frame off its feet. Ned hit the wall behind him hard enough to drive the air from his lungs. He snapped his weapon open again and spun the cylinder to a loaded chamber. The Blighter came up again, mouth gaping in a savage hiss, momentarily torn between Ned and Steve. Steve threw his pistol, striking it in the face, and it came at him with angry violence. Steve fell back, holding his booted feet up in the air to meet her, and as she fell on him, he kicked with the hard soles of his riding boots, breaking her jaw. She grabbed at his leg, trying to bite through the leather of his boot with her largely useless mouth, while he tried to shake her off.

Joe had dragged Dan back against the wall. "Come on!" he screamed. "Come on, you filthy evil bastard!"

The Blighter charged. Joe held Dan by his shirt, "Wait, wait!" - and just as the Blighter was upon them, he thrust Dan one way and he dived the other. The creature crashed into the wall where they had been, and instantly Joe was behind it, trying to ram its head into the wall. "Dan!" he yelled, and Dan added his weight, and grunting they fought the Blighter as it tried to turn to bite them. But they couldn't hold it - it put its hands up against the wall and pushed and spun, and the two men went flying, going down in a tangle of harness and tools stacked near the wall.

Ned cocked his pistol and was over by Steve in three long strides, looking for a clear shot in the tangle of arms and legs. Steve sighed to himself, and held his leg out high and perfectly still. The Blighter fell on it, bringing her hungry mouth down onto the torn remnants of Steve's trousers, and in that quieter moment, Ned pressed the barrel against her temple and pulled the trigger, and the side of her head spattered across the room.

Behind them, Joe came up from the pile of equipment with a shovel in his hands, and as the big male came ploughing in after them, he deftly stepped to the side, swinging the shovel and connecting with the end of the long wooden splinter still lodged in its mouth, driving the point in and up into its brain. With a final gurgle, the Blighter slumped to its knees and crashed sideways onto the floor.

Ned pushed himself up on his feet and stalked to where Macauley lay slumped. He raised the pistol as he came, and the manager just had time to raise an arm weakly, and say, "No!" before Ned squeezed the trigger and the hammer hit home. There was an empty click, and Ned paused, and then raised the pistol with a look of puzzlement. He shook his head, blinked, and thrust the gun back into his belt. Macauley collapsed.

"Boys? Is everyone alright?"

"Yes, Ned," they answered, coming together into the middle of the shed.

"Let's get outside. Into the clean air."

They shoved Macauley before them, and limped outside. Up on the veranda, Mrs Fitzgerald sobbed as she saw the manager pushed to his knees in the dirt. The gang lifted their shirts and pant legs, showing each other their skin in a well-practised drill. Though all were bleeding from cuts and scrapes, none had been bitten by the two Blighters.

"That was a close one," said Dan. Steve nodded emphatically.

"We need to think about this some more," said Joe. "It's very risky. Even with guns."

"We're not giving up," said Ned.

"No. But we could even the odds some more. I've been thinking - the old Chinese bloke I used to live near, Ah Feng, he showed me some books when I was a boy. I couldn't read the writing, of course, but I could look at the pictures. They were about these old wars in China, and there were some pictures of armour. Ned, I reckon we could make some ourselves, to protect us."

"Yes," said Dan, "and maybe everyone in the district could make some... but what would we make it out of?"

"Leather?" asked Steve, pointing to his boots. There were clear teeth marks in them, but they had not been cut through.

"Make ploughshares into swords..." murmured Ned.

"What's that?"

"Boys, we'll talk about it later. Joe, it's a good idea. A very good idea. But right now, we have to decide what we are doing here."

The gang turned to look at Macauley.

"I warned you..." muttered the manager.

"That you did." Ned looked at the others. "It was my fault,

boys. I'm sorry. But when I saw that poor girl, well, she looked just like..."

"Yes," nodded Joe, "I could see it, too." They both glanced at Steve, who nodded solemnly.

"I should have stopped to think that of course, no Blighter was going to sit there with a live girl in there with it."

"I thought maybe it was full."

"Do they ever get full?" asked Dan.

"No," said Macauley, "they're always hungry. But if they can't walk about, and can't see or hear anything, they kind of shut down. That's why I told you to be quiet."

"Shut up!" spat Ned. "It's because they are so bloody dangerous, men like you can't be allowed to keep them like some kind of prize exhibit."

"What shall we do with him?" asked Joe.

Ned stared at Macauley. "The penalty for harbouring Blighters should be death."

"No!" cried Mrs Fitzgerald.

"Death?" asked Macauley. "Aye, well, I suppose the man with the gun gets to make the rules."

"Aye, well, I suppose he must if he wants to stop the men with the money having it all their own way, at the expense of the rest of us."

"Ned," said Dan. "Are we to be executioners now? Killing the undead is one thing, but this?"

"Don't go soft, little brother. Remember these bastards have our own dear ma rotting in gaol..."

"I am remembering her, Ned, and thinking what she would say if she could see you like this. I saw you pull the trigger in there, Ned. Please. There has to be some difference between us and them."

"Let him say his piece," said Joe. "Let him explain why he had them, and then we can decide if he should die."

Steve and Dan nodded, and Ned said to Macauley, "Go on, then. Explain."

"But no pressure, right?" said the manager.

"You made this situation."

"Well, to be fair, it was the owners. Messrs.Younghusband and Lyle."

"Who are they?"

Macauley laughed. "Well, I doubt you would move much in their circles."

"Less lip, you!" shouted Dan.

"They are very wealthy men, but not the sort you would see appearing in the society pages. They keep to themselves. Look, I telegraphed them after we caught the first Blighter-"

"One of these? Or you mean there were more?"

"There was another before these two. One of my boundary riders found it. Got itself caught up in the barbed wire on an outstation. He came and got me, and a whole bunch of us went out to have a look. I mean, we had all heard stories... Well, it was a pretty sad specimen. Don't know how long it had been wandering, or where from, but it was pretty desiccated by the time it got here. Like tanned leather stretched over bone. Anyway, we managed to rope it and pull it off the fence, and I brought it back here. You see, I had an idea, looking at how it just kept standing there, pulling against the wire... If we could work out a way to use them, to harness that energy... I wrote to the owners, letting them know what I had, and explaining my ideas, and they were down here like a shot. They were fascinated by it. We had it chained in that shed, and they wanted to test it by sticking it with a pitchfork, that kind of thing. It had not fear, and felt no pain. Over the next week, we tried rigging up a harness for it, and getting it behind a plough, or a buggy, but it was practically falling apart by then. The owners had to return to Melbourne, but promised me they'd help continue the experiment. They were back in a month, and they brought that big bugger you just killed with them, chained and nailed in a box. They didn't tell me where they got it, and I didn't like to ask. It was much fresher, which meant it was much stronger, and more mobile. And hungrier. We had the devil of a time trying to control it. I tried rigid bars to hold it in place, blinders so it couldn't look sideways, even had one of the younger lads running in front of it, getting it to follow. And it worked - we could get him dragging that plough for hours on end. Not very straight, but these were early days. Can you imagine what this would mean? Unlimited power! You could find ways to harness them in factories, to train carriages... The possibilities..."

"And what about the girl?" asked Ned quietly.

"Ah. Well. I first have to tell you that we worked out how to keep the male Blighter in good repair. If you feed them meat regularly, you slow down the decomposition process."

"What the hell did you feed them?" asked Dan.

"Lamb, mostly. The only thing is, you have to give them their prey live. They aren't as interested if it's already dead. I thought if we could remove their teeth, they'd be safer to work with, but they need them to eat... "

"Ah, Jesus!"

"Now, Messrs. Lyle and Younghusband are intelligent men. They figured that if one appetite remains in place, why not another? They wanted to see if there was another way to get Blighters... Whether it was possible to breed them..."

"Tell me," said Ned, "that girl was already dead before you put her in there with that thing."

"She was! I swear it! We aren't barbarians. But don't you see? This is a new field of science, of agricultural science! We will all be rich!"

"Oh? Promised to share the wealth, did they, the owners? Going to make all the workers part of the company?"

"That's right. How'd you know?"

"Because it's how their kind always corrupts decent working folk. They rub their filthy bloody money all over you and the stench of it infects your brains. Jesus, man, listen to yourself!"

"And what about you, then? Who are you to set yourself up as judge and jury?"

"Don't forget executioner..."

"Ha! Exactly! You ride around, shooting the odd Blighter, and think you are helping people? You think you can win this that way? Blighters are a part of life now, friend. We had better find a way to use them, because there is no getting rid of them now. That ship has sailed."

"Aye, and when was that? You seem to know an awful lot about them. Where did they come from? Did your masters let you in on their dark little secret?"

Macauley frowned. "No one knows for sure. They just started appearing..."

"Macauley, please! You can do better than that!"

"I don't know! If you know, you tell me."

"What happened to the natives who used to live here?"

"What?" The manager frowned. "The natives? They went away..."

"And what drove them away, do you think? What happened that meant all this land was available for your masters to squat on and claim as their own?"

"Oh come now. They wouldn't have... You don't know the gentlemen!"

"Not necessarily your masters, Macauley - but men of their ilk. Did I say 'men'? There are probably better terms than that for them."

Macauley fell silent, staring down at the dust of the yard. He chewed his lip.

"I've heard enough," said Dan. He drew his revolver and stepped forward. "I've changed my mind. I say death it is."

"No." Joe shook his head. "I say no."

Steve looked at Dan, and slowly shook his head.

"Well?" Dan asked Ned.

"I think," said Ned slowly, "I think there is another way. To really hurt the bastards, and not just by cutting the strings on their puppets. You, Macauley, where do you do the banking for the station?"

"Euroa..."

Ned smiled broadly. "So there it is. Boys, once Mr Macauley here has been kind enough to write us a big fat cheque, we'll go and make a withdrawal."

"That's theft."

"No, that's compensation."

Macauley was propelled into his office inside the station house, and compelled to write out a suitably large amount. He was then taken and shoved inside the storeroom with the other men. Joe was picked to stay and stand guard, since they didn't want to risk Mrs Fitzgerald letting them out early, but neither did they feel it was right locking the old girl up. They all had mothers, after all.

"Don't worry about me," said Joe, sitting back on the veranda and filling his pipe. "But you boys be careful."

They took one of the station's carts for the journey into town. Dan suggested they find the Blighter harness and have Macauley pull them to Euroa himself, but Ned said the whole point of taking the cart was to be less inconspicuous, not more.

"But we can have a go at putting him through his paces when we get back, if you like."

It was mid-afternoon when they pulled into town. The bank was situated on a corner, just up from the railway station. While there was a police station in town too, they weren't unduly worried as it was only staffed by a single trooper. Steve sat with the cart, keeping the horses quiet, as Ned and Dan walked up to the closed door. Through the frosted glass, they could make out two tellers sitting behind the counter, heads buried in their ledgers. Ned rapped at the glass. The two men looked up, and one pointed up at the clock mounted on the wall. Ned knocked again, and waved the cheque. The figures appeared to confer, and then one slid off his stool and came over to the door, opening it a few inches.

"Sorry, gents, bank is closed for the afternoon."

"I just have this cheque here to cash," said Ned. "Won't take you long."

"Sorry, all the cash is locked away for the day. We can't access it."

"Who can?"

"Only the manager, Mr Scott."

"Well, go get him then."

"You can see him tomorrow morning." The teller went to close the door. Ned stuck his foot in the way. The teller looked down at it in surprise.

"You don't understand. I'm Ned Kelly, and we're coming in."

Ned gave the door a shove, and the teller stumbled back. The two brothers quickly stepped through and closed the door behind them. They drew their pistols.

"Let's discuss customer service, shall we?"

"What the devil is going on?" A middle-aged man appeared from a door at the back of the room. Ned waved his pistol.

"A withdrawal. You Mr Scott?"

The man went pale, but he managed a slight nod. "Don't shoot me. Oh my dear wife..."

"Don't worry, she isn't a widow yet. Just do as we say. I have a generous cheque here from Mr Macauley, out on Faithfulls

Creek station. If you would be so good as to cash it, we'll be on our way."

The manager, Scott, appeared frozen. Ned lost patience and strode over to him, taking his hand and stuffing the cheque into it. "Now get to it."

With shaking hands, the manager pulled a ring of keys from his pocket and they followed him to the safe. It took him several attempts to line the key up properly and get it in the keyhole. The safe door swung open on oiled hinges.

"Oh," said Ned.

"Ned! So much cash!"

Scott reached in, and counted out in notes the amount written on the cheque. There was a lot of cash left. Ned licked his lips, and glanced at Dan, who swallowed, and nodded.

"You may as well throw in all the rest," said Ned thickly.

The tellers fetched some bags, and the notes were duly stacked inside, and they all helped carry them out to the cart, where a nervous Steve Hart sat. His eyes bugged when he saw how many bags they were carrying.

"What about them?" asked Dan. "Lock 'em in?"

Ned shook his head. "I reckon they'd be discovered too quick. Let's take them back to the station with us. Come on boys, all aboard."

The two tellers hopped onto the back of the cart, perching amongst the money bags and hugging their knees. The manager hesitated. "Um, my wife is expecting me back shortly..." He gestured to the upstairs of the bank, where his living quarters were situated.

"More the merrier," said Ned, and soon they were trotting back to the station, with the addition of a confused Mrs Scott, a toddler in her arms. Joe was sitting where they had left him.

"Let's have everyone out," said Ned.

Their prisoners were gathered on the veranda and told to

watch while Steve and Dan dragged various pieces of harness, some covered in blackened blood, from the shed. Macauley was called down, and he stood stiffly while the gang fussed over cinching him into the straps he himself had devised. There was a leather helmet with blinkers, and a pitted wooden bit to go between his teeth. The manager clenched his jaw.

"Now go on and be a good boy," said Ned. "Open wide."

There were grumblings from some of the men on the veranda, but Joe had the shotgun trained on them and no one moved.

"You have your sympathies all wrong," Ned told them. "You don't understand what is going on here..."

"Ned." Steve has pointing into the distance. Back towards Euroa, there was a haze of dust in the air. "Horses coming."

"Damn it. Alright, everyone back inside. Explanations will have to wait for another day."

They pushed their collection of hostages back inside the storeroom and locked the door.

"Now, Missus," Ned said to Mrs Fitzgerald. "Don't you go opening that door for three hours."

The housekeeper nodded grimly. "I give me word."

The gang trooped outside, raiding the station gun cabinet on the way. They were able to increase their arsenal with another pair of rifles and a shotgun.

"Mr Kelly?" Mrs Fitzgerald had followed them outside. "I want you to know I think you have a black heart, Edward Kelly."

Ned nodded. "Seems fitting, Mrs Fitzgerald. But if I had the time, I'd make you see that circumstance makes the man."

He tipped his hat to her, and they rode off.

A little later, they clattered into the farmer's yard. He stood squinting as Ned dismounted, carrying over one of the bags of money.

"Compensation," he said, holding it aloft. The farmer's face split into a gap-toothed grin. "Now, you must keep in mind that we can't give it all to you, lovely as that would be. There are a lot of people hurting out there. So I'm asking you to think carefully - how many chickens did you lose?"

The farmer nodded seriously. "Two dozen."

Ned frowned, but counted out a fair price. But as he swung back into the saddle, the farmer called out, "Oh, Mr Kelly? I think I made a mistake..."

Ned smiled at Dan as the farmer jogged over and stood by his stirrup.

"It were nearer three dozen, actually..."

NINETEEN

"You're smiling," said Ned.

"And it isn't easy," I said, pulling my nearly empty bottle of laudanum from my pocket. "I'm in a lot of pain. Though this does help..."

"Care to share the joke?"

"I'm not laughing at you, I promise you. It's just... humans. Things are always more complicated than they appear, aren't they? And people are just so basically...fallible. Even you."

"Me?"

"Yes. Taking all the money. How much did you end up keeping yourselves?"

"Some. We did give a lot of it away. Helping people get back on their feet. Giving them the means to buy arms so they could defend themselves. Of course, then the authorities claimed we were arming the population to bring on a revolution, and started locking up anyone who looked like they were supporting us."

"Is that when Maggie's husband was arrested?"

"That came a bit later, but yes, he was caught up in it. Shall we continue?"

"Actually, I think I need to go. I'm feeling pretty wretched.

And you don't look so good yourself. Are you cold?" I had noticed Ned shivering.

"I'm just feeling a bit... unwell. Come back tomorrow?"

"Of course. I have to hear how this all finishes."

"How this all finishes..."

"I meant, the events leading up to your capture. Glenrowan. I want to hear about that."

He nodded, eyes going distant. What did he see?

"Actually, there is one more errand I'd like to take care of today, and I think you may be able to help. Do you know where I can get some ammunition?"

He looked at me. "You have a gun? Really?"

"Don't look so surprised. How do you think I stopped my friends in Beechworth from stomping me to death?"

"Do you know who they were, RM?"

I shrugged, and began the slow process of dragging myself to my feet. As well as my cracked ribs and bruises, all my other muscles seemed to have set like cement. "My guess is your committal didn't quite go to plan, thanks to me. I assume someone was trying to make sure I wouldn't be readily available for your actual trial back here."

"Be careful, RM. There is a lot riding on this. We need to make sure it all comes out at the trial."

"All those reporters, yes, I know. Foreign press, too, here for the Exhibition. So... bullets?"

"Go to Rosiers," Ned said with laugh. "On Elisabeth Street. But for God's sake, don't say Ned sent you."

"What's the joke?"

"Oh, Tom and Maggie got some ammunition from him for us. You see, getting guns was easy enough, but we never seemed to have enough cartridges. And we had trouble getting hold of them in Benalla and Beechworth. So Tom and Maggie came in on the train and spun some story about a hunting trip, and bought a good big lot for us. Rosier had everything but shells for one of the rifles we picked up, and told them to come back later. Luckily, Maggie smelled a rat, and they took what they had and left. We found out later that Rosier went straight to the police and they had the place staked out that whole afternoon. It would be nice to think he got the chance to help us out again, in however small a way."

I left Ned sitting amid the refuse of his cell, and limped back to the gate. I ran into Quinn, the senior warder on the way out, and barked at him to be sure to replace the furniture in Kelly's cell immediately, or I would make it my business to ensure the whole city knew they had him sleeping on the cold floor. Quinn looked at me venomously, but shouted for the warders to get busy and fetch a new cot.

Outside, I limped my way slowly down La Trobe, then turned onto Elisabeth Street. I didn't have the shop number, but made my way south towards the river, and found it located at number sixty-six. 'JW Rosier', said the sign out the front, 'gun-maker.' I pushed open the door, and a small bell rang above my head. The shop was narrow, but quite deep, and the air was heavy with the smell of steel and gun oil. The walls were lined with dozens of rifles and shotguns.

"Be right with you, sir!" called a heavyset man from behind the far end of the counter. He had the dour look of a Scottish Presbyterian minister. This would be Rosier, then.

I drifted along the racks, and saw that as well as the usual assortment of sporting pieces, and solid farmer's guns, Rosier had an array of military firearms as well. Sniders, Martini Henrys, even Prussian needleguns. I stopped to look at an odd looking shotgun lying on the bench.

"Now, how can I help?" asked the man, coming down to stand before me on the other side of the counter. He picked up the gun off the counter and went to put it away.

"Interesting looking shotgun," I said.

"I doubt you would be interested in this piece, sir. Now, something for hunting, is it? Fowling piece?"

I gestured at the gun in his hands. "May I?"

He hesitated, and then handed it over. I looked at it curiously. It wasn't a shotgun at all.

"My own design," he said after a moment. "Double barrelled rifle. Fifty calibre."

I whistled. "Get many elephants in these parts, do you?"

He scowled, and held his hands out for the gun. I handed it back, and he stooped and tucked it away in a cupboard.

"Sell many of those?"

"Special orders," he said, "for the police."

I nodded. "They look just the thing for..." I stopped, and he looked at me, frowning. "Well," I continued, "it is actually ammunition I am after. For this." I dug around in my valise and pulled out my derringer.

"Ah," he said, "your wife's?"

Bastard.

"Mine, actually. It misfired recently and the cartridge is stuck."

He took it from me, snapping it open and inspecting it closely. "Yes, I see." He shuffled to a workbench, and put on a pair of spectacles. With some needle nosed pliers, he pulled the offending cartridge free and studied it, no doubt noting its cheapness. He worked the action a few time, then tinkered some more. "It's a little better. It's the second chamber. If you leave it with me, I can fix it properly."

"I'd rather not. I'm...uh... heading out of town. The first chamber will work?"

"Yes. And the second should. Come out the back."

I had no choice, as he went off, taking my pistol with him, and a box of shells he pulled off a shelf. There was a small kitchen out the back, a storeroom, and then a heavy back door that opened onto a small yard surrounded by high brick walls. There were a series of simple targets set up against the far wall. He loaded the derringer, squinted down the barrel, and quickly jerked the trigger twice, the reports echoing around us.

"Works fine!" I said, eyeing one of the targets, which now had a couple of extra holes in it. He was a good shot.

"That time," he said. "But the second chamber is likely to misfire again, I warn you."

I had spotted something off to the side. "What do you think of the sight?" I asked him. "Is it true?"

"It's just a simple sight," he grumbled. "Not much can go wrong with it. Not like you'd do much distance shooting with this anyway..."

But he dutifully started reloading and lining up with the target again. I walked quickly over to a pile of wooden boards stacked against the wall, about six feet long and three wide, riddled with bullet holes. I pulled the first one back, and saw a rough human shape sketched on it in charcoal. There weren't many facial features - except for a mouthful of teeth like daggers. Usually, when practising on a man-shaped target, the shooter is encouraged to aim at the body. In this case, the majority of the bullet holes were grouped around the head.

"What are you doing?"

I dropped the board back and swung around guiltily. "Nothing. Just looking..."

"Well, don't. That's none of your business." He stared at me, and, guessing we were done, I headed back into the building and through to the store, feeling his eyes on the back of my head the whole way. He wrapped the box of bullets in brown paper, and placed it and the derringer in front of me. The simple trans-actions of business seemed to calm him, and he asked, "You are sure I can't interest you in a more... useful pistol?" He gestured to a case of Colts and Webleys.

"I'm content with this," I said, counting out some notes. I put the pistol in one pocket, and the bullets in the other, and then picked up my bag. "Rosier. French, isn't it?"

He glared at me. "English."

I nodded, sporting my best unconvinced expression, and took my leave. It was late afternoon, and I was feeling sick and sore, and home - such as it was - seemed a long way away. It was definitely a cab day. Thankfully, I did not have long to wait before an empty one came by, and I sank gratefully back into the cracked upholstery for the ride back to Fitzroy. I even paid the cabbie with a real sense of gratitude, and was also happy to be able to enter the house and creak up the stairs without feeling the need to hide from Mrs Mackie.

My room was a mess, things thrown about from when I left... what, three days ago? Seemed longer. A lot had happened. I sank onto my unmade bed and pulled my bottle from my pocket, but it was practically empty. I drained what there was, even sticking my tongue into the neck to get what I could. Then, with sudden inspiration, I threw my door open and crossed to Rawson's, and knocked sharply upon it.

"What? What's that?" came his voice from within.

"Rawson, it's me."

The door opened, revealing my florid neighbour. He was unshaven, his collar open and suspenders hanging loose.

"Well, well! Haven't seen you in a bit, old mate... Jesus, what happened to you?"

"Long story. Look, I need your help..."

"Anything, old mate, anything. Come in!" He stepped back, but his room smelled worse than mine. "I've just been... learning my lines."

"Do you know where I can get some more of this?" I handed

him my bottle, which he took and held at arm's reach, squinting at the label, then opened and sniffed.

"I don't think you ought to be mucking around with this, old chap. Come and have some wine instead."

"I'll buy you a bottle of red if you can tell me where to get more of this."

He rubbed his jaw, whiskers rasping, and nodded. I was wrong when I was talking to Ned - some people are easy to understand. There was a boy - Italian, I think - who lived downstairs with his family. Rawson used him for errands, and now hollered down the stairwell for him. I don't know why, but Mrs Mackie never complained about the noise Rawson made. I wondered if perhaps they had a closer relationship than I realised - but would she really choose him over me? The idea was depressing. The boy bounded up the stairs, and Rawson gave him my money and a folded slip of paper. I had to listen to another ten minutes of the actor's lies about his career, and then the boy returned, a dark red bottle for Rawson, and a smaller rectangular bottle for me. I thanked them both and retreated into my room, pulling the stopper free and taking a swig. The sharp edge of pain that had been sawing at me dulled, grew distant. I set the bottle down, kicked off my boots, and swung my feet up onto the bed.

I dreamed.

I was back in London, or some dreary shire - Oxford or Cambridge - in a ballroom at night. The room was packed, and stuffy. I leaned against a wall, my collar too tight, sharp elbows of jabbering matrons poking me in the ribs as they cackled with each other. The floor was full of couples; it looked like one of those tedious coming out balls at the start of a season, when the next crop of pale, timid leeches would be powdered and sprayed and sent hunting to snare a suitable income. It was the sort of event my father would drag me to, and I had long ago learned the only way to make it bearable, was to take a small pipe of opium before I went. Just enough to take the edge off, not enough to be reduced to a drooling buffoon - though, really, who would notice - or else I'd most likely cop a flogging from Father. All the way there in the coach I would have his yellow teeth barking at me, "Why can't you..." and "You had better..."

As I stood there now, head spinning, I felt in my pocket but groaned to find I was without my pipe. I craned my neck, pulling at my collar, my back wet with sweat, and realised I was looking about for Maggie. But of course she would not be here, this was England. And then I spied a vapid pale bloodsucker coming my way, pale eyes fixed hungrily upon me, and somehow at the urging and shoving of the matrons about me, I was forced into her arms and out onto the floor. She stared at me, her eyes without a spark, and I shivered as I took her cold bony fingers in mine. The music reeled, and we spun amongst the dancers, and all the while she stared at me. I tried glancing about the room to lessen the tension of it, but the sight of all that tightly buttoned lust and desperation was sickening to me, so I instead tried drawing her closer, so my head was beside hers. Her hair smelled of cloying powder.

The music took on a discordant note, and at once, I began to be buffeted by other dancers. At first, it was just a bump or two, the sort of thing that naturally happened when the room was too small for the company, but then the impacts grew heavier, knocking me hard, and I finally turned to snarl a warning. And then I saw that what I had taken for dancing was an orgy of monstrous eating. Each pair that I had taken to be dancers were in fact pairs of Blighters, locked together in unholy embraces, each tearing at the other with their savage teeth, taking chunks of flesh from cheeks and noses. And through the middle of this charnel house, I danced, till I felt a peculiar pull at my shoulder, and turned my head to see my awful partner was undead as well, and gnawing on my flesh. I screamed and tried to thrust her from me, but we were held tight in that monstrous pack, and she gripped me with inhuman strength. I punched at her, and wrenched, to no avail, and then realised there was only one way to make her stop, and in savage desperation, sunk my head and closed my teeth around the soft grey flesh of her throat-

I woke.

Jesus fucking Christ.

Oh Maggie...

I awoke feeling perfectly wretched. My body had seized into a tangled collection of pain. One would have thought you would start to feel better a couple of days later, not worse, but it was like the more my muscles and tissue considered the assault, the more they tightened in outrage. My mouth was dry and disgusting, and when I tottered over to my sideboard, trailing blankets, I found no water in my jug. My bladder was screaming at me, too, but rather than use my pot, I took my jug and staggered downstairs and through to the privy out the back of the house. I set the jug outside before entering the ammonia-reeking outhouse, and sighed happily as my internal pressure eased. There was an old pump in the backyard, and I stuck my head under it and gasped as a few pulls sent a jet of cold water gushing over me. I scrubbed at my face - God, I needed a proper shave - and then made my way slowly back up to my room.

I neatened myself up as best I could, but was aware that I was beginning to look more like my surroundings - down at heel, working class. I would have to find a tailor I had not visited yet and procure some new clothes. My finances were starting to run low again, but money from Father should have been appearing in my account shortly. I needed cheering up, and coffee, and bacon. I heard the Robert Burns put on a good breakfast.

Of course, I was going to see Maggie. I had seen how my bruises looked in the mirror in my room, and, if I was honest, hoped that they may awaken some sympathy in her. Assuming, of course, that it wasn't her who had set the ruffians upon me. I wanted to catch her before she went out, so it made sense to head straight there.

It seemed a full stomach was in order, so I did indeed have breakfast first. A layer of bacon fat and toast did wonders for my queasy insides, and several hot coffees began to awaken my brain from its drugged fug.

Feeling far surer of myself, I breezed through to the reception area of the hotel and talked the old chap there into telling me which room Mrs Skillion was staying in. The stairs leading up to the next floor reminded me of my physical state. The air seemed to change, too, become thicker somehow, and not just from the musty staleness of the hallway - spilled beer and tobacco smoke. I couldn't force enough into my lungs. I waded through it to the door of her room, and, unbidden, the memory of our last time together crawled into my mind.

I do not want to think about this.

It was nothing. A turn, that's all. Don't judge me based on one stupid moment.

I rested my forehead against the door, and fancied I could feel her life force behind that thin layer of wood. Was she sleeping? Or dressing? Or even sitting there now, waiting? Could she feel me here on the other side, and was even now rising and rushing forward, like magnets-

"Don't do it."

I turned. Tom Lloyd was there, standing in the doorway of the next room down. He shook his head, and held a finger up to his lips. I stared at him, and slowly raised my hand, fist ready to pound on the door. Go on, my posture said, what are you going to do? But instead of coming for me, he sagged back against the doorway, and he shook his head again, more in sorrow than in command. I let my hand fall. He stood upright, and motioned me to his room. I surreptitiously brushed my pocket with my fingers, feeling the comforting weight of the derringer, then left Maggie's doorway and walked past him into his room.

It was very tidy. Too tidy, as if he was scared to touch anything in there, which he probably was, the stupid country bumpkin. He closed the door quietly behind us, and we faced each other.

"Christ. What happened to you?"

I touched my puffed and tender face. "Bet you wish you did it."

He snorted once.

"Look, do you mind if I sit down?" Without waiting for an answer, I sank into an armchair. He remained standing. "I had some trouble in Beechworth. I was half thinking you set them on me."

He shook his head. "I'm a man who takes care of his own business. If I wanted you beaten, I'd beat you myself. But Maggie told me to leave you alone..."

At the mention of her name, my eyes flicked to the wall dividing the rooms, a movement he couldn't help but notice.

"Just leave her alone, can't you?"

"I..." I said. I what? "What... What did she say?"

"Not much. Just that she wanted nothing more to do with you, that I was right about you being a wrong 'un, but I was to leave you be. She said you were your own worse punishment."

Quite the judge of character.

"I need to talk to her..."

"No, you don't." He came and sat on the bed, leaning forward with his elbows on his knees, staring at me intently.

"Think about it. Just think about it for a minute. What kind of future do you think you have together, even if she wanted to be with you? Are you planning on taking her back to Sydney when all this is over? Or England? Do you think she would be happy so far from her family? Jesus, her ma is in prison here."

"And her husband," I put in acidly.

"And what about her children? You know she has children, right? Are you going to be a father to them?"

Me?

"You haven't thought this through at all. I can see it in your face."

"Maybe you just want me out of the picture, eh, Lloyd? So you can have a clear run yourself?"

He winced at my rising volume, and gestured at me to keep it down.

"It's not a competition," he said.

"Looks like a three way race to me," I snarled. "You, me, her poor bloody husband... Oh, and we may as well add Gaunson in too..." I stopped. He was gently shaking his head.

"I'm already with her."

"What do you mean?"

"I mean, we're living together. Now. We spend our nights together in her room. I dress in here. She's with me, and I'm taking care of her."

"Her husband..." I choked out.

"Doesn't want anything to do with her or her family. Once he's out of jail, we won't be seeing a sight of him."

I noticed I was wringing my hands. I thrust them into my pockets instead.

Ah. What do we have here...

"This has been tremendous hard for her. And she likes to carry on like she's strong, and she is, but under all that, all that flashness, there's... a little girl. And I care for her deeply.

So I don't want anything making it worse for her. Including you."

The distance between us is short.

"You seem like a... like a gentleman. So I'm asking for your word that you will let her be. Let me take care of her..."

He fell silent, his big head tilted forward.

Now might I do it, pat.

Why not? So easy to slide my hand out of my pocket, and just show him what I am holding... Almost like an experiment, just to see what might happen. Would he launch himself at me? Or stare in disbelief, or cry and beg? Wet himself? A simple act and there would be no Tom Lloyd with Maggie. And then... And then...

Her pale, still body.

An open well.

Monster.

I stood. I strode to the door without a backwards glance. I was through it, and down the hall, and I didn't look at her door once. Didn't look to see if it was cracked open. Down the stairs and out onto the street. Turned right towards the city. Walking, feet pounding the pavement.

I don't know why I didn't shoot him. I don't know what it was. But it wasn't mercy, I know that.

TWENTY

"Where were we?" Ned did not look too good. His cell was back in order, and he was in his customary place, sitting on his bed with his legs stretched out before him. He appeared a little feverish to me, something about his eyes. But then, I didn't look good either, and had no doubt my eyes were a little dilated from the laudanum.

"You had taken up bank robbery."

A ghost of a smile crossed his face. "Ah, yes. There was another after that. Jerilderie. That was good sport. They had a police station with two troopers. We bailed them up first and locked them in their own cell, and then Dan and I dressed in their uniforms and walked around town. No one said anything, which shows just how unfriendly troopers generally are. We called in on the bank and took about two thousand pounds."

I must have made some involuntary noise, because he glanced across at me. "It wasn't for us to keep and spend, Remittance Man. It was to fund the fight. We used that money to buy more ammunition and guns. I bought my repeating carbine with that. Ridiculously dangerous gun – sometimes all six chambers can go off at once, but we were always looking to increase our firepower."

"You didn't think about expanding the gang, in that case?"

"Well," he said, "there was Aaron. He was always there on the edge of things. Ended up playing a much larger role than any of us thought he would - him included, I suspect."

"So what did happen with him?"

"He was living on a run not far from Joe's ma. Nice little place. He would have been much better off if he'd just focussed on farming that, instead of pushing himself forward as he did. Well. We'd been using him occasionally, for messages and such. And Joe dropped in on him for a drink and a pipe when he could. Anyway, after Jerilderie, I got it into my head I wanted to tell my side of the story to the people. I wrote out a letter, with Joe's help, explaining how the government had unleashed the Blighted on the Aboriginal people, and how the Blighters were now spreading slowly into settled areas. Joe suggested I give it to Aaron, so he could feel part of things... So I got it to him and told him to take it to a newspaperman."

"And was it published?"

"Jesus Christ! The rotten fucker!"

The fire exploded in sparks and ash as Ned kicked it savagely. The other three leapt away, trying to cover their tin mugs of tea with their hands. Maggie stood, biting her lip while holding White Foot's bridle.

"Now, Ned," said Joe, "could you not go kicking the fire to death again?"

"Don't you start!" Ned stabbed a finger at him. "I know he's your mate, Joe, though God only knows why apart from habit. Look at this!"

He shook the crumpled newspaper he held in his hand.

"Anyone could have changed your letter. Why would Aaron do that?"

"But it isn't just that, Joe," said Dan. "What about Euroa? How did the police turn up so quick? And then again at Jerilderie, they were right behind us again."

"And further back," said Ned, "Stringybark? The whole of the Wombat Ranges, and troopers turn up at Stringybark?"

"Well, maybe he wasn't careful enough. Maybe he sometimes drinks a bit too much and says the wrong thing in the wrong company..."

"Maybe," said Ned. "Maybe he's a damned traitor."

Joe frowned, shaking his head. "But Aaron... I... I just can't..."

"Well, go see him," said Maggie. "Go and hear what he has to say."

"Why not?" asked Joe. "Why not give him a chance to explain, to answer to all of it?"

Ned nodded. "We'll have to be careful. We'll have to go at night. I don't want to be ambushed. But we'll do it. We'll hear what he has to say."

The others nodded. Joe stepped away, but Ned stopped him with a hand on his arm.

"But Joe - if we don't like what he says? If he is a turncoat?"

"Then I'll shoot the bastard myself."

They waited till later in the day, then rode for Aaron's property, timing the journey so that the most risky legs would be under the cover of darkness. They went well armed, in case of encounters with either troopers or Blighters. At Ned's insistence, they stopped at the closest cabin to Aaron's and compelled the owner, a German named Weekes, to come with them. They dismounted some distance from the small hut, noting the subdued light of a lamp within. Steve was designated to watch the horses, and the other three frogmarched Weekes up to the door.

With Joe digging a shotgun into his back, Weekes called out, "Aaron! Aaron, I must talk mit you!"

There was a pause, and then Weekes called out again. "Aaron! Help me, I am lost!"

Again they waited, then a faint voice from inside said, "Go away."

Ned leaned over and hissed in Weekes' ear. The German nodded. "Iz there a problem, Aaron? Iz there anyone else in there viz you? Aaron?"

"Go away..."

Ned and Joe exchanged a look, and Joe shoved the German aside. Together they strode up and banged on the door.

"Aaron! It's Joe! Open the bloody door!"

"Joe?"

There was the sound of something toppling over, and a curse, and then the door cracked open, pale light within silhouetting Aaron, shivering and wrapped in a blanket. "Joe... Jesus!"

Spotting Ned and Dan, and the guns, Aaron grabbed the door and tried to slam it closed, the blanket dropping from his shoulders, revealing his shirt plastered wetly to his body. Joe stuck his foot in the way, and Ned leaned past to give the door a mighty kick. Aaron was sent sprawling inside, dragging a chair down with him. There was a shriek from within.

The gang poured in, weapons at the ready, but there was only Aaron lying gasping on the floor, and a pale teenage girl standing in the corner, holding her hands over her mouth. The room was rank with the smell of fever and corruption.

"Jesus, girl. Go home to your ma," said Ned. "This is no place for you."

"No. She's my wife," rasped Aaron.

"Wife? For God's sake, Aaron, she's a child."

Joe reached down with one hand and hauled Aaron up, helping him back to his cot, which was dishevelled and stained. "What in hell is going on, Aaron? What's wrong with you?"

"Take his shirt off," said Ned.

Joe looked at him, then, grimacing, grabbed a handful of Aaron's shirt and wrenched it up and over his head, tearing the cloth as he did so. Aaron howled, and the girl collapsed in tears.

"I didn't know what to do!" sobbed the girl. "I ain't seen nothing like it!"

Aaron held his arm, gingerly, gasping. There was a hideous wound on his forearm, blackened and weeping. Bright red blood trickled where a scab had been torn away. The wound stank. Dark, straining veins showed on Aaron's pale emaciated body, crossing his chest and limbs like a spider's web.

"Bitten," said Ned, and his rifle arced up into place.

"Wait," said Joe thickly, and he pushed Ned back a little. He placed his shotgun on the table, and righted a chair next to the cot. He sat. "Aaron... Aaron, what's happened?"

Aaron looked at him, and then squeezed his eyes shut as tears leaked down his face. His breathing was fast and high in his chest. He shook his head. "You won't understand..."

"Talk to me. It's me, Joe."

A shrill laugh burst from the sick man. "But you're with him! You're always with him! It used to be you and me... but then he came along, and you liked him better. You always liked him better..."

Ned snorted, and Joe shot him a look. Aaron stared at Ned over Joe's shoulder. "There he is. Mr Undead Kelly himself. Come to put a bullet in my brain." He started crying anew.

"No one," started Joe, then faltered, looking at Aaron's mutilated arm. "No one is going to..."

"Don't shoot me," whispered Aaron. "Oh, Joe."

"What happened? Who did this to you?"

"Hare. It was Hare..."

They met in Benalla, seemingly by chance.

In fact, chance played little part in it. Hare had inherited old Nicholson's plan of wooing an informer, and had noticed Sherrit previously, as part of the Greta Mob, and filed his face away in his memory. Discrete inquiries around town had provided a name, and so when he saw Sherrit skulking about one day, he engineered a meeting. Seeming to bump into Aaron on the sidewalk, he got to talking with him, coaxing the young man out of his initial reticence, and eventually invited him for a drink.

Aaron paused long enough to lick his dry lips, and then agreed. He hesitated at the door of O'Learys, the amount of polished wood inside giving him pause. But Hare jollied him through and over to a discrete table away from the windows, and Sherrit was impressed with how the waiters knew Hare and the deferential attention they gave him, and Aaron by extension. And he was impressed, though he wouldn't have admitted it, by Hare's easy way with them, and with him as well.

He suddenly found himself halfway through a second beer, and talking about horses, with Steve Hart's name in his mouth...

"Go on," said Hare. He took an unhurried sip of his own beer, smacking the foam off his moustache with relish.

"I was just going to say that he - Steve - is one of the best riders you'll see in these parts. If you want to see good riding."

"Ah," said Hare, "but will I? Will I get the chance to see him?"

Aaron shrugged, spinning his beer glass around on the wet polished wood of the table.

"Such a shame. To have such a promising young man mixed up with... well, you know who I mean."

Aaron swallowed hard, keeping his eyes down. Here it comes, he thought. Here comes the question.

"Well," said Hare, draining his glass in one long swallow, "best be getting back to it. No, take your time, Aaron. Don't rush it on my account. See you around."

And he walked out, leaving Sherrit sitting puzzled and almost wishing the conversation had continued.

After that, they seemed to run into each other more frequently. Hare always had a friendly smile, but he was discrete, never doing it in such a public place that Aaron should feel nervous about who was watching.

Then one day, Aaron may have let slip that he had some information, and was wondering if it could be made worth his while to talk. Hare left him in no doubt that would be the case. And so, parties of armed police were able to focus their attention on the Wombat Ranges, rather than beating the bush across the whole region.

That night, Aaron drank himself into a stupor, and in his drunken state, before he passed out, punched himself in the head repeatedly, over and over: "Stupid! Stupid! Stupid!"

The next day, afflicted with a crippling hangover, and half expecting to be shot down at any moment, he paid his first call on Maggie, Ellen, and the rest, and in a gushing need to atone, worked hard for them, cutting firewood and wiring up felled fence posts. And as he drank deep mouthfuls of water brought to him by the girls, felt his fear and guilt start to melt away, and he pictured what life would be like if he could live like this, the king amongst the maidens, and he felt a happiness that was all too foreign to him.

And once the first piece of information had been given, it was easy to give the next. And so on. And there was something to be said for the feeling a bloke got in his chest when the super-intendent came asking for his advice about where else to look. That was a feeling worth bottling. And so, more opportunities to feel it had to be created.

We could set a watch on Joe Byrne's house, he suggested. Where his old ma is living. Joe was always soft for his ma, he'd be sure to come calling on her sometime. Probably at night.

And so a watch was set - Aaron and a squad of troopers, hiding out in the bush around the Byrne property. It was winter, and icy cold in the bush, but Aaron never much minded the cold, and enjoyed the comparative discomfort of the troopers, swearing beneath their blankets and furs. They never saw a hide of Joe or any of the others, but Aaron didn't mind. He didn't give it much thought, but he knew that once the gang was caught, his usefulness was at an end. Oh yes, he was a realist enough to know that Hare would never treat him the same after. It wasn't like they could become friends...

One night, Hare came to check on how the trap was going. Aaron heard him blundering about in the dark, and smiled to himself at the superintendent's lack of bushcraft.

"Where the hell is Sherrit?" he heard Hare ask.

"Dunno, sir," came the mournful reply from a trooper, teeth chattering. "He's around 'ere somewhere. Disappears like a bloody black, that one."

"Sherrit? Sherrit?" Hare's hisses carried through the cold night air as loudly as if he were shouting.

"I'm here," said Aaron, standing up from behind the log he had partially dug himself under.

"Jesus!" said Hare, and then tramped over. He squinted at Aaron. "Don't you have a coat? Or a blanket?"

"I don't mind the cold."

Hare shook his head. "You're a tough one." He turned and stared at the Byrne house in the distance, a patch of deeper darkness in the gloom. "Hope the bloody Kelly's are as cold. What about it, Aaron? Are they as tough as you?"

"Oh, I could lick the two young ones, Dan and Steve," said Aaron. "And I could always beat Joe, ever since we was kids."

"And what about Ned?"

"Ned... Ned's different. There's not many can beat Ned."

"Well, I certainly aim to."

Aaron said nothing.

"You don't think I can? Well, I have a secret weapon." Aaron saw Hare's teeth gleam in the darkness.

After an hour or so, Hare left them to it. But Joe and the gang didn't come that night, and not long after Mrs Byrne herself found them. She would suddenly appear in her doorway and yell out into the night, "He's not here, you idiots. Go and get warm somewhere. Or stay and catch your death of cold, see if I care." And after that, the trap was dissolved.

Then came news of the murders at Stringybark.

He rode into Benalla in some trepidation. And he was right to worry. This was a different Hare who met him. There was something reptilian and cold about the way his heavy lids came down over his eyes. He barely nodded to Aaron, then suggested they take a walk. He led the way along the street, more publicly than before, and Aaron was left to jog to catch up, glancing around nervously to see who may be watching. Hare led him to the police station, but instead of entering, they walked around the back, and up behind the outbuildings to a lone shed right at the rear. Somewhere along the way, a sergeant had fallen into step behind them. At the door to the shed - secured with a large padlock - Hare stopped and spun around.

"I'm going to need more, Aaron."

"Superintendent, I tell you all I know, honestly."

"All? Hmm. I wonder." Hare felt in his pocket and retrieved

a key. Aaron watched him insert it into the lock and turn it with a snap.

"If I'd known exactly where they were, I'd have told you, I swear."

"Well, Aaron, the thing is, generalities aren't cutting it anymore. I've had three troopers killed and another, well, rendered useless. Combined, that doesn't make me look very good. I need specifics. I need detail. I have a special train standing by and a plan in place. But I need to know exactly where they are."

"I don't know more than I'm telling you..."

"Then you'll find out more."

He laughed. "They aren't going to trust me with more information. Ned always keeps me at arm's length..."

"Then you'll have to find a way to get closer." Hare pushed the door open. It was dark and gloomy inside. A stench rolled out of the windowless interior, forcing Aaron back a step. He bounced off the sergeant, who was standing right behind him. He put a hand over his mouth.

"What is in there? Roo skins?"

"Take a look. You get used to the smell."

Aaron peered into the dark. It looked like the small interior was divided by some kind of metal grill. Something shifted in the darkness. "I don't think I want to..."

Strong hands gripped his arms and thrust him forward.

"But I insist," said Hare.

They propelled him inside before he had a chance to muster any real resistance, and pulled the door shut behind them. It was very dark, and the smell pressed against his face. There was a gurgling groan from behind the bars.

"What was that?" he hissed.

"That," said Hare, striking a flint and lighting a lamp, "is Constable Fitzpatrick. Say hello to the Constable, Aaron."

He raised the lamp, and Aaron saw the thing standing behind the bars. It saw him in the same moment and charged forward, colliding hard with the barrier, arms reaching through the gaps. It was true it wore a ragged blue uniform, but the rest of it was inhuman. In the flickering lamplight, all Aaron could see were its wide, dead eyes, devoid of any feelings except an unmistakable hunger, and its gaping mouth, black and scabbed. Aaron recoiled from the grasping hands with their grey mottled flesh and broken fingernails.

"I think he likes you, Aaron."

"Is... is that a Blighter?"

"No, Aaron. Fitzpatrick is just sleeping off a bender. What do you think?"

"...Horrible..."

Suddenly Hare and the sergeant grabbed him again and pushed him forwards, towards the hideous undead thing. He screamed no, no, no! Feet scrabbling on the dirt floor. They held him just outside of its reach, just so the fingertips hooked a bare inch from his face, and the thing pressed its head so hard between the gap in the bars that he feared it would burst.

"The choice is simple, Aaron," hissed Hare in his ear. "Get us some more information, or I'll lock you in there with Fitzpatrick. And don't think I won't do it. He needs some nourishment, does poor old Fitz. He's starting to look the worse for wear."

They let him drop to his knees, and he didn't even notice the stain spreading across his crotch...

"Still," said Joe after a moment, "you should have left my mother out of it, Aaron. That wasn't nice, staking out her house like that."

"I'm sorry," whispered Aaron, and then a coughing fit shook him to his core, until he spat black bloodied phlegm onto the bed.

"How did you get bitten?" asked Ned.

Aaron looked at him, tried to focus on him, but brought his gaze back to Joe. "That Hare is a demon. He kept at me, and at me. I thought maybe I should move away, but where could I go? I don't know anyone anywhere else... I tried making things up, but he could always tell when I was lying. So I kept trying to see you, Joe, to find out what I could. But I never wanted them to catch you. Not you."

Joe held his tongue, and nodded.

"I was able to tell them you were going to be around Euroa way, but they missed you, which is what I wanted, Joe, but Hare... They took me back there. I thought they were only going to try to give me a scare again, and I didn't want to see that... that thing, that bloody Blighter again, but I thought I could suck it up and get through. And I was thinking that maybe after that I'd come and join you... But it wasn't like last time. Hare was furious. You'd just done Jerilderie, too, and made the traps look like fools. You gave me that letter, the one you wanted put in the paper. I had to give them something, Joe, so I gave them that. And Hare seemed pleased - he said they'd put a story in the paper alright, set you up as a crackpot rebel, he said. I said, but if you change it, they'll blame me. They'll come for me. And he just stared at me, with his damned lizard eyes."

Aaron's face creased in distress, and tears rolled from his red eyes.

"They pushed me right up against the cage. I tried to fight them, but they took me by surprise. And then that monster grabbed me - it got hold of my arm and pulled it inside. God, it was so strong. I was screaming and cursing at it, but it latched on. Oh God, it bit hard. It pulled and ripped, and it tore a piece of my arm off. They let me go then, dropped me. And all I could see was that foul bloody thing chewing on my skin..."

―――――

"There," said Hare. "Now get out of town, Aaron. Go home. And don't come back. My men will have orders to shoot you on sight if you do."

Aaron held his stinging arm, looking in horror at the bright blood trickling from between his fingers. "Why did you do that?"

Hare grinned, his teeth seeming as large as those belonging to the Blighter. Aaron couldn't help but flinch. "A little gift for Kelly and the boys, when they come calling. With my compliments. And that's just for starters. Wait until they see what else I've got in store for them..."

―――――

"What's going to happen?" whispered Aaron.

"You're going to die, mate," said Joe.

"No..."

"It's always the same when one of them bites you. The fever... then you die. And then..."

"What?" asked Aaron, but the horror in his eyes showed he knew what the answer would be.

"You come back as one of them. You become a Blighter."

Aaron's face crumpled again, and he looked at the ceiling, and cried. "Oh, God... Oh, God..."

Ned stepped forward, cocking his rifle. "Well, let's put him out of his misery."

Aaron shrieked, and Joe jumped to his feet, placing his hand in Ned's chest. "Wait!"

Ned looked down at Joe's hand. "Wait for what, Joe? Look at

him. He'll be gone soon. And then he'll be back. It's kinder to do it now."

"Don't shoot me..." moaned Aaron.

"I know, I know!" said Joe. "Just... Can't you... Leave him to me, alright?"

Ned paused, then nodded and stepped back. Joe let his arm fall, and then slowly lowered himself back onto the edge of Aaron's cot. He patted the dying man on the arm. "It's alright, Aaron. Calm down, mate. But listen... You're Blighted. You are going to turn into one of those things. That's what Hare wanted, he hoped you'd already be one when we got here and attack us. But you're stronger than that, aren't you, mate? You held on."

"Yes. I was always the strong one, eh, Joe?"

"That's right. And you need to be strong again now. We have to take care of you, Aaron. We can't have you roaming the countryside biting people. Not with my own ma not far down the road. And think of your young missus there. We can stop all that, but we need to put a bullet in your head."

"Joe..."

"But I'll wait till you've died, Aaron. I promise you. I'll be the one to do it, and I'll wait til you've died."

"Joe." Ned stirred.

"We wait," said Joe flatly.

And the wait wasn't long. Whether their arrival and the excitement hastened the Blight's onset wasn't clear, but soon after, Aaron's breath came in shallower and shallower bursts, and his eyes rolled back into his head. With a final ragged breath, he shook once and went still. The girl, who had been sitting mutely in the corner, jumped up with a cry and ran to him, but stopped beside his wretched, sweaty corpse and flapped her hands. Steve and Dan took her by the arms and gently pulled her away, and outside.

"Well," said Joe thickly, and pulled his revolver clear.

"Wait," said Ned.

"Why?"

"I want to see how long it takes."

"What?"

"I want to see how long it takes for him to come back."

Joe shook his head. "You're a cold bastard sometimes, Edward Kelly." And he pressed his pistol to the side of Aaron's head and pulled the trigger.

TWENTY-ONE

"So. Not your finest moment."

Ned shrugged and didn't meet my eye.

"What was in the paper? What was it they published?"

"Oh, it was only excerpts - or what were supposed to be excerpts from my letter. They had me trying to justify my crimes and railing against the treatment of Irish Catholics by the English and Irish Protestants. Actually, that is something I like to talk about, so they had me down pretty pat there. But they took out anything to do with the government introduction of Blighters, of course."

"Did you really think the paper would print that stuff anyway?"

"I did, Remittance Man. I like to think there is still a free press in this country. It can't all be owned by the rich and be nothing but a mouthpiece for those who seek to repress the majority for their own gains."

We fell silent, he leaning against the wall with his eyes now closed, a sheen of sweat on his forehead and upper lip, me on the hard wooden chair by the new small table the warders had provided. No cushion, of course. My presence now seemed tolerated by the staff at best. Mind you, my friend the laudanum bottle made all the difference to my comfort level.

"Are you ready for the trial?" I asked him, to make conversation.

"Yes."

"I suppose I should go see Gaunson. Haven't spoken to him since Beechworth." I stood, and packed my notes. I glanced at Ned, but he almost looked asleep. I knocked on the door and waited for the familiar tread of the warder.

"Remittance Man? Just make sure I get my say on the stand. That's all I want."

"Don't worry," I said, and left the gaol.

It was early afternoon when I came out onto the street. I walked to Gaunson's law office but was told he was having lunch. Going by the lateness of the hour, it was either a long lunch, a late lunch, or he was actually hiding in his office. I took a punt on it being either of the former, and went along to the Club. It took some talk and a little cash to gain admittance from the doorman - I believe he did recognize me, but used my bruised appearance to extort some shillings from me. I headed purposely towards the private dining room where I had last seen the old bastard with Maggie. Once inside a place like that, generally no one asks questions if you look like you know where you are going. I paused outside the door, and could indeed hear Gaunson's voice. I wondered what I would say if it was Maggie. I pushed the door open - but it was a man.

"Charles!" said Gaunson. He and his guest looked me over. "Oh my goodness. I wasn't expecting you."

"Don't you want to ask me what happened?"

"Unless you fell down a staircase, repeatedly," observed the stranger, "it would be a safe bet to say you copped a thrashing."

"A thrashing? But from whom, Charles?"

"Didn't you hear about it back at the hotel?"

"No!"

I studied his blank face, but simply could not tell if there was guile there or not. "You didn't wonder why I didn't come back to Melbourne with you?"

He went red and shifted uneasily. "Well, Charles. I thought... Well, I was with Maggie, and she said not to worry about you. What happened?"

"I made some new friends. Look, I wanted to talk to you about the trial, but..." I looked at the other man.

"Oh, Charles, this is Binden. We've taken him on to act as barrister."

"Oh? We have, have we?"

"Yes, Charles. Yes, we have. Maggie agreed that-"

"Agreed? It was your idea then?"

"Maggie agreed that we need some extra support to take on Smyth. Not that your own displays were without...some merit. But we need less fireworks, if you like, and more..."

"More icy calm and dogged determination," said Binden, with an effected swagger. He held out his hand to me. "Pleased to meet you, Charles."

Dogged determination? This jackass had no idea what I had been through since working on this case. I shook his hand, though.

"Excellent!" beamed Gaunson. "Now, with the trial starting the day after tomorrow-"

"What? But I haven't even finished taking down Ned's whole statement!"

"Not to worry," said Binden, "we have enough to be getting on with."

"But you don't have all the facts! He hasn't told me about Glenrowan!"

"You mean his arrest? That doesn't even figure in the charges, Charles. It isn't important."

"It is. Something happened out there. Something very much important. Look, Gaunson, you were at the committal - you heard them. None of the troopers who were there were available and Hare-"

"So?" asked Binden. He snorted. I could grow to detest this man. "If they are unavailable, they are unavailable. What are you suggesting Ned and the gang killed them? Then where are the charges?"

"No, I don't think that. I think... I think..." I stopped. I couldn't say it. Looking at their plump, whiskered faces, I just couldn't say it.

"Now listen, Charles," said Binden in what was supposed to be a soothing tone, but made me really want to punch him, "It will be fine. You'll have plenty of time to finish the deposition if you wish. I'll get an adjournment straight away, as soon as the case starts. I simply need more time to chew through the facts."

Gaunson nodded. "There are an awful lot of facts."

"Gaunson tried to get an adjournment at Beechworth."

"Well," smiled Binden, "I do know a thing or two about getting an adjournment. I didn't get to where I am today by not securing the odd adjournment when I wanted one." He winked at Gaunson, and they both laughed together. "You look a little stressed to me, Charles. Why not give yourself the afternoon off? Leave your cares with me. I have your notes. I have plenty to go on with for now. Have you been to the Exhibition yet?"

I stared for a moment, unsure what he was talking about, then it clicked. Of course, the Melbourne Exhibition. Supposedly showcasing the greatness of the colony. Ever since the Crystal Exhibition in London, every man and his dog wanted to do an exhibition. At this point, Gaunson pulled out his billfold and passed me some notes. Must have been feeling guilty. I didn't let my mind travel too far down that path, to consider what exact things he may feel guilty about. It didn't bear thinking about.

I left them sipping their port and chewing on their cigars - God, it made me feel like an adolescent again, being brought into the study with the men after dinner, where they could examine me on my knowledge of Latin and Empire. Out on the street, I walked aimlessly for a while, then found myself drifting in the direction of Carlton Gardens. Soon the Exhibition Hall came into view - after all, its dome made it the tallest building in the city. Why not? I thought.

At the entrance, there was a small queue lining up for admission, and I joined it. It cost a shilling to get in. I noted a family group lined up ahead of me. Usually, I would have worked at sneaking in with them - old granny was up the back, in the care of a miserable spotted adolescent: it would have been no work at all to nudge him aside and take her elbow, then engineer a trip as she was passing through the gate. Then, in the hubbub of righting her and saving others from the sight of her bloomers - no doubt the pimpled lad would be struck dumb with horror - make my escape inside. Instead, I found myself holding back, and handing over my shilling.

Within the gardens and the halls lay displays from across the globe: Germany, France, Prussia, Britain, even the USA. But the largest amount of goods came, of course, from the colony of Victoria itself. I perused good honest British carpets and upholstery, Yankee barbed wire and electric lights, and a tinkling fountain gifted by the Frogs. There was lace and furniture, rifles, carriages, and huge brutal steam engines. And everywhere, there were people. Talking, pointing, scratching their idiot heads, standing slack jawed. Couples spooning. Gangs of bachelors sauntering along, full of flashness, hunting the tribes of young ladies with their sidelong glances and breathless, whispering giggles behind their hands.

My head was beginning to spin. It was hard to take in the scale of it all. I sought refuge in a kiosk inside the hall - I should have been warned by the morose look of the existing customers, but paid good money for a sandwich like pasteboard and a cup of lukewarm dregs they were laughingly calling coffee. The stodge filled me, yet a hollow ache lingered. I found myself in a small room back by the main door, where the visitor's book sat, itself a huge volume of finest handmade paper. My eyes trawled down the entries, meaningless names and comments like "grand!" and "glorious!" and "spiffing!" Seized with a desire to make my mark, somehow, I took up the pen, and wrote my own name, my real name, on the page, safe amid the hundreds of others. In the comment section I wrote, "Glory is fleeting."

I found the stairs leading up to the viewing platform around the dome, and though my heaving lungs punished my ribs, I made my way up there. There were people here, too, but it was possible to find a spare bit of railing, and lean there looking over the city. All that commotion.

I wanted to shout at them all. Don't you know what's out there? Don't you know what evil is here, now, nestling in the bosom of your fellow man? None of these trinkets are worth a damn. If you want a real exhibition of our progress and where it has taken us... If you got what you deserve...

A vision passed across my eyes. A city of flame and screams. Panicked shoppers and sight-seeing visitors fleeing. Doors smashing down in dance halls, in restaurants, in churches, and the undead pouring in to devour and spread the Blight across the whole city. Red blood and black bile splashing in the streets like rain. Knives and forks pausing over plates of red rare beef in the Club, whiskers quivering, leather shoes slipping on marble stairs as flesh torn fingers catch at pant legs, the great and good brought down, blood and claret pooling on the floor into a rich gravy.

How would they all fair? Rossier, coming out of his shop, bristling with guns: shooting them down as they came at him, until he was overcome. Rawson, trying to stuff himself under his bed as they came pounding up the stairs, a dead and ravenous Mrs Mackie at their head. Castieau, pen still scratching as they burst into his office... Hare, running, throwing other innocents behind him in his desperation to escape... All the others, everyone I knew, running, dying, *rising*...

Maggie, looking out the hotel window at the growing tide of death in the street, until Tom took her in his arms and tenderly drew her away...

I walked home slowly, morose and lonely. I ran into Rawson at the foot of the stairs, evidently returning from a trip out back to the lavatory. He seemed surprised to see me.

"Hello, old chap. Just in now, are you? Thought you were already back."

I grabbed his arm. "What?"

"I thought you were back. I thought I heard you banging about in your room."

"When? Just then?"

"No, a little earlier."

I looked up the shadowy stairwell. Of course they knew where I lived. Of course they weren't going to leave me alone. "What about just now as you came downstairs? Did you hear anything then?"

He reddened. "I'm afraid I've been out the back for a while. Trouble with the plumbing, you see." He patted his stomach.

My lip curled. I really hated anyone talking about their bowels. "Listen, Rawson, do me a favour. Take my key and see if anyone is still up there, would you?"

"Not in any trouble, are you, old boy? Creditors? Jealous husband?"

"Just do it! Please!"

I followed behind him, but ducked out of sight on the floor below, listening to him let himself into my room. I hoped not to hear a gunshot, or the sound of a violent struggle, for he was an affable chap, and luckily soon enough, he was back on the landing, whistling me up.

"You're not going to like it..."

He was right. Someone had turned my small room upside down. It had been none too clean when I had left, but now... What had they been looking for? Or was this another warning? Either way, I couldn't stay here any longer. I was going to have to run for it. I thanked Rawson and closed the door on his inquisitive face, and set about sorting through the debris. Thankfully, they had not found where I had stashed my derringer, in a hole in the mattress. Since the attack on me, I was all too aware of the danger I faced if I was perceived to be continuing to meddle. They had tried to lead me astray with tipoffs, drugged me, beat me... surely if it came to it, killing me must be the next step. And I could hardly rely on my name to keep me safe. I had resolved to carry my gun with me, but this was easier said than done. I couldn't take it into the gaol as they may search me. I had hidden it once in a drain near the prison, but was worried it would be found. So this morning I had slit my thin mattress and hidden the pistol and extra cartridges inside it. Now it lay on the floor where it had been flipped during the search, but luckily, the gun was so light that the searcher had not noticed its additional weight - quite a surprise, considering the cheapness of the mattress.

I had started shoving all my clothes in my valise, and my papers, when I realised I was probably better off appearing to maintain this abode. If I disappeared, they would search for me.

If they thought they knew where I was, and were complacent enough to think they could lay their hands on me whenever they wanted, then that may play into my hands somehow. What I needed was some sort of bolthole where I could sleep safe and sound. Somewhere I could escape to when the trial was on and the storm broke.

What I fancied was a classy hotel, with clean cotton sheets and young maids to ogle, but with the Exhibition on, not to mention Ned's upcoming trial, I doubted I would be able to find a room in the city. Besides which, I needed somewhere more low key.

First, I needed it to get dark. I spent a couple of troubled hours sitting on my chair, sipping at my bottle, with my loaded derringer in my lap. Rawson knocked at one point, asking if I wanted a drink, but I stayed silent until he went down to dinner.

Did I look at all heroic, sitting there, gun at the ready, bruises on my face? As I sat, a letter composed itself in my mind. Dear Father, it began... You like to believe yourself a fine judge of character, figuring you can find the measure of a man from his handshake and how well he meets your eye... Yet, you wrote me off so early. So finally. And maybe once, I was something lesser, but are we all not clay in the hands of the gods? Might there not be some chance that I, even I, could be shaped anew?

Who is to say, if the cosmic hands have pulled more gently at some, that they are in any way the better men for it? And if the pull is too great on others and they are torn asunder, who is it who can stand in judgment unless they, too, have felt the unravelling of all that they are?

Would you recognize me, Father? Sitting in the growing dark, ready for violence if it should come to it, all for the sake of a doomed Irishman and his fantastic stories of courage and murder? Strange it should be the dry involvement of men like you that gives credence to his tale. I may struggle cynically with stories of selfless action, but tell me about the darkness lurking in the hearts of men and I hear the bell of truth ring. For does not my own darkness howl in return?

It was dark enough.

I opened my door a fraction, confirming that Rawson was safely tucked away in his room. I went down the stairs as quietly as I could, and turned down the dark passage, passed the dining room, and slipped out to the backyard. I passed the outhouse - thankfully unoccupied - and looked over the paling fence into the shadowy backyard of the house next door. It appeared empty as ours – but did they have a dog? Christ, had I ever heard a dog? I couldn't remember, but I didn't want to go out by my own back gate in case it was being watched. I hoisted myself up onto the fence, which swayed alarmingly - wood rot, I suppose - and heaved myself over. I crouched, listening, but there was nothing there, no guard dog, no bohemian female artist either. Down I went, out the back gate into the inky lane behind the house. I stood silently in the dark for a few moments, letting my eyes adjust further to the gloom, and then walked as quickly and quietly as I could down the lane. Snatches of voices came from the houses towering around me - a baby crying, a woman yelling out for her sons to come in, a man raging at someone or nothing, a party singing...

...something stirring in the dark ahead of me...

My hand went to the gun in my pocket. A human form levered itself stiffly up off the ground from behind a pile of refuse. It was too dark to make it out clearly, but in the moon-light, its skin appeared to be dark, and it shuffled forward, straight towards me.

...If ever one of them gets loose in the city...

I caught a flash of white teeth in a dark face, and pulled my pistol clear, whipping it up and aiming at the oncoming figure.

Visions of those teeth tearing at my flesh filled my mind, yet I did not pull the trigger. I just wanted to see...

"Stop," I croaked, "I have a gun."

The figure stopped, swaying. Did they understand English? I couldn't remember if Ned had mentioned that.

"Where?" came a voice, low and hoarse.

"Here." I tilted the barrel in the weak light, trying to show it.

"Dat's not a gun. Dat's just your thumb."

"My thumb isn't black," I said stupidly.

"Mine is," said the figure, and shuffled forwards to show me. It was indeed as dark as he said.

He was a native, of course. Not some nightmare come to feast on me. My God, the combination of the mad Irishman's tales and laudanum was getting to me. He was the first Aboriginal I had seen up close. Not that this one seemed that fine a specimen. His clothes were ragged, and he smelt of alcohol.

"You got any money, mister?"

"No," I said, and kept walking, holding the derringer down by my side in case he should try to rob me. I realised he was following me.

"Where you goin'?"

I stopped, and in an instant, spun and had the gun thrust up under his jaw. "Have you been watching me?"

"No, boss..."

"Are you sure? No one paid you to watch that house back down there?"

"Nobody pay me nothin'."

I stared into his rheumy eyes, saw the defeat there, and suddenly felt sick. I stepped away, but he stood slightly cowed still, as if I might still strike him or do him harm.

"What tribe are you?" I asked.

He glanced up at me. "No tribe," he muttered.

"No? But you haven't always lived in the city have you?"

"No," he said quietly.

"Did you," I asked, "did you ever hunt Blighters?"

His eyes widened. He looked at me blankly, and then started to edge away along the wall.

"Wait! You know something about them, don't you? I was told they were used to kill your people - is that what happened to your tribe?"

"I don't want no trouble, I'm goin'..."

"I'll give you money."

That stopped him. He stood for a moment, hesitant, swaying, then turned back to face me. "What you want to know?"

"So... they are real? You've seen them?"

He nodded. "Never-fall-down-fellas."

"That's right, that's what Ned said your people called them. He said, he said that it was you, the natives, who have been protecting us from them for years."

"Not you. The land. Them fellas got no place on it."

"Why are you here?"

"Nobody left," he laughed mirthlessly. "Now I got to live on white fellas' land. Until I fall down."

I handed him some money, my fingers brushing his as he took it and stowed it in a pocket without even looking at it. He nodded at me once, and then resumed his limping way down the lane.

I myself continued for another couple of blocks, then came out onto a street. I found a hotel, The Standard - standard indeed, a dull affair, block-like in design, but they had a room and took the name I gave at face value. Inside a small, tidy bedroom on the upper floor, I was able to lie back and let my muscles begin to unknot themselves slowly.

Sleep, such as it was, was a long time coming.

TWENTY-TWO

Passing through the gates of the gaol, I felt a great heaviness enveloping me. A sense of coming to the end, but not met with any joy or expectation of release. No, there was a curious darkness ahead - I could see the trial, but beyond that, I had no sense of what may come, what I would do.

I suppose the feeling could have been due to my abuse of the laudanum bottle. My ribs and contusions were still very sore, and I still did not want to face them without chemical assistance. On top of that, I had taken a roundabout route to the gaol that morning, slipping down laneways until I found a cab, then being dropped some distance from the gaol, then again skittering down back passages like some city rat until I had to come out onto Russel Street as near as possible to the front gate. Would anyone actually try to stop me? Rather not take that chance.

I was admitted as grumpily as usual - no change there - and as I walked towards the cellblock, my neck prickled. I glanced around and up, and saw Castieau staring down at me from his office window. I waved at him cheerily, and one of his arms flinched as if to wave back, but then he put them both behind his back. I fancied I could see his lips tighten and go white with strain. Really, he should thank me for giving him more ammunition for his book.

My nostrils twitched as I entered the cell. It stank of sweat. Ned had the look of someone who had spent the night in fevered discomfort - shirt damply clinging to his chest, blankets kicked to the bottom of his cot.

"Has the doctor seen you?"

"I don't want him." His voice was rough. He coughed to clear it.

"Look, if you aren't feeling up to it..."

"Sit down, Remittance Man."

Good. I didn't really want to leave. I wanted to hear the end.

"We knew that Hare had his pet Blighter," he began without preamble. "And his special train, ready to move on us from Benalla. So we told the German, Weekes, that we were going to raid Beechworth. We said we were going to rob the banks, burn the station and courthouse, and arm anyone who wanted to join us."

"I guess that got Hare's attention alright."

"Yes. Just the kind of armed uprising he had me threatening in that letter. Meanwhile, we loaded our armour into a cart-"

"Wait, wait," I said, "you haven't told me about the armour."

"Oh, right." Ned rubbed his temples with his fingertips. "It's hard to keep all the details in order in my head..."

"Too many facts, eh?"

"What?"

"Nothing. So... the armour?"

It had been Joe's idea, after the near misses in the fight with the Blighted at Faithfulls Creek. Back in the Wombat Ranges, he drew sketches on bark using charcoal, showing them some basic armour designs, modelled on what he could remember of the colourful prints in old Ah Feng's books.

"Why not just thick leather, like Steve said?" asked Dan.

"Because it won't just be the Blighter," said Ned. "There'll be troopers, too. It would be better if it could be bite proof and bullet proof."

"But how will the troopers be able to control a Blighter? Just because it was Fitzpatrick doesn't mean it is going to take orders, is it? They can't be trained like that, can they?"

"Remember the Wildman," said Joe. "they had that on chains. Maybe they'll try the same thing."

Iron armour was going to prove difficult. A first attempt using sheets from an old water tank seemed tough enough to withstand teeth and fingers, but bullets passed through it easily. Ned's earlier words about ploughshares and swords proved prophetic - the best source of iron proved to be the mould boards on ploughs. With the help of Maggie on Whitefoot, word spread amongst their sympathisers - or at least those not currently locked up, accused of plotting sedition, rebellion and terrorism - and she was able to deliver a growing pile. It was a big sacrifice for the local farmers. Those known to be unsympathetic to the cause, or staunch disbelievers of the threat of the Blighted, also contributed – albeit unwillingly. They simply came out some morning to harness up their horses, only to find the cutting blade from their plough removed and spirited away in the night.

With the advice of a local blacksmith, they built a bush forge and heated the curled blades, smashing them flat with the help of a green tree log they dropped on the glowing iron. They shaped and cut the plates with hammers and chisels, beating them into breastplates, back plates, helmets, and swinging shields to protect their groins.

"I don't want one of these," said Joe, practising walking in one of the suits. The groin guard flapped against his thighs. "That's really irritating."

"More irritating than getting shot in the balls?" asked Ned.

"I'll be right," said Joe, "I'd rather be able to move more easily."

They had Maggie buy them long thick coats, and leather gloves. They modelled the whole panoply for her.

"Jesus," breathed Maggie. "I don't know what's scarier - the Blighters or you lot."

Ned pulled his helmet off. He wore a cloth cap underneath. "With this, we can take on an army of Blighters. And traps. We can show what we, the people, are capable of. We can bring all of them to their knees. All we need is the right situation to use it."

"And that was Glenrowan?"

Ned nodded. "Yes. We sent Weekes off to do his part, and rode out to set the trap. Glenrowan was a good spot, because the line curves there, above a culvert. We thought if we could derail the train there, it would go crashing down the bank and should pulverise anyone on board. We could stand on the top of the slope and gun down anyone or anything that survived. What?"

"I didn't say anything."

"But you're thinking it, aren't you?"

I shifted uncomfortably. I really could have used a new cushion. "It just sounds so... cold blooded. Even if, as you say, Hare had Fitzpatrick with them..."

"You think we were playing or something? You don't under-stand the significance of this at all. This was war, Remittance

Man. No mercy, no compassion. Just get the bloody job done. You think I liked it?"

Yes, Ned, on some level I think you bloody did. But I didn't say that out loud. "So what happened?"

"So what happened?" he repeated, eyes far away. "It all went to hell, that's what happened. And Steve and Joe and...and Dan...they all died. But maybe, maybe...not for nothing."

The gang rode into Glenrowan early on Sunday morning. Tom Lloyd was bringing the cart with the armour and extra guns and ammunition, and would meet them later.

The stationmaster, Stanistreet, was standing on the platform as he liked to do first thing, drinking a cup of tea, when he glanced up and noticed the four horsemen dismount further up the line and stand looking at the tracks.

"This can't be good," he said to himself as he watched them kick at the rails, then turn and look in his direction. He threw the dregs of his tea onto the tracks as they trotted towards him, waiting and watching the steam rise from the icy metal rails.

"I'm Ned Kelly," said one of the men, drawing a pistol. "And you are going to help us tear up these tracks."

Stanistreet scratched at his scalp beneath his hat. "I know more about tickets and timetables than track wrecking, I'm afraid to say."

"Who's in the house?" asked Ned.

"My wife and children. We don't want any trouble, now."

Ned grimaced. "We'll have to have them out of there, soon. Where are your tools?"

Stanistreet led them to a box containing an assortment of hammers, chisels, and saws. The gang rummaged through it, taking out the heaviest hammers.

"You'll need proper bars if you want to shift the tracks. And more men, I'd wager."

Ned looked at him, and then looked about. He pointed at the closest house. "Who lives there?"

"That's Reardon, and his wife and children."

"Get them out here, Joe."

Joe jogged off towards the house. Stanistreet sucked his teeth. "There's a few fettlers camped down the track a ways. They'll have the muscle and the tools you're looking for."

At a nod from Ned, Steve and Dan mounted their horses and cantered off in the direction the stationmaster had indicated.

"What exactly are you meaning to do? If I may ask?" he regretted the words as soon as he uttered them, for Ned turned a look on him that was as cold as the grave.

"Save the colony," he snapped, "that's what we're going to do."

As the sun rose higher above the distant hill line, and the low lying mist burned off, the gang collected a group of half a dozen men or so, who were led up the tracks to the bend by Ned and Joe, and put to work unbolting a section of rail and levering it clear. The women and children were kept at the station by Dan and Steve. It was chilly, but the workers soon worked up a sweat. When they were done, Ned paced along the ruined section, then jogged down the line in the direction of Benalla, and studied the track from a distance.

"Excellent," he said, jogging back. "Top notch. Breakfast is on me. Where's a good place?"

"The Jones Hotel is nice," said one of the fettlers, pointing to a simple clapboard structure, fronted by a simple split rail fence, some way off from the station. "That Mrs Jones, she knows how to put on a spread."

"Lead the way!" called Ned, and he and the other three gang

members ushered their prisoners towards the hotel, where the first tendrils of smoke were beginning to rise from the chimney. At the sound of their voices, an iron-haired woman appeared on the veranda, wiping her hands on her apron, a teenage boy peering from behind her shoulder.

"Morning!" said Ned cheerfully. "Breakfast all round please, Mrs Jones."

The proprietress eyed them, especially noting the guns of the four young men. "Don't have much. But we can do bacon, tea, and toast."

"Please."

The group settled themselves on the veranda and inside the front room. Ned's good cheer slowly rubbed off on the others - the hostages found their captors amiable, and the whole experience quite exciting. Besides, it was a Sunday, and there wasn't much else to do. The only one who couldn't relax was Stanistreet. He kept thinking about that distant piece of ruined track. He wondered what his duty was in this situation. He wondered if he'd made a mistake, slipping the pistol into the back of his trousers back at the station house when no one was looking. He wiped his sleeve across his face - he was sweating, despite the chill air.

As other townsfolk appeared, they too were added to the number of hostages. At one point, a buggy came past, driven by a serious-faced young man, with two women and a number of children as passengers. Joe stepped into their path and bailed them up.

"And who are you?" asked Ned, as they joined the crowd inside the hotel.

"Thomas Curnow," said the young man, "I'm the schoolmaster."

"And I'm Ned Kelly. I kill the undead."

"Undead?" said Curnow. "Oh."

"You're sure of this?" asked Hare.

The German nodded. "Dey said Beechworth."

Hare allowed himself a moment of stillness, to savour the moment. A thrill ran through his stomach. He wondered if he should visit the lavatory first. Plenty of time for that. "Sergeant Steele!" he called.

"Sir?"

"It's happening. Gather the men."

"Listen," said Ned. The crowd before him numbered more than forty. "I ask for your patience. There is a thing we have to do, and for your own safety, you must all stay here at the hotel. Nobody must leave. I give you my word that no harm will come to any of you, so long as you obey that instruction. Disobey, however, and God have mercy on your soul, and those of them you hold dear."

The engine driver tried a lever, tapped a gauge, and yelled down to Hare, "She's ready, Superintendent!"

"And about bloody time!" Hare stood beside the locomotive, steam swirling about him. He perused the thirty or so troopers before him.

"Men," he said, "this is a moment for the history books. Today spells the end of the Kelly gang forever. We're going to run them to ground, surround them, and then... obliterate them."

The troopers cheered. It had been a hard few months, gathering up the Kelly supporters, putting up with the insults, the jeers, the spitting. Now was payback. Sergeant Steele jumped from the single carriage and saluted. "Trunk is secured, sir."

"Excellent. Right, all aboard. Nobody touch the trunk. Sergeant, you are riding up front with me. Grab that shotgun, would you?"

As the troopers clambered aboard, Steele climbed up into the driver's compartment at the back of the locomotive behind Hare. "Why are we riding in here, sir? More comfy in the carriage."

Hare tapped his nose. "Plans and stratagems, Sergeant. Plans and stratagems. Best possible speed, please, Mr McFie."

Tom Lloyd arrived with the cart. "Where do you want it, Ned?"

Ned looked over towards the railway line, thinking. "We'll hear the train coming a mile off. May as well put it in here, in the hotel."

Several of the men were given the job of helping lug the clanging armour, the armfuls of rifles, and boxes of cartridges, into one of the small bedrooms at the back of the hotel. Tom himself carried in a keg of blasting powder, placing it carefully behind the bar.

"Thanks, Tom," said Ned. "Now get yourself out of here. When this is over, there are going to be some big changes around these parts. Be ready."

The children played games out the front of the hotel, enjoying the unexpected party. Ned joined them, playing at hop-step-jump - they cheered him on as he drove himself to greater and greater distances. Even some of the adults joined in the applause.

Stanistreet maneuvered himself over beside Curnow. "I don't like this, Thomas."

"No," said Curnow, glancing around carefully - none of the rest of the gang were nearby. "But what can we do? The man is quite mad. Undead?"

"I don't know," said Stanistreet, "I have heard some strange rumours... but the thing is, he means to wreck a police train, I'm sure of it. He means to kill a lot of men, Thomas. I have to do something. Listen, I... I have a gun."

"John, don't start anything, I beg you. I have my wife and sister to consider, not to mention the children. Besides, surely the train drivers will be watching for such things..."

Stanistreet shook his head. "Not if it's dark. Not if it's on a bend, where they can't see far enough ahead. I tell you, it will be a bloody massacre."

Curnow shot a worried glance at the stationmaster, taking in his strained white face. "Shit," he said softly to himself, and walked slowly back over to his wife. He placed an arm around her shoulders and squeezed.

"Quite an adventure, isn't it, Thomas? To be held to ransom by highwayman. I can't wait to write to mother."

"Bushrangers," murmered Curnow distractedly, "the correct term is bushrangers."

The day wore on, and the crowd became listless. After their good cheer of the morning, the gang became increasingly tense. For one thing, none of them got a chance to rest. They had to supervise trips out to the hotel outhouse, and keep a count on all the people. Finally, as the afternoon began to cool, Ned ordered everyone inside the hotel, and the front door was locked.

There was a piano in the front room, and Mrs Jones was exhorted to come out from behind the counter and play. She settled herself at the keyboard, cracked her fingers, and launched into a lively tune. The children, finding new energy, leapt straight up and danced, and soon a number of feet were tapping time. Dan grabbed Steve, and dragged him into the middle of the floor. They began a jig, marked by Steve occasionally trying to dodge away and sit down, and Dan dragging him back up again. The crowd laughed and clapped. Steve finally took refuge behind Curnow, holding the schoolmaster in front of himself like a shield. Dan took hold of him, instead.

"Let's dance, teacher."

"Gladly," said Curnow, but then held his ground, "though, sadly, I've got the wrong footwear on." He pointed down at his boots. "Now, if I had my dancing shoes, I'd show you a thing or two."

"Oh, really? Where are your shoes?"

"At my home. Quite nearby... I could nip home and get them."

"Let's go!"

"And maybe I could be permitted to take my family home? I give you my word they will stay put. They'll just go to bed, they're quite tired."

Dan shook his head. "I don't think so. You'll have to ask Ned."

Steve took that opportunity to duck away, and Dan made a grab for him. Curnow sidled over next to Ned, who was watching with a faint smile on his face.

"I just want you to know," said Curnow in his ear, "that I thoroughly support what you are doing."

"Thank you, schoolmaster," said Ned. "Maybe after tonight, you will be able to teach the truth about what has been going on."

"Nothing would give me greater pleasure." Curnow looked around the throng. He spotted Stanistreet biting his nails in the opposite corner. "I feel I should warn you, that the station master has a concealed weapon."

Ned's head swivelled, and he stared into Curnow's eyes. "Much obliged." He caught Joe's attention, and the two of them eased their way over towards Stanistreet. Curnow watched them, as they drifted over, seemingly deep in relaxed conversation, then suddenly they bowled forwards and seized Stanistreet, and slammed him against the wall. Mrs Jones stopped playing. Joe pulled the revolver from where it sat wetly in the small of Stanistreet's back. They spun him back to face them.

"And just what did you have planned for that?" spat Ned, and Joe cocked the gun and stuck it against the man's temple. His wife screamed.

"Please..." he whispered, and a dark stain appeared at the front of his trousers. He sagged down onto the floor.

"Ah, let him be." said Ned in disgust, and stomped off. Joe reached down and tapped Stanistreet on the head with the pistol barrel, then stuck it in his belt.

"Thank you again," said Ned to Curnow, who was watching Mrs Stanistreet try to comfort her husband, while avoid getting any of his urine on her dress. "God knows what might have happened if that idiot tried anything."

"Like I said, I'm on your side. The... the Blighted are indeed a grave threat to us all." Curnow waited a full minute before then saying, "I wonder if I might ask a small favour in return?"

Ned bent his head, and listened.

Curnow shepherded his wife, sister, and children out into the cold night air. The children were whining, overtired and not wanting to leave the fun, and Curnow was short with them, having had to run the gauntlet of jealous and disapproving stares from some of the other hostages. Stanistreet had shot him a particularly venomous glare, but no matter, wasn't the schoolmaster always hated deep down? He herded his family back to their house almost at a run, demanding they stay inside with the doors locked and no lights on.

"Give me your scarf!" he shouted at his sister, and grabbed a candle from the stand just inside their front door. When he was sure the door was shut and locked, and no one could be seen within, he set out at a jog in the direction of the tracks.

There was the whistle of a train in the distance. Curnow broke into an awkward sprint.

The gang members looked at each other. "So," said Ned, and they walked into the back of the hotel where their gear sat.

"Must you?" hissed Hare.

"Safety regulations," said the driver, McFie. "Warns anyone on the track in the dark."

"Anyone on the track in the dark deserves what they get. No more whistles, thank you, McFie."

"Suit yourself," shrugged the driver, "it's your train."

"Come on, come on." Curnow worked frantically to light the candle, his sister's red scarf held under his chin. He couldn't get it to catch. The matches kept blowing out. His shaking fingers spilled matches. "Come on! Jesus fucking Christ, come on!"

Dressing in the armour in a small bedroom was difficult. Ned paused to pull a long green sash from his coat pocket and wind it around his waist.

"You still have that old thing?" said Dan with a smile, but Ned only nodded once, oddly embarrassed.

Once the breast and back plates were strapped on, they had to pull over the top the thick coats, and put on the leather gloves. They felt the weight of it as they bent to pick up their helmets and guns.

"Listen for the crash, boys," said Ned. "Not long now. Then we go down there and finish it."

"Warning light!" cried McFie, and he hauled on the brake. Wheels locked, but the mass of the train kept it grinding forward, squealing, sparks showering. Hare and Steele, unprepared, crashed into the stoker, and all three went down in a heap.

"What the hell!" cried Hare, scrabbling to his feet. "What did you stop for?"

"There!" McFie pointed. A small red light was bobbing towards them out of the darkness. "There was someone on the tracks."

The train finally coasted to a stop, and a man appeared gasping and blowing beside the engine. "Oh, thank God!" cried Curnow. "Thank God!"

The gang stood on the veranda, staring into the quiet darkness. Each held his helmet in one arm, and a rifle in the other. Revolvers were tucked into the deep pockets of their coats. Inside, the crowd was silent, too.

"What happened?" asked Dan. "Did we not hear it?"

"There was no bloody crash," said Joe bitterly.

"Curnow," said Ned. "You bloody little bastard."

"Constable Stanton!" bellowed Hare.

"Sir?" came the muffled response from inside the carriage.

"Open the trunk! Time to distribute the...uh... extra weapons!"

Hare reached up and locked the carriage door from the outside.

"What are you doing?" asked Steele, white faced.

"Improvising," snapped Hare. "Now go and lock the other door. Run, damn you!"

Steele hesitated for a moment, and then bolted to the far end of the carriage.

"What's going on?" asked Curnow. "Aren't you going to arrest Kelly?"

"Arrest him?" snarled Hare. "I'm going to eat him alive!"

Inside the carriage came a cry of surprise, then horror, then a high pitched scream.

"Good God," said Curnow. A spray of something wet and dark arced across the closest window. The teacher took a step away, tripped, and went sprawling down onto his backside in the scree. More screams came from inside the carriage, and the door shook violently.

"Let us out! Let us out!" screamed the men inside.

Steele stuck his fingers in his ears as he leaned grimacing against the far door. The screaming moved steadily up the carriage, a terrible chorus taken up by voice after voice. There was a pistol shot, but only one, as Hare had ordered all guns unloaded for the journey. Whoever managed to load his revolver had time only to pull the trigger once before his life was torn away. Slowly, horribly, the screams gave way to groaning.

"Dear God," murmured Curnow, "what have I done?"

"You've done your colony a great bloody favour," laughed Hare. "Cheer up, you'll be remembered forever for this!"

And all at once, the carriage was still. No more desperate screams of pain and horror rent the night air. There was only a steady drip as blood beaded from beneath the doors and dropped, steaming slightly, onto the cold iron tracks below.

"Back to me, now, Sergeant."

Steele paused to vomit onto the ground, then roughly wiped his mouth and ran back to the locomotive.

"Shove over, McFie. We're coming back up in there with you. Come on, Steele."

"Right behind you, sir."

"What about me?" asked Curnow. "Should I come up too?"

"No, you wait down there."

"Wait? For what?"

"You'll see. Shouldn't be too long."

––––––––

It was a still night. The screams had carried clearly to the men standing on the veranda.

"Jesus Christ," said Joe.

"Dan. Steve. Get everyone into the back room. Tell them to keep the lights off and stay away from the windows."

"Ned? What do you think is happening?"

"The moment we've been waiting for."

Joe looked at the grim expression on his friend's face, and felt a shiver like ice water run down his spine. "The moment?"

"Every war needs its last battle, Joe. Or its first."

"Which is this?" asked Joe, but Ned only smiled.

––––––––

"Uh, Superintendent?"

"What is it, schoolmaster?"

"I think some of your men are still alive. I can hear them moving."

Hare nodded slowly. He pulled his revolver out of his holster and snapped it open, checking that all the chambers were loaded.

"Should we do something?"

"Yes," said Hare. "Open up that door and have a look. Go on, it's alright. I'm sure the danger is passed."

"Um, sir?"

"Shut up, Sergeant. All of you shut up and keep down. If you want to live to see the dawn."

Hare peeked out and watched Curnow walk up to the door of the carriage. He could hear the stumblings and stirrings within the carriage, now. "Have a quick look in," he called down to Curnow, "and then you are free to go home."

Curnow reached out with a tremulous hand, flipped the lock, and gripped the cold iron in his sweat-slippery hand. He tugged downwards, and the latch disengaged, the door pulled open-

-and amidst a splattering stream of blood the ragged torn things inside spilled outwards with a roar of desperate hunger. Curnow screamed and went down under several of the mutilated clawing bodies as they fell from the door upon him, but was temporarily saved by their very numbers, for none was able to get a grip on him. He clawed desperately backwards, kicking out at their reaching fingers and clashing mouths with his boots. But no blow, no matter how he felt it crunch into bone, made them hesitate at all. As they pulled free of each other, and more came lurching to the door and falling clear, he saw that all were sprayed with bloody gore and showed the signs of a violent death. This one had its throat torn out. That one was missing most of its face. Another was disembowelled, tripping over its own drooping loops of gut. Others were missing lips and noses, or fingers from their hands. One had a clear bullet wound in the middle of its chest, the hole going all the way through, but despite all these injuries, on they came. And then, with a stench of old death, one appeared in the doorway even worse than the others - where they were ripped and bloody, this one was rotted and foul. It appeared to wear the tatters of a uniform, but it was so caked in rusty stains and filth it was hard to tell. It was much more emaciated than the others, looking like it must have crawled from some unholy grave, a skeleton covered in leathered skin - all except its belly, which was swollen. Its lipless teeth were stained bright crimson.

It was too much. The horror of it all was too great. Curnow felt the energy drain from his limbs. But then he heard someone hissing his name...

"Curnow! Run for the town! Lead them to Kelly!"

It was Hare. Curnow could see him peeking from the driver's compartment. None of the undead appeared to have noticed the men huddled in there - they were too intent on him. He glanced back over his shoulder at the darkened buildings of Glenrowan.

"My family is back there..."

"Lead them to Kelly! We'll shoot them all dead once they've killed him! Your family will be safe! Now run!"

A hand plucked at Curnow's pants, its owner was crawling towards him, face a noseless, bloody mask. Curnow could stand no more. With a final kick he clawed to his feet and ran back a few paces.

"You promise?" he yelled. "You promise?"

"Yes! Go! Oh, shit..."

One of the dead had heard Hare's voice, and turned questioningly towards the engine. Hare sank out of sight. Curnow had never felt more alone. He backed away, trying to think. It was like he was a magnet - as he moved, he drew them after him. There must have been a score or more of them now, and their foul leader was amongst them, pushing through them and breaking into a shambling trot. What to do? What to do?

"Hey!" he shouted. "They're in there! In the train!"

But the Blighters just kept coming. They didn't understand his pointing. All they understood was that his warm wet flesh would satisfy for a while the burning aching emptiness they felt inside.

Curnow turned and ran. The Blighters followed. All but one - if he had time to look, the school master may have been gladdened to see one creature pulling itself up into the locomotive, until a coal shovel swung down out of the darkness and cleaved its head in two.

Curnow ran. He needed to distract them. He needed them to find another target. He needed the Kelly's. He ran for the hotel.

The undead followed, leaving a trail of gore and tatters of flesh in their wake. The newly Blighted troopers stumbled forward on rubbery knees, still with the flexibility of the living, but still coming to terms with the dark primitive messages emanating from deep inside their brains. The undead Fitzpatrick followed as quickly as he could, on stiffened jerking legs, belching charnel air from the meat sitting in his rotting gut.

When some minutes had passed, and no more Blighters emerged from the carriage, four heads appeared one by one from the rear of the locomotive.

"Right," said Hare. "You two are deputised. Find a rifle. Sergeant Steele, shotgun at the ready, please."

The sergeant waited for the two train crew to scramble into the carriage. The sound of them retching as they dug through the bloody shambles for guns carried clearly to the police. "Sir," he said, "what were you going to do if that Curnow fellow hadn't come along? How were you going to set the men... the Blighters onto Kelly?"

"No need to worry about that now, Sergeant. Come on!"

"Just as I thought. I just want to say you're a bastard, sir."

"Duly noted. Now keep your eyes and ears open. We don't want to overtake them."

The first fusillade of gunshots erupted from the town.

The gang crouched in the front room of the hotel, peering out of the windows. Dawn was not too far away, and in the meantime, the moonlight was cold and clear. The murmur of voices came from the back room, where the hostages had been told to take cover. Just then, a lone figure came dashing out of the darkness towards the inn.

"Help!" screamed Curnow. "Help! They're after me!"

He bolted through the opening in the simple split rail fence that surrounded the front of the hotel and ran up to the door. He rattled the handle and pounded on the thick planking, all the while looking back over his shoulder for the nightmare he knew was after him

"Open up! Hurry!"

"Shoot him or let him in?" Joe asked Ned.

"Let's leave him - he can act as bait so we can see how many are out there."

"Help! Help! For the love of God!" Curnow rained blows on the thick planking of the door, but it was solid and held. He spun around, shrinking back into the doorframe. A whimper escaped his lips.

There was a patch of deeper darkness moving across the ground. There came a low moaning - dead air escaping useless lungs. Curnow looked around desperately. He chewed his lip, looking at the distance, then leapt off the veranda and charged to the front corner of the fence. His movement drew the Blighters away from the gate - they surged instead towards him.

Curnow waved his arms above his head. "That's right! Over here!" He looked back over his shoulder, "Now shoot them! Shoot them!"

The other three looked at Ned. He shook his head. "Wait. He might lead some off."

The undead bunched against the railing, reaching for Curnow, those behind pressing into those at the front, all desperate to get to him. He saw the wood begin to bow under the pressure.

"Fuck!" he screamed, and bolted for the other corner. "For fuck's sake, shoot them!"

Inside, the children smirked to hear such language coming from their teacher. Curnow stopped in the other corner, blowing hard. The undead were following the fence line down towards him, but the pressure of the group pushed some in through the gate. He was going to be trapped.

"Kelly, God damn you! What are you waiting for?"

He looked around desperately. He could vault the fence and run, but where could he go? And what if the creatures spread out through the town? Would his dear family be safe? The gang weren't going to let him inside, either, that much was plain... Would they really stand by and watch him be torn to shreds? He couldn't believe that was possible.

A hand swiped at his pant leg - a Blighter was on its belly, thrusting under the fence. Curnow ran toward the front door again, but then stopped, and dropped to his knees.

"What's he doing?" whispered Dan. "Run, you idiot!"

Curnow knelt, his hands clasped trembling together, eyes

screwed tightly shut. "The Lord is my shepherd... The Lord is my shepherd..."

He heard the swift susurration of clumsy feet kicking through the dust behind him, heard the rumbling groans... How long would it take? How much would it hurt? Could he be strong?

A hand like iron gripped his shoulder. Liquid dripped onto his head and neck as something foul bent over him-

A shot rang out amid shattering glass, and there was a wet explosion as the monster's head burst above him.

Ned looked across at Steve, who stood aiming through the broken window, rifle smoking.

"Oh, Steve..."

The younger man wouldn't meet his eye. "A short life," he said "but a merry one." Outside, the horde of Blighters had paused, heads lifting towards the hotel, focussing on the source of the noise.

"Well, that's that then," said Ned. "Helmets on, boys. It's been nice knowing you."

A volley of shots boomed from the front of the inn, and the closest Blighters were hacked down - two shot through the head, another punched backwards off its feet, head almost severed by a bullet through the neck. Curnow felt fluid and wet fragments spatter across his back - he crawled forward, keeping low, hearing the dreadful tearing zip of bullets passing just over his head. He didn't stop until his head crunched into the wall of the inn, then he turned, following it until he came to the corner then crawled around the side. He jumped up and ran for the back of the property. "Thank you God," he mumbled, "Thank you God."

Steve and Dan had fired a pair of breech loading rifles apiece, while Joe worked the lever on his Spencer rifle and Ned shot off all the chambers of his six shot Colt carbine. Gunsmoke hazed the air in front of the inn, and the undead were a tangled disarray of bodies, some still, others - most - struggling to climb over and pull clear, driven to get to the noise inside the building.

Inside, four men were swearing, struggling to reload their weapons with shaking fingers encased in thick leather gloves. The two breechloaders were easiest, and Steve and Dan were back at the windows as the first Blighter was mounting the stairs. They fired together and its head disintegrated, the body thrown back into the yard. Another tripped over it, but there were more coming on, a wave of cold dead flesh, curling fingers, dead eyes and gnashing teeth.

"Barricade the windows!" yelled Ned.

They seized chairs, and tables, but the undead were already at the openings, reaching inside. At his window, Ned spun and thrust himself backwards into the opening, presenting his armoured and coat clad back to the Blighters. He smashed his helmet backwards, knocking one back out of the window. He braced himself, wincing at the sound of fingers clawing at the metal of his armour. Joe rushed up, a chair in one hand and a shotgun in the other. He shoved the gun over Ned's shoulder, the twin barrels disappearing into one creature's red and black maw. He fired - "Shit!" yelled Ned - and the Blighter was slammed away, clearing a momentary space. Joe dropped the gun, and as Ned stumbled clear, jammed the chair in the space. Ned slid another to him, and another, and he swiftly rammed them together into a tangled wooden barricade.

At the other window, Steve was swinging one rifle like a club, knocking the undead back through the window as Dan shoved a pile of furniture together. "Now!" he cried, and Steve threw his gun aside to help block the opening.

Outside, the undead flowed up to the front of the inn, scrabbling with torn fingers or stumps at the door, clawing at the chairs, trying to thrust their heads through the spaces they could find. At this range, the gang could draw their revolvers and fire into the gaps. No time to always aim for heads, just shoot to tear the bodies apart and render them less dangerous, even though those hit in the first volleys were still dragging themselves forward across the gore-streaked yard. The front door groaned under the pressure of bodies - Joe took his second pistol, aimed at head height and fired all six shots, the bullets tearing through the thick wood and smacking into the skulls of the closest Blighters.

Others flowed around the sides of the building.

Ned pulled his helmet off, and yanked his gloves off with his teeth. He threw his Colt rifle and several pistols onto a table, ammunition spilling across the floor. He shoved cartridges into the empty chambers as fast as he could.

"Joe!" he called. "Come with me."

Joe stepped back cautiously. Their hasty barricade was holding for now - a mass of splintered furniture and body parts and slippery bodily fluids. "What are you planning?"

"I'm going outside. I'm going to draw some of them away."

"Ned!" cried Dan. "No! Don't go out there!"

"You saw how many there were. They're going to get in here sooner or later, unless I take the pressure off. Don't worry, they aren't going to get me. I'll lead them away, kill as many as I can, then circle back here. Don't shoot me! Joe..."

There was a scream from the back room, and the sound of splintering glass.

Ned pointed at Dan and Steve. "Stay here! Joe!"

The two dashed around the counter and through the door into the narrow passage separating the two parts of the building. Townspeople were shoving in as well from the back of the house, crying in horror.

"Get out of the way!" bellowed Ned, dragging men and women aside. The screams continued.

In the back, they found Mrs Jones on her knees before a smashed window, her teenage son being dragged out headfirst by two Blighters. The boy was too horrified to make a sound. Ned and Joe dropped their guns and rushed forward; seizing the boy by the legs and pulling him back in a dreadful game of tug-of-war. Now the boy screamed, sawed by glass, staring in beseeching terror at Ned.

"Someone shoot them!" roared Ned, but no one listened. "Joe!"

Joe let go, and dived for their dropped guns, coming up with a pistol, but too late as the boy was wrenched free of Ned's grip and disappeared through the window with a final despairing wail.

"No!" cried Joe, and he was half out the window himself, firing wildly, the sound deafening in the small room.

"My boy!" screamed Mrs Jones. "Oh, my boy!"

"I'm sorry!" Joe dropped to his knees. He dragged his helmet off and dashed it to the floor. Ned grabbed him, hauled him up. "To the door, Joe. Go! Some of you, block this window! You!"

He grabbed hold of the closest man, recognizing him as one of the fettlers. He shoved him toward the blood streaked window frame. "Barricade it, now!"

Firing resumed from the front of the hotel. "Joe!" cried Dan. "Hurry up! We need you!"

Ned lowered his helmet over his head, stuffed a revolver in both coat pockets, and took up his Colt rifle in one hand and another pistol in the other. He stood at the back door.

"Now!" he cried. Joe thrust the door open, shoving aside a pair of Blighters who were just outside. Ned stepped through, firing the revolver as he went, two shots into the head of one, two into the other. Joe hesitated for one last second as Ned strode into the gloom, and then slammed the door shut.

Outside, for Ned the world shrank to the thin view afforded

by his helmet. His ears were ringing still from the shotgun blast so near his head. The only thing he could clearly hear was his own ragged breathing. He turned the corner, and entered a maelstrom.

Joe grabbed his helmet and guns and ran for the front room - but a cry brought him skidding to a halt - the fettler Ned had put to work was frantically trying to pull his arm clear. He had most of the window blocked, but one Blighter had thrust a head and arm through the gap and grabbed him. Even now, it was gnawing on the man's arm. Joe levelled his pistol and fired, taking the monster between the eyes. It slumped, and the fettler fell back into the room. Joe stepped forward and kicked at the body, pushing it clear.

"Help me!" he cried, and Stanistreet jumped forward, helping thrust a bed against the window.

Joe looked down at the fettler, cradling his bleeding arm. "Close your eyes," he said.

"What?"

There was no time. Joe pointed the pistol at the man's head.

"No!" the fettler and Stanistreet cried at the same time.

Joe pulled the trigger.

Outside, Ned was in a storm at sea. A cyclone. Shapes rushed at him from all sides, slamming into him, and his armour rang like a bell. He staggered backwards and forwards, fighting to keep his footing as the undead came swarming at him. He ground his teeth and thrust forwards, swinging his weapons like clubs, drawing a pack of Blighters in his wake away from the hotel. From inside his helmet, all he could see were nightmarish visions of gaping mouths and teeth, and dead, dead eyes. Then he glimpsed something pale up ahead - a big fallen gum tree. He fought to get through to it, get his back to it, turn and face the undead.

Joe ran into the front room just as the door gave way. A

handful of undead blundered into the room. Dan and Steve turned from the window as this fresh onslaught came at them, desperately clubbing at them with their rifles. Joe came forward at a run, hurling his helmet at the back of one's head, causing it to stumble, drawing another pistol and firing, not caring where he hit them, just struggling to take them down, and give the others some time. He got to the door, and fired into the face of another Blighter as it tried to enter. He shoved the door closed, and leaned against it - then screamed in pain and horror - a fallen Blighter had reared up and sunk its teeth into his inner thigh, right by his groin. He ground the pistol into its eye and pulled the trigger, but the chamber clicked empty. He wailed, and beat at the thing with the pistol butt, smashing its face into pulp and bone fragments, and it tore away, a chunk of his thigh, a piece of him, triumphantly in its teeth. Bright arterial blood sprayed across it.

Dan and Steve had beaten the remaining Blighters to death, and now took the chance to reload. They hadn't noticed what had happened to him. Joe held the wound tight, but blood continued to spurt from between his fingers.

"Hey," he said to them, but his voice came out so weak. He tried to call again, but the room was spinning and the armour was so heavy and he was so tired. He slid down the doorway to the floor.

Ned fired the two shots left in his pistol, then raised his Colt rifle and fired off another three or four shots, switching from target to target. There was a small space around him now, the standing Blighters having to trip their way over the bodies of their foul comrades. Ned looked around, it was lighter now, the sun was slowly rising. How many more, he wondered. He caught sight of a small group hanging back, behind the rest of the dead...

"Don't get too close," said Hare. "We don't want them to notice us."

"No bloody fear," muttered McFie, the driver. He and the engineer huddled almost in each other's arms behind the two troopers, rifles clutched to their chests.

"Sir!" said Steele. "Look! There's one there! Is that...?"

"Kelly," snarled Hare. "I bet it's him. *Hey, Kelly!*"

"Sir, don't!"

"How do you like that, Kelly?"

They saw the figure stiffen and bring his rifle to bear.

"Oh, shit..." said Hare. He started to raise his pistol. The range was long.

Ned fired. Hare's pistol flew from his hand and his arm jerked. He stared at it – blood ran from a hole in his wrist.

"I don't believe it..." he mumbled. "He shot me."

"Sir! Come away!" Steele grabbed him, and dragged him back away from the inn.

Ned aimed carefully at the retreating group. One more shot before he was down to his pistols... But a Blighter charged at him from the side - this one fouler than the rest, rotted and stinking. It grabbed his arm and bit into his glove-covered fingers. Ned cried out, feeling its teeth grind and crack the bones of his hand. The rifle dropped from his grasp, and still the thing gnawed, seeking to break through the leather of his glove. It shook him like a dog. Ned clawed at his pocket, pulling free a revolver. The thing gave up on his hand and lunged at his face, its head smashing into his helmet. For a moment, he was eye to eye with it, looking into dark depths that held nothing but a roiling ferocious hunger. Yet... He frowned.

"Fitzpatrick..."

The thing bit at his eye slit, its arms locked about him, and he felt with the end of his pistol for its head. He fired, and its rotten head exploded, a dark mist spraying through into his helmet, into his eyes, and mouth. He coughed, spat, kicking the corpse away. He could hardly catch a breath; the foul stuff was in his nose. He blundered backwards, moving to get behind the dead tree. He needed a minute, just a minute...

Joe stood up.

"Joe!" cried Dan. "There's more coming! Block the door! Joe!"

Joe stumbled towards him.

"What are you doing? Shit! Steve!"

Steve looked over - Dan was curled in a ball on the floor, shoving Joe off with his feet. It didn't make sense - then he noticed the river of blood Joe had left in his wake, and he went cold.

"Steve! Get him off me! Shoot him!"

Steve aimed his pistol with his weary arm. He let it drop.

"Joe, stop it! Joe!" Surely, thought Dan, as the strength faded from his legs - Christ, how long since they had last slept? Surely, there was some spark of Joe remaining. "Joe. Please..."

But the face he knew so well, now so transformed, came closer and closer-

With a metallic clang, Steve jammed Joe's helmet back onto his head. The newly dead Joe bent to bite Dan, but only succeeded in slamming the helmet into the younger Kelly's head. Together, Dan and Steve shoved him aside and looked at each other: Blighters were scrabbling at the windows, and Joe was staggering back to his feet, an echoing moan coming from inside his armour.

"Let's put him out," said Dan. "They won't touch him. Not now he is one of them." Steve nodded. They ducked in low and fast under Joe's waving arms, and propelled him towards the door. Steve snatched in open, and with a last kick, Dan sent their friend staggering out onto the veranda and down the steps. There was a rattle as the barricades in one of the windows finally collapsed inwards, and a Blighter started climbing through.

"That's got it," said Sergeant Steele, tightening the sling around Hare's shoulder. "How's it feel?"

"Like I've been shot in the wrist." hissed Hare. "Come on, we're going back."

"Is that wise, sir? Why don't we stay back here until it's over? And fully light? Then we can pick off the survivors - whoever they may be..."

"What the bloody hell is that?" shrieked McFie.

They looked where he was pointing - something was coming for them out of the morning mist, an indistinct shape, lurching, inhuman.

"Oh calm down, man. It's only a Blighter. Take it down."

Hare aimed his pistol with his left hand and started firing, the others wincing at the discharge. They heard the sounds of the bullets striking the creature, and they saw it stagger, but on it came. Hare frowned.

"Don't wait for my invitation," he said to the two railwaymen. They both stepped forward, aiming tremulous barrels at the approaching monster.

"Oh, give it to me," snapped Steele, and he took the rifle from the engineer, who retreated gratefully to the back of the group. Steele aimed, and fired. The figure spun and staggered back four or five steps, but then resumed its relentless stalking.

"Fuck me!" said Steele. He snatched the other rifle from the open-mouthed McFie, sighted carefully at the head, and fired. This time the Blighter went down, flat on its back. Steele grunted in satisfaction.

"Good shot, Sergeant. This one must have a particularly thick skull and small brain. Irish, I suppose."

McFie squealed like a kettle and pointed again. The Blighter was climbing to its feet.

"It's the bunyip!"

"It's not the bloody bunyip! It's...," said Hare. "It's..."

The creature was upon them, smoking, tendrils of mist sweeping along with it, its head a misshapen block. The two crewmen screamed and took to their heels, sprinting back towards the train.

"It's one of the gang, sir! In armour! And Blighted, too!"

Hare's eyes narrowed. "Let's bring it down then, Sergeant. You've got the shotgun. Blow its feet off. Then we can see who it is."

Ned jerked awake with a start, slumped over the log. How long had he been asleep? It didn't seem possible, with the moans of the undead and the rattle of gunfire. His body ached all over, and his head was spinning - more likely he'd passed out, then. He cautiously lifted his head and glanced about, but there did not appear to be any Blighters nearby - he had been hidden behind the tree. Digging in his coat pocket he found his other pistol - he had to hold it left-handed, the fingers on his right were swollen and unresponsive. He started circling around through the trees, to come out near the front of the inn.

Dan and Steve fell back behind the counter. With the door and one window open, they couldn't hold position. As they reloaded their pistols, the other barricade gave way with a crash. The front veranda was crowded with undead, clamouring to get in.

"What do we do?" asked Steve.

"We must get the people out. But we'll have to hold the Blighters here, otherwise they'll be amongst them and it'll be a slaughter." Dan stuck his head into the back room, "Hey! Listen to me! You have a chance if you make a run for it out the back now. Go quick and quiet and don't stop! Understand?"

The men, women and children sitting rigid with terror on the floor stared at him. Stanistreet was the first to stand. It took him several attempts to speak. "Thank you. We..."

"Just go," said Dan, and then he shut the door and rejoined Steve. "Oh," he said.

The front room was full of Blighters. Steve was facing them, busily splashing the contents of a kerosene cask around the bar, and over the dead.

"You go, too," said Steve.

Dan shook his head. "No. Joe's dead, Ned must be dead. I don't want to be alone."

He snatched up the spare lamps from behind the bar, smashing them. "Last drinks! Last drinks, gentlemen! Oh." He spotted the cask of blasting powder. He picked it up, and smashed it down, breaking it open like an egg.

Steve had to duck as a Blighter grabbed at him; he knelt down behind the bar. Dan squatted down beside him.

"I don't want to burn," said Dan.

"Don't want to be eaten," said Steve.

Dan held up his pistol. "Shall we?"

Steve nodded grimly, holding up his. "Do each other?"

"On three," said Dan. He looked up - terrible faces were looming over the bar, hands reaching for them.

They knelt together, cocking the hammers of their guns, gently pressing the barrel up under each other's chin. Steve pulled a handful of matches from his pocket.

"Dan, I..." said Steve.

Dan smiled. "No long speeches now, Stevey."

Hands pulled at them. Figures clambered over, were poised above them.

Steve struck the matches in his hands. The phosphorous flared brightly. Together they counted: "One, two, three-"

Two pistols fired. Two men slumped to the floor. The burning matches fell upon the wooden floor, into a puddle of kerosene and gunpowder.

WHOOMPH

Ned came out of the trees - something was wrong - the yard and front of the inn was strewn with maybe eight or ten bodies, but where were the rest? Then he saw the blank gaping maw of the open door and defenceless windows-

"No," he said, "No!"

He jogged forward. There was a crowd inside, he could see that. Two shots rang out - still time, save them – but the world went orange before his eyes. A fierce wind beat at him, and he staggered backwards. Flames shot out of the windows and door-way, licking at the tinder dry slab walls and shingle roof.

"*DAN!*"

Indistinct figures blundered about in the orange world inside the inn, colliding with each other, falling, crawling, stop-ping. Ned strode for the doorway - a hellish creature of flame and blackened skin and ash-white bone came at him, and he smashed it aside. The flames caught at his coat and he cried out and tore it from him. He spun back to the doorway, but it was too late, he stepped forward anyway: Dan on the bush track, the boy in the river. Ma, Maggie, heat beating at him, why couldn't he do it, but he just couldn't force his cowardly body inside. Just do it, just do it, but instead, reeling back, coughing, defeated, iron an oven around him, reeling back, back, back...

A funeral pyre. Thick smoke roiling into the sky. Cracking falling timbers covering the sound of the desperate cry of the man falling to his knees.

Ned slumped. There was still his pistol in his hand. He raised it, shaking, pressed the barrel up underneath his helmet, right to his jaw-

-there came the dull boom of a shotgun, somewhere behind him.

"Hare," he snarled. And pushed himself to his feet.

"Good," said Hare. "Now go and find some rope or wire or something, so we can secure him. Pity it wasn't Kelly himself."

Hare stepped back from the mangled form of Joe's undead body as it continued to try to crawl towards him on the ruin of its limbs. He waited until it almost reached him, and then stepped neatly back again.

"You just don't give up, do you?" he mused. "Extraordinary. Fitzpatrick was a sad specimen in comparison. What I could do with an army of you... "

He looked up at the column of smoke rising into the air.

A shot rang out, whining close by his head. He jumped. Another armour clad figure was limping towards him, this one aiming a pistol at him.

"*Hare!*" it shouted.

"Kelly?" Hare held his good arm up, and dropped his empty pistol. "Don't shoot. I'm disarmed. And wounded."

"*You think that's going to save you?*"

"Save me?" said Hare. "I don't know about that. But it might buy me a little time."

Ned halted, body heaving, but he kept his aim true. He cocked the hammer.

"I believe you know Joe Byrne." Hare gestured with his head.

Ned stared at the ruination of his friend. He was glad of the helmet as hot tears sprang to his eyes. He aimed his pistol at the back of Joe's poor head and squeezed the trigger. Goodbye, Joe. He looked at Hare. "You evil bastard. You are going to pay for that."

"Ah," said Hare, "but not to you. Now, Sergeant."

Ned knew in an instant and squeezed the trigger, but a shotgun boomed and his legs gave way beneath him. His shot went wide. Hare was on him in a flash, wrenching the pistol out of his grip. Other hands roughly pulled his helmet clear, and the barrels of the shotgun hovered over his face.

"Got you," snarled Hare. "Got you, Kelly." He laughed.

"No matter," said Ned softly, watching the smoke rise in the air. "No matter."

A train whistle blew shrilly in the distance.

TWENTY-THREE

I walked slowly back to the hotel, barely taking in the crowds who pushed by me. My soul felt sickened. So much death and murder. It was hard to take in. All those people... At least now I knew what had happened to the officers, why they couldn't be trotted out as witnesses. Nor could Hare claim the Kelly gang had murdered them all - how would that look?

And Dan, and Steve, and Joe. And the fettler, and the poor teenage boy...

"Did the rest of the people get away?" I'd asked him in the heavy silence that lay over us like a shroud at the end of his story. He'd shrugged, not meeting my eye. "And was it... was it worth it, do you think?" I'd asked, my voice shaking, and he looked up then.

"Was it worth it?" he said, and though he was there in the cell with me, his eyes were miles away, stinging from smoke and sweat and blood, as troopers surrounded him. As they dragged twisted bodies from the ruins of the inn, including two that had fallen on top of each other behind the bar, almost as if in each other's arms. As they posed for photographs beside Joe's body, strung up in a doorway. "No," he said, "not yet."

Back at The Standard, I bought a bottle of whiskey and took it up to my room. Dangerous to combine it with laudanum, probably, but I hardly cared. My heart and mind felt sick and soiled, and all I wanted was a few hours of blankness. But no matter how much I gulped down, I remained disappointingly clear-headed, the alcohol instead sitting sourly in my stomach, till I threw up the half bottle I'd drunk into my wash basin.

I lay back on my bed but sleep eluded me. Sometime around midnight, I pulled my boots on and went walking. My feet led me down dark streets until I found myself outside the Robbie Burns. There were drinkers carousing in the public bar, but I didn't go in. Instead, I walked around to the back lane, and looked up at the windows of the bedrooms. I could count along and work out which was hers. It was dark, as was Lloyd's. Was she sleeping? Or lying there awake, thinking of the trial starting tomorrow? Was he with her? Were they moving together as one? Was she thinking, even a little, of me?

Dawn found me already up and ready. I had cleaned my suit as best I could, and the laundry at The Standard had done a reasonable job on my better - couldn't call it 'best' - shirt. I looked at my reflection in the small mirror: battered, bruised... Hopefully, a metaphor for what was about to befall the government of this colony. I leaned in and touched my hair – was that a touch of grey? As I left, an urge struck me, and I unrolled my derringer from the sock it was hiding in and slipped it into my pocket. This morning was the last chance they had to stop me getting to the trial.

Finding a cab was difficult in that area at that time of the morning, and I was almost resigned to walking when a battered little vehicle pulled by an old nag passed me at pace only slightly faster than my own weary limp. The driver, whose long face made him look eerily like some distant relative of his horse, nodded without speaking when I asked him to convey me to the courthouse, and I climbed gratefully inside despite the stench of mould in the interior. My ribs were aching, which I hoped was a sign that they were on the mend, rather than that I was not giving the healing process the care it needed.

The Supreme Court was essentially attached to the gaol itself. It was early when Charon dropped me off - a good hour or so before the trial started. I had my last sheets of notes folded in my pocket ready to give to Gaunson and Binden. I felt exposed standing outside on the street, but didn't want to go inside and sit by myself. Instead I crossed the road and tucked myself away in an alcove where I could watch who arrived.

I had only been standing there for about a quarter of an hour when a smart carriage pulled up, and a man got out on the far side. As it pulled away, I saw who it was: Hare. He was wearing his blue uniform, and had the same heavy lidded lizard eyes I recalled from Beechworth. He glanced around the street, and up at the courthouse, flexing the fingers on his right hand. Good, I thought, I hope it bloody aches. He drew a watch out of his pocket, snapped it shut, and proceeded to walk off down the street. Here he was, one of the key actors, alone. On an impulse, I followed, keeping well back and ready to turn away if he should turn around. Down on the next corner was a neat pub, where the court and gaol clerks liked to have a beer. He went in. I waited a few minutes, and followed.

Inside, he was perched on a stool at a small round table, staring at a beer sitting before him.

I slid onto the seat next to him, jamming the barrel of the derringer into his side below the table. My jaw was so tight I could barely open it to speak. "You evil bastard. You evil bastard, Hare."

He looked at me, then down at the pistol, then finally back to at his beer.

"Is it true? The things he told me you did - I'm giving you a chance now, damn it - is it true? I should shoot you down right here."

He took a slow sip, licked foam off his moustache. "Either pull the trigger or go away."

A second of silence passed us by. A spasm passed through my finger and retreated.

"I thought so. Go away, would you, there's a good chap."

He went to lift his glass again, and, hissing, I ground the barrel painfully into his side, at last causing him to glance at me. But I did not pull the trigger.

"It's what you deserve."

He laughed then. A deep belly laugh that made the publican and the couple of old soaks at the bar look up.

"You don't really want to kill me. If you wanted me dead, you'd have picked a better spot than this to do it. No." He swivelled to look at me. "No, this is something else." He stared at me with his unblinking snake eyes. "I know your dirty little secret."

"You don't know me..." I mumbled.

"You want to know, don't you?" He nodded. "It isn't that you're outraged. You aren't some avenging assassin. You just want to know." He smiled coldly. "You want to know if they are real."

My voice was caught in my throat. I could feel my fingers holding the gun were filmed with sweat.

"Do you want to see one?" he asked me. "Do you want to see a Blighter?"

"The trial..." I croaked stupidly.

"Oh, don't worry about that. Smyth and your fellow will drone on for hours. Plenty of time to get back." He bent his head towards mine. "I've got one close by."

I couldn't help but glance around the room.

"Oh, don't be a fool. It isn't here. I have it somewhere safe. Well?" he asked. "Do you want to see? Do you want to see what life beyond death is really like, as opposed to that nonsense that gets spouted from the pulpits?"

I licked dry lips. "Where?"

"Close enough. Though we'll have to take a cab." He glanced down meaningfully at my gun. I hesitated, and then slipped it into my pocket, still pointing at him. He shook his head. "Alright then. Let's go."

Out on the street, I stood a little behind him as he flagged down a cab. Up the street, I could see people arriving for the trial. What the hell was I doing? I should go there now, give my notes to Binden and talk strategy. Instead, I followed Hare into the back of the cab. I missed the address he gave to the driver, but we were soon trotting down the street towards the river.

On Flinders Street we took a right hand turn, following the Yarra along its course. I half expected we would turn up Spencer Street, but instead the cab clip clopped on into the western part of the city. This is where the West Melbourne swamp was reclaimed. They were in the process of widening the river, so new docks could be built. As it was, ships had to anchor down in Hobson's Bay, and have their cargo unloaded into lighters to be rowed up the river. Pity help the merchants who had shipped valuables all the way from England and Europe, only to have it dropped into the bottom of a river boat by some drunken lout calling himself a skiffsman - and charging a fortune for the privilege.

A foul miasma hung over this part of the city. Here, along the muddy banks of the river, you could find abattoirs and bone grinders, wool workers and tanneries, candle makers and tallow renderers. All were pouring their liquid filth into the river, and all thickening the air with the stench of rot. It was certainly a handy place to stash a body, undead or otherwise. I frowned.

Hare sat gazing out the window with his flat eyes. I sat across from him, my gun still covering him from within my pocket. His lack of fear made me feel slightly ridiculous, like some private detective in a penny dreadful. I shook myself - that may have seemed my lot previously, to live my life like a cheap forgettable character - not even that, a bit part, a cipher - but I was determined that the next two days would see me play a part in something meaningful. And this was surely part of it. To see at last... To know...

"Why do it?" I asked Hare. He slowly turned his gaze on me, as if faintly bemused that I should speak to him. Finally he spoke.

"The ends justify the means."

"That's it? That's your driving philosophy?"

"First look, then we can discuss your moral objections to my methods. We're here."

I looked out in surprise. We had stopped outside a ware-house-like building that the signage proclaimed to be an abat-toir. There was no one about as we climbed from the cab. Hare handed the driver some coins and told him to return in half an hour. While we waited for him to pull away, I studied the grim front of the building - there was a notice tacked to the door. I walked over and found it to be a closure order from the police, threatening arrest for anyone who entered the premises. Hare appeared at my side.

"There was a recent murder here. Makes for a convenient cover story. No one will come here."

He pushed the door open, and gestured me inside. I shook my head, pointing with my gun. He smirked and strode into the gloomy interior. I followed him past several closed doors, then we came out into a large room at the back of the building, backing onto the river. It was high ceilinged, but shadowy and close. The air stank, and the wooden floor was slippery with fat, dung, and blood. Chains and hooks hung from wooden beams, and pens lined the walls. The killing floor.

"It's fitting, no?" said Hare. "After all, the Blight reveals us for what we truly are: nothing but meat."

"Where is it?" I asked. Damn my voice for quavering.

"Down there." He pointed to the rear of the room. There was an open trapdoor of some kind, I could see light coming up it, and hear the lap of the river below. "Down the offal chute."

I was pulled towards it. The wood around it was dyed with blood. Pieces of tissue and fat were wedge in cracks between the floorboards. The opening yawned like a mouth – what secrets did it have to tell? I peered down the chute: all I could see was the sluggish brown surface of the river, light playing off spinning pools of grease and oil. "There's nothing-"

He hit me. My head exploded and I staggered, the derringer going off in my pocket as my finger jerked involuntarily. I tried to protect my head with my other arm, but he stepped in and struck me again, something – maybe a police truncheon - in his hand. My world tilted, and I pitched forward, head first down the chute. I tried to grab at the sides, but my fingers dug futilely at the fat-slicked walls. I plunged down into the foul water, disappearing beneath the surface. The water felt thick and diseased. I struggled, my boots and suit instantly waterlogged and heavy. I fought for the surface, and came up to find myself already swept past the abattoir, and away. I tried to strike out for the shore, but my jacket wetly wrapped around me, and my ribs screamed. I tried to take a deep breath and the brown river water filled my mouth and nose. I coughed, vomited, bitter bile burning my throat. I rolled onto my back and tried to kick, waves lapping over my face. My legs were leaden, the effort impossible.

"Help..." I croaked.

The boy in the creek. The puppy in the well.

I went under again, fought back up again. I didn't know which direction to turn. I slammed hard into something unyielding, and cried out as my ribs rasped together. I wrapped my arms around it - some kind of pylon. Some structure - a dock - stretching out over the river. The current pushed and pulled at me, sliding me around the slimy pole, until I slipped off. But where there was one pylon there must be more - I thrashed around, windmilling my arms until my knuckles cracked against another fat post. I grabbed at it, wrapping myself to it like a lover. It was dark and gloomy beneath the dock, but I could see other pylons leading the way to shore. All I had to do was make it to the next one over, and so on. I wanted to rest, but already could feel all the strength draining from my arms. I tried to throw myself across to the next, but the river took hold of me in its foul embrace again and I passed it, but was able to grab the next, and so work myself one section closer to the bank. I repeated this once more, praying that the dock would not run out before I was in the shallows. And finally, there I was splashing out of knee deep water onto a dirt embankment. There was a ladder set here, leading up to the street level. I looked up. It was impossible. I tried to take hold, but slid down, down, onto the welcoming dirt at its base. Blackness, like a tide, took me.

I dreamed.

I had been buried alive. I scratched at the thick wood of my casket, fingernails tearing on the rough wood. I scrabbled in the wet grave dirt, clawing at it weakly, and my breath coming in short hot pants. Water must have leaked in, drenching my shroud, and I shivered and shook, teeth clacking in my skull. Forgotten. Alone.

I was on a pyre, roasting. No matter how I squirmed, I could not escape the heat.

I was in Hell. It was what I deserved.

I awoke. My head throbbed, and I cracked my eyes open to see sunlight playing on rough timbers above me. I could hear the lap of water, and the voices of men above me, laughing at some joke. I sat up, body stiff and sore. I was lying on the dirt embankment beneath the dock. I noticed something was digging uncomfortably into my side, and found that my jacket was twisted under me, the derringer still caught snugly in my pocket. My head swam. I reached up and gingerly touched the back of my head, finding a pair of egg shaped lumps. I was lucky he hadn't fractured my skull. I crawled to the ladder, and slowly dragged myself up it.

"Glory be!" cried a voice. "Boys! Look at this feller!"

Rough hands helped haul me up the final rungs and sat me on a coil of rope. A bottle of something was placed to my lips and burning liquor hissed down my throat. I coughed and sputtered and they laughed, thumping my back good-naturedly.

"What the hell were you doing down there?"

I eyed them - they were a tough looking bunch. I took a chance. "Pushed in by a copper."

They grumbled and cursed, blasting the wretched bloody traps and their abuse of the working man.

"What time is it?" I asked. "I have to get to court."

They laughed. "You late for your case?"

"I'm helping Ned Kelly," I said.

"Didn't his trial start yesterday?" asked one.

A cold thrill ran through me. "What day is it?"

"Friday."

It wasn't possible. I had got into the cab with Hare on Thursday morning.

"I have to go."

I pushed through them, though they called to me to wait, have something to eat before I left. I broke into a limping jog back up the river. I couldn't believe it - I had been unconscious down there more than a day. Though, I reflected, a diet based mostly on laudanum, coupled with stress, fever, poor sleep and several cases of physical assault could probably do that to you. I had to get back for the trial. The second day? My God, Binden and Gaunson were probably conducting the defence even now.

I passed the abattoir Hare had lured me to - stupid, stupid - and continued on towards the city centre. I hit Flinders Street, and was forced by a painful stitch in my side to slow to a walk. I wanted a cab, but looked in such a state I doubted any would stop for me. People stared at me as I passed them, but for once, I could not care. Finally, I was at Russell Street - still nine city blocks to go. I had to stop, bent over, vomiting a small mouthful of bile into the gutter as men and women cursed me and walked wide berths around me.

There were cabs here, and I had to try my luck, holding out my hand and shouting as the first few drove right past me. I stepped out into the road and finally one stopped, and I threw myself into the back seat, shouting at the driver to get me to the courthouse as quickly as possible. I sat retching in the back, every nerve urging the vehicle to go faster, but the traffic was quite heavy and our progress seemed so slow. Two blocks short, I had enough. I kicked the door open and jumped down, swearing as a shockwave went through my poor ribs. I threw some coins at the surprised driver, and narrowly avoided being crushed beneath a massive wagon. I ignored the shouts and limped to the sidewalk, then ran for the court.

I could see people out the front, people walking away, two

men were arguing. And there was Gaunson, standing by the road, holding up his hand to hail a cab.

"Gaunson!"

"Charles!" he cried. "Where have you been? What became of you?"

I grabbed him by his lapels, sending us both staggering. "The trial! What's going on?"

"All over, I'm afraid, old boy."

My mind reeled. "Over? That can't be..."

"Well, it is. Justice Barry just handed down the sentence. Death, I'm afraid, but we always thought-"

I shook him. "Ned's testimony! What did Ned say?"

"Why, nothing. We didn't put him on the stand."

"*What?*"

"Give me a little credit, Charles. He was sick. I should think I know better than to allow a feverish client to testify. I should think I know better than that. No telling what he may say... Charles!"

I threw him aside and sprinted into the courthouse. I barged through the interior wooden doors - clerks were packing up papers, last stragglers were debating the verdict, Smyth was standing shaking the hands of his supporters. At the far end of the room, the internal door was closing on warders and a flash of prison yellow.

"*NED!*" I ran forward, a trooper stepped in my way and caught me. "*NED!*"

A hint of bearded face and defeated eye as the door closed. People stared.

"*I'M SORRY! NED, I'M SORRY!*"

They left me alone, to sag into one of the benches, my head in my hands. Smyth swept past me, with a sniff and a smirk. This couldn't be how it ended. I pushed myself back onto my feet and back outside. The day was there, people going about their business, totally unaware of the wicked whirrings of money, law and state. I needed a reporter. Looking about, I spotted Binden up the road, standing beside an expensive looking carriage. He was talking to whoever was inside through an open door. An arm extended from within, and shook his hand, and he smiled and stepped away to hail a cab. I started trotting up the street. Binden disappeared inside a cab, which pulled away smartly, but the black carriage still sat by the sidewalk. I felt in my pocket for my pistol as I drew up to it. I yanked the door open and climbed inside.

"Hello, HP," I said, "who's your friend?"

HP had the grace to appear a little shocked at my intrusion. His eyes bugged in his great leonine face. His fellow passenger - an aging skeleton of a man, skin thin and tight across the bones of his face, dressed in a very expensive suit - regarded me through murderous slitted eyes. A dangerous man. I pulled the derringer free of my pocket so they could both see it.

"My boy," said HP. "You don't know what you are doing. There is no need for this. It's over."

"Is it?"

"So this is the young pup?" growled the other man. "Don't seem to get the message, do you?"

"Apparently not," I said. "And you are?"

He smiled coldly. "I'm Henry Dang-"

"Steady!" said HP. "No need for that."

"I don't care if he knows who I am."

"Still and all," said HP. "We've gone to a lot of trouble to keep this quiet..."

I shook my head. "It won't work. The story will come out. Hell, even if it doesn't, one day a Blighter will walk into the city, and there won't be any way you can hush that up."

"We'll see," said Henry, eyes glittering.

"Yes, we will," I said, and pointed at HP. "And then you lot will be accountable."

Henry barked. "You think it was them? The government? Boy, the governments of these colonies couldn't organise a fuck in a brothel. It was us, the squatters, who took this situation in hand, saw what had to be done and did it. Squatters make the wealth. Squatters made this colony. Not parliaments."

"Steady on," said HP.

"Oh, shut up, Parkes, you old fart. You know it's true. We'd still be up to our eyeballs in blacks if we waited for you to do anything. You should thank the Black Association for what we've done."

My mind was reeling. "What the hell is the Black Association?"

"A group of like-minded men, men of influence, who are prepared to lead the way."

"You mean by committing genocide?"

He stared at me with his cold eyes. "You know some big words, don't you, boy? But you don't know anything. Everything this colony has is owed to us."

"Evil fucker, aren't you?" I pointed my derringer into his face.

"Wait!" cried HP.

"You think this will change anything?" snarled Henry.

"Worth a try," I said, and pulled the trigger.

The hammer struck home. It misfired.

They both at least flinched. No one can face death with that much equanimity.

Henry recovered fast, though, and laughed. "And that about sums you up, doesn't it? You wet squib."

I kicked at the carriage door, causing it to fly open. HP grabbed my arm as I slid out.

"By the way," he said, and smiled wolfishly. "We know who you really are. Your poor father, he must be so disappointed."

The blood drained from my face. I thought I'd been so careful...

"We can take you anytime we want. You can't get away. You're trapped." And then he said a name.

I smiled and slammed the door.

"That isn't me," I said, and turned and walked away into the city.

The prison pulled me back, a huge bluestone magnet. It was late afternoon. I'd been walking aimlessly, restlessly. Trying to decide whether to get drunk, or not, or... I didn't know. I'd gone back to The Standard, and spent some time prying the misfired cartridge out of the second barrel of the derringer. Useless fucking thing. Should have had the gunsmith fix it when I had the chance. I cleaned the mud and grit off it, reloaded it, and hid it back inside the mattress, which I had slit in the same manner as my other, back at Mrs Mackie's.

But finally, I was pulled back to the gaol, to face him.

"William?"

I spun around. I was just about to walk up and knock on the gate when her voice brought me up short. There she stood, another young woman at her elbow, both wan, both watching me with tear-darkened eyes.

"Maggie. I..." I took a step towards her. She held up her hand and I stopped in my tracks.

"Are you going to see Ned?"

"If they let me. Maggie, I'm so sorry. I didn't..."

"Can you do something for me?"

"Anything." Everything. All things.

"Make sure he gets this." She nodded at the girl beside her. "Ettie?"

The girl looked to her, then at me, biting her lip. She rushed over to me, holding out her hand. I opened mine, and she dropped something into it and burst into tears, hurrying back over behind Maggie. I looked in my hand. It was a ring. A gold ring.

"Will you see he gets that?"

"It's a wedding ring," I said.

"That's right. This is his wife, Ettie."

And I saw it, then. The hole in his story. The yawning chasm where his words continually skittered across the surface. His love. Here she was. Here she had always been, kept on the edge, shielded. It was like looking at a series of paintings, or photographic plates, and realising someone had been carefully painted over or scratched away, and once you saw the space where they had been standing, it was all too clear where they should have been. There she was, riding with Maggie to see him in the Wombat Ranges. There she was, visiting with Ellen and the girls when Fitzpatrick came. Ettie Hart. Steve's sister. The girl in the pen at Faithfull's Creek had looked just like her.

He was a man, just a man, after all.

I closed my hand around the ring, and put it in my pocket. "I'll get it to him. Is there anything you want me to tell him?"

"Tell him," said Maggie, "Tell him..." Her eyes brimmed with tears.

"Maggie..."

"No!" The hand again, cutting the space between us, denying anything. She patted the air. "Just do that, William. Give him the ring. And tell him to die like a Kelly." She placed her arm around the girl, who sobbed on her shoulder, and led her gently away.

My hands were shaking as I pounded on the gate. They

made me wait for a full quarter of an hour while they sent to confirm with Castieau whether I was allowed to see the prisoner. Finally, the word came back, and the warders reported it to me with glee: "I don't give a damn. He can go hang along with Kelly if he likes." So I had lost a fan there - but at least they let me in.

At his cell, I paused for only the smallest of moments before going in. Ned was in his customary spot, sitting on his cot, his face in his hands. I could see them shaking. The door closed behind me, and I walked to the wooden chair and sat down.

"What happened?" he asked, from behind his hands.

"It was Hare," I told him wearily. "And others... I don't think they were ever going to let you speak."

"No. I tried. Demanded my right to be heard, but they bundled me away every time. I gave up in the end. Stupid, really, to think..."

He fell silent.

"Scheherazade," I said softly, "with no more tales to tell."

"I have a request," he said.

"Yes?"

"Did you say you had a gun, Remittance Man?"

"Yes."

"Do you have it here now?"

"No... It's back in my room."

He finally looked at me then. "There's something I need you to do. I want you to bring it to the execution tomorrow. And just before they drop me through the trap, I want you to shoot me in the head."

"*What*? Why?"

His eyes, her eyes. Both set the perfect hooks for the holes in my heart. How they pulled at me.

"Haven't you guessed?"

I shook my head, frowning in confusion.

"The Blight. I've got the Blight."

I jumped to my feet, sending the chair clattering to the floor.

"Calm down. I've had it the whole time we've been talking."

"You were bitten?"

"No. It was when I got Fitzpatrick all over my face. I breathed it in, or swallowed it, I don't know. But it's been burning away at me - slower than if I'd been bitten, much slower. But I fear that when I'm dead... Remittance Man, I don't want to end up like that. Not after everything... So I need you to promise to bring your gun and shoot me in the head."

"They'll tear me apart..."

"Look!" he said sharply. "Do you know what will happen if I... If one of them gets loose in a city? Didn't you listen when I told you about Glenrowan? You have to do it, damn it. You... You're my only hope."

"Surely if you tell them-"

"I'm not telling them anything!" He was on his feet, and on me, in a second. And behind his fever bright eyes, I could indeed believe I saw something malevolently brewing. "You do it! You step up and be a man, and you do it!"

There are manly things.

"Alright," I said. "Alright."

"Give me your word then, damn you. As a man of honour, do you promise?"

Who was he talking to? Who was he reaching for?

"As a man of honour," I told him, "I promise to shoot a bullet into your brain."

He calmed, and sank back onto the cot. I couldn't stand to be there any longer. I stood, and then remembered, and pulled the ring from my pocket.

"Here. From Ettie." I tossed it to him. "You might have told me about her. You might have shared that with me."

"No," he said, the ring cupped in his hands. "She wasn't for you. She is just for me."

And then they couldn't get me out of there fast enough for my liking, to escape the sound of his choking, strangled sobs.

The execution was set for ten o'clock the next morning. A crowd of several thousand seemed to have gathered outside the gaol for the occasion, spilling out onto the road. They were a mixture of supporters and the curious, watched over by a large group of sour-faced constables. Were they really worried some final rescue attempt would be launched that would pluck Ned from the reach of Justice?

I joined the file of pressmen entering the gaol. I had pen and paper in my hand, a bribe in one pocket and my derringer awkwardly stuffed in my boot. As it was, I had no need of disguise, as I was recognized by my old comrade, the Ancient Mariner, and waved through. The reporters I was with naturally assumed I was one of them.

One of them glanced back past me out the gate, shaking his head at a crowd of flash young toughs at the front of the mob. "Fools," he said. "They think the poor bastard lived some kind of wild, free life - all he really had was the life of a hunted animal."

I nodded as if in agreement, but his words bit at me. We were herded into the newer wing of the gaol, where the gallows sat up on the first gallery. All there was to it was a wide wooden beam with a noose attached, sited over a simple trap door. Once the rope was about your neck and the bolt pulled free, you had an eight-foot drop to the floor below. Not that you'd hit the ground, quite. I could not envision how anything would induce me to stand still on that trap. I shuddered, picturing myself being dragged there, leaving a trail of piss in my wake. Wasn't that the fate that awaited me, though, if I went through with this mad plan? For that was the nature of the law, wasn't it, probably to find me guilty of murdering a man who was moments from death. A sudden thought struck me - suppose I wait until he drops, and then shoot him? What could they charge me with then? Interfering with a corpse? But no, once I was apprehended and they realised who I was, I doubted I would ever walk free.

There were about thirty or forty of us crowded around - as well as reporters, there were various officials, detectives, and constables. Castieau was there, of course, puffed up with importance. I maneuvered so as to have a large number of people between me and him.

Then the moment arrived. A cell door opened and Ned was led out, in his familiar prison garb, but with a white cap perched on his head. He looked pale. At the same moment, another cell opened and the hangman came out. He was a grey haired fellow with a muscular build – another convict. He walked up to Ned swiftly and pinioned his arms with a strap around his elbows. I saw Ned say something to him, but the hangman simply shrugged. A priest was beside Ned, either chanting or speaking in his ear.

Around me, the reporters jostled and whispered to each other in a hissing susurration. I saw Ned look towards us, eyes scanning the throng. I carefully stepped behind a tall pressman. Now was the time. I reached towards my ankle - we were pressed fairly tight and it was hard to bend to reach my gun, I couldn't get to it. I stood back up and started to squeeze myself through to one side, where I might have a better chance. But I was far away - for a pocket pistol. I couldn't be sure from this distance.

Ned was led onto the trap. His step did not falter, damn him. His lips moved, and all the pressman turned to each other and asked, "What'd he say? What'd he say?" The hangman placed the noose around his neck, and cinched it into position where it would break his neck. The white cap was pulled down over his face.

And then I was free, wasn't I, because the real truth was that I was never going to do it, and without his eyes to see me, to damn me, I could stand by and do nothing. The gun had been an awkward lie all the way from the hotel, a fact I had to keep running from as my monster stirred restlessly in my chest, a hard pressing reminder of my true nature.

The hangman stepped across to the bolt. Ned stiffened, as if taking in a deep breath. Jesus Christ, don't call out to me, don't call out to me-

The hangman yanked back the bolt, and Ned Kelly plummeted to the floor below, jerking to a sudden stop four feet off the ground.

A sigh stirred through the crowd. A moment of stillness, then pencils scratched, and the pressman turned to speak to their friends and colleagues, and the crowd began to pull apart. And a man's life had ceased in an instant. A story ended. I stared at the taught rope, gently swinging. Shouldn't there be more? How could such a moment be so... small.

They left him hanging for half an hour, while the crowd slowly thinned, then a handcart was manoeuvred beneath his body, and he was cut down and laid in it. A pair of young warders wheeled him from the wing. I kept to the back, not stepping forward as some of the others did to inspect the crumpled form in the cart. The great Undead Kelly.

Undead indeed... Was he?

None of the warders seemed particularly in charge of corralling the press, so it was a simple enough matter to detach myself and slink after the departed cart. Out in the yard, I watched them disappear into the low building that must have housed the hospital wing. No one appeared to be about as I walked as purposefully as I could across the yard, hoping I looked busy enough that no warder would question me.

Once through the doors, though, I wasn't sure where they went. The corridor stretched in both directions, and doors led off it at regular intervals. I didn't fancy having to slink along, peering into all of them one after another. That was sure to get me noticed. And what could I tell them I was doing? Making sure the man they just hanged stayed dead?

It hit me then, the craziness of it. I'd been as infected by this lunatic idea as surely as Norris and the rest. Was this what I had come to? Was I actually here with the idea that I was going to see Ned rise from the dead? I walked slowly down the corridor, trailing the fingers of one hand along the cool plastered wall. I turned a corner, and found a stairwell leading down. The hand-cart was parked to one side.

I descended the stairs. It was dark down there, but light glowed from the cracks around a set of doors. I pressed my head against them, but could hear nothing inside, no voices. I bent and pulled my derringer clear of my boot, flexing my foot several times now that the painful thing was out. I placed it in my coat pocket and swung the door open.

Inside was a cool bricked room, lined with shelves. A stained table was positioned in the middle, well lit by a number of lamps. And on the table lay Ned. He was naked, his prison garb tossed in an untidy heap in the corner. A man stood over him, his back to me, wearing a white apron. Something was wrong - something looked wrong, the way the head was sitting. Then I realised that of course his neck had to have been broken by the hanging.

"You're early," said the man, without turning around.

"Ah," I said, fingers tightening on the gun in my pocket.

"Fascinating study," the man said. "Phrenology."

"Hmmm," I said, stepping into the room and letting the door close behind me.

"You'll have to wait, though. Chap from the waxworks has been hired to do a death mask, and he isn't here yet. But I've already separated the head."

"...What?"

I looked again at the body. The head was too far away. He'd cut the head off.

He finished what he was doing and turned around. "You are the phrenologist, aren't you?"

"Yes."

"We'll have to shave the head so Kreitmayer can get a good mould. Care to help?" He opened a drawer and started sorting through, pulling out clippers, and a straight razor.

I drifted over to the table. Ned looked like nothing so much as a piece of meat. His face did not look like it was sleeping, or at rest, or any of the other euphemisms people liked to use to hold the fear of death at bay. He looked... empty. Maybe cutting his head off had stopped the Blight? But he had been so sure about the need to destroy the brain...

"Happy to hold it while I shave it?"

I reached out trembling fingers and sank them into his hair. It felt like normal hair. I lifted, grunted, surprised at the weight of it. "Actually, I need to take it now."

He laughed. "Wish I could, old boy. Can't wait to get started, eh? Don't blame you - fascinating case. But I'm under strict orders - death mask first, then you can have it."

"No," I said, pulling the derringer from my pocket. "I really need to take it now."

He saw the gun, and choked. "But... But..."

"Get me a bag. Or something. Now."

With shaking hands, he clattered about, and then held out a

white cloth bag. I lowered Ned's head inside it. "Now kneel down."

"Please... Don't..." He knelt down.

"If you come outside that door in the next ten minutes, I'll shoot you, understand?"

He nodded, spit bubbling on his lips. I took up the bag with its grisly load and backed to the door, keeping the gun trained on him. I stepped through backwards, then turned and ran. I bolted up the stairs, slid around the corner and raced for the door. I only just remembered to stop long enough to shove the pistol back into my pocket, then took a breath, and stepped out. I walked briskly towards the distant gate, the head banging against my leg as I went. My teeth ground together - I expected any minute to hear a shout behind me.

It was my old friend, the Ancient Mariner, at the gate. "What are you still doing here?" he asked.

"I'm going now."

He glanced at the bag, which I dangled behind my leg. He shrugged, and opened the gate.

"Hey!" someone shouted, and I spun around. But it was only one warder calling across to another.

"Someone's mighty jumpy," opined my friend, watching me.

I fairly shoved him aside and was out onto the street. I trotted across the road and headed down Victoria, fighting not to break into a run. I turned down a side street as soon as I could, the knots in my shoulders only slightly relaxing as I plunged deeper into Fitzroy. I wanted to be inside, off the street, as soon as possible. It was only when I was striding up the lane behind Mrs Mackie's boarding house that I realised I had unthinkingly headed back to my old abode. I couldn't stay here - they knew about me here. I hovered in the alley - no, I had to go to The Standard. I turned to go-

A man was shambling towards me. I went to run, then I

realised it was just the Aboriginal beggar from the other night. I went to walk by him.

"Loose change, boss?" he asked. "Wait, I know you."

"Yes, hello," I said, and kept walking. He followed.

"What you got there?"

"Nothing. Go away."

His fingers caught at my sleeve. "What you got there?" His voice was hard as iron.

I turned. He was frowning now, and he seemed to have grown. His fingers were locked in my sleeve. I swung the bag. It caught him a blow on the side of the head and he staggered and let me go. I whipped the derringer out of my pocket and slammed it down on his skull. He fell to the ground. I glanced around - no one had seen. I pocketed the gun again and fled.

Back at The Standard, I clattered up the stairs to my room. Inside, I dropped the bag by the door, and pulled the curtains closed. I sagged against the wall, sliding down until my legs were stretched out before me on the floor. I closed my eyes, trying to control my ragged breath and thudding heart. I rubbed at my chest.

I don't know how long I would have sat there, but I became increasingly aware of the bag and its macabre contents sitting on the floor not far from me. Unable to stand the gloom of the room, I creaked upright and lit the lamp. Shadows leapt across the walls. I dragged a chair and small table into the middle of the room, and placed the lamp on it. I found the half-empty bottle of whiskey and uncapped it with trembling fingers, gulping down great burning mouthfuls until I choked and spluttered it across it the room. I wiped my arm across my mouth and looked at the bag where it lay by the door. It was stained now, a wet pinkish mark spreading across it. I took it up, held it open above the table and shook it, and Ned's head fell out and bounced upon the wood. I gagged.

Mustering my courage, I gripped it by the hair again and sat in on the wadded-up bag, and when it threatened to topple over, wedged it upright with a couple of books. I took off my jacket, placing my pistol on the table, and sat in the chair.

"Face to face again," I said to the head. I laughed, nervously.

The dead eyes opened.

I yelped and jumped backward, almost tipping out of the chair. I sat back up - surely not - but yes, the eyes were open and staring at me with what could only be called utter malice.

"My God," I whispered. "It is true. It's all true."

All of it. The boy on the track. Fighting the Wildman. Stringybark. Faithfulls Creek. Glenrowan. All of it true.

And I almost laughed, for I suddenly felt so much lighter, almost giddy. What was this? Relief? Why?

Because...

Because it meant he had not lied to me.

The mouth opened and worked, the thick tongue squirming repulsively within. The complete *wrongness* of it, I hadn't expected that. Something in our brain or soul, recoiling...Shaking, I reached for the whiskey bottle, unable to take my eyes off the head. My fingertips snagged the bottle awkwardly, and it tipped, fell, whiskey flooding across the table and onto my lap. I cursed, and jumped up, grabbing a handful of paper, mopping it back away-

-a savage pain in my arm - I pull away - the head attached, its teeth sunk into the flesh of my forearm - I swear and shake it, won't let go, then grip and pull at it, and shriek as it comes away, and stare in disbelief at the strip of skin between its teeth. I hold my arm in the light, and there is the confirmation - bitten, I've been bitten.

I crash down into my chair. The head lies on its side on the table, watching me, and I swear it is smiling with savage glee. I grab the derringer and press the barrel right between its eyes, and pull the trigger, and shoot a bullet right in Ned Kelly's brain, just as I had promised to do. The head skittered and bounced off the table, rolling across the floor in a trail of matter and shattered bone.

Bitten... I've been bitten.

How long?

Step up and be a man, said Ned. I looked at the derringer, smoke drifting from one barrel. The other was still loaded. I lifted it with a shaking hand, and pressed it to my temple.

Maggie...

My mind was reeling, sweeping. My chest ached. Do it do it do it.

I...

Red faces and cigar smoke. Greedy laughter. The girls with the hunted eyes.

can't...

It might misfire. Pull the trigger and it might misfire. Let Fate speak. Let God speak. Let someone else make the fucking decision. The barrel shakes, sliding across my sweat slicked head.

My mind is whirling.

Jesus

I only wanted to be free.

If one ever gets loose in the city...

That about sums you up, doesn't it?

You bastards, you should have left me alone. It's what you deserve.

If one ever gets loose...

How long? Already I fancied I could feel something black raging through my blood. The monster in my chest finally uncaged.

Evolution.

Warm soft body against my chest

Maggie
No more pain, no more fear.
Mother
monstrous, she said, monstrous boy
A free man
Such a free man
how long

I threw the gun across the room

Let it come, let it come

Such
    is
    life

ACKNOWLEDGMENTS

Thanks to Shane, Rob and Russ for their interest, enthusiasm and criticism.

Thanks also to Shane and Jo at Tar & Feather for helping this book to return from the dead.

And many thanks to my wife, Sandra, for her belief in me – and in zombies.

ALSO BY TIMOTHY BOWDEN

Freaks and Greeks

Know Thyself. 490BC: One small city in Ancient Greece is in the midst of a revolution. A unique idea has taken hold: that power should be held not by kings, not by the wealthy, but by the ordinary citizens themselves. They call it *demos kratia*.

But it may soon be swept away, before it has a chance to take hold. For a plague is spreading across the ancient world... A sickness that brings the dead back from the afterlife. And when they return, they are *hungry*.

The Egyptian pharaohs unleashed it in their greed for immortality. The Persian kings spread it in their hunger for empire. Now it will fall to one man, Miltiades of Athens, to rise above the clash of class and race, and his own self doubt, to keep this small flame of freedom alive. But he must be careful: power is infectious.

The forces are gathering. The final battle is set to begin. A desperate race for survival...

At Marathon.